PENGUIN POPULAR CLASSICS

THE CORAL ISLAND
BY R. M. BALLANTYNE

ROBERT MICHAEL BALLANTYNE (1825–94). A prolific story-teller, he was particularly noted for the thrilling action adventures he wrote for young boys, most famously *The Coral Island*.

Robert Michael Ballantyne was born in Edinburgh in April 1825. He was the nephew of the famous Ballantyne brothers, who worked closely with Sir Walter Scott: James in the highly flourishing printing businesss and John in the less successful publishing and bookselling firm. Robert Ballantyne began his career working for the Hudson's Bay Company for six years and in 1848 he published his adventurous diary, *Hudson's Bay: or Every-Day Life in the Wilds of North America*. He then worked for Constable, the printing firm, about which he wrote *Personal Reminiscences in Bookmaking* in 1893. In 1856 he published his first adventure story, *Snowflakes and Sunbeams: or the Young Fur Traders*, which was soon after known only by its subtitle. He became a pioneer writer of adventure stories for boys, all set in exotic places with masculine and virtuous heroes. To discover authentic background for his stories Robert Ballantyne travelled widely, to Norway, Canada, Algeria and elsewhere, and he gained a deeper knowledge of the countries by taking a variety of jobs, including fireman and miner. He wrote over eighty novels, all extremely popular, which included *The Coral Island* (1858), *Martin Rattler, or a Boy's Adventure in the Forests of Brazil* (1858), *The Dog Crusoe* (1860), *The Gorilla Hunters* (1862) and *Black Ivory* (1873). Robert Michael Ballantyne died in 1894.

The Coral Island is Ballantyne's most enduringly popular and best-remembered action adventure. Set in the South Seas, it is based on Ballantyne's own experiences of the Pacific Ocean. It stands out from the restrictive Victorian era as a novel of exhilarating freedom and excitement; read by both children and adults as an escape from the 'real' world.

PENGUIN POPULAR CLASSICS

THE
CORAL ISLAND

R. M. BALLANTYNE

PENGUIN BOOKS
A PENGUIN/GODFREY CAVE EDITION

PENGUIN BOOKS

Published by the Penguin Group
Penguin Books Ltd, 27 Wrights Lane, London w8 5tz, England
Penguin Books USA Inc., 375 Hudson Street, New York, New York 10014, USA
Penguin Books Australia Ltd, Ringwood, Victoria, Australia
Penguin Books Canada Ltd, 10 Alcorn Avenue, Toronto, Ontario, Canada m4v 3b2
Penguin Books (NZ) Ltd, 182–190 Wairau Road, Auckland 10, New Zealand

Penguin Books Ltd, Registered Offices: Harmondsworth, Middlesex, England

First published 1858
Published in Penguin Popular Classics 1995
1 3 5 7 9 10 8 6 4 2

Printed in England by Clays Ltd, St Ives plc

PREFACE

I WAS a boy when I went through the wonderful adventures herein set down. With the memory of my boyish feelings strong upon me, I present my book specially to boys, in the earnest hope that they may derive valuable information, much pleasure, great profit, and unbounded amusement from its pages.

One word more. If there is any boy or man who loves to be melancholy and morose, and who cannot enter with kindly sympathy into the regions of fun, let me seriously advise him to shut my book and put it away. It is not meant for him.

RALPH ROVER.

THE CORAL ISLAND

CHAPTER I

The beginning—My early life and character—I thirst for adventure
in foreign lands, and go to sea.

ROVING has always been, and still is, my ruling
passion, the joy of my heart, the very sunshine
of my existence. In childhood, in boyhood, and in
man's estate, I have been a rover ; not a mere rambler
among the woody glens and upon the hill-tops of
my own native land, but an enthusiastic rover
throughout the length and breadth of the wide,
wide world.

It was a wild, black night of howling storm,
the night in which I was born on the foaming bosom
of the broad Atlantic Ocean. My father was a sea-
captain ; my grandfather was a sea-captain ;
my great-grandfather had been a marine. Nobody
could tell positively what occupation *his* father
had followed ; but my dear mother used to assert
that he had been a midshipman, whose grandfather,
on the mother's side, had been an admiral in the

royal navy. At any rate, we knew that, as far back
as our family could be traced, it had been intimately
connected with the great watery waste. Indeed
this was the case on both sides of the house ; for
my mother always went to sea with my father on his
long voyages, and so spent the greater part of her
life upon the water.

Thus it was, I suppose, that I came to inherit a
roving disposition. Soon after I was born, my
father, being old, retired from a seafaring life, pur-
chased a small cottage in a fishing village on the
west coast of England, and settled down to spend
the evening of his life on the shores of that sea which
had for so many years been his home. It was not
long after this that I began to show the roving spirit
that dwelt within me. For some time past my
infant legs had been gaining strength, so that I came
to be dissatisfied with rubbing the skin off my chubby
knees by walking on them, and made many attempts
to stand up and walk like a man ; all of which
attempts, however, resulted in my sitting down
violently and in sudden surprise. One day I took
advantage of my dear mother's absence to make
another effort ; and, to my joy, I actually succeeded
in reaching the doorstep, over which I tumbled into
a pool of muddy water that lay before my father's
cottage door. Ah, how vividly I remember the
horror of my poor mother when she found me sweltering in the mud amongst a group of cackling ducks,
and the tenderness with which she stripped off my
dripping clothes and washed my dirty little body !

From this time forth my rambles became more frequent, and, as I grew older, more distant, until at last I had wandered far and near on the shore and in the woods around our humble dwelling, and did not rest content until my father bound me apprentice to a coasting vessel, and let me go to sea.

For some years I was happy in visiting the seaports, and in coasting along the shores of my native land. My Christian name was Ralph, and my comrades added to this the name of Rover, in consequence of the passion which I always evinced for travelling. Rover was not my real name, but as I never received any other, I came at last to answer to it as naturally as to my proper name ; and as it is not a bad one, I see no good reason why I should not introduce myself to the reader as Ralph Rover. My shipmates were kind, good-natured fellows, and they and I got on very well together. They did, indeed, very frequently make game of and banter me, but not unkindly ; and I overheard them sometimes saying that Ralph Rover was a " queer, old-fashioned fellow." This, I must confess, surprised me much, and I pondered the saying long, but could come at no satisfactory conclusion as to that wherein my old-fashionedness lay. It is true I was a quiet lad, and seldom spoke except when spoken to. Moreover, I never could understand the jokes of my companions even when they were explained to me : which dullness in apprehension occasioned me much grief ; however, I tried to make up for it by smiling and looking pleased when I observed that they were laughing at some witticism which I had failed to detect. I was also very fond of inquiring into the nature of things and their causes, and often fell into fits of abstraction while thus engaged in my mind. But in all this I saw nothing that did not seem to be exceedingly natural, and could by no means understand why my comrades should call me " an old-fashioned fellow."

Now, while engaged in the coasting trade, I fell in with many seamen who had travelled to almost every quarter of the globe ; and I freely confess that my heart glowed ardently within me as they recounted their wild adventures in foreign lands—the dreadful storms they had weathered, the appalling dangers they had escaped, the wonderful creatures they had seen both on the land and in the sea, and the interesting lands and strange people they had visited. But of all the places of which they told me, none captivated and charmed my imagination so much as the Coral Islands of the Southern Seas. They told me of thousands of beautiful fertile islands that had been formed by a small creature called the coral insect, where summer reigned nearly all the year round ; where the trees were laden with a constant harvest of luxuriant fruit ; where the climate was almost perpetually delightful ; yet where, strange to say, men were wild, bloodthirsty savages, excepting in those favoured isles to which the gospel of our Saviour had been conveyed. These exciting accounts had so great an effect upon my mind, that, when I reached the age of fifteen, I resolved to make a voyage to the South Seas.

I had no little difficulty at first in prevailing on my dear parents to let me go ; but when I urged on my father that he would never have become a great captain had he remained in the coasting trade, he saw the truth of what I said, and gave his consent. My dear mother, seeing that my father had made up his mind, no longer offered opposition to my wishes. " But oh, Ralph," she said, on the day I bade her adieu, " come back soon to us, my dear boy ; for we are getting old now, Ralph, and may not have many years to live."

I will not take up my reader's time with a minute account of all that occurred before I took my final leave of my dear parents. Suffice it to say that my father placed me under the charge of an old messmate of his own, a merchant captain, who was on the point of sailing to the South Seas in his own ship, the *Arrow*. My mother gave me her blessing and a small Bible ; and her last request was, that I would never forget to read a chapter every day, and say my prayers ; which I promised, with tears in my eyes, that I would certainly do.

Soon afterwards I went on board the *Arrow*, which was a fine large ship, and set sail for the islands of the Pacific Ocean.

CHAPTER II

IT was a bright, beautiful, warm day when our ship spread her canvas to the breeze, and sailed for the regions of the south. Oh, how my heart bounded with delight as I listened to the merry chorus of the sailors while they hauled at the ropes and got in the anchor! The captain shouted; the men ran to obey; the noble ship bent over to the breeze, and the shore gradually faded from my view, while I stood looking on with a kind of feeling that the whole was a delightful dream.

The first thing that struck me as being different from anything I had yet seen during my short career on the sea, was the hoisting of the anchor on deck, and lashing it firmly down with ropes, as if we had now bid adieu to the land for ever, and would require its services no more.

"There, lass," cried a broad-shouldered jack-tar, giving the fluke of the anchor a hearty slap with his hand after the housing was completed—" there, lass, take a good nap now, for we shan't ask you to kiss the mud again for many a long day to come!"

And so it was. That anchor did not " kiss the mud " for many long days afterwards ; and when at last it did, it was for the last time !

There were a number of boys in the ship, but two of them were my special favourites. Jack Martin was a tall, strapping, broad-shouldered youth of eighteen, with a handsome, good-humoured, firm face. He had had a good education, was clever and hearty and lion-like in his actions, but mild and quiet in disposition. Jack was a general favourite, and had a peculiar fondness for me. My other companion was Peterkin Gay. He was little, quick, funny, decidedly mischievous, and about fourteen years old. But Peterkin's mischief was almost always harmless, else he could not have been so much beloved as he was.

" Hallo, youngster ! " cried Jack Martin, giving me a slap on the shoulder, the day I joined the ship, " come below, and I'll show you your berth. You and I are to be messmates, and I think we shall be good friends, for I like the look o' you."

Jack was right. He and I and Peterkin afterwards became the best and staunchest friends that ever tossed together on the stormy waves.

I shall say little about the first part of our voyage. We had the usual amount of rough weather and calm ; also we saw many strange fish rolling in the sea, and I was greatly delighted one day by seeing a shoal of flying-fish dart out of the water and skim through the air about a foot above the surface. They were pursued by dolphins—which feed on them—and one flying-fish in its terror flew over the ship, struck on the rigging, and fell upon the deck. Its wings were just fins elongated, and we found that they could never fly far at a time, and never mounted into the air like birds, but skimmed along the surface of the sea. Jack and I had it for dinner, and found it remarkably good.

When we approached Cape Horn, at the southern extremity of America, the weather became very cold and stormy, and the sailors began to tell stories about the furious gales and the dangers of that terrible cape.

" Cape Horn," said one, " is the most horrible headland I ever doubled. I've sailed round it twice already, and both times the ship was a'most blow'd out o' the water."

" I've been round it once," said another, " an' that time the sails were split, and the ropes frozen in the blocks, so that they wouldn't work, and we wos all but lost."

" An' I've been round it five times," cried a third, " an' every time wos wuss than another, the gales wos so treemendous ! "

" And I've been round it no times at all," cried Peterkin, with an impudent wink of his eye, " an' *that* time I wos blow'd inside out ! "

Nevertheless, we passed the dreaded cape without much rough weather, and, in the course of a few weeks afterwards, were sailing gently before a warm tropical breeze over the Pacific Ocean. Thus we proceeded on our voyage, sometimes bounding merrily before a fair breeze, at other times floating calmly on the glassy wave and fishing for the curious inhabitants of the deep,—all of which, although the sailors thought little of them, were strange, and interesting, and very wonderful to me.

At last we came among the Coral Islands of the Pacific, and I shall never forget the delight with which I gazed—when we chanced to pass one—at the pure, white, dazzling shores, and the verdant palm trees, which looked bright and beautiful in the sunshine. And often did we three long to be landed on one, imagining that we should certainly find perfect happiness there ! Our wish was granted sooner than we expected.

One night, soon after we entered the tropics, an awful storm burst upon our ship. The first squall of wind carried away two of our masts, and left only the foremast standing. Even this, however, was more than enough, for we did not dare to hoist a rag of sail on it. For five days the tempest raged in all its fury. Everything was swept off the decks except one small boat. The steersman was lashed to the wheel, lest he should be washed away, and we all gave ourselves up for lost. The captain said that he had no idea where we were, as we had been blown far out of our course ; and we feared much that we might get among the dangerous coral reefs which are so numerous in the Pacific. At daybreak on the sixth morning of the gale we saw land ahead. It was an island encircled by a reef of coral on which the waves broke in fury. There was calm water within.

this reef, but we could see only one narrow opening into it. For this opening we steered, but ere we reached it a tremendous wave broke on our stern, tore the rudder completely off, and left us at the mercy of the winds and waves.

" It's all over with us now, lads ! " said the captain to the men. " Get the boat ready to launch ; we shall be on the rocks in less than half an hour."

The men obeyed in gloomy silence, for they felt that there was little hope of so small a boat living in such a sea.

" Come, boys," said Jack Martin, in a grave tone, to me and Peterkin, as we stood on the quarterdeck awaiting our fate—" come, boys ; we three shall stick together. You see it is impossible that the little boat can reach the shore, crowded with men. It will be sure to upset, so I mean rather to trust myself to a large oar. I see through the telescope that the ship will strike at the tail of the reef, where the waves break into the quiet water inside ; so if we manage to cling to the oar till it is driven over the breakers, we may perhaps gain the shore. What say you ; will you join me ? "

We gladly agreed to follow Jack, for he inspired us with confidence, although I could perceive, by the sad tone of his voice, that he had little hope ; and indeed, when I looked at the white waves that lashed the reef and boiled against the rocks as if in fury, I felt that there was but a step between us and death. My heart sank within me ; but at that moment my thoughts turned to my beloved mother, and I remembered those words, which were among the last that she said to me : " Ralph, my dearest child, always remember in the hour of danger to look to your Lord and Saviour Jesus Christ. He alone is both able and willing to save your body and your soul." So I felt much comforted when I thought thereon.

The ship was now very near the rocks. The men were ready with the boat, and the captain beside them giving orders, when a tremendous wave came towards us. We three ran towards the bow to lay hold of our oar, and had barely reached it when the wave fell on the deck with a crash like thunder. At the same moment the ship struck, the fore-mast broke off close to the deck and went over the side, carrying the boat and men along with it. Our oar got entangled with the wreck, and Jack seized an axe to cut it free ; but owing to the motion of the ship, he missed the cordage, and struck the axe deep into the oar. Another wave, however, washed it clear of the wreck. We all seized hold of it, and the next instant we were struggling in the wild sea. The last thing I saw was the boat whirling in the surf, and all the sailors tossed into the foaming waves. Then I became insensible.

On recovering from my swoon, I found myself lying on a bank of soft grass, under shelter of an overhanging rock, with Peterkin on his knees by my side, tenderly bathing my temples with water, and endeavouring to stop the blood that flowed from a wound in my forehead.

CHAPTER III

THERE is a strange and peculiar sensation experienced in recovering from a state of insensibility, which is almost indescribable : a sort of dreamy, confused consciousness ; a half-waking half-sleeping condition, accompanied with a feeling of weariness, which, however, is by no means disagreeable. As I slowly recovered and heard the voice of Peterkin inquiring whether I felt better, I thought that I must have overslept myself, and should be sent to the mast-head for being lazy ; but before I could leap up in haste, the thought seemed to vanish suddenly away, and I fancied that I must have been ill. Then a balmy breeze fanned my cheek, and I thought of home, and the garden at the back of my father's cottage, with its luxuriant flowers, and the sweet-scented honeysuckle that my dear mother trained so carefully upon the trellised porch. But the roaring of the surf put these delightful thoughts to flight, and I was back again at sea, watching the dolphins and the flying-fish, and reefing topsails off the wild and stormy Cape Horn. Gradually the roar of the surf became louder and more distinct. I thought of being wrecked far, far away from my native land, and slowly opened my eyes to meet those of my companion Jack, who, with a look of intense anxiety, was gazing into my face.

" Speak to us, my dear Ralph," whispered Jack tenderly. " Are you better now ? "

I smiled and looked up, saying, " Better ! why, what do you mean, Jack ? I'm quite well."

" Then what are you shamming for, and frightening us in this way ? " said Peterkin, smiling through his tears ; for the poor boy had been really under the impression that I was dying.

I now raised myself on my elbow, and putting my hand to my forehead, found that it had been cut pretty severely, and that I had lost a good deal of blood.

" Come, come, Ralph," said Jack, pressing me gently backward, " lie down, my boy ; you're not right yet. Wet your lips with this water ; it's cool and clear as crystal. I got it from a spring close at hand. There now, don't say a word, hold your tongue," said he, seeing me about to speak. " I'll tell you all about it, but you must not utter a syllable till you have rested well."

" Oh, don't stop him from speaking, Jack ! " said Peterkin, who, now that his fears for my safety were removed, busied himself in erecting a shelter of broken branches in order to protect me from the wind ; which, however, was almost unnecessary, for the rock beside which I had been laid com-

pletely broke the force of the gale. "Let him speak,
Jack; it's a comfort to hear that he's alive, after
lying there stiff and white and sulky for a whole
hour, just like an Egyptian mummy.—Never saw
such a fellow as you are, Ralph; always up to
mischief. You've almost knocked out all my
teeth and more than half choked me, and now you
go shamming dead! It's very wicked of you, indeed
it is."

While Peterkin ran on in this style, my faculties
became quite clear again, and I began to understand
my position. "What do you mean by saying I
half choked you, Peterkin?" said I.

"What do I mean? Is English not your mother-
tongue, or do you want me to repeat it in French, by
way of making it clearer? Don't you remember—"

"I remember nothing," said I, interrupting him,
"after we were thrown into the sea."

"Hush, Peterkin!" said Jack; "you're exciting
Ralph with your nonsense.—I'll explain it to you.
You recollect that, after the ship struck, we three
sprang over the bow into the sea: well, I noticed
that the oar struck your head and gave you that
cut on the brow, which nearly stunned you, so
that you grasped Peterkin round the neck without
knowing apparently what you were about. In doing
so you pushed the telescope—which you clung to
as if it had been your life—against Peterkin's
mouth—"

"Pushed it against his mouth!" interrupted
Peterkin; "say crammed it down his throat. Why,

there's a distinct mark of the brass rim on the back of my gullet at this moment ! "

" Well, well, be that as it may," continued Jack, " you clung to him, Ralph, till I feared you really would choke him. But I saw that he had a good hold of the oar ; so I exerted myself to the utmost to push you towards the shore, which we luckily reached without much trouble, for the water inside the reef is quite calm."

" But the captain and crew, what of them ? " I inquired anxiously.

Jack shook his head.

" Are they lost ? "

" No, they are not lost, I hope, but I fear there is not much chance of their being saved. The ship struck at the very tail of the island on which we are cast. When the boat was tossed into the sea it fortunately did not upset, although it shipped a good deal of water, and all the men managed to scramble into it ; but before they could get the oars out, the gale carried them past the point and away to leeward of the island. After we landed I saw them endeavouring to pull towards us ; but as they had only one pair of oars out of the eight that belong to the boat, and as the wind was blowing right in their teeth, they gradually lost ground. Then I saw them put about and hoist some sort of sail—a blanket, I fancy, for it was too small for the boat—and in half an hour they were out of sight."

" Poor fellows ! " I murmured sorrowfully.

" But the more I think about it, I've better hope

of them," continued Jack, in a more cheerful tone. " You see, Ralph, I've read a great deal about these South Sea Islands, and I know that in many places they are scattered about in thousands over the sea, so they're almost sure to fall in with one of them before long."

" I'm sure I hope so," said Peterkin earnestly. " But what has become of the wreck, Jack ? I saw you clambering up the rocks there while I was watching Ralph. Did you say she had gone to pieces ? "

" No, she has not gone to pieces, but she has gone to the bottom," replied Jack. " As I said before, she struck on the tail of the island and stove in her bow ; but the next breaker swung her clear, and she floated away to leeward. The poor fellows in the boat made a hard struggle to reach her, but long before they came near her she filled and went down. It was after she had foundered that I saw them trying to pull to the island."

There was a long silence after Jack had ceased speaking, and I have no doubt that each was revolving in his mind our extraordinary position. For my part, I cannot say that my reflections were very agreeable. I knew that we were on an island, for Jack had said so, but whether it was inhabited or not I did not know. If it should be inhabited, I felt certain, from all I had heard of South Sea Islanders, that we should be roasted alive and eaten. It it should turn out to be uninhabited, I fancied that we should be starved to death. " Oh," thought I, " if the ship had only stuck on the rocks we might have done pretty well, for we could have obtained provisions from her, and tools to enable us to build a shelter; but now—alas! alas! we are lost!" These last words I uttered aloud in my distress.

"Lost! Ralph?" exclaimed Jack, while a smile overspread his hearty countenance. "Saved, you should have said. Your cogitations seem to have taken a wrong road, and led you to a wrong conclusion."

"Do you know what conclusion *I* have come to?" said Peterkin. "I have made up my mind that it's capital—first rate—the best thing that ever happened to us, and the most splendid prospect that ever lay before three jolly young tars. We've got an island all to ourselves. We'll take possession in the name of the king; we'll go and enter the service of its black inhabitants. Of course we'll rise, naturally, to the top of affairs. White men always do in savage countries. You shall be king, Jack; Ralph, prime minister; and I shall be—"

"The court-jester," interrupted Jack.

"No," retorted Peterkin; "I'll have no title at all. I shall merely accept a highly responsible situation under government; for you see, Jack, I'm fond of having an enormous salary and nothing to do."

"But suppose there are no natives?"

"Then we'll build a charming villa, and plant a lovely garden round it, stuck all full of the most splendiferous tropical flowers, and we'll farm the land, plant, sow, reap, eat, sleep, and be merry."

"But to be serious," said Jack, assuming a grave

expression of countenance, which I observed always had the effect of checking Peterkin's disposition to make fun of everything, " we are really in rather an uncomfortable position. If this is a desert island, we shall have to live very much like the wild beasts, for we have not a tool of any kind, not even a knife."

" Yes, we have *that*," said Peterkin, fumbling in his trousers pocket, from which he drew forth a small penknife with only one blade, and that was broken.

" Well, that's better than nothing. But come," said Jack, rising ; " we are wasting our time in *talking* instead of *doing*.—You seem well enough to walk now, Ralph.—Let us see what we have got in our pockets, and then let us climb some hill and ascertain what sort of island we have been cast upon, for, whether good or bad, it seems likely to be our home for some time to come."

CHAPTER IV

We examine into our personal property, and make a happy
  discovery—Our island described—Jack proves himself to
  be learned and sagacious above his fellows—Curious discoveries—Natural lemonade !

WE now seated ourselves upon a rock, and began to
examine into our personal property. When we
reached the shore, after being wrecked, my companions had taken off part of their clothes and spread
them out in the sun to dry ; for although the gale
was raging fiercely, there was not a single cloud in
the bright sky. They had also stripped off most part
of my wet clothes and spread them also on the
rocks. Having resumed our garments, we now
searched all our pockets with the utmost care, and
laid their contents out on a flat stone before us ; and
now that our minds were fully alive to our condition,
it was with no little anxiety that we turned our
several pockets inside out, in order that nothing
might escape us. When all was collected together,
we found that our worldly goods consisted of the
following articles :—

First, A small penknife with a single blade broken
off about the middle and very rusty, besides having
two or three notches on its edge. (Peterkin said of

this, with his usual pleasantry, that it would do for a saw as well as a knife, which was a great advantage.) Second, An old German-silver pencil-case without any lead in it. Third, A piece of whip-cord about six yards long. Fourth, A sailmaker's needle of a small size. Fifth, A ship's telescope, which I happened to have in my hand at the time the ship struck, and which I had clung to firmly all the time I was in the water. Indeed it was with difficulty that Jack got it out of my grasp when I was lying insensible on the shore. I cannot understand why I kept such a firm hold of this telescope. They say that a drowning man will clutch at a straw. Perhaps it may have been some such feeling in me, for I did not know that it was in my hand at the time we were wrecked. However, we felt some pleasure in having it with us now, although we did not see that it could be of much use to us, as the glass at the small end was broken to pieces. Our sixth article was a brass ring which Jack always wore on his little finger. I never understood why he wore it, for Jack was not vain of his appearance, and did not seem to care for ornaments of any kind. Peterkin said " it was in memory of the girl he left behind him ! " But as he never spoke of this girl to either of us, I am inclined to think that Peterkin was either jesting or mistaken. In addition to these articles we had a little bit of tinder, and the clothes on our backs. These last were as follows :—

Each of us had on a pair of stout canvas trousers, and a pair of sailors' thick shoes. Jack wore a red

flannel shirt, a blue jacket, and a red Kilmarnock
bonnet or nightcap, besides a pair of worsted socks,
and a cotton pocket-handkerchief, with sixteen
portraits of Lord Nelson printed on it, and a union-
jack in the middle. Peterkin had on a striped flannel
shirt—which he wore outside his trousers, and belted
round his waist, after the manner of a tunic—and a
round black straw hat. He had no jacket, having
thrown it off just before we were cast into the sea ;
but this was not of much consequence, as the climate
of the island proved to be extremely mild,—so much
so, indeed, that Jack and I often preferred to go about
without our jackets. Peterkin had also a pair of white
cotton socks, and a blue handkerchief with white
spots all over it. My own costume consisted of a blue
flannel shirt, a blue jacket, a black cap, and a pair of
worsted socks, besides the shoes and canvas trousers
already mentioned. This was all we had, and besides these things we had nothing else ; but when we
thought of the danger from which we had escaped,
and how much worse off we might have been had the
ship struck on the reef during the night, we felt very
thankful that we were possessed of so much, although,
I must confess, we sometimes wished that we had had
a little more.

While we were examining these things and talking
about them, Jack suddenly started and exclaimed,—

" The oar ! we have forgotten the oar."

" What good will that do us ? " said Peterkin ;
" there's wood enough on the island to make a thousand oars."

" Ay, lad," replied Jack ; " but there's a bit of hoop iron at the end of it, and that may be of much use to us."

" Very true," said I, " let us go fetch it ; " and with that we all three rose and hastened down to the beach. I still felt a little weak from loss of blood, so that my companions soon began to leave me behind ; but Jack perceived this, and, with his usual considerate good nature, turned back to help me. This was now the first time that I had looked well about me since landing, as the spot where I had been laid was covered with thick bushes, which almost hid the country from our view. As we now emerged from among these and walked down the sandy beach together, I cast my eyes about, and truly my heart glowed within me and my spirits rose at the beautiful prospect which I beheld on every side. The gale had suddenly died away, just as if it had blown furiously till it dashed our ship upon the rocks, and had nothing more to do after accomplishing that. The island on which we stood was hilly, and covered almost everywhere with the most beautiful and richly-coloured trees, bushes, and shrubs, none of which I knew the names of at that time, except, indeed, the cocoa-nut palms, which I recognized at once from the many pictures that I had seen of them before I left home. A sandy beach of dazzling whiteness lined this bright green shore, and upon it there fell a gentle ripple of the sea. This last astonished me much, for I recollected that at home the sea used to fall in huge billows on the shore long after a storm had subsided. But on casting my glance out to sea the cause became apparent. About a mile distant from the shore I saw the great billows of the ocean rolling like a green wall, and falling with a long, loud roar upon a low coral reef, where they were dashed into white foam and flung up in clouds of spray. This spray sometimes flew exceedingly high, and every here and there a beautiful rainbow was formed for a moment among the falling drops. We afterwards found that this coral reef extended quite round the island, and formed a natural breakwater to it. Beyond this the sea rose and tossed violently from the effects of the storm ; but between the reef and the shore it was as calm and as smooth as a pond.

My heart was filled with more delight than I can express at sight of so many glorious objects, and my thoughts turned suddenly to the contemplation of the Creator of them all. I mention this the more gladly, because at that time, I am ashamed to say, I very seldom thought of my Creator, although I was constantly surrounded by the most beautiful and wonderful of His works. I observed, from the expression of my companion's countenance, that he too derived much joy from the splendid scenery, which was all the more agreeable to us after our long voyage on the salt sea. There the breeze was fresh and cold, but here it was delightfully mild ; and when a puff blew off the land, it came laden with the most exquisite perfume that can be imagined. While we thus gazed, we were startled by a loud " Huzza ! " from Peterkin, and on looking towards the edge of

the sea, we saw him capering and jumping about like
a monkey, and ever and anon tugging with all his
might at something that lay upon the shore.

"What an odd fellow he is, to be sure!" said Jack,
taking me by the arm and hurrying forward. "Come,
let us hasten to see what it is."

"Here it is, boys, hurrah! come along. Just what
we want," cried Peterkin, as we drew near, still tugging with all his power. "First rate; just the very
ticket!"

I need scarcely say to my readers that my companion Peterkin was in the habit of using very
remarkable and peculiar phrases. And I am free to
confess that I did not well understand the meaning
of some of them—such, for instance, as "the very
ticket;" but I think it my duty to recount everything
relating to my adventures with a strict regard to
truthfulness in as far as my memory serves me; so
I write, as nearly as possible, the exact words that
my companion spoke. I often asked Peterkin to
explain what he meant by "ticket," but he always
answered me by going into fits of laughter. However,
by observing the occasions on which he used it, I
came to understand that it meant to show that
something was remarkably good or fortunate.

On coming up we found that Peterkin was vainly
endeavouring to pull the axe out of the oar, into which,
it will be remembered, Jack struck it while endeavouring to cut away the cordage among which it had
become entangled at the bow of the ship. Fortunately
for us the axe had remained fast in the oar, and even

now all Peterkin's strength could not draw it out of the cut.

" Ah ! that is capital indeed," cried Jack, at the same time giving the axe a wrench that plucked it out of the tough wood. " How fortunate this is ! It will be of more value to us than a hundred knives, and the edge is quite new and sharp."

" I'll answer for the toughness of the handle at any rate," cried Peterkin ; " my arms are nearly pulled out of the sockets. But see here, our luck is great. There is iron on the blade." He pointed to a piece of hoop iron as he spoke, which had been nailed round the blade of the oar to prevent it from splitting.

This also was a fortunate discovery. Jack went down on his knees, and with the edge of the axe began carefully to force out the nails. But as they were firmly fixed in, and as the operation blunted our axe, we carried the oar up with us to the place where we had left the rest of our things, intending to burn the wood away from the iron at a more convenient time.

" Now, lads," said Jack, after we had laid it on the stone which contained our little all, " I propose that we should go to the tail of the island, where the ship struck, which is only a quarter of a mile off, and see if anything else has been thrown ashore. I don't expect anything, but it is well to see. When we get back here it will be time to have our supper and prepare our beds."

" Agreed ! " cried Peterkin and I together, as, in-

deed, we would have agreed to any proposal that
Jack made ; for besides his being older and much
stronger and taller than either of us, he was a very
clever fellow, and I think would have induced people
much older than himself to choose him for their
leader, especially if they required to be led on a bold
enterprise.

Now, as we hastened along the white beach, which
shone so brightly in the rays of the setting sun that
our eyes were quite dazzled by its glare, it suddenly
came into Peterkin's head that we had nothing to eat
except the wild berries which grew in profusion at
our feet.

" What shall we do, Jack ? " said he, with a rueful
look ; " perhaps they may be poisonous ! "

" No fear," replied Jack confidently ; " I have
observed that a few of them are not unlike some of
the berries that grow wild on our own native hills.
Besides, I saw one or two strange birds eating them
just a few minutes ago, and what won't kill the birds
won't kill us. But look up there, Peterkin," continued
Jack, pointing to the branched head of a cocoa-nut
palm. " There are nuts for us in all stages."

" So there are ! " cried Peterkin, who, being of a
very unobservant nature, had been too much taken
up with other things to notice anything so high above
his head as the fruit of a palm tree. But whatever
faults my young comrade had, he could not be blamed
for want of activity or of animal spirits. Indeed,
the nuts had scarcely been pointed out to him when
he bounded up the tall stem of the tree like a squirrel,

and in a few minutes returned with three nuts, each
as large as a man's fist.

"You had better keep them till we return," said
Jack. "Let us finish our work before eating."

"So be it, captain; go ahead," cried Peterkin,
thrusting the nuts into his trousers pocket. "In fact
I don't want to eat just now, but I would give a good
deal for a drink. Oh that I could find a spring! but
I don't see the smallest sign of one hereabouts.—I say,
Jack, how does it happen that you seem to be up to
everything? You have told us the names of half a
dozen trees already, and yet you say that you were
never in the South Seas before."

"I'm not up to *everything*, Peterkin, as you'll find
out ere long," replied Jack, with a smile; "but I have
been a great reader of books of travel and adventure
all my life, and that has put me up to a good many
things that you are, perhaps, not acquainted with."

"O Jack, that's all humbug. If you begin to lay
everything to the credit of books, I'll quite lose my
opinion of you," cried Peterkin, with a look of contempt. "I've seen a lot o' fellows that were *always*
poring over books, and when they came to try to *do*
anything, they were no better than baboons!"

"You are quite right," retorted Jack; "and I
have seen a lot of fellows who never looked into books
at all, who knew nothing about anything except the
things they had actually seen, and very little they
knew even about these. Indeed, some were so ignorant that they did not know that cocoa nuts grew on
cocoa-nut trees!"

I could not refrain from laughing at this rebuke, for there was much truth in it, as to Peterkin's ignorance.

"Humph! maybe you're right," answered Peterkin; "but I would not give *tuppence* for a man of books, if he had nothing else in him."

"Neither would I," said Jack; "but that's no reason why you should run books down, or think less of me for having read them. Suppose now, Peterkin, that you wanted to build a ship, and I were to give you a long and particular account of the way to do it, would not that be very useful?"

"No doubt of it," said Peterkin, laughing.

"And suppose I were to write the account in a letter instead of telling you in words, would that be less useful?"

"Well—no, perhaps not."

"Well, suppose I were to print it, and send it to you in the form of a book, would it not be as good and useful as ever?"

"Oh, bother! Jack, you're a philosopher, and that's worse than anything!" cried Peterkin, with a look of pretended horror.

"Very well, Peterkin, we shall see," returned Jack, halting under the shade of a cocoa-nut tree. "You said you were thirsty just a minute ago; now jump up that tree and bring down a nut—not a ripe one, bring a green, unripe one."

Peterkin looked surprised, but seeing that Jack was in earnest, he obeyed.

" Now cut a hole in it with your penknife, and clap it to your mouth, old fellow," said Jack.

Peterkin did as he was directed, and we both burst into uncontrollable laughter at the changes that instantly passed over his expressive countenance. No sooner had he put the nut to his mouth, and thrown back his head in order to catch what came out of it, than his eyes opened to twice their ordinary size with astonishment, while his throat moved vigorously in the act of swallowing. Then a smile and a look of intense delight overspread his face, except, indeed, the mouth, which, being firmly fixed to the hole in the nut, could not take part in the expression ; but he endeavoured to make up for this by winking at us excessively with his right eye. At length he stopped, and, drawing a long breath, exclaimed,—

" Nectar ! perfect nectar ! I say, Jack, you're a Briton—the best fellow I ever met in my life.—Only taste that ! " said he, turning to me and holding the nut to my mouth. I immediately drank, and certainly I was much surprised at the delightful liquid that flowed copiously down my throat. It was extremely cool, and had a sweet taste, mingled with acid ; in fact, it was the likest thing to lemonade I ever tasted, and was most grateful and refreshing. I handed the nut to Jack, who, after tasting it, said, " Now, Peterkin, you unbeliever, I never saw or tasted a cocoa nut in my life before, except those sold in shops at home ; but I once read that the green nuts contain that stuff, and you see it is true ! "

"And pray," asked Peterkin, "what sort of 'stuff' does the ripe nut contain?"

"A hollow kernel," answered Jack, "with a liquid like milk in it; but it does not satisfy thirst so well as hunger. It is very wholesome food, I believe."

"Meat and drink on the same tree!" cried Peterkin; "washing in the sea, lodging on the ground,—and all for nothing! My dear boys, we're set up for life; it must be the ancient Paradise,—hurrah!" and Peterkin tossed his straw hat in the air, and ran along the beach hallooing like a madman with delight.

We afterwards found, however, that these lovely islands were very unlike Paradise in many things. But more of this in its proper place.

We had now come to the point of rocks on which the ship had struck, but did not find a single article, although we searched carefully among the coral rocks, which at this place jutted out so far as nearly to join the reef that encircled the island. Just as we were about to return, however, we saw something black floating in a little cove that had escaped our observation. Running forward, we drew it from the water, and found it to be a long, thick leather boot, such as fishermen at home wear; and a few paces further on we picked up its fellow. We at once recognized these as having belonged to our captain, for he had worn them during the whole of the storm, in order to guard his legs from the waves and spray that constantly washed over our decks. My first thought on seeing them was that our dear captain had been drowned ; but Jack soon put my mind more at rest on that point, by saying that if the captain had been drowned with the boots on, he would certainly have been washed ashore along with them, and that he had no doubt whatever he had kicked them off while in the sea, that he might swim more easily.

Peterkin immediately put them on, but they were so large that, as Jack said, they would have done for boots, trousers, and vest too. I also tried them, but although I was long enough in the legs for them, they were much too large in the feet for me : so we handed them to Jack, who was anxious to make me keep them ; but as they fitted his large limbs and feet as if they had been made for him, I would not hear of it, so he consented at last to use them. I may remark, however, that Jack did not use them often, as they were extremely heavy.

It was beginning to grow dark when we returned to our encampment ; so we put off our visit to the top of a hill till next day, and employed the light that yet remained to us in cutting down a quantity of boughs and the broad leaves of a tree of which none of us knew the name. With these we erected a sort of rustic bower, in which we meant to pass the night. There was no absolute necessity for this, because the air of our island was so genial and balmy that we could have slept quite well without any shelter ; but we were so little used to sleeping in the open air, that we did not quite relish the idea of lying down without any covering over us ; besides, our bower would shelter us from the night-dews or rain, if any

should happen to fall. Having strewed the floor
with leaves and dry grass, we bethought ourselves of
supper.

But it now occurred to us, for the first time, that
we had no means of making a fire.

" Now, there's a fix !—what shall we do ? " said
Peterkin, while we both turned our eyes on Jack, to
whom we always looked in our difficulties. Jack
seemed not a little perplexed.

" There are flints enough, no doubt, on the beach,"
said he, " but they are of no use at all without a steel.
However, we must try." So saying, he went to the
beach, and soon returned with two flints. On one
of these he placed the tinder, and endeavoured to
ignite it ; but it was with great difficulty that a very
small spark was struck out of the flints, and the
tinder, being a bad, hard piece, would not catch.
He then tried the bit of hoop iron, which would not
strike fire at all ; and after that the back of the axe,
with no better success. During all these trials
Peterkin sat with his hands in his pockets, gazing
with a most melancholy visage at our comrade, his
face growing longer and more miserable at each
successive failure.

" Oh dear ! " he sighed ; " I would not care a
button for the cooking of our victuals—perhaps
they don't need it—but it's so dismal to eat one's
supper in the dark, and we have had such a capital
day that it's a pity to finish off in this glum style.
Oh, I have it ! " he cried, starting up : " the spy-
glass—the big glass at the end is a burning-glass ! "

" You forget that we have no sun," said I.

Peterkin was silent. In his sudden recollection of the telescope he had quite overlooked the absence of the sun.

" Ah, boys, I've got it now ! " exclaimed Jack, rising and cutting a branch from a neighbouring bush, which he stripped of its leaves. " I recollect seeing this done once at home. Hand me the bit of whip-cord." With the cord and branch Jack soon formed a bow. Then he cut a piece, about three inches long, off the end of a dead branch, which he pointed at the two ends. Round this he passed the cord of the bow, and placed one end against his chest, which was protected from its point by a chip of wood ; the other point he placed against the bit of tinder, and then began to saw vigorously with the bow, just as a blacksmith does with his drill while boring a hole in a piece of iron. In a few seconds the tinder began to smoke ; in less than a minute it caught fire ; and in less than a quarter of an hour we were drinking our lemonade and eating cocoa nuts round a fire that would have roasted an entire sheep, while the smoke, flames, and sparks flew up among the broad leaves of the overhanging palm trees, and cast a warm glow upon our leafy bower.

That night the starry sky looked down through the gently-rustling trees upon our slumbers, and the distant roaring of the surf upon the coral reef was our lullaby.

CHAPTER V

Morning, and cogitations connected therewith—We luxuriate in the sea, try our diving powers, and make enchanting excursions among the coral groves at the bottom of the ocean—The wonders of the deep enlarged upon.

WHAT a joyful thing it is to awaken, on a fresh glorious morning, and find the rising sun staring into your face with dazzling brilliancy! to see the birds twittering in the bushes, and to hear the murmuring of a rill, or the soft hissing ripples as they fall upon the seashore! At any time and in any place such sights and sounds are most charming, but more especially are they so when one awakens to them, for the first time, in a novel and romantic situation, with the soft sweet air of a tropical climate mingling with the fresh smell of the sea, and stirring the strange leaves that flutter overhead and around one, or ruffling the plumage of the stranger birds that fly inquiringly around, as if to demand what business we have to intrude uninvited on their domains. When I awoke on the morning after the shipwreck, I found myself in this most delightful condition; and as I lay on my back upon my bed of leaves, gazing up through the branches of the cocoa-nut trees into the clear blue sky, and watched the few fleecy clouds that passed slowly across it, my heart expanded more and more with an exulting gladness, the like of which I had never felt before. While I meditated, my thoughts again turned to the great and kind Creator of this beautiful world, as they had done on the previous day, when I first beheld the sea and the coral reef, with the mighty waves dashing over it into the calm waters of the lagoon.

While thus meditating, I naturally bethought me of my Bible, for I had faithfully kept the promise, which I gave at parting to my beloved mother, that I would read it every morning; and it was with a feeling of dismay that I remembered I had left it in the ship. I was much troubled about this. However, I consoled myself with reflecting that I could keep the second part of my promise to her—namely, that I should never omit to say my prayers. So I rose quietly, lest I should disturb my companions, who were still asleep, and stepped aside into the bushes for this purpose.

On my return I found them still slumbering, so I again lay down to think over our situation. Just at that moment I was attracted by the sight of a very small parrot, which Jack afterwards told me was called a paroquet. It was seated on a twig that overhung Peterkin's head, and I was speedily lost in admiration of its bright green plumage, which was mingled with other gay colours. While I looked I observed that the bird turned its head slowly from side to side and looked downwards, first with the one eye and then with the other. On glancing downwards I observed that Peterkin's

mouth was wide open, and that this remarkable
bird was looking into it. Peterkin used to say that
I had not an atom of fun in my composition, and that
I never could understand a joke. In regard to the
latter, perhaps he was right ; yet I think that, when
they were explained to me, I understood jokes as
well as most people. But in regard to the former
he must certainly have been wrong, for this bird
seemed to me to be extremely funny ; and I could
not help thinking that, if it should happen to faint,
or slip its foot, and fall off the twig into Peterkin's
mouth, he would perhaps think it funny too ! Suddenly the paroquet bent down its head and uttered
a loud scream in his face. This awoke him, and,
with a cry of surprise, he started up, while the
foolish bird flew precipitately away.

" Oh you monster ! " cried Peterkin, shaking his
fist at the bird. Then he yawned, and rubbed his
eyes, and asked what o'clock it was.

I smiled at this question, and answered that, as
our watches were at the bottom of the sea, I could
not tell, but it was a little past sunrise.

Peterkin now began to remember where we were.
As he looked up into the bright sky and snuffed the
scented air, his eyes glistened with delight, and he
uttered a faint " Hurrah ! " and yawned again.
Then he gazed slowly round, till, observing the
calm sea through an opening in the bushes, he
started suddenly up as if he had received an electric
shock, uttered a vehement shout, flung off his
garments, and, rushing over the white sands,

plunged into the water. The cry awoke Jack, who rose on his elbow with a look of grave surprise; but this was followed by a quiet smile of intelligence on seeing Peterkin, in the water. With an energy that he only gave way to in moments of excitement, Jack bounded to his feet, threw off his clothes, shook back his hair, and, with a lion-like spring dashed over the sands and plunged into the sea with such force as quite to envelop Peterkin in a shower of spray. Jack was a remarkably good swimmer and diver, so that after his plunge we saw no sign of him for nearly a minute; after which he suddenly emerged, with a cry of joy, a good many yards out from the shore. My spirits were so much raised by seeing all this that I, too, hastily threw off my garments and endeavoured to imitate Jack's vigorous bound; but I was so awkward that my foot caught on a stump, and I fell to the ground; then I slipped on a stone while running over the sand, and nearly fell again, much to the amusement of Peterkin, who laughed heartily, and called me a " slow coach," while Jack cried out, "Come along, Ralph, and I'll help you." However, when I got into the water I managed very well, for I was really a good swimmer, and diver too. I could not, indeed, equal Jack, who was superior to any Englishman I ever saw; but I infinitely surpassed Peterkin, who could only swim a little, and could not dive at all.

While Peterkin enjoyed himself in the shallow water and in running along the beach, Jack and I swam out into the deep water and occasionally

dived for stones. I shall never forget my surprise
and delight on first beholding the bottom of the sea.
As I have before stated, the water within the reef
was as calm as a pond ; and, as there was no wind,
it was quite clear, from the surface to the bottom, so
that we could see down easily even at a depth of
twenty or thirty yards. When Jack and I dived in
shallower water, we expected to have found sand and
stones, instead of which we found ourselves in what
appeared really to be an enchanted garden. The
whole of the bottom of the lagoon, as we called the
calm water within the reef, was covered with coral
of every shape, size, and hue. Some portions were
formed like large mushrooms ; others appeared like
the brain of a man, having stalks or necks attached
to them ; but the most common kind was a species
of branching coral, and some portions were of a lovely
pale pink colour, others pure white. Among this
there grew large quantities of seaweed of the richest
hues imaginable, and of the most graceful forms ;
while innumerable fishes—blue, red, yellow, green,
and striped—sported in and out amongst the flower-
beds of this submarine garden, and did not appear
to be at all afraid of our approaching them.

On darting to the surface for breath, after our
first dive, Jack and I rose close to each other.

" Did you ever in your life, Ralph, see anything so
lovely ? " said Jack, as he flung the spray from his hair.

" Never," I replied. " It appears to me like fairy
realms. I can scarcely believe that we are not
dreaming."

"Dreaming!" cried Jack; "do you know, Ralph, I'm half tempted to think that we really are dreaming. But if so, I am resolved to make the most of it, and dream another dive; so here goes—down again, my boy!"

We took the second dive together, and kept beside each other while under water; and I was greatly surprised to find that we could keep down much longer than I ever recollect having done in our own seas at home. I believe that this was owing to the heat of the water, which was so warm that we afterwards found we could remain in it for two and three hours at a time without feeling any unpleasant effects such as we used to experience in the sea at home. When Jack reached the bottom, he grasped the coral stems, and crept along on his hands and knees, peeping under the seaweed, and among the rocks. I observed him also pick up one or two large oysters, and retain them in his grasp, as if he meant to take them up with him; so I also gathered a few. Suddenly he made a grasp at a fish with blue and yellow stripes on its back, and actually touched its tail, but did not catch it. At this he turned towards me and attempted to smile; but no sooner had he done so than he sprang like an arrow to the surface, where, on following him, I found him gasping and coughing, and spitting water from his mouth. In a few minutes he recovered, and we both turned to swim ashore.

"I declare, Ralph," said he, "that I actually tried to laugh under water."

"So I saw," I replied; "and I observed that you

very nearly caught that fish by the tail. It would have done capitally for breakfast if you had."

" Breakfast enough here," said he, holding up the oysters, as we landed and ran up the beach.— " Hallo, Peterkin ! here you are, boy. Split open these fellows while Ralph and I put on our clothes. They'll agree with the cocoa nuts excellently, I have no doubt."

Peterkin, who was already dressed, took the oysters, and opened them with the edge of our axe, exclaiming, " Now, that *is* capital. There's nothing I'm so fond of."

" Ah ! that's lucky," remarked Jack. " I'll be able to keep you in good order now, Master Peterkin. You know you can't dive any better than a cat. So, sir, whenever you behave ill, you shall have no oysters for breakfast."

" I'm very glad that our prospect of breakfast is so good," said I, " for I'm very hungry."

" Here, then, stop your mouth with that, Ralph," said Peterkin, holding a large oyster to my lips. I opened my mouth and swallowed it in silence, and really it was remarkably good.

We now set ourselves earnestly about our preparations for spending the day. We had no difficulty with the fire this morning, as our burning-glass was an admirable one ; and while we roasted a few oysters and ate our cocoa nuts, we held a long, animated conversation about our plans for the future. What those plans were, and how we carried them into effect, the reader shall see hereafter.

CHAPTER VI

An excursion into the interior, in which we make many valuable and interesting discoveries—We get a dreadful fright—The bread-fruit tree—Wonderful peculiarity of some of the fruit-trees—Signs of former inhabitants.

OUR first care, after breakfast, was to place the few articles we possessed in the crevice of a rock at the farther end of a small cave which we discovered near our encampment. This cave, we hoped, might be useful to us afterwards as a storehouse. Then we cut two large clubs off a species of very hard tree which grew near at hand. One of these was given to Peterkin, the other to me, and Jack armed himself with the axe. We took these precautions because we purposed to make an excursion to the top of the mountains of the interior, in order to obtain a better view of our island. Of course we knew not what dangers might befall us by the way, so thought it best to be prepared.

Having completed our arrangements and carefully extinguished our fire, we sallied forth and walked a short distance along the sea-beach, till we came to the entrance of a valley, through which flowed the rivulet before mentioned. Here we turned our backs on the sea and struck into the interior.

The prospect that burst upon our view on entering
the valley was truly splendid. On either side of us
there was a gentle rise in the land, which thus formed
two ridges, about a mile apart, on each side of the
valley. These ridges—which, as well as the low
grounds between them, were covered with trees and
shrubs of the most luxuriant kind—continued to
recede inland for about two miles, when they joined
the foot of a small mountain. This hill rose rather
abruptly from the head of the valley, and was likewise entirely covered even to the top with trees,
except on one particular spot near the left shoulder,
where was a bare and rocky place of a broken and
savage character. Beyond this hill we could not
see, and we therefore directed our course up the
banks of the rivulet towards the foot of it, intending to climb to the top, should that be possible, as,
indeed, we had no doubt it was.

Jack being the wisest and boldest among us, took
the lead, carrying the axe on his shoulder. Peterkin,
with his enormous club, came second, as he said he
should like to be in a position to defend me if any
danger should threaten. I brought up the rear, but,
having been more taken up with the wonderful and
curious things I saw at starting than with thoughts
of possible danger, I had very foolishly left my club
behind me. Although, as I have said, the trees
and bushes were very luxuriant, they were not so
thickly crowded together as to hinder our progress
among them. We were able to wind in and out, and
to follow the banks of the stream quite easily,

although, it is true, the height and thickness of the foliage prevented us from seeing far ahead. But sometimes a jutting-out rock on the hillsides afforded us a position whence we could enjoy the romantic view and mark our progress towards the foot of the hill. I was particularly struck, during the walk, with the richness of the undergrowth in most places, and recognized many berries and plants that resembled those of my native land, especially a tall, elegantly-formed fern, which emitted an agreeable perfume. There were several kinds of flowers, too, but I did not see so many of these as I should have expected in such a climate. We also saw a great variety of small birds of bright plumage, and many paroquets similar to the one that awoke Peterkin so rudely in the morning.

Thus we advanced to the foot of the hill without encountering anything to alarm us, except, indeed, once, when we were passing close under a part of the hill which was hidden from our view by the broad leaves of the banana trees, which grew in great luxuriance in that part. Jack was just preparing to force his way through this thicket, when we were startled and arrested by a strange pattering or rumbling sound which appeared to us quite different from any of the sounds we had heard during the previous part of our walk.

" Hallo ! " cried Peterkin, stopping short and grasping his club with both hands, " what's that ? "

Neither of us replied ; but Jack seized his axe in his right hand, while with the other he pushed aside the broad leaves and endeavoured to peer amongst them.

" I can see nothing," he said, after a short pause. " I think it—"

Again the rumbling sound came, louder than before, and we all sprang back and stood on the defensive. For myself, having forgotten my club, and not having taken the precaution to cut another, I buttoned my jacket, doubled my fists, and threw myself into a boxing attitude. I must say, however, that I felt somewhat uneasy; and my companions afterwards confessed that their thoughts at this moment had been instantly filled with all they had ever heard or read of wild beasts and savages, torturings at the stake, roastings alive, and such like horrible things. Suddenly the pattering noise increased with tenfold violence. It was followed by a fearful crash among the bushes, which was rapidly repeated, as if some gigantic animal were bounding towards us. In another moment an enormous rock came crashing through the shrubbery, followed by a cloud of dust and small stones, and flew close past the spot where we stood, carrying bushes and young trees along with it.

" Pooh ! is that all ? " exclaimed Peterkin, wiping the perspiration off his forehead. " Why, I thought it was all the wild men and beasts in the South Sea Islands galloping on in one grand charge to sweep us off the face of the earth, instead of a mere stone tumbling down the mountain side."

" Nevertheless," remarked Jack, " if that same

stone had hit any of us, it would have rendered the charge you speak of quite unnecessary, Peterkin."

This was true, and I felt very thankful for our escape. On examining the spot more narrowly, we found that it lay close to the foot of a very rugged precipice, from which stones of various sizes were always tumbling at intervals. Indeed the numerous fragments lying scattered all around might have suggested the cause of the sound, had we not been too suddenly alarmed to think of anything.

We now resumed our journey, resolving that, in our future excursions into the interior, we would be careful to avoid this dangerous precipice.

Soon afterwards we arrived at the foot of the hill, and prepared to ascend it. Here Jack made a discovery which caused us all very great joy. This was a tree of a remarkably beautiful appearance, which Jack confidently declared to be the celebrated bread-fruit tree.

" Is it celebrated ? " inquired Peterkin, with a look of great simplicity.

" It is," replied Jack.

" That's odd, now," rejoined Peterkin ; " I never heard of it before."

" Then it's not so celebrated as I thought it was," returned Jack, quietly squeezing Peterkin's hat over his eyes ; " but listen, you ignorant boobie ! and hear of it now."

Peterkin readjusted his hat, and was soon listening with as much interest as myself, while Jack told us that this tree is one of the most valuable in the islands

of the south ; that it bears two, sometimes three,
crops of fruit in the year ; that the fruit is very like
wheaten bread in appearance, and that it constitutes
the principal food of many of the islanders.

" So," said Peterkin, " we seem to have everything
ready prepared to our hands in this wonderful island—
lemonade ready bottled in nuts, and loaf-bread growing on the trees ! "

Peterkin, as usual, was jesting ; nevertheless it
is a curious fact that he spoke almost the literal
truth.

" Moreover," continued Jack, " the bread-fruit
tree affords a capital gum, which serves the natives
for pitching their canoes ; the bark of the young
branches is made by them into cloth ; and of the
wood, which is durable and of a good colour, they
build their houses. So you see, lads, that we have
no lack of material here to make us comfortable, if
we are only clever enough to use it."

" But are you sure that that's it ? " asked Peterkin.

" Quite sure," replied Jack ; " for I was particularly interested in the account I once read of it, and
I remember the description well. I am sorry, however, that I have forgotten the descriptions of many
other trees which I am sure we have seen to-day, if
we could but recognize them. So you see, Peterkin,
I'm not up to everything yet."

" Never mind, Jack," said Peterkin, with a grave,
patronizing expression of countenance, patting his
tall companion on the shoulder—" never mind, Jack ;
you know a good deal for your age. You're a clever

boy, sir—a promising young man ; and if you only
go on as you have begun, sir, you will——"

The end of this speech was suddenly cut short
by Jack tripping up Peterkin's heels and tumbling
him into a mass of thick shrubs, where, finding himself comfortable, he lay still, basking in the sunshine,
while Jack and I examined the bread-fruit tree.

We were much struck with the deep, rich green
colour of its broad leaves, which were twelve or
eighteen inches long, deeply indented, and of a glossy
smoothness, like the laurel. The fruit, with which it
was loaded, was nearly round, and appeared to be
about six inches in diameter, with a rough rind,
marked with lozenge-shaped divisions. It was of
various colours, from light pea-green to brown and
rich yellow. Jack said that the yellow was the
ripe fruit. We afterwards found that most of the
fruit-trees on the island were evergreens, and that we
might, when we wished, pluck the blossom and the
ripe fruit from the same tree. Such a wonderful
difference from the trees of our own country surprised us not a little. The bark of the tree was
rough and light-coloured ; the trunk was about two
feet in diameter, and it appeared to be twenty feet
high, being quite destitute of branches up to that
height, where it branched off into a beautiful and
umbrageous head. We noticed that the fruit hung
in clusters of twos and threes on the branches ; but
as we were anxious to get to the top of the hill,
we refrained from attempting to pluck any at that
time.

Our hearts were now very much cheered by our good fortune, and it was with light and active steps that we clambered up the steep sides of the hill. On reaching the summit, a new and if possible a grander prospect met our gaze. We found that this was not the highest part of the island, but that another hill lay beyond, with a wide valley between it and the one on which we stood. This valley, like the first, was also full of rich trees, some dark and some light green, some heavy and thick in foliage, and others light, feathery, and graceful, while the beautiful blossoms on many of them threw a sort of rainbow tint over all, and gave to the valley the appearance of a garden of flowers. Among these we recognized many of the bread-fruit trees, laden with yellow fruit, and also a great many cocoa-nut palms. After gazing our fill we pushed down the hillside, crossed the valley, and soon began to ascend the second mountain. It was clothed with trees nearly to the top, but the summit was bare, and in some places broken.

While on our way up we came to an object which filled us with much interest. This was the stump of a tree that had evidently been cut down with an axe ! So, then, we were not the first who had viewed this beautiful isle. The hand of man had been at work there before us. It now began to recur to us again that perhaps the island was inhabited, although we had not seen any traces of man until now ; but a second glance at the stump convinced us that we had not more reason to think so now than formerly ; for the surface of the wood was quite decayed, and partly covered with fungus and green matter, so that it must have been cut many years ago.

" Perhaps," said Peterkin, " some ship or other has touched here long ago for wood, and only taken one tree."

We did not think this likely, however, because, in such circumstances, the crew of a ship would cut wood of small size, and near the shore ; whereas this was a large tree, and stood near the top of the mountain. In fact, it was the highest large tree on the mountain, all above it being wood of very recent growth.

" I can't understand it," said Jack, scratching the surface of the stump with his axe. " I can only suppose that the savages have been here and cut it for some purpose known only to themselves. But, hallo ! what have we here ? "

As he spoke, Jack began carefully to scrape away the moss and fungus from the stump, and soon laid bare three distinct traces of marks, as if some inscription or initials had been cut thereon. But although the traces were distinct, beyond all doubt, the exact form of the letters could not be made out. Jack thought they looked like J. S., but we could not be certain. They had apparently been carelessly cut, and long exposure to the weather had so broken them up that we could not make out what they were. We were exceedingly perplexed at this discovery, and stayed a long time at the place conjecturing what these marks could have been, but without avail ; so, as the day was advancing, we left it, and quickly reached the top of the mountain.

We found this to be the highest point of the island, and from it we saw our kingdom lying, as it were, like a map around us. As I have always thought it impossible to get a thing properly into one's understanding without comprehending it, I shall beg the reader's patience for a little while I describe our island, thus, shortly :—

It consisted of two mountains ; the one we guessed at 500 feet ; the other, on which we stood, at 1,000. Between these lay a rich, beautiful valley, as already said. This valley crossed the island from one end to the other, being high in the middle and sloping on each side towards the sea. The large mountain sloped on the side farthest from where we had been wrecked, gradually towards the sea ; but although, when viewed at a glance, it had thus a regular sloping appearance, a more careful observation showed that it was broken up into a multitude of very small vales, or rather dells and glens, intermingled with little rugged spots and small but abrupt precipices here and there, with rivulets tumbling over their edges and wandering down the slopes in little white streams, sometimes glistening among the broad leaves of the bread-fruit and cocoa-nut trees, or hiding altogether beneath the rich underwood. At the base of this mountain lay a narrow bright green plain or meadow, which terminated abruptly at the shore. On the other side of the island, whence we had come, stood the smaller hill, at the foot of which diverged three valleys ; one being that which we had ascended, with a smaller vale on each side of it, and separated from it by the two ridges before mentioned. In these smaller valleys there were no streams, but they were clothed with the same luxuriant vegetation.

The diameter of the island seemed to be about ten miles, and as it was almost circular in form, its circumference must have been thirty miles—perhaps a little more, if allowance be made for the numerous bays and indentations of the shore. The entire island was belted by a beach of pure white sand, on which laved the gentle ripples of the lagoon. We now also observed that the coral reef completely encircled the island ; but it varied its distance from it here and there, in some places being a mile from the beach, in others a few hundred yards, but the average distance was half a mile. The reef lay very low, and the spray of the surf broke quite over it in many places. This surf never ceased its roar, for however calm the weather might be, there is always a gentle swaying motion in the great Pacific, which, although scarce noticeable out at sea, reaches the shore at last in a huge billow. The water within the lagoon, as before said, was perfectly still. There were three narrow openings in the reef : one opposite each end of the valley which I have described as crossing the island ; the other opposite our own valley, which we afterwards named the Valley of the Wreck. At each of these openings the reef rose into two small green islets, covered with bushes and having one or two cocoa-nut palms on each. These islets were very singular, and appeared as if planted expressly for the purpose of marking the channel into the lagoon. Our

captain was making for one of these openings the day
we were wrecked, and would have reached it too, I
doubt not, had not the rudder been torn away. Within the lagoon were several pretty, low coral islands,
just opposite our encampment ; and immediately
beyond these, out at sea, lay about a dozen other
islands, at various distances, from half a mile to ten
miles ;—all of them, as far as we could discern,
smaller than ours and apparently uninhabited. They
seemed to be low coral islands, raised but little above
the sea, yet covered with cocoa-nut trees.

All this we noted, and a great deal more, while we
sat on the top of the mountain. After we had satisfied
ourselves we prepared to return ; but here again we
discovered traces of the presence of man. These
were a pole or staff and one or two pieces of wood
which had been squared with an axe. All of these
were, however, very much decayed, and they had
evidently not been touched for many years.

Full of these discoveries we returned to our encampment. On the way we fell in with the traces of
some four-footed animal, but whether old or of recent
date none of us were able to guess. This also tended
to raise our hopes of obtaining some animal food
on the island, so we reached home in good spirits,
quite prepared for supper, and highly satisfied with
our excursion.

After much discussion, in which Peterkin took the
lead, we came to the conclusion that the island was
uninhabited, and went to bed.

CHAPTER VII

Jack's ingenuity—We get into difficulties about fishing, and
get out of them by a method which gives us a cold bath—
Horrible encounter with a shark.

FOR several days after the excursion related in the
last chapter we did not wander far from our encampment, but gave ourselves up to forming plans for the
future and making our present abode comfortable.

There were various causes that induced this state
of comparative inaction. In the first place, although
everything around us was so delightful, and we could
without difficulty obtain all that we required for our
bodily comfort, we did not quite like the idea of set-
tling down here for the rest of our lives, far away from
our friends and our native land. To set energetically about preparations for a permanent residence
seemed so like making up our minds to saying adieu
to home and friends for ever, that we tacitly shrank
from it, and put off our preparations, for one reason
and another, as long as we could. Then there was a
little uncertainty still as to there being natives on the
island, and we entertained a kind of faint hope that a
ship might come and take us off. But as day after

day passed and neither savages nor ships appeared, we gave up all hope of an early deliverance, and set diligently to work at our homestead.

During this time, however, we had not been altogether idle. We made several experiments in cooking the cocoa nut, most of which did not improve it. Then we removed our goods, and took up our abode in the cave, but found the change so bad that we returned gladly to the bower. Besides this, we bathed very frequently, and talked a great deal ; at least Jack and Peterkin did—I listened. Among other useful things, Jack, who was ever the most active and diligent, converted about three inches of the hoop iron into an excellent knife. First he beat it quite flat with the axe. Then he made a rude handle, and tied the hoop iron to it with our piece of whip-cord, and ground it to an edge on a piece of sandstone. When it was finished he used it to shape a better handle, to which he fixed it with a strip of his cotton handkerchief—in which operation he had, as Peterkin pointed out, torn off one of Lord Nelson's noses. However, the whip-cord, thus set free, was used by Peterkin as a fishing-line. He merely tied a piece of oyster to the end of it. This the fish were allowed to swallow, and then they were pulled quickly ashore. But as the line was very short and we had no boat, the fish we caught were exceedingly small.

One day Peterkin came up from the beach, where he had been angling, and said in a very cross tone, " I'll tell you what, Jack, I'm not going to be hum-bugged with catching such contemptible things any longer. I want you to swim out with me on your back, and let me fish in deep water."

" Dear me, Peterkin ! " replied Jack, " I had no idea you were taking the thing so much to heart, else I would have got you out of that difficulty long ago. Let me see,"—and Jack looked down at a piece of timber on which he had been labouring, with a peculiar gaze of abstraction, which he always assumed when trying to invent or discover any-thing.

" What say you to building a boat ? " he inquired, looking up hastily.

" Take far too long," was the reply ; " can't be bothered waiting. I want to begin at once ! "

Again Jack considered. " I have it ! " he cried. " We'll fell a large tree and launch the trunk of it in the water, so that when you want to fish you've nothing to do but to swim out to it."

" Would not a small raft do better ? " said I.

" Much better ; but we have no ropes to bind it together with. Perhaps we may find something here-after that will do as well, but in the meantime let us try the tree."

This was agreed on, so we started off to a spot not far distant, where we knew of a tree that would suit us, which grew near the water's edge. As soon as we reached it Jack threw off his coat, and, wielding the axe with his sturdy arms, hacked and hewed at it for a quarter of an hour without stopping. Then he paused, and while he sat down to rest I continued the work. Then Peterkin made a vigorous attack on it, so that when Jack renewed his powerful blows, a few minutes' cutting brought it down with a terrible crash.

" Hurrah ! now for it," cried Jack ; " let us off with its head."

So saying he began to cut through the stem again, at about six yards from the thick end. This done, he cut three strong, short poles or levers from the stout branches, with which to roll the log down the beach into the sea ; for, as it was nearly two feet thick at the large end, we could not move it without such helps. With the levers, however, we rolled it slowly into the sea.

Having been thus successful in launching our vessel, we next shaped the levers into rude oars or paddles, and then attempted to embark. This was easy enough to do ; but after seating ourselves astride the log, it was with the utmost difficulty we kept it from rolling round and plunging us into the water. Not that we minded that much, but we preferred, if possible, to fish in dry clothes. To be sure, our trousers were necessarily wet, as our legs were dangling in the water on each side of the log ; but as they could be easily dried, we did not care. After half an hour's practice we became expert enough to keep our balance pretty steadily. Then Peterkin laid down his paddle, and having baited his line with a whole oyster, dropped it into deep water.

" Now then, Jack," said he, " be cautious ; steer clear o' that seaweed. There ! that's it ; gently now, gently. I see a fellow at least a foot long down there coming to—ha! that's it! Oh bother! he's off."

"Did he bite?" said Jack, urging the log onwards a little with his paddle.

"Bite? ay! He took it into his mouth, but the moment I began to haul he opened his jaws and let it out again."

"Let him swallow it next time," said Jack, laughing at the melancholy expression of Peterkin's visage.

"There he's again," cried Peterkin, his eyes flashing with excitement. "Look out! Now then! No! Yes! No! Why, the brute *won't* swallow it!"

"Try to haul him up by the mouth, then," cried Jack. "Do it gently."

A heavy sigh and a look of blank despair showed that poor Peterkin had tried and failed again.

"Never mind, lad," said Jack, in a voice of sympathy; "we'll move on, and offer it to some other fish." So saying, Jack plied his paddle; but scarcely had he moved from the spot, when a fish with an enormous head and a little body darted from under a rock and swallowed the bait at once.

"Got him this time—that's a fact!" cried Peterkin, hauling in the line. "He's swallowed the bait right down to his tail, I declare. Oh what a thumper!"

As the fish came struggling to the surface, we leaned forward to see it, and overbalanced the log. Peterkin threw his arms round the fish's neck, and in another instant we were all floundering in the water!

A shout of laughter burst from us as we rose to the surface like three drowned rats, and seized hold of

the log. We soon recovered our position, and sat more
warily while Peterkin secured the fish, which had
wellnigh escaped in the midst of our struggles. It
was little worth having, however ; but, as Peterkin
remarked, it was better than the smouts he had been
catching for the last two or three days ; so we laid it
on the log before us, and having re-baited the line,
dropped it in again for another.

Now, while we were thus intent upon our sport,
our attention was suddenly attracted by a ripple on
the sea, just a few yards away from us. Peterkin
shouted to us to paddle in that direction, as he thought
it was a big fish, and we might have a chance of catching it. But Jack, instead of complying, said, in a
deep, earnest tone of voice, which I never before
heard him use, " Haul up your line, Peterkin ; seize
your paddle ; quick,—it's a shark ! "

The horror with which we heard this may well be
imagined, for it must be remembered that our legs
were hanging down in the water, and we could not
venture to pull them up without upsetting the log.
Peterkin instantly hauled up the line, and grasping
his paddle, exerted himself to the utmost, while we
also did our best to make for shore. But we were a
good way off, and the log being, as I have before said,
very heavy, moved but slowly through the water.
We now saw the shark quite distinctly swimming
round and round us, its sharp fin every now and then
protruding above the water. From its active and un-
steady motions, Jack knew it was making up its mind
to attack us, so he urged us vehemently to paddle

for our lives, while he himself set us the example. Suddenly he shouted, " Look out ! there he comes ! " and in a second we saw the monstrous fish dive close under us, and turn half over on his side. But we all made a great commotion with our paddles, which no doubt frightened it away for that time, as we saw it immediately after circling round us as before.

" Throw the fish to him," cried Jack, in a quick, suppressed voice ; " we'll make the shore in time yet if we can keep him off for a few minutes."

Peterkin stopped one instant to obey the command, and then plied his paddle again with all his might. No sooner had the fish fallen on the water than we observed the shark to sink. In another second we saw its white breast rising ; for sharks only turn over on their sides when about to seize their prey, their mouths being not at the point of their heads like those of other fish, but, as it were, under their chins. In another moment his snout rose above the water ; his wide jaws, armed with a terrific double row of teeth, appeared. The dead fish was engulfed, and the shark sank out of sight. But Jack was mistaken in supposing that it would be satisfied. In a few minutes it returned to us, and its quick motions led us to fear that it would attack us at once.

" Stop paddling," cried Jack suddenly. " I see it coming up behind us. Now, obey my orders *quickly*. Our lives may depend on it. Ralph, Peterkin, do your best to *balance the log*. Don't look out for the shark. Don't glance behind you. Do nothing but balance the log."

Peterkin and I instantly did as we were ordered, being only too glad to do anything that afforded us a chance or a hope of escape, for we had implicit confidence in Jack's courage and wisdom. For a few seconds, that seemed long minutes to my mind, we sat thus silently; but I could not resist glancing backward, despite the orders to the contrary. On doing so, I saw Jack sitting rigid like a statue, with his paddle raised, his lips compressed, and his eyebrows bent over his eyes, which glared savagely from beneath them down into the water. I also saw the shark, to my horror, quite close under the log, in the act of darting towards Jack's foot. I could scarce suppress a cry on beholding this. In another moment the shark rose. Jack drew his leg suddenly from the water, and threw it over the log. The monster's snout rubbed against the log as it passsed, and revealed its hideous jaws, into which Jack instantly plunged the paddle, and thrust it down its throat. So violent was this act that Jack rose to his feet in performing it; the log was thereby rolled completely over, and we were once more plunged into the water. We all rose, sputtering and gasping, in a moment.

" Now, then, strike out for shore," cried Jack.— " Here Peterkin, catch hold of my collar, and kick out with a will."

Peterkin did as he was desired, and Jack struck out with such force that he cut through the water like a boat; while I, being free from all encumbrance, succeeded in keeping up with him. As we had by this time drawn pretty near to the shore, a few minutes more sufficed to carry us into shallow water ; and, finally, we landed in safety, though very much exhausted, and not a little frightened by our terrible adventure.

CHAPTER VIII

The beauties of the bottom of the sea tempt Peterkin to dive—
How he did it—More difficulties overcome—The Water
Garden—Curious creatures of the sea—The tank—Candles
missed very much, and the candle-nut tree discovered—
Wonderful account of Peterkin's first voyage—Cloth found
growing on a tree—A plan projected and arms prepared for
offence and defence—A dreadful cry.

OUR encounter with the shark was the first great
danger that had befallen us since landing on this
island, and we felt very seriously affected by it,
especially when we considered that we had so often
unwittingly incurred the same danger before while
bathing. We were now forced to take to fishing again
in the shallow water, until we should succeeed in con-
structing a raft. What troubled us most, however,
was, that we were compelled to forego our morning
swimming excursions. We did, indeed, continue to
enjoy out bathe in the shallow water, but Jack and
I found that one great source of our enjoyment was
gone, when we could no longer dive down among the
beautiful coral groves at the bottom of the lagoon.
We had come to be so fond of this exercise, and to take
such an interest in watching the formations of coral
and the gambols of the many beautiful fish amongst
the forests of red and green seaweeds, that we had

become quite familiar with the appearance of the fish and the localities that they chiefly haunted. We had also become expert divers. But we made it a rule never to stay long under water at a time. Jack told me that to do so often was bad for the lungs, and, instead of affording us enjoyment, would ere long do us a serious injury. So we never stayed at the bottom as long as we might have done, but came up frequently to the top for fresh air, and dived down again immediately. Sometimes, when Jack happened to be in a humorous frame, he would seat himself at the bottom of the sea on one of the brain-corals, as if he were seated on a large paddock-stool, and then make faces at me, in order, if possible, to make me laugh under water. At first, when he took me unawares, he nearly succeeded, and I had to shoot to the surface in order to laugh ; but afterwards I became aware of his intentions, and being naturally of a grave disposition, I had no difficulty in restraining myself. I used often to wonder how poor Peterkin would have liked to be with us ; and he sometimes expressed much regret at being unable to join us. I used to do my best to gratify him, poor fellow, by relating all the wonders that we saw ; but this, instead of satisfying, seemed only to whet his curiosity the more, so one day we prevailed on him to try to go down with us. But although a brave boy in every other way, Peterkin was very nervous in the water, and it was with difficulty we got him to consent to be taken down, for he could never have managed to push himself down to the bottom without assistance. But no

sooner had we pulled him down a yard or so into the
deep clear water, than he began to struggle and kick
violently ; so we were forced to let him go, when he
rose out of the water like a cork, gave a loud gasp and
a frightful roar, and struck out for the land with the
utmost possible haste.

Now all this pleasure we were to forego, and when
we thought thereon, Jack and I felt very much
depressed in our spirits. I could see, also, that
Peterkin grieved and sympathized with us, for when
talking about this matter he refrained from jesting
and bantering us upon it.

As, however, a man's difficulties usually set him
upon devising methods to overcome them, whereby
he often discovers better things than those he may
have lost, so this our difficulty induced us to think
of searching for a large pool among the rocks, where
the water should be deep enough for diving, yet so
surrounded by rocks as to prevent sharks from getting
at us. And such a pool we afterwards found, which
proved to be very much better than our most sanguine
hopes anticipated. It was situated not more than
ten minutes' walk from our camp, and was in the
form of a small deep bay or basin, the entrance to
which, besides being narrow, was so shallow that no
fish so large as a shark could get in, at least not unless
he should be a remarkably thin one.

Inside of this basin, which we called our Water
Garden, the coral formations were much more
wonderful, and the seaweed plants far more lovely
and vividly coloured, than in the lagoon itself.

And the water was so clear and still that, although
very deep, you could see the minutest object at
the bottom. Besides this, there was a ledge of rock
which overhung the basin at its deepest part, from
which we could dive pleasantly, and whereon
Peterkin could sit and see not only all the wonders
I had described to him, but also Jack and me
creeping amongst the marine shrubbery at the
bottom, like—as he expressed it—" two great
white sea-monsters." During these excursions of
ours to the bottom of the sea, we began to get
an insight into the manners and customs of its inhabitants, and to make discoveries of wonderful
things, the like of which we never before con-
ceived. Among other things, we were deeply
interested with the operations of the little coral
insect, which, I was informed by Jack, is supposed
to have entirely constructed many of the numerous
islands in the Pacific Ocean. And certainly, when
we considered the great reef which these insects had
formed round the island on which we were cast, and
observed their ceaseless activity in building their
myriad cells, it did at first seem as if this might be
true ; but then, again, when I looked at the mountains
of the island, and reflected that there were thousands
of such, many of them much higher, in the South
Seas, I doubted that there must be some mistake
here. But more of this hereafter.

I also became much taken up with the manners
and appearance of the anemones, and star-fish, and
crabs, and sea-urchins, and such like creatures ; and

was not content with watching those I saw during
my dives in the Water Garden, but I must needs
scoop out a hole in the coral rock close to it, which
I filled with salt water, and stocked with sundry
specimens of anemones and shell-fish, in order to
watch more closely how they were in the habit of
passing their time. Our burning-glass also now became a great treasure to me, as it enabled me to magnify, and so to perceive more clearly the forms and
actions of these curious creatures of the deep.

Having now got ourselves into a very comfortable
condition, we began to talk of a project which we had
long had in contemplation—namely, to travel entirely
round the island ; in order, first, to ascertain whether
it contained any other productions which might be
useful to us ; and, second, to see whether there might
be any place more convenient and suitable for our
permanent residence than that on which we were now
encamped. Not that we were in any degree dissatisfied with it ; on the contrary, we entertained quite
a home-feeling to our bower and its neighbourhood ;
but if a better place did exist, there was no reason
why we should not make use of it. At any rate, it
would be well to know of its existence.

We had much earnest talk over this matter. But
Jack proposed that, before undertaking such an
excursion, we should supply ourselves with good
defensive arms ; for as we intended not only to go
round all the shore, but to ascend most of the
valleys, before returning home, we should be likely
to meet in with, he would not say *dangers*, but at

least with everything that existed on the island, whatever that might be.

"Besides," said Jack, " it won't do for us to live on cocoa nuts and oysters always. No doubt they are very excellent in their way, but I think a little animal food now and then would be agreeable as well as good for us ; and as there are many small birds among the trees, some of which are probably very good to eat, I think it would be a capital plan to make bows and arrows, with which we could easily knock them over."

"First-rate ! " cried Peterkin. " You will make the bows, Jack, and I'll try my hand at the arrows, The fact is, I'm quite tired of throwing stones at the birds. I began the very day we landed, I think, and have persevered up to the present time, but I've never hit anything yet."

"You forget," said I, " you hit me one day on the shin."

"Ah, true," replied Peterkin, " and a precious shindy you kicked up in consequence. But you were at least four yards away from the impudent paroquet I aimed at ; so you see what a horribly bad shot I am."

"But," said I, " Jack, you cannot make three bows and arrows before to-morrow, and would it not be a pity to waste time, now that we have made up our minds to go on this expedition ? Suppose that you make one bow and arrow for yourself, and we can take our clubs ? "

"That's true, Ralph. The day is pretty far advanced, and I doubt if I can make even one bow before dark. To be sure, I might work by firelight, after the sun goes down."

We had, up to this time, been in the habit of going to bed with the sun, as we had no pressing call to work o' nights; and, indeed, our work during the day was usually hard enough—what between fishing, and improving our bower, and diving in the Water Garden, and rambling in the woods; so that when night came we were usually very glad to retire to our beds. But now that we had a desire to work at night, we felt a wish for candles.

"Won't a good blazing fire give you light enough?" inquired Peterkin.

"Yes," replied Jack, "quite enough; but then it will give us a great deal more than enough of heat in this warm climate of ours."

"True," said Peterkin; "I forgot that. It would roast us."

"Well, as you're always doing that at any rate," remarked Jack, "we could scarcely call it a change. But the fact is, I've been thinking over this subject before. There is a certain nut growing in these islands which is called the candle-nut, because the natives use it instead of candles, and I know all about it, and how to prepare it for burning—"

"Then why don't you do it?" interrupted Peterkin. "Why have you kept us in the dark so long, you vile philosopher?"

"Because," said Jack, "I have not seen the tree yet, and I'm not sure that I should know either the tree or the nuts if I did see them. You see, I forget the description."

"Ah! that's just the way with me," said Peterkin, with a deep sigh. "I never could keep in my mind for half an hour the few descriptions I ever attempted to remember. The very first voyage I ever made was caused by my mistaking a description, or forgetting it, which is the same thing. And a horrible voyage it was. I had to fight with the captain the whole way out, and made the homeward voyage by swimming!"

"Come, Peterkin," said I, "you can't get even *me* to believe that."

"Perhaps not, but it's true notwithstanding," returned Peterkin, pretending to be hurt at my doubting his word.

"Let us hear how it happened," said Jack, while a good-natured smile overspread his face.

"Well, you must know," began Peterkin, "that the very day before I went to sea I was greatly taken up with a game at hockey, which I was playing with my old schoolfellows for the last time before leaving them.—You see I was young then, Ralph." Peterkin gazed, in an abstracted and melancholy manner, out to sea.—"Well, in the midst of the game, my uncle, who had taken all the bother and trouble of getting me bound 'prentice and rigged out, came and took me aside, and told me that he was called suddenly away from home, and would not be able to see me aboard, as he had intended. 'However,' said he, 'the captain knows you are coming, so that's not of much consequence; but as you'll have to find the ship yourself, you must remember her name and description. D'ye hear, boy?' I certainly did hear, but I'm afraid I did not understand, for my mind was so taken up with the game, which I saw my side was losing, that I began to grow impatient, and the moment my uncle finished his description of the ship, and bade me good-bye, I bolted back to my game, with only a confused idea of three masts, and a green-painted tafferel, and a gilt figure-head of Hercules with his club at the bow. Next day I was so much cast down with everybody saying good-bye, and a lot o' my female friends cryin' horribly over me, that I did not start for the harbour, where the ship was lying among a thousand others, till it was almost too late. So I had to run the whole way. When I reached the pier, there were so many masts, and so much confusion, that I felt quite humblebumbled in my faculties. 'Now,' said I to myself, 'Peterkin, you're in a fix.' Then I fancied I saw a gilt figure-head and three masts, belonging to a ship just about to start; so I darted on board, but speedily jumped on shore again, when I found that two of the masts belonged to another vessel, and the figure-head to a third! At last I caught sight of what I made sure was it—a fine large vessel just casting off her moorings. The tafferel was green. Three masts—yes, that must be it—and the gilt figure-head of Hercules. To be sure, it had a three-pronged pitchfork in its hand instead of a club; but that

might be my uncle's mistake, or perhaps Hercules
sometimes varied his weapons. ' Cast off ! ' roared
a voice from the quarter-deck. ' Hold on ! ' cried
I, rushing frantically through the crowd. ' Hold
on ! hold on ! ' repeated some of the bystanders,
while the men at the ropes delayed for a minute.
This threw the captain into a frightful rage ; for some
of his friends had come down to see him off, and
having his orders contradicted so flatly was too much
for him. However, the delay was sufficient. I took
a race and a good leap ; the ropes were cast off ;
the steam-tug gave a puff, and we started. Suddenly the captain walks up to me : ' Where did you
come from, you scamp, and what do you want here ? '

" ' Please, sir,' said I, touching my cap, ' I'm your
new 'prentice come aboard.'

" ' New 'prentice ! ' said he, stamping ; ' I've got
no new 'prentice. My boys are all aboard already.
This is a trick, you young blackguard. You've run
away, you have ; ' and the captain stamped about
the deck and swore dreadfully ; for, you see, the
thought of having to stop the ship and lower a boat
and lose half an hour, all for the sake of sending a
small boy ashore, seemed to make him very angry.
Besides, it was blowin' fresh outside the harbour, so
that to have let the steamer alongside to put me into
it was no easy job. Just as we were passing the pierhead, where several boats were rowing into the
harbour, the captain came up to me.

" ' You've run away, you blackguard,' he said,
giving me a box on the ear.

"'No I haven't,' said I angrily; for the box was by no means a light one.

"'Hark'ee, boy, can you swim?'

"'Yes,' said I.

"'Then do it;' and seizing me by my trousers and the nape of my neck, he tossed me over the side into the sea. The fellows in the boats at the end of the pier backed their oars on seeing this; but observing that I could swim, they allowed me to make the best of my way to the pierhead.—So you see, Ralph, that I really did swim my first homeward voyage."

Jack laughed, and patted Peterkin on the shoulder.

"But tell us about the candle-nut tree," said I; "you were talking about it."

"Very true," said Jack, "but I fear I can remember little about it. I believe the nut is about the size of a walnut; and I think that the leaves are white, but I am not sure."

"Eh! ha! hum!" exclaimed Peterkin, "I saw a tree answering to that description this very day."

"Did you?" cried Jack. "Is it far from this?"

"No, not half a mile."

"Then lead me to it," said Jack, seizing his axe.

In a few minutes we were all three pushing through the underwood of the forest, headed by Peterkin.

We soon came to the tree in question, which, after Jack had closely examined it, we concluded must be the candle-nut tree. Its leaves were of a beautiful silvery white, and formed a fine contrast to the dark-green foliage of the surrounding trees. We immediately filled our pockets with the nuts, after which Jack said,—

" Now, Peterkin, climb that cocoa-nut tree and cut me one of the long branches."

This was soon done, but it cost some trouble, for the stem was very high, and as Peterkin usually pulled nuts from the younger trees, he was not much accustomed to climbing the high ones. The leaf or branch was a very large one, and we were surprised at its size and strength. Viewed from a little distance, the cocoa-nut tree seems to be a tall, straight stem, without a single branch except at the top, where there is a tuft of feathery-looking leaves, that seem to wave like soft plumes in the wind. But when we saw one of these leaves or branches at our feet, we found it to be a strong stalk, about fifteen feet long, with a number of narrow, pointed leaflets ranged alternately on each side. But what seemed to us the most wonderful thing about it was a curious substance resembling cloth, which was wrapped round the thick end of the stalk, where it had been cut from the tree. Peterkin told us that he had the greatest difficulty in separating the branch from the stem on account of this substance, as it was wrapped quite round the tree, and, he observed, round all the other branches, thus forming a strong support to the large leaves while exposed to high winds. When I call this substance cloth, I do not exaggerate. Indeed, with regard to all the things I saw during my eventful career in the South Seas, I have been exceedingly careful not to exaggerate, or in any way to mislead or deceive my readers. This cloth, I say, was remarkably like to coarse brown cotton cloth. It had a seam or fibre down the centre of it, from which diverged other fibres, about the size of a bristle. There were two layers of these fibres, very long and tough, the one layer crossing the other obliquely, and the whole was cemented together with a still finer fibrous and adhesive substance. When we regarded it attentively, we could with difficulty believe that it had not been woven by human hands. This remarkable piece of cloth we stripped carefully off, and found it to be above two feet long by a foot broad, and we carried it home with us as a great prize.

Jack now took one of the leaflets, and, cutting out the central spine or stalk, hurried back with it to our camp. Having made a small fire, he baked the nuts slightly, and then peeled off the husks. After this he wished to bore a hole in them, which, not having anything better at hand at the time, he did with the point of our useless pencil-case. Then he strung them on the cocoa-nut spine, and on putting a light to the topmost nut, we found to our joy that it burned with a clear, beautiful flame ; upon seeing which, Peterkin sprang up and danced round the fire for at least five minutes in the excess of his satisfaction.

" Now, lads," said Jack, extinguishing our candle,

" the sun will set in an hour, so we have no time to lose. I shall go and cut a young tree to make my bow out of, and you had better each of you go and select good strong sticks for clubs, and we'll set to work at them after dark."

So saying he shouldered his axe and went off, followed by Peterkin ; while I took up the piece of newly-discovered cloth, and fell to examining its structure. So engrossed was I in this that I was still sitting in the same attitude and occupation when my companions returned.

" I told you so ! " cried Peterkin, with a loud laugh.—" O Ralph, you're incorrigible. See, there's a club for you. I was sure, when we left you looking at that bit of stuff, that we would find you poring over it when we came back, so I just cut a club for you as well as for myself."

" Thank you, Peterkin," said I. " It was kind of you to do that, instead of scolding me for a lazy fellow, as I confess I deserve."

" Oh, as to that," returned Peterkin, " I'll blow you up yet, if you wish it ; only it would be of no use if I did, for you're a perfect mule ! "

As it was now getting dark we lighted our candle, and placing it in a holder, made of two crossing branches, inside of our bower, we seated ourselves on our leafy beds and began to work.

" I intend to appropriate the bow for my own use," said Jack, chipping the piece of wood he had brought with his axe. " I used to be a pretty fair shot once.—But what's that you're doing ? " he

added, looking at Peterkin, who had drawn the end
of a long pole into the tent, and was endeavouring
to fit a small piece of the hoop-iron to the end of it.

"I'm going to enlist into the Lancers," answered
Peterkin. "You see, Jack, I find the club rather
an unwieldy instrument for my delicately-formed
muscles, and I flatter myself I shall do more execution with a spear. "

"Well, if length constitutes power," said Jack,
"you'll certainly be invincible."

The pole which Peterkin had cut was full twelve
feet long, being a very strong but light and tough
young tree, which merely required thinning at the
butt to be a serviceable weapon.

"That's a very good idea," said I.

"Which—this ? " inquired Peterkin, pointing to
the spear.

"Yes," I replied.

"Humph ! " said he ; "you'd find it a pretty
tough and matter-of-fact idea if you had it stuck
through your gizzard, old boy ! "

"I mean the idea of making it is a good one,"
said I, laughing. "And, now I think of it, I'll
change my plan, too. I don't think much of a club,
so I'll make me a sling out of this piece of cloth.
I used to be very fond of slinging, ever since I read
of David slaying Goliath the Philistine, and I was
once thought to be expert at it."

So I set to work to manufacture a sling. For a
long time we all worked very busily without speaking. At length Peterkin looked up. "I say, Jack,

I'm sorry to say I must apply to you for another strip of your handkerchief, to tie on this rascally head with. It's pretty well torn at any rate, so you won't miss it."

Jack proceeded to comply with this request, when Peterkin suddenly laid his hand on his arm and arrested him.

" Hist, man," said he, " be tender ; you should never be needlessly cruel if you can help it. Do try to shave past Lord Nelson's mouth without tearing it, if possible ! Thanks. There are plenty more handkerchiefs on the cocoa-nut trees."

Poor Peterkin ! with what pleasant feelings I recall and record his jests and humorous sayings now !

While we were thus engaged, we were startled by a distant but most strange and horrible cry. It seemed to come from the sea, but was so far away that we could not clearly distinguish its precise direction. Rushing out of our bower, we hastened down to the beach and stayed to listen. Again it came quite loud and distinct on the night air,— a prolonged, hideous cry, something like the braying of an ass. The moon had risen, and we could see the islands in and beyond the lagoon quite plainly, but there was no object visible to account for such a cry. A strong gust of wind was blowing from the point whence the sound came, but this died away while we were gazing out to sea.

" What can it be ? " said Peterkin, in a low whisper, while we all involuntarily crept closer to each other.

" Do you know," said Jack, " I have heard that mysterious sound twice before, but never so loud as to-night. Indeed it was so faint that I thought I must have merely fancied it, so, as I did not wish to alarm you, I said nothing about it."

We listened for a long time for the sound again, but as it did not come, we returned to the bower and resumed our work.

" Very strange," said Peterkin, quite gravely.— " Do you believe in ghosts, Ralph ? "

" No," I answered, " I do not. Nevertheless I must confess that strange, unaccountable sounds, such as we have just heard, make me feel a little uneasy."

" What say you to it, Jack ? "

" I neither believe in ghosts nor feel uneasy," he replied. " I never saw a ghost myself, and I never met with any one who had ; and I have generally found that strange and unaccountable things have almost always been accounted for, and found to be quite simple, on close examination. I certainly can't imagine what *that* sound is ; but I'm quite sure I shall find out before long, and if it's a ghost, I'll— I'll—"

" Eat it," cried Peterkin.

" Yes, I'll eat it ! Now, then, my bow and two arrows are finished ; so if you're ready we had better turn in."

By this time Peterkin had thinned down his spear and tied an iron point very cleverly to the end of it ; I had formed a sling, the lines of which were

composed of thin strips of the cocoa-nut cloth, plaited;
and Jack had made a stout bow, nearly five feet long,
with two arrows, feathered with two or three large
plumes which some bird had dropped. They had
no barbs, but Jack said that if arrows were well
feathered they did not require iron points, but would
fly quite well if merely sharpened at the point;
which I did not know before.

"A feathered arrow without a barb," said he,
"is a good weapon, but a barbed arrow without
feathers is utterly useless."

The string of the bow was formed of our piece of
whip-cord, part of which, as he did not like to cut it,
was rolled round the bow.

Although thus prepared for a start on the morrow,
we thought it wise to exercise ourselves a little in the
use of our weapons before starting, so we spent the
whole of the next day in practising. And it was well
we did so, for we found that our arms were very imperfect, and that we were far from perfect in the use
of them. First, Jack found that the bow was much
too strong, and he had to thin it. Also the spear
was much too heavy, and so had to be reduced in
thickness, although nothing would induce Peterkin
to have it shortened. My sling answered very well,
but I had fallen so much out of practice that my first
stone knocked off Peterkin's hat, and narrowly
missed making a second Goliath of him. However,
after having spent the whole day in diligent practice,
we began to find some of our former expertness returning—at least Jack and I did. As for Peterkin,

being naturally a neat-handed boy, he soon handled his spear well, and could run full tilt at a cocoa nut, and hit it with great precision once out of every five times.

But I feel satisfied that we owed much of our rapid success to the unflagging energy of Jack, who insisted that, since we had made him captain, we should obey him ; and he kept us at work from morning till night, perseveringly, at the same thing. Peterkin wished very much to run about and stick his spear into everything he passed ; but Jack put up a cocoa nut, and would not let him leave off running at that for a moment, except when he wanted to rest. We laughed at Jack for this, but we were both convinced that it did us much good.

That night we examined and repaired our arms ere we lay down to rest, although we were much fatigued, in order that we might be in readiness to set out on our expedition at daylight on the following morning.

CHAPTER IX

Prepare for a journey round the island—Sagacious reflections—
Mysterious appearances and startling occurrences.

SCARCELY had the sun shot its first ray across the
bosom of the broad Pacific, when Jack sprang to his
feet, and, hallooing in Peterkin's ear to awaken him,
ran down the beach to take his customary dip in the
sea. We did not, as was our wont, bathe that morning in our Water Garden, but, in order to save time,
refreshed ourselves in the shallow water just opposite
the bower. Our breakfast was also dispatched without loss of time, and in less than an hour afterwards
all our preparations for the journey were completed.

In addition to his ordinary dress, Jack tied a belt
of cocoa-nut cloth round his waist, into which he
thrust the axe. I was also advised to put on a belt
and carry a short cudgel or bludgeon in it ; for, as
Jack truly remarked, the sling would be of little use
if we should chance to come to close quarters with
any wild animal. As for Peterkin, notwithstanding
that he carried such a long, and I must add, fright-
ful-looking spear over his shoulder, we could not
prevail on him to leave his club behind ; " for," said
he, " a spear at close quarters is not worth a button."
I must say that it seemed to me that the club was,
to use his own style of language, not worth a button-
hole ; for it was all knotted over at the head, some-

thing like the club which I remember to have observed in picture-books of Jack the Giant-Killer, besides being so heavy that he required to grasp it with both hands in order to wield it at all. However, he took it with him, and in this manner we set out upon our travels.

We did not consider it necessary to carry any food with us, as we knew that wherever we went we should be certain to fall in with cocoa-nut trees ; having which we were amply supplied, as Peterkin said, with meat and drink and pocket-handkerchiefs ! I took the precaution, however, to put the burning-glass into my pocket, lest we should want fire.

The morning was exceedingly lovely. It was one of that very still and peaceful sort which made the few noises that we heard seem to be *quiet* noises (I know no other way of expressing this idea)—noises which, so far from interrupting the universal tran- quillity of earth, sea, and sky, rather tended to reveal to us how quiet the world round us really was. Such sounds as I refer to were, the peculiarly melan- choly—yet, it seemed to me, cheerful—plaint of sea- birds floating on the glassy water or sailing in the sky, also the subdued twittering of little birds among the bushes, the faint ripples on the beach, and the solemn boom of the surf upon the distant coral reef. We felt very glad in our hearts as we walked along the sands side by side. For my part, I felt so deeply overjoyed that I was surprised at my own sensations, and fell into a reverie upon the causes of happiness. I came to the conclusion that a state of profound peace and repose, both in regard to outward objects and within the soul, is the happiest condition in which man can be placed ; for although I had many a time been most joyful and happy when engaged in bustling, energetic, active pursuits or amusements, I never found that such joy or satisfaction was so deep or so pleasant to reflect upon as that which I now experienced. And I was the more confirmed in this opinion when I observed, and indeed was told by himself, that Peterkin's happiness was also very great ; yet he did not express this by dancing as was his wont, nor did he give so much as a single shout, but walked quietly between us with his eye sparkling, and a joyful smile upon his countenance. My reader must not suppose that I thought all this in the clear and methodical manner in which I have set it down here. These thoughts did indeed pass through my mind, but they did so in a very confused and indefinite manner, for I was young at that time, and not much given to deep reflection. Neither did I consider that the peace whereof I write is not to be found in this world—at least in its perfection, although I have since learned that by religion a man may attain to a very great degree of it.

I have said that Peterkin walked along the sands between us. We had two ways of walking together about our island. When we travelled through the woods, we always did so in single file, as by this method we advanced with greater facility, the one treading in the other's footsteps. In such cases Jack always took the lead, Peterkin followed, and I brought up the rear. But when we travelled along the sands, which extended almost in an unbroken line of glistening white round the island, we marched abreast, as we found this method more sociable, and every way more pleasant. Jack, being the tallest, walked next the sea, and Peterkin marched between us, as by this arrangement either of us could talk to him or he to us, while if Jack and I happened to wish to converse together, we could conveniently do so over Peterkin's head. Peterkin used to say, in reference to this arrangement, that had he been as tall as either of us, our order of march might have been the same; for as Jack often used to scold him for letting everything we said to him pass in at one ear and out at the other, his head could of course form no interruption to our discourse.

We were now fairly started. Half a mile's walk conveyed us round a bend in the land which shut out our bower from view, and for some time we advanced at a brisk pace without speaking, though our eyes were not idle, but noted everything, in the woods, on the shore, or in the sea, that was interesting. After passing the ridge of land that formed one side of our valley—the Valley of the Wreck— we beheld another small vale lying before us in all the luxuriant loveliness of tropical vegetation. We had, indeed, seen it before from the mountain-top, but we had no idea that it would turn out to be so much more lovely when we were close to it. We were about to commence the exploration of this valley, when Peterkin stopped us, and directed our attention to a very remarkable appearance in advance along the shore.

" What's yon, think you ? " said he, levelling his spear, as if he expected an immediate attack from the object in question, though it was full half a mile distant.

As he spoke, there appeared a white column above the rocks, as if of steam or spray. It rose upwards to a height of several feet, and then disappeared. Had this been near the sea, we would not have been so greatly surprised, as it might in that case have been the surf, for at this part of the coast the coral reef approached so near to the island that in some parts it almost joined it. There was, therefore, no lagoon between, and the heavy surf of the ocean beat almost up to the rocks. But this white column appeared about fifty yards inland. The rocks at the place were rugged, and they stretched across the sandy beach into the sea. Scarce had we ceased expressing our surprise at this sight, when another column flew upwards for a few seconds, not far from the spot where the first had been seen, and disappeared ; and so, at long, irregular intervals, these strange sights recurred. We were now quite sure that the columns were watery or composed of spray, but what caused them we could not guess, so we determined to go and see.

In a few minutes we gained the spot, which was very rugged and precipitous, and, moreover, quite damp with the falling of the spray. We had much ado to pass over dryshod. The ground also was full of holes here and there. Now, while we stood

anxiously waiting for the reappearance of these
waterspouts, we heard a low, rumbling sound near us,
which quickly increased to a gurgling and hissing
noise, and a moment afterwards a thick spout of
water burst upwards from a hole in the rock, and
spouted into the air with much violence, and so close
to where Jack and I were standing that it nearly
touched us. We sprang aside, but not before a cloud
of spray descended, and drenched us both to the skin.

Peterkin, who was standing farther off, escaped
with a few drops, and burst into an uncontrollable
fit of laughter on beholding our miserable plight.

" Mind your eye ! " he shouted eagerly, " there
goes another ! " The words were scarcely out of his
mouth when there came up a spout from another hole,
which served us exactly in the same manner as before.

Peterkin now shrieked with laughter ; but his
merriment was abruptly put a stop to by the gurgling
noise occurring close to where he stood.

" Where'll it spout this time, I wonder ? " he said,
looking about with some anxiety, and preparing to
run. Suddenly there came a loud hiss or snort ; a
fierce spout of water burst up between Peterkin's
legs, blew him off his feet, enveloped him in its spray,
and hurled him to the ground. He fell with so much
violence that we feared he must have broken some
of his bones, and ran anxiously to his assistance ;
but fortunately he had fallen on a clump of tangled
herbage, in which he lay sprawling in a most deplor-
able condition.

It was now our turn to laugh ; but as we were not

yet quite sure that he was unhurt, and as we knew not when or where the next spout might arise, we assisted him hastily to jump up and hurry from the spot.

I may here add, that although I am quite certain that the spout of water was very strong, and that it blew Peterkin completely off his legs, I am not quite certain of the exact height to which it lifted him, being somewhat startled by the event, and blinded partially by the spray, so that my power of observation was somewhat impaired for the moment.

"What's to be done now?" asked Peterkin ruefully.

"Make a fire, lad, and dry ourselves," replied Jack.

"And here is material ready to our hand," said I, picking up a dried branch of a tree, as we hurried up to the woods.

In about an hour after this mishap our clothes were again dried. While they were hanging up before the fire, we walked down to the beach, and soon observed that these curious spouts took place immediately after the fall of a huge wave, never before it; and, moreover, that the spouts did not take place excepting when the billow was an extremely large one. From this we concluded that there must be a subterraneous channel in the rock into which the water was driven by the larger waves, and finding no way of escape except through these small holes, was thus forced up violently through them. At any rate, we could not conceive any other reason for these strange waterspouts, and as this seemed a very simple and probable one, we forthwith adopted it.

" I say, Ralph, what's that in the water ? is it a shark ? " said Jack, just as we were about to quit the place.

I immediately ran to the overhanging ledge of rock, from which he was looking down into the sea, and bent over it. There I saw a very faint pale object of a greenish colour, which seemed to move slightly while I looked at it.

" It's like a fish of some sort," said I.

" Hallo, Peterkin ! " cried Jack, " fetch your spear ; here's work for it."

But when we tried to reach the object, the spear proved to be too short.

" There now," said Peterkin, with a sneer, " you were always telling me it was too long."

Jack now drove the spear forcibly towards the object, and let go his hold ; but although it seemed to be well aimed, he must have missed, for the handle soon rose again ; and when the spear was drawn up, there was the pale green object in exactly the same spot, slowly moving its tail.

" Very odd," said Jack.

But although it was undoubtedly very odd, and although Jack and all of us plunged the spear at it repeatedly, we could neither hit it nor drive it away, so we were compelled to continue our journey without discovering what it was. I was very much perplexed at this strange appearance in the water, and could not get it out of my mind for a long time afterwards. However, I quieted myself by resolving that I would pay a visit to it again at some more convenient season.

CHAPTER X

OUR examination of the little valley proved to be altogether most satisfactory. We found in it not only trees similar to those we had already seen in our own valley, but also one or two others of a different species. We had also the satisfaction of discovering a peculiar vegetable, which Jack concluded must certainly be that of which he had read as being very common among the South Sea islanders, and which was named *taro*. Also we found a large supply of yams, and another root like a potato in appearance. As these were all quite new to us, we regarded our lot as a most fortunate one, in being thus cast on an island which was so prolific and so well stored with all the necessaries of life. Long afterwards we found out that this island of ours was not better in these respects than thousands of other islands in those seas. Indeed, many of them were much richer and more productive ; but that did not render us the less grateful for our present good fortune. We each put one of these roots in our pocket, intending to use them for our supper ; of which more hereafter. We also saw many beautiful birds here, and traces of some

four-footed animal again. Meanwhile the sun began
to descend, so we returned to the shore, and pushed
on round the spouting rocks into the next valley.
This was that valley of which I have spoken as running
across the entire island. It was by far the largest
and most beautiful that we had yet looked upon.
Here were trees of every shape and size and hue which
it is possible to conceive of, many of which we had
not seen in the other valleys ; for, the stream in this
valley being larger, and the mould much richer than
in the Valley of the Wreck, it was clothed with a more
luxuriant growth of trees and plants. Some trees
were dark glossy green, others of a rich and warm
hue, contrasting well with those of a pale light green,
which were everywhere abundant. Among these
we recognized the broad dark heads of the bread-
fruit, with its golden fruit ; the pure, silvery foliage
of the candle-nut, and several species which bore a
strong resemblance to the pine ; while here and
there, in groups and in single trees, rose the tall forms
of the cocoa-nut palms, spreading abroad, and
waving their graceful plumes high above all the rest,
as if they were a superior race of stately giants keeping guard over these luxuriant forests. Oh, it was
a most enchanting scene ! and I thanked God for
having created such delightful spots for the use of man.

Now, while we were gazing around us in silent
admiration, Jack uttered an exclamation of surprise,
and pointing to an object a little to one side of us,
said,—

" That's a banyan tree."

" And what's a banyan tree ? " inquired Peterkin, as we walked towards it.

" A very curious one, as you shall see presently," replied Jack. " It is called the *aoa* here, if I recollect rightly, and has a wonderful peculiarity about it. What an enormous one it is, to be sure ! "

" *It !* " repeated Peterkin ; " why, there are dozens of banyans here ! What do you mean by talking bad grammar ? Is your philosophy deserting you, Jack ? "

" There is but one tree here of this kind," returned Jack, " as you will perceive if you will examine it." And, sure enough, we did find that what we had supposed was a forest of trees was in reality only one. Its bark was of a light colour, and had a shining appearance, the leaves being lance-shaped, small, and of a beautiful pea-green. But the wonderful thing about it was that the branches, which grew out from the stem horizontally, sent down long shoots or fibres to the ground, which, taking root, had themselves become trees, and were covered with bark like the tree itself. Many of these fibres had descended from the branches at various distances, and thus supported them on natural pillars, some of which were so large and strong that it was not easy at first to distinguish the offspring from the parent stem. The fibres were of all sizes and in all states of advancement, from the pillars we have just mentioned to small cords which hung down and were about to take root, and thin brown threads still far from the ground, which swayed about with every motion of wind. In short, it seemed to us that, if there were only space afforded to it, this single tree would at length cover the whole island.

Shortly after this we came upon another remarkable tree, which, as its peculiar formation afterwards proved extremely useful to us, merits description. It was a splendid chestnut, but its proper name Jack did not know. However, there were quantities of fine nuts upon it, some of which we put in our pockets. But its stem was the wonderful part of it. It rose to about twelve feet without a branch, and was not of great thickness : on the contrary, it was remarkably slender for the size of the tree ; but, to make up for this, there were four or five wonderful projections in this stem, which I cannot better describe than by asking the reader to suppose that five planks two inches thick and three feet broad had been placed round the trunk of the tree, with their *edges* closely fixed to it, from the ground up to the branches, and that these planks had been covered over with the bark of the tree and incorporated with it. In short they were just natural buttresses, without which the stem could not have supported its heavy and umbrageous top. We found these chestnuts to be very numerous. They grew chiefly on the banks of the stream, and were of all sizes.

While we were examining a small tree of this kind, Jack chipped a piece off a buttress with his axe, and found the wood to be firm and easily cut. He then struck the axe into it with all his force, and very soon split it off close to the tree, first, however, having cut it across transversely above and below. By this means he satisfied himself that we could now obtain short planks, as it were already sawn, of any size and thickness that we desired ; which was a very great discovery indeed, perhaps the most important we had yet made.

We now wended our way back to the coast, intending to encamp near the beach, as we found that the musquitoes were troublesome in the forest. On our way we could not help admiring the birds which flew and chirped around us. Among them we observed a pretty kind of paroquet, with a green body, a blue head, and a red breast ; also a few beautiful turtle-doves, and several flocks of wood-pigeons. The hues of many of these birds were extremely vivid—bright green, blue, and scarlet being the prevailing tints. We made several attempts throughout the day to bring down one of these, both with the bow and the sling—not for mere sport, but to ascertain whether they were good for food. But we invariably missed, although once or twice we were very near hitting. As evening drew on, however, a flock of pigeons flew past. I slung a stone into the midst of them at a venture, and had the good fortune to kill one. We were startled, soon after, by a loud whistling noise above our heads ; and on looking up, saw a flock of wild ducks making for the coast. We watched these, and observing where they alighted, followed them up until we came upon a most lovely blue lake, not more than two hundred yards long, imbosomed in verdant trees. Its placid surface, which reflected every leaf and stem as if in a mirror, was covered with various

100 THE CORAL ISLAND

species of wild ducks, feeding among the sedges and broad-leaved water-plants which floated on it, while numerous birds like water-hens ran to and fro most busily on its margin. These all with one accord flew tumultuously away the instant we made our appearance. While walking along the margin we observed fish in the water, but of what sort we could not tell.

Now, as we neared the shore, Jack and I said we would go a little out of our way, to see if we could procure one of those ducks; so, directing Peterkin to go straight to the shore and kindle a fire, we separated, promising to rejoin him speedily. But we did not find the ducks, although we made a diligent search for half an hour. We were about to retrace our steps, when we were arrested by one of the strangest sights that we had yet beheld.

Just in front of us, at the distance of about ten yards, grew a superb tree, which certainly was the largest we had yet seen on the island. Its trunk was at least five feet in diameter, with a smooth gray bark; above this the spreading branches were clothed with light green leaves, amid which were clusters of bright yellow fruit, so numerous as to weigh down the boughs with their great weight. This fruit seemed to be of the plum species, of an oblong form, and a good deal larger than the magnum bonum plum. The ground at the foot of this tree was thickly strewn with the fallen fruit, in the midst of which lay sleeping, in every possible attitude, at least twenty hogs of all ages and sizes, apparently quite surfeited with a recent banquet.

Jack and I could scarce restrain our laughter as we gazed at these coarse, fat, ill-looking animals while they lay groaning and snoring heavily amid the remains of their supper.

"Now, Ralph," said Jack, in a low whisper, "put a stone in your sling—a good big one—and let fly at that fat fellow with his back toward you. I'll try to put an arrow into yon little pig."

"Don't you think we had better put them up first?" I whispered; "it seems cruel to kill them while asleep."

"If I wanted *sport*, Ralph, I would certainly set them up; but as we only want *pork*, we'll let them lie. Besides, we're not sure of killing them; so, fire away."

Thus admonished, I slung my stone with so good aim that it went bang against the hog's flank as if against the head of a drum; but it had no other effect than that of causing the animal to start to its feet, with a frightful yell of surprise, and scamper away. At the same instant Jack's bow twanged, and the arrow pinned the little pig to the ground by the ear.

"I've missed after all," cried Jack, darting forward with uplifted axe, while the little pig uttered a loud squeal, tore the arrow from the ground, and ran away with it, along with the whole drove, into the bushes and disappeared, though we heard them screaming long afterwards in the distance.

"That's very provoking, now," said Jack, rubbing the point of his nose.

"Very," I replied, stroking my chin.

"Well, we must make haste and rejoin Peterkin," said Jack. "It's getting late." And without further remark we threaded our way quickly through the woods towards the shore.

When we reached it, we found wood laid out, the fire lighted and beginning to kindle up, with other signs of preparation for our encampment, but Peterkin was nowhere to be found. We wondered very much at this; but Jack suggested that he might have gone to fetch water: so he gave a shout to let him know that we had arrived, and sat down upon a rock; while I threw off my jacket, and seized the axe, intending to split up one or two billets of wood. But I had scarce moved from the spot when, in the distance, we heard a most appalling shriek, which was followed up by a chorus of yells from the hogs, and a loud hurrah.

"I do believe," said I, "that Peterkin has met with the hogs."

"When Greek meets Greek," said Jack, soliloquizing, "then comes the tug of—"

"Hurrah!" shouted Peterkin in the distance.

We turned hastily towards the direction whence the sound came, and soon descried Peterkin walking along the beach towards us with a little pig transfixed on the end of his long spear!

"Well done, my boy!" exclaimed Jack, slapping him on the shoulder when he came up; "you're the best shot amongst us."

"Look here, Jack!" cried Peterkin, as he disengaged the animal from his spear. "Do you recognize that hole?" said he, pointing to the pig's ear: "and are you familiar with this arrow, eh?"

" Well, I declare ! " said Jack.

" Of course, you do," interrupted Peterkin ; " but pray restrain your declarations at this time, and let's have supper, for I'm uncommonly hungry, I can tell you : and it's no joke to charge a whole herd of swine with their great-grandmother bristling like a giant porcupine at the head of them ! "

We now set about preparing supper ; and, truly, a good display of viands we made, when all was laid out on a flat rock in the light of the blazing fire. There was, first of all, the little pig ; then there were the taro-root, and the yam, and the potato, and six plums ; and, lastly, the wood-pigeon. To these Peterkin added a bit of sugar-cane, which he had cut from a little patch of that plant which he had found not long after separating from us ; " and," said he, " the patch was somewhat in a square form, which convinces me it must have been planted by man."

" Very likely," replied Jack. " From all we have seen, I'm inclined to think that some of the savages must have dwelt here long ago."

We found no small difficulty in making up our minds how we were to cook the pig. None of us had ever cut up one before, and we did not know exactly how to begin ; besides, we had nothing but the axe to do it with, our knife having been forgotten. At last Jack started up and said,—

" Don't let us waste more time talking about it, boys.—Hold it up, Peterkin. There, lay the hind leg on this block of wood—so ; " and he cut it off, with a large portion of the haunch, at a single blow of the axe. " Now the other—that's it." And having thus cut off the two hind legs, he made several deep gashes in them, thrust a sharp-pointed stick through each, and stuck them up before the blaze to roast. The wood-pigeon was then split open, quite flat, washed clean in salt water, and treated in a similar manner. While these were cooking, we scraped a hole in the sand and ashes under the fire, into which we put our vegetables, and covered them up.

The taro-root was of an oval shape, about ten inches long and four or five thick. It was of a mottled-gray colour, and had a thick rind. We found it somewhat like an Irish potato, and exceedingly good. The yam was roundish, and had a rough brown skin. It was very sweet and well flavoured. The potato, we were surprised to find, was quite sweet, and exceedingly palatable, as also were the plums ; and, indeed, the pork and pigeon too, when we came to taste them. Altogether this was decidedly the most luxurious supper we had enjoyed for many a day. Jack said it was out-of-sight better than we ever got on board ship ; and Peterkin said he feared that if we should remain long on the island, he would infallibly become a glutton or an epicure : whereat Jack remarked that he need not fear that, for he was *both* already ! And so, having eaten our fill, not forgetting to finish off with a plum, we laid ourselves comfortably down to sleep upon a couch of branches, under the overhanging ledge of a coral rock.

CHAPTER XI

WHEN we awoke on the following morning, we found that the sun was already a good way above the horizon ; so I came to the conclusion that a heavy supper is not conducive to early rising. Nevertheless, we felt remarkably strong and well, and much disposed to have our breakfast. First, however, we had our customary morning bathe, which refreshed us greatly.

I have often wondered very much in after years that the inhabitants of my own dear land did not make more frequent use of this most charming ele- ment, water—I mean in the way of cold bathing. Of course, I have perceived that it is not convenient for them to go into the sea or the rivers in winter, as we used to do on the Coral Island ; but then I knew from experience that a large washing-tub and a sponge do form a most pleasant substitute. The feelings of freshness, of cleanliness, of vigour, and extreme hilarity, that always followed my bathes in the

sea, and even, when in England, my ablutions in the
wash-tub, were so delightful, that I would sooner
have gone without my breakfast than without my
bathe in cold water. My readers will forgive me
for asking whether they are in the habit of bathing
thus every morning ; and if they answer " No,"
they will pardon me for recommending them to begin
at once. Of late years, since retiring from the
stirring life of adventure which I have led so long in
foreign climes, I have heard of a system called the
cold-water cure. Now, I do not know much about
that system, so I do not mean to uphold it, neither
do I intend to run it down. Perhaps, in reference
to it, I may just hint that there may be too much of
a good thing. I know not ; but of this I am quite
certain, that there may also be too little of a good
thing ; and the great delight I have had in cold bathing during the course of my adventurous career in-
clines me to think that it is better to risk taking too
much than to content one's self with too little. Such
is my opinion, derived from much experience ; but
I put it before my readers with the utmost diffidence
and with profound modesty, knowing that it may
possibly jar with their feelings of confidence in their
own ability to know and judge as to what is best and
fittest in reference to their own affairs. But to
return from this digression, for which I humbly
crave forgiveness :

We had not advanced on our journey much above
a mile or so, and were just beginning to feel the
pleasant glow that usually accompanies vigorous

exercise, when, on turning a point that revealed to us a new and beautiful cluster of islands, we were suddenly arrested by the appalling cry which had so alarmed us a few nights before. But this time we were by no means so much alarmed as on the previous occasion, because, whereas at that time it was night, now it was day; and I have always found, though I am unable to account for it, that daylight banishes many of the fears that are apt to assail us in the dark.

On hearing the sound, Peterkin instantly threw forward his spear.

"Now, what can it be?" said he, looking round at Jack. "I tell you what it is: if we are to go on being pulled up in a constant state of horror and astonishment, as we have been for the last week, the sooner we're out o' this island the better, notwithstanding the yams and lemonade, and pork and plums!"

Peterkin's remark was followed by a repetition of the cry, louder than before.

"It comes from one of these islands," said Jack.

"It must be the ghost of a jackass, then," said Peterkin, "for I never heard anything so like."

We all turned our eyes towards the cluster of islands, where, on the largest, we observed curious objects moving on the shore.

"Soldiers they are—that's flat!" cried Peterkin, gazing at them in the utmost amazement.

And, in truth, Peterkin's remark seemed to me to

be correct ; for, at the distance from which we saw
them, they appeared to be an army of soldiers.
There they stood, rank and file, in lines and in
squares, marching and counter-marching, with blue
coats and white trousers. While we were looking at
them, the dreadful cry came again over the water,
and Peterkin suggested that it must be a regiment
sent out to massacre the natives in cold blood. At
this remark Jack laughed and said,—

" Why, Peterkin, they are penguins ! "

" Penguins ? " repeated Peterkin.

" Ay, penguins, Peterkin, penguins—nothing more
or less than big sea-birds, as you shall see one of these
days, when we pay them a visit in our boat, which
I mean to set about building the moment we return
to our bower."

" So, then, our dreadful yelling ghosts and our
murdering army of soldiers," remarked Peterkin,
" have dwindled down to penguins—big sea-birds !
Very good. Then I propose that we continue our
journey as fast as possible, lest our island should be
converted into a dream before we get completely
round it."

Now, as we continued on our way, I pondered
much over this new discovery, and the singular
appearance of these birds, of which Jack could only
give us a very slight and vague account ; and I
began to long to commence to our boat, in order
that we might go and inspect them more narrowly.
But by degrees these thoughts left me, and I began
to be much taken up again with the interesting

peculiarities of the country which we were passing through.

The second night we passed in a manner somewhat similar to the first, at about two-thirds of the way round the island, as we calculated, and we hoped to sleep on the night following at our bower. I will not here note so particularly all that we said and saw during the course of this second day, as we did not make any further discoveries of great importance. The shore along which we travelled, and the various parts of the woods through which we passed, were similar to those which have been already treated of. There were one or two observations that we made, however, and these were as follows :—

We saw that, while many of the large fruit-bearing trees grew only in the valleys, and some of them only near the banks of the streams, where the soil was peculiarly rich, the cocoa-nut palm grew in every place whatsoever ; not only on the hillsides, but also on the seashore, and even, as has been already stated, on the coral reef itself, where the soil, if we may use the name, was nothing better than loose sand mingled with broken shells and coral rock. So near to the sea, too, did this useful tree grow, that in many places its roots were washed by the spray from the breakers. Yet we found the trees growing thus on the sands to be quite as luxuriant as those growing in the valleys, and the fruit as good and refreshing also. Besides this, I noticed that on the summit of the high mountain, which we once more ascended at a different point from our first ascent, were found abundance of shells and broken coral formations ; which Jack and I agreed proved either that this island must have once been under the sea, or that the sea must once have been above the island. In other words, that as shells and coral could not possibly climb to the mountain-top, they must have been washed upon it while the mountain-top was on a level with the sea. We pondered this very much ; and we put to ourselves the question, " What raised the island to its present height above the sea ? " But to this we could by no means give to ourselves a satisfactory reply. Jack thought it might have been blown up by a volcano ; and Peterkin said he thought it must have jumped up of its own accord ! We also noticed, what had escaped us before, that the solid rocks of which the island was formed were quite different from the live coral rocks on the shore, where the wonderful little insects were continually working. They seemed, indeed, to be of the same material—a substance like limestone ; but while the coral rocks were quite full of minute cells in which the insects lived, the other rocks inland were hard and solid, without the appearance of cells at all. Our thoughts and conversations on this subject were sometimes so profound that Peterkin said we should certainly get drowned in them at last, even although we were such good divers ! Nevertheless we did not allow his pleasantry on this and similar points to deter us from making our notes and observations as we went along.

We found several more droves of hogs in the woods,

but abstained from killing any of them, having more than sufficient for our present necessities. We saw also many of their footprints in this neighbourhood. Among these we also observed the footprints of a smaller animal, which we examined with much care, but could form no certain opinion as to them. Peterkin thought they were those of a little dog, but Jack and I thought differently. We became very curious on this matter, the more so that we observed these footprints to lie scattered about in one locality, as if the animal which had made them was wandering round about in a very irregular manner, and without any object in view. Early in the forenoon of our third day we observed these footprints to be much more numerous than ever, and in one particular spot they diverged off into the woods in a regular beaten track, which was, however, so closely beset with bushes that we pushed through it with difficulty. We had now become so anxious to find out what animal this was and where it went to, that we determined to follow the track, and, if possible, clear up the mystery. Peterkin said, in a bantering tone, that he was sure it would be cleared up, as usual, in some frightfully simple way, and prove to be no mystery at all !

The beaten track seemed much too large to have been formed by the animal itself, and we concluded that some larger animal had made it, and that the smaller one made use of it. But everywhere the creeping plants and tangled bushes crossed our path, so that we forced our way along with some difficulty.

Suddenly, as we came upon an open space, we heard a faint cry, and observed a black animal standing in the track before us.

"A wild cat!" cried Jack, fitting an arrow to his bow, and discharging it so hastily that he missed the animal, and hit the earth about half a foot to one side of it. To our surprise the wild cat did not fly, but walked slowly towards the arrow, and snuffed at it.

"That's the most comical wild cat I ever saw!" cried Jack.

"It's a tame wild cat, I think," said Peterkin, levelling his spear to make a charge.

"Stop!" cried I, laying my hand on his shoulder; "I do believe the poor beast is blind. See, it strikes against the branches as it walks along. It must be a very old one;" and I hastened towards it.

"Only think," said Peterkin, with a suppressed laugh, "of a superannuated wild cat!"

We now found that the poor cat was not only blind, or nearly so, but extremely deaf, as it did not hear our footsteps until we were quite close behind it. Then it sprang round, and putting up its back and tail, while the black hair stood all on end, uttered a hoarse mew and a fuff.

"Poor thing!" said Peterkin, gently extending his hand, and endeavouring to pat the cat's head. "Poor pussy; chee, chee, chee; puss, puss puss; cheetie pussy!"

No sooner did the cat hear these sounds than all signs of anger fled, and advancing eagerly to

Peterkin, it allowed itself to be stroked, and rubbed itself against his legs, purring loudly all the time, and showing every symptom of the most extreme delight.

"It's no more a wild cat than I am!" cried Peterkin, taking it in his arms; "it's quite tame.— Poor pussy, cheetie pussy!"

We now crowded around Peterkin, and were not a little surprised, and, to say truth, a good deal affected, by the sight of the poor animal's excessive joy. It rubbed its head against Peterkin's cheek, licked his chin, and thrust its head almost violently into his neck, while it purred more loudly than I ever heard a cat purr before, and appeared to be so much overpowered by its feelings, that it occasionally mewed and purred almost in the same breath. Such demonstrations of joy and affection led us at once to conclude that this poor cat must have known man before, and we conjectured that it had been left either accidentally or by design on the island many years ago, and was now evincing its extreme joy at meeting once more with human beings. While we were fondling the cat and talking about it, Jack glanced round the open space in the midst of which we stood.

"Hallo!" exclaimed he; "this looks something like a clearing. The axe has been at work here. Just look at these tree-stumps."

We now turned to examine these, and without doubt we found trees that had been cut down here and there, also stumps and broken branches; all of

which, however, were completely covered over with
moss, and bore evidence of having been in this
condition for some years. No human footprints
were to be seen either on the track or among the
bushes, but those of the cat were found everywhere. We now determined to follow up the track
as far as it went, and Peterkin put the cat down;
but it seemed to be so weak, and mewed so very
pitifully, that he took it up again and carried it
in his arms, where in a few minutes it fell sound
asleep.

About ten yards further on, the felled trees became
more numerous, and the track, diverging to the right,
followed for a short space the banks of a stream.
Suddenly we came to a spot where once must
have been a rude bridge, the stones of which were
scattered in the stream, and those on each bank
entirely covered over with moss. In silent surprise
and expectancy we continued to advance, and, a
few yards further on, beheld, under the shelter of
some bread-fruit trees, a small hut or cottage. I
cannot hope to convey to my readers a very correct
idea of the feelings that affected us on witnessing this
unexpected sight. We stood for a long time in silent
wonder, for there was a deep and most melancholy
stillness about the place that quite overpowered us;
and when we did at length speak, it was in subdued
whispers, as if we were surrounded by some awful
or supernatural influence. Even Peterkin's voice,
usually so quick and lively on all occasions, was
hushed now; for there was a dreariness about this

silent, lonely, uninhabited cottage—so strange in its
appearance, so far away from the usual dwellings of
man, so old, decayed, and deserted in its aspect—
that fell upon our spirits like a thick cloud, and
blotted out as with a pall the cheerful sunshine that
had filled us since the commencement of our tour
round the island.

The hut or cottage was rude and simple in its
construction. It was not more than twelve feet
long by ten feet broad, and about seven or eight
feet high. It had one window, or rather a small
frame in which a window might perhaps once have
been, but which was now empty. The door was
exceedingly low, and formed of rough boards, and
the roof was covered with broad cocoa-nut and plantain leaves. But every part of it was in a state of
the utmost decay. Moss and green matter grew in
spots all over it. The woodwork was quite perforated
with holes ; the roof had nearly fallen in, and appeared to be prevented from doing so altogether by
the thick matting of creeping plants and the interlaced branches which years of neglect had allowed
to cover it almost entirely ; while the thick, luxuriant
branches of the bread-fruit and other trees spread
above it, and flung a deep, sombre shadow over the
spot, as if to guard it from the heat and the light
of day. We conversed long and in whispers about
this strange habitation ere we ventured to approach
it ; and when at length we did so, it was, at least on
my part, with feelings of awe.

At first Jack endeavoured to peep in at the window,

but from the deep shadow of the trees already mentioned, and the gloom within, he could not clearly discern objects ; so we lifted the latch and pushed open the door. We observed that the latch was made of iron, and almost eaten away with rust. In the like condition were also the hinges, which creaked as the door swung back. On entering, we stood still and gazed around us, while we were much impressed with the dreary stillness of the room. But what we saw there surprised and shocked us not a little. There was no furniture in the apartment save a little wooden stool and an iron pot, the latter almost eaten through with rust. In the corner farthest from the door was a low bedstead, on which lay two skeletons, embedded in a little heap of dry dust. With beating hearts we went forward to examine them. One was the skeleton of a man, the other that of a dog, which was extended close beside that of the man, with its head resting on his bosom.

Now we were very much concerned about this discovery, and could scarce refrain from tears on beholding these sad remains. After some time, we began to talk about what we had seen, and to examine in and around the hut, in order to discover some clue to the name or history of this poor man, who had thus died in solitude, with none to mourn his loss save his cat and his faithful dog. But we found nothing—neither a book nor a scrap of paper. We found, however, the decayed remnants of what appeared to have been clothing, and an old axe. But none of these things bore marks of any kind :

and, indeed, they were so much decayed as to convince us that they had lain in the condition in which we found them for many years.

This discovery now accounted to us for the tree-stump at the top of the mountain with the initials cut on it ; also for the patch of sugar-cane and other traces of man which we had met with in the course of our rambles over the island. And we were much saddened by the reflection that the lot of this poor wanderer might possibly be our own, after many years' residence on the island, unless we should be rescued by the visit of some vessel or the arrival of natives. Having no clue whatever to account for the presence of this poor human being in such a lonely spot, we fell to conjecturing what could have brought him there. I was inclined to think that he must have been a shipwrecked sailor, whose vessel had been lost here, and all the crew been drowned except himself and his dog and cat. But Jack thought it more likely that he had run away from his vessel, and had taken the dog and cat to keep him company. We were also much occupied in our minds with the wonderful difference between the cat and the dog. For here we saw that while the one perished like a loving friend by its master's side, with its head resting on his bosom, the other had sought to sustain itself by prowling abroad in the forest, and had lived in solitude to a good old age. However, we did not conclude from this that the cat was destitute of affection, for we could not forget its emotions on first meeting with us ; but we saw from this that

the dog had a great deal more of generous love in
its nature than the cat, because it not only found it
impossible to live after the death of its master, but
it must needs, when it came to die, crawl to his side
and rest its head upon his lifeless breast.

While we were thinking on these things, and examining into everything about the room, we were
attracted by an exclamation from Peterkin.

" I say, Jack," said he, " here is something that
will be of use to us."

" What is it ? " said Jack, hastening across the
room.

" An old pistol," replied Peterkin, holding up the
weapon, which he had just pulled from under a heap
of broken wood and rubbish that lay in a corner.

" That, indeed, might have been useful," said
Jack, examining it, " if we had had any powder ;
but I suspect the bow and the sling will prove more
serviceable."

" True, I forgot that," said Peterkin ; " but we
may as well take it with us, for the flint will serve
to strike fire with when the sun does not shine."

After having spent more than an hour at this
place without discovering anything of further interest,
Peterkin took up the old cat, which had lain very
contentedly asleep on the stool whereon he had
placed it, and we prepared to take our departure.
In leaving the hut Jack stumbled heavily against the
door-post, which was so much decayed as to break
across, and the whole fabric of the hut seemed ready
to tumble about our ears. This put into our heads

that we might as well pull it down, and so form a mound over the skeleton. Jack, therefore, with his axe, cut down the other door-post; which, when it was done, brought the whole hut in ruins to the ground—a grave being thus formed to the bones of the poor recluse and his dog. Then we left the spot, having brought away the iron pot, the pistol, and the old axe, as they might be of much use to us hereafter.

During the rest of this day we pursued our journey, and examined the other end of the large valley, which we found to be so much alike to the parts already described, that I shall not recount the particulars of what we saw in this place. I may, however, remark that we did not quite recover our former cheerful spirits until we arrived at our bower, which we did late in the evening, and found everything just in the same condition as we had left it three days before.

CHAPTER XII

Something wrong with the tank—Jack's wisdom and Peterkin's
impertinence—Wonderful behaviour of a crab—Good wishes
for those who dwell far from the sea—Jack commences to build
a little boat.

REST is sweet as well for the body as for the mind.
During my long experience, amid the vicissitudes
of a chequered life, I have found that periods of
profound rest at certain intervals, in addition to the
ordinary hours of repose, are necessary to the well-
being of man. And the nature as well as the period
of this rest varies, according to the different tem-
peraments of individuals, and the peculiar circumstances in which they may chance to be placed. To
those who work with their minds, bodily labour is
rest. To those who labour with the body, deep sleep
is rest. To the downcast, the weary, and the sorrow-
ful, joy and peace are rest. Nay, further, I think that
to the gay, the frivolous, the reckless, when sated
with pleasures that cannot last, even sorrow proves
to be rest of a kind, although, perchance, it were
better that I should call it relief than rest. There is,
indeed, but one class of men to whom rest is denied
—there is no rest to the wicked. At this I do but
hint, however, as I treat not of that rest which is

spiritual, but, more particularly, of that which applies to the mind and to the body.

Of this rest we stood much in need on our return home, and we found it exceedingly sweet when we indulged in it after completing the journey just related. It had not, indeed, been a very long journey; nevertheless we had pursued it so diligently that our frames were not a little prostrated. Our minds were also very much exhausted in consequence of the many surprises, frequent alarms, and much profound thought to which they had been subjected; so that when we lay down on the night of our return under the shelter of the bower, we fell immediately into very deep repose. I can state this with much certainty, for Jack afterwards admitted the fact, and Peterkin, although he stoutly denied it, I heard snoring loudly at least two minutes after lying down. In this condition we remained all night and the whole of the following day without awaking once, or so much as moving our positions. When we did awake it was near sunset, and we were all in such a state of lassitude that we merely rose to swallow a mouthful of food. As Peterkin remarked, in the midst of a yawn, we took breakfast at tea-time, and then went to bed again, where we lay till the following forenoon.

After this we arose very greatly refreshed, but much alarmed lest we had lost count of a day. I say we were much alarmed on this head, for we had carefully kept count of the days since we were cast upon our island, in order that we might remember the

Sabbath-day, which day we had hitherto with one
accord kept as a day of rest, and refrained from all
work whatsoever. However, on considering the
subject, we all three entertained the same opinion
as to how long we had slept, and so our minds were
put at ease.

We now hastened to our Water Garden to enjoy
a bathe, and to see how did the animals which I had
placed in the tank. We found the garden more
charming, pellucid, and inviting than ever, and
Jack and I plunged into its depths and gambolled
among its radiant coral groves, while Peterkin wallowed at the surface, and tried occasionally to kick
us as we passed below. Having dressed, I then
hastened to the tank ; but what was my surprise and
grief to find nearly all the animals dead, and the
water in a putrid condition ! I was greatly distressed at this, and wondered what could be the
cause of it.

" Why, you precious humbug," said Peterkin,
coming up to me, " how could you expect it to be
otherwise ? When fishes are accustomed to live
in the Pacific Ocean, how can you expect them to
exist in a hole like that ? "

" Indeed, Peterkin," I replied, " there seems to
be truth in what you say. Nevertheless, now I
think of it, there must be some error in your reason-
ing ; for if I put in but a few very small animals,
they will bear the same proportion to this pond that
the millions of fish bear to the ocean."

" I say, Jack," cried Peterkin, waving his hand,

" come here, like a good fellow. Ralph is actually talking philosophy. Do come to our assistance, for he's out o' sight beyond me already ! "

" What's the matter ? " inquired Jack, coming up, while he endeavoured to scrub his long hair dry with a towel of cocoa-nut cloth.

I repeated my thoughts to Jack, who, I was happy to find, quite agreed with me. " The best plan," he said, " will be to put very few animals at first into your tank, and add more as you find it will bear them. And look here," he added, pointing to the sides of the tank, which, for the space of two inches above the water-level, were incrusted with salt, " you must carry your philosophy a little further, Ralph. That water has evaporated so much that it is too salt for anything to live in. You will require to add *fresh* water now and then, in order to keep it at the same degree of saltness as the sea."

" Very true, Jack ; that never struck me before," said I.

" And now I think of it," continued Jack, " it seems to me that the surest way of arranging your tank so as to get it to keep pure and in good condition, will be to *imitate* the ocean in it : in fact, make it a miniature Pacific. I don't see how you can hope to succeed unless you do that."

" Most true," said I, pondering what my companion said. " But I fear that that will be very difficult."

" Not at all," cried Jack, rolling his towel up into a ball and throwing it into the face of Peterkin, who had been grinning and winking at him during

the last five minutes—" not at all. Look here.
There is water of a certain saltness in the sea ; well,
fill your tank with sea-water, and keep it at that
saltness by marking the height at which the water
stands on the sides. When it evaporates a little,
pour in *fresh* water from the brook till it comes up
to the mark, and then it will be right, for the salt
does not evaporate with the water. Then there's
lots of seaweed in the sea ; well, go and get one or
two bits of seaweed, and put them into your tank.
Of course the weed must be alive, and growing to
little stones ; or you can chip a bit off the rocks
with the weed sticking to it. Then, if you like, you
can throw a little sand and gravel into your tank, and
the thing's complete."

" Nay, not quite," said Peterkin, who had been
gravely attentive to this off-hand advice—" not quite;
you must first make three little men to dive in it
before it can be said to be perfect ; and that would
be rather difficult, I fear, for two of them would
require to be philosophers. But hallo ! what's
this ?—I say, Ralph, look here. There's one o'
your crabs up to something uncommon. It's performing the most remarkable operation for a crab
I ever saw—taking off its coat, I do believe, before
going to bed ! "

We hastily stooped over the tank, and certainly
were not a little amused at the conduct of one of the
crabs which still survived its companions. It was
one of the common small crabs, like to those that
are found running about everywhere on the coasts

of England. While we gazed at it, we observed its back to split away from the lower part of its body, and out of the gap thus formed came a soft lump which moved and writhed unceasingly. This lump continued to increase in size until it appeared like a bunch of crab's legs ; and, indeed, such it proved in a very few minutes to be, for the points of the toes were at length extricated from the hole in its back, the legs spread out, the body followed, and the crab walked away quite entire, even to the points of its nipper-claws, leaving a perfectly entire shell behind it, so that, when we looked, it seemed as though there were two complete crabs instead of one.

"Well," exclaimed Peterkin, drawing a long breath, "I've *heard* of a man jumping out of his skin and sitting down in his skeleton in order to cool himself, but I never expected to *see* a crab do it ! "

We were, in truth, much amazed at this spectacle, and the more so when we observed that the new crab was larger than the crab that it came out of. It was also quite soft, but by next morning its skin had hardened into a good shell. We came thus to know that crabs grow in this way, and not by the growing of their shells, as we had always thought before we saw this wonderful operation.

Now I considered well the advice which Jack had given me about preparing my tank, and the more I thought of it the more I came to regard it as very sound and worthy of being acted on. So I forthwith put his plan in execution, and found it to answer excellently well, indeed much beyond my expectation ; for I found that after a little experience had taught me the proper proportion of seaweed and animals to put into a certain amount of water, the tank needed no further attendance ; and, moreover, I did not require ever afterwards to renew or change the sea-water, but only to add a very little fresh water from the brook, now and then, as the other evaporated. I therefore concluded that if I had been suddenly conveyed, along with my tank, into some region where there was no salt sea at all, my little sea and my sea-fish would have continued to thrive and to prosper notwithstanding. This made me greatly to desire that those people in the world who live far inland might know of my wonderful tank, and, by having materials like to those of which it was made conveyed to them, thus be enabled to watch the habits of those most mysterious animals that reside in the sea, and examine with their own eyes the wonders of the great deep.

For many days after this, while Peterkin and Jack were busily employed in building a little boat out of the curious natural planks of the chestnut-tree, I spent much of my time in examining with the burning-glass the marvellous operations that were constantly going on in my tank. Here I saw those anemones, which cling, like little red, yellow, and green blobs of jelly, to the rocks, put forth, as it were, a multitude of arms and wait till little fish or other small animalcules unwarily touched them, when they would instantly seize them, fold arm after arm round their victims, and so engulf them in their stomachs. Here I saw the ceaseless working of those little coral insects whose efforts have incrusted the islands of the Pacific with vast rocks and surrounded them with enormous reefs. And I observed that many of these insects, though extremely minute, were very beautiful, coming out of their holes in a circle of fine threads, and having the form of a shuttlecock. Here I saw curious little barnacles opening a hole in their backs and constantly putting out a thin feathery hand, with which, I doubt not, they dragged their food into their mouths. Here, also, I saw those crabs which have shells only on the front of their bodies, but no shell whatever on their remarkably tender tails, so that, in order to find a protection to them, they thrust them into the empty shells of whelks, or some such fish, and when they grow too big for one, change into another. But, most curious of all, I saw an animal which had the wonderful power, when it became ill, of casting its stomach and its teeth away from it, and getting an entirely new set in the course of a few months! All this I saw, and a great deal more, by means of my tank and my burning-glass; but I refrain from setting down more particulars here, as I have still much to tell of the adventures that befell us while we remained on this island.

CHAPTER XIII

Notable discovery at the spouting cliffs—The mysterious green monster explained—We are thrown into unutterable terror by the idea that Jack is drowned—The Diamond Cave.

" COME, Jack," cried Peterkin, one morning about three weeks after our return from our long excursion, " let's be jolly to-day, and do something vigorous. I'm quite tired of hammering and bammering, hewing and screwing, cutting and butting, at that little boat of ours, that seems as hard to build as Noah's ark. Let us go on an excursion to the mountain-top, or have a hunt after the wild ducks, or make a dash at the pigs. I'm quite flat—flat as bad ginger-beer—flat as a pancake ; in fact, I want something to rouse me, to toss me up, as it were. Eh ! what do you say to it ? "

" Well," answered Jack, throwing down the axe with which he was just about to proceed towards the boat, " if that's what you want, I would recommend you to make an excursion to the waterspouts. The last one we had to do with tossed you up a considerable height ; perhaps the next will send you higher, who knows, if you're at all reasonable or moderate in your expectations ! "

" Jack, my dear boy," said Peterkin gravely,

"you are really becoming too fond of jesting. It's a thing I don't at all approve of, and if you don't give it up, I fear that, for our-mutual good, we shall have to part."

"Well, then, Peterkin," replied Jack, with a smile, "what would you have?"

"Have?" said Peterkin; "I would *have* nothing. I didn't say I wanted to *have*; I said that I wanted to *do*."

"By-the-bye," said I, interrupting their conversation, "I am reminded by this that we have not yet discovered the nature of yon curious appearance that we saw near the waterspouts, on our journey round the island. Perhaps it would be well to go for that purpose."

"Humph!" ejaculated Peterkin, "I know the nature of it well enough."

"What was it?" said I.

"It was of a *mysterious* nature, to be sure!" said he, with a wave of his hand, while he rose from the log on which he had been sitting and buckled on his belt, into which he thrust his enormous club.

"Well, then, let us away to the waterspouts," cried Jack, going up to the bower for his bow and arrows; "and bring your spear, Peterkin. It may be useful."

We now, having made up our minds to examine into this matter, sallied forth eagerly in the direction of the waterspout rocks, which, as I have before mentioned, were not far from our present place of abode. On arriving there we hastened down to the edge of the rocks and gazed over into the sea, where we observed the pale-green object still distinctly visible, moving its tail slowly to and fro in the water.

" Most remarkable ! " said Jack.

" Exceedingly curious ! " said I.

" Beats everything ! " said Peterkin.

" Now, Jack," he added, " you made such a poor figure in your last attempt to stick to that object, that I would advise you to let me try it. If it has got a heart at all, I'll engage to send my spear right through the core of it ; if it hasn't got a heart, I'll send it through the spot where its heart ought to be."

" Fire away, then, my boy," replied Jack, with a laugh.

Peterkin immediately took the spear, poised it for a second or two above his head, then darted it like an arrow into the sea. Down it went straight into the centre of the green object, passed quite through it, and came up immediately afterwards, pure and unsullied, while the mysterious tail moved quietly as before !

" Now," said Peterkin gravely, " that brute is a heartless monster ; I'll have nothing more to do with it."

" I'm pretty sure now," said Jack, " that it is merely a phosphoric light ; but I must say I'm puzzled at its staying always in that exact spot."

I also was much puzzled, and inclined to think with Jack that it must be phosphoric light, of which luminous appearance we had seen much while on our voyage to those seas. " But," said I, " there is

nothing to hinder us trom diving down to it, now
that we are sure it is not a shark."

" True," returned Jack, stripping off his clothes ;
" I'll go down, Ralph, as I'm better at diving than
you are.—Now, then, Peterkin, out o' the road ! "
Jack stepped forward, joined his hands above his
head, bent over the rocks, and plunged into the sea.
For a second or two the spray caused by his dive hid
him from view ; then the water became still, and we
saw him swimming far down in the midst of the
green object. Suddenly he sank below it, and vanished altogether from our sight ! We gazed anxiously
down at the spot where he had disappeared for nearly
a minute, expecting every moment to see him rise
again for breath ; but fully a minute passed, and still
he did not reappear. Two minutes passed ! and
then a flood of alarm rushed in upon my soul, when
I considered that, during all my acquaintance with
him, Jack had never stayed under water more than
a minute at a time ; indeed seldom so long.

" O Peterkin ! " I said, in a voice that trembled
with increasing anxiety, " something has happened.
It is more than three minutes now." But Peterkin
did not answer, and I observed that he was gazing
down into the water with a look of intense fear
mingled with anxiety, while his face was overspread with a deadly paleness. Suddenly he sprang
to his feet and rushed about in a frantic state,
wringing his hands and exclaiming, " O Jack, Jack !
he is gone ! It must have been a shark, and he is
gone for ever ! "

For the next five minutes I know not what I did; the intensity of my feelings almost bereft me of my senses. But I was recalled to myself by Peterkin seizing me by the shoulder and staring wildly into my face, while he exclaimed, " Ralph! Ralph! perhaps he has only fainted. Dive for him, Ralph! "

It seemed strange that this did not occur to me sooner. In a moment I rushed to the edge of the rocks, and, without waiting to throw off my garments, was on the point to spring into the waves, when I observed something black rising up through the green object. In another moment Jack's head rose to the surface, and he gave a wild shout, flinging back the spray from his locks, as was his wont after a dive. Now we were almost as much amazed at seeing him reappear, well and strong, as we had been at first at his non-appearance; for, to the best of our judgment, he had been nearly ten minutes under water, perhaps longer, and it required no exertion of our reason to convince us that this was utterly impossible for mortal man to do and retain his strength and faculties. It was, therefore, with a feeling akin to superstitious awe that I held down my hand and assisted him to clamber up the steep rocks. But no such feeling affected Peterkin. No sooner did Jack gain the rocks and seat himself on one, panting for breath, than he threw his arms round his neck and burst into a flood of tears. " O Jack, Jack! " said he, " where were you? What kept you so long? "

After a few moments Peterkin became composed

enough to sit still and listen to Jack's explanation, although he could not restrain himself from attempting to wink every two minutes at me, in order to express his joy at Jack's safety. I say he attempted to wink, but I am bound to add that he did not succeed ; for his eyes were so much swollen with weeping, that his frequent attempts only resulted in a series of violent and altogether idiotical contortions of the face, that were very far from expressing what he intended. However, I knew what the poor fellow meant by it, so I smiled to him in return, and endeavoured to make believe that he was winking.

" Now, lads," said Jack, when we were composed enough to listen to him, " yon green object is not a shark ; it is a stream of light issuing from a cave in the rocks. Just after I made my dive, I observed that this light came from the side of the rock above which we are now sitting ; so I struck out for it, and saw an opening into some place or other that appeared to be luminous within. For one instant I paused to think whether I ought to venture. Then I made up my mind and dashed into it. For you see, Peterkin, although I take some time to tell this, it happened in the space of a few seconds, so that I knew I had wind enough in me to serve to bring me out o' the hole and up to the surface again. Well, I was just on the point of turning—for I began to feel a little uncomfortable in such a place—when it seemed to me as if there was a faint light right above me. I darted upwards, and found my head out of water. This relieved me greatly, for I now felt that I could take in air enough to enable me to return the way I came. Then it all at once occurred to me that I might not be able to find the way out again ; but, on glancing downwards, my mind was put quite at rest by seeing the green light below me streaming into the cave, just like the light that we had seen streaming out of it, only what I now saw was much brighter.

" At first I could scarcely see anything as I gazed around me, it was so dark ; but gradually my eyes became accustomed to it, and I found that I was in a huge cave, part of the walls of which I observed on each side of me. The ceiling just above me was also visible, and I fancied that I could perceive beautiful glittering objects there ; but the farther end of the cave was shrouded in darkness. While I was looking around me in great wonder, it came into my head that you two would think I was drowned ; so I plunged down through the passage again in a great hurry, rose to the surface, and— here I am ! "

When Jack concluded his recital of what he had seen in this remarkable cave, I could not rest satisfied till I had dived down to see it ; which I did, but found it so dark, as Jack had said, that I could scarcely see anything. When I returned, we had a long conversation about it, during which I observed that Peterkin had a most lugubrious expression on his countenance.

" What's the matter, Peterkin ? " said I.

"The matter?" he replied. "It's all very well for you two to be talking away like mermaids about the wonders of this cave, but you know I must be content to hear about it, while you are enjoying yourselves down there like mad dolphins. It's really too bad."

"I'm very sorry for you, Peterkin, indeed I am," said Jack, "but we cannot help you. If you would only learn to dive—"

"Learn to fly, you might as well say!" retorted Peterkin, in a very sulky tone.

"If you would only consent to keep still," said I, "we would take you down with us in ten seconds."

"Hum!" returned Peterkin; "suppose a salamander was to propose to you 'only to keep still,' and he would carry you through a blazing fire in a few seconds, what would you say?"

We both laughed and shook our heads, for it was evident that nothing was to be made of Peterkin in the water. But we could not rest satisfied till we had seen more of this cave; so, after further consultation, Jack and I determined to try if we could take down a torch with us, and set fire to it in the cavern. This we found to be an undertaking of no small difficulty, but we accomplished it at last by the following means:—First, we made a torch of a very inflammable nature out of the bark of a certain tree, which we cut into strips, and, after twisting, cemented together with a kind of resin or gum, which we also obtained from another tree; neither of which trees, however, was known by name to Jack. This, when prepared, we wrapped up in a great number of plies of cocoa-nut cloth, so that we were confident it could not get wet during the short time it should be under water. Then we took a small piece of the tinder, which we had carefully treasured up lest we should require it, as before said, when the sun should fail us ; also, we rolled up some dry grass and a few chips, which, with a little bow and drill, like those described before, we made into another bundle, and wrapped it up in cocoa-nut cloth. When all was ready we laid aside our garments, with the exception of our trousers, which, as we did not know what rough scraping against the rocks we might be subjected to, we kept on.

Then we advanced to the edge of the rocks, Jack carrying one bundle, with the torch, I the other, with the things for producing fire.

"Now don't weary for us, Peterkin, should we be gone some time," said Jack ; "we'll be sure to return in half an hour at the very latest, however interesting the cave should be, that we may relieve your mind."

"Farewell!" said Peterkin, coming up to us with a look of deep but pretended solemnity, while he shook hands and kissed each of us on the cheek. "Farewell! and while you are gone I shall repose my weary limbs under the shelter of this bush, and meditate on the changefulness of all things earthly, with special reference to the forsaken condition of a poor shipwrecked sailor boy!" So saying, Peterkin waved his hand, turned from us, and cast himself upon the ground with a look of melancholy resignation, which was so well feigned that I would have thought it genuine had he not accompanied it with a gentle wink. We both laughed, and, springing from the rocks together, plunged head first into the sea.

We gained the interior of the submarine cave without difficulty, and, on emerging from the waves, supported ourselves for some time by treading water, while we held the two bundles above our heads. This we did in order to let our eyes become accustomed to the obscurity. Then, when we could see sufficiently, we swam to a shelving rock, and landed in safety. Having wrung the water from our trousers, and dried ourselves as well as we could under the circumstances, we proceeded to ignite the torch. This we accomplished without difficulty in a few minutes ; and no sooner did it flare up than we were struck dumb with the wonderful objects that were revealed to our gaze. The roof of the cavern just above us seemed to be about ten feet high, but grew higher as it receded into the distance, until it was lost in darkness. It seemed to be made of coral, and was supported by massive columns of the same material. Immense icicles (as they appeared to us) hung from it in various places. These, however, were formed, not of ice, but of a species of limestone, which seemed to flow in a liquid form towards the point of each, where it became solid. A good many drops fell, however, to the rock below, and these formed little cones, which rose to meet the points above. Some of them had already met, and thus we saw how the pillars were formed, which at first seemed to us as if they had been placed there by some human architect to support the roof. As we advanced further in, we saw that the floor was composed of the same material as the pillars ; and it presented the curious appearance of ripples, such as are formed on water when gently ruffled by the wind. There were several openings on either hand in the walls, that seemed to lead into other caverns ; but these we did not explore at this time. We also observed that the ceiling was curiously marked in many places, as if it were the fretwork of a noble cathedral ; and the walls, as well as the roof, sparkled in the light of our torch, and threw back gleams and flashes, as if they were covered with precious stones. Although we proceeded far into this cavern, we did not come to the end of it ; and we were obliged to return more speedily than we would otherwise have done, as our torch was nearly expended. We did not observe any openings in the roof, or any indications of places whereby light might enter ; but near the entrance to the cavern stood an immense mass of pure white coral rock, which caught and threw back the little light that found an entrance through the cave's mouth, and thus produced, we conjectured, the pale-green object which had first attracted our attention. We concluded, also, that the reflecting power of this rock was that which gave forth the dim light that faintly illumined the first part of the cave.

Before diving through the passage again, we extinguished the small piece of our torch that remained and left it in a dry spot ; conceiving that we might possibly stand in need of it, if at any future time we should chance to wet our torch while diving into the cavern. As we stood for a few minutes after it was out, waiting till our eyes became accustomed to the gloom, we could not help remarking the deep, intense stillness and the unutterable gloom of all around us ; and as I thought of the stupendous dome above, and the countless gems that had sparkled in the torchlight a few minutes before, it came into my mind to consider how strange it is that God should make such wonderful and exquisitely beautiful works never to be seen at all, except, indeed, by chance visitors such as ourselves.

I afterwards found that there were many such caverns among the islands of the South Seas, some of them larger and more beautiful than the one I have just described.

" Now, Ralph, are you ready ? " said Jack, in a low voice, that seemed to echo up into the dome above.

" Quite ready."

" Come along, then," said he ; and plunging off the ledge of the rock into the water, we dived through the narrow entrance. In a few seconds we were panting on the rocks above, and receiving the congratulations of our friend Peterkin.

CHAPTER XIV

IT was quite a relief to us to breathe the pure air and to enjoy the glad sunshine after our long ramble in the Diamond Cave, as we named it ; for although we did not stay more than half an hour away, it seemed to us much longer. While we were dressing, and during our walk home, we did our best to satisfy the curiosity of poor Peterkin, who seemed to regret, with lively sincerity, his inability to dive.

There was no help for it, however, so we condoled with him as we best could. Had there been any great rise or fall in the tide of these seas, we might perhaps have found it possible to take him down with us at low water ; but as the tide never rose or fell more than eighteen inches or two feet, this was impossible.

This peculiarity of the tide—its slight rise and fall —had not attracted our observation till some time after our residence on the island. Neither had we observed another curious circumstance until we had been some time there. This was the fact that the tide rose and fell with constant regularity, instead of being affected by the changes of the moon as in

our own country, and as it is in most other parts
of the world—at least in all those parts with which
I am acquainted. Every day and every night, at
twelve o'clock precisely, the tide is at the full ; and
at six o'clock every morning and evening it is ebb.
I can speak with much confidence on this singular
circumstance, as we took particular note of it, and
never found it to alter. Of course, I must admit,
we had to guess the hour of twelve midnight, and I
think we could do this pretty correctly ; but in
regard to twelve noon we are quite positive, because
we easily found the highest point that the sun reached
in the sky by placing ourselves at a certain spot
whence we observed the sharp summit of a cliff resting against the sky, just where the sun passed.

Jack and I were surprised that we had not noticed
this the first few days of our residence here, and
could only account for it by our being so much taken
up with the more obvious wonders of our novel situation. I have since learned, however, that this want
of observation is a sad and very common infirmity
of human nature, there being hundreds of persons
before whose eyes the most wonderful things are
passing every day, who nevertheless are totally ignorant of them. I therefore have to record my sympathy with such persons, and to recommend to them
a course of conduct which I have now for a long time
myself adopted—namely, the habit of forcing my
attention upon *all* things that go on around me, and
of taking some degree of interest in them, whether
I feel it naturally or not. I suggest this the more

earnestly though humbly, because I have very frequently come to know that my indifference to a thing
has generally been caused by my ignorance in regard
to it.

We had much serious conversation on this subject
of the tides ; and Jack told us, in his own quiet, philo-
sophical way, that these tides did great good to the
world in many ways, particularly in the way of
cleansing the shores of the land, and carrying off the
filth that was constantly poured into the sea there-
from ; which, Peterkin suggested, was remarkably
tidy of it to do. Poor Peterkin could never let slip
an opportunity to joke, however inopportune it might
be : which at first we found rather a disagreeable
propensity, as it often interrupted the flow of very
agreeable conversation—and, indeed, I cannot too
strongly record my disapprobation of this tendency
in general—but we became so used to it at last that
we found it no interruption whatever ; indeed,
strange to say, we came to feel that it was a necessary
part of our enjoyment (such is the force of habit),
and found the sudden outbursts of mirth, resulting
from his humorous disposition, quite natural and
refreshing to us in the midst of our more serious
conversations. But I must not misrepresent Peterkin.
We often found, to our surprise, that he knew many
things which we did not ; and I also observed that
those things which he learned from experience were
never forgotten. From all these things I came at
length to understand that things very opposite and
dissimilar in themselves, when united, do make an

agreeable whole ; as, for example, we three on this our island, although most unlike in many things, when united, made a trio so harmonious that I question if there ever met before such an agreeable triumvirate. There was, indeed, no note of discord whatever in the symphony we played together on that sweet Coral Island ; and I am now persuaded that this was owing to our having been all tuned to the same key—namely, that of *love* ! Yes, we loved one another with much fervency while we lived on that island ; and, for the matter of that, we love each other still.

And while I am on this subject, or rather the subject that just preceded it—namely, the tides—I may here remark on another curious natural phenomenon. We found that there was little or no twilight in this island. We had a distinct remembrance of the charming long twilight at home, which some people think the most delightful part of the day, though for my part I have always preferred sunrise ; and when we first landed, we used to sit down on some rocky point or eminence, at the close of our day's work, to enjoy the evening breeze ; but no sooner had the sun sunk below the horizon than all became suddenly dark. This rendered it necessary that we should watch the sun when we happened to be out hunting ; for to be suddenly left in the dark while in the woods was very perplexing, as, although the stars shone with great beauty and brilliancy, they could not pierce through the thick umbrageous boughs that interlaced above our heads.

But to return. After having told all we could to Peterkin about the Diamond Cave under Spouting Cliff, as we named the locality, we were wending our way rapidly homewards, when a grunt and a squeal were borne down by the land breeze to our ears.

" That's the ticket ! " was Peterkin's remarkable exclamation, as he started convulsively and levelled his spear.

" Hist ! " cried Jack ; " these are your friends, Peterkin. They must have come over expressly to pay you a friendly visit, for it is the first time we have seen them on this side the island."

" Come along ! " cried Peterkin, hurrying towards the wood, while Jack and I followed, smiling at his impatience.

Another grunt and half a dozen squeals, much louder than before, came down the valley. At this time we were just opposite the small vale which lay between the Valley of the Wreck and Spouting Cliff.

" I say, Peterkin," cried Jack, in a hoarse whisper.

" Well, what is't ? "

" Stay a bit, man. These grunters are just up there on the hillside. If you go and stand with Ralph in the lee of yon cliff, I'll cut round behind and drive them through the gorge, so that you'll have a better chance of picking out a good one. Now, mind you pitch into a fat young pig, Peterkin," added Jack, as he sprang into the bushes.

" Won't I, just ! " said Peterkin, licking his lips, as we took our station beside the cliff. " I feel quite a tender affection for young pigs in my heart. Perhaps it would be more correct to say in my s—"

"There they come!" cried I, as a terrific yell from Jack sent the whole herd screaming down the hill. Now Peterkin, being unable to hold back, crept a short way up a very steep grassy mound, in order to get a better view of the hogs before they came up; and just as he raised his head above its summit, two little pigs, which had outrun their companions, rushed over the top with the utmost precipitation. One of these brushed close past Peterkin's ear; the other, unable to arrest its headlong flight, went, as Peterkin himself afterwards expressed it, "bash" into his arms with a sudden squeal, which was caused more by the force of the blow than the will of the animal, and both of them rolled violently down to the foot of the mound. No sooner was this reached than the little pig recovered its feet, tossed up its tail, and fled shrieking from the spot. But I slung a large stone after it, which, being fortunately well aimed, hit it behind the ear, and felled it to the earth.

"Capital, Ralph! that's your sort!" cried Peterkin, who, to my surprise and great relief, had risen to his feet, apparently unhurt, though much dishevelled. He rushed franticly towards the gorge, which the yells of the hogs told us they were now approaching. I had made up my mind that I would abstain from killing another, as, if Peterkin should be successful, two were more than sufficient for our wants at the present time. Suddenly they all burst forth—two or three little round ones in advance, and an enormous old sow with a drove of hogs at her heels.

"Now, Peterkin," said I, "there's a nice little fat one ; just spear it."

But Peterkin did not move ; he allowed it to pass unharmed. I looked at him in surprise, and saw that his lips were compressed, and his eyebrows knitted as if he were about to fight with some awful enemy.

"What is it ? " I inquired, with some trepidation.

Suddenly he levelled his spear, darted forward, and, with a yell that nearly froze the blood in my veins, stabbed the old sow to the heart. Nay, so vigorously was it done that the spear went in at one side and came out at the other !

"O Peterkin ! " said I, going up to him, "what have you done ? "

"Done ! I've killed their great-great-grandmother, that's all," said he, looking with a somewhat awe-struck expression at the transfixed animal.

"Hallo ! what's this ? " said Jack, as he came up. "Why, Peterkin, you must be fond of a tough chop. If you mean to eat this old hog, she'll try your jaws, I warrant. What possessed you to stick *her*, Peterkin ? "

"Why, the fact is I want a pair of shoes."

"What have your shoes to do with the old hog ? " said I, smiling.

"My present shoes have certainly nothing to do with her," replied Peterkin ; "nevertheless she will have a good deal to do with my future shoes. The fact is, when I saw you floor that pig so neatly, Ralph, it struck me that there was little use in killing another. Then I remembered all at once that I had long wanted some leather or tough substance to make shoes of, and this old grandmother seemed so tough that I just made up my mind to stick her, and you see I've done it ! "

" That you certainly have, Peterkin," said Jack, as he was examining the transfixed animal.

We now considered how we were to carry our game home, for, although the distance was short, the hog was very heavy. At length we hit on the plan of tying its four feet together, and passing the spear handle between them. Jack took one end on his shoulder, I took the other on mine, and Peterkin carried the small pig.

Thus we returned in triumph to our bower, laden, as Peterkin remarked, with the glorious spoils of a noble hunt. As he afterwards spoke in similarly glowing terms in reference to the supper that followed, there is every reason to believe that we retired that night to our leafy beds in a high state of satisfaction.

CHAPTER XV

Boat-building extraordinary—Peterkin tries his hand at cookery, and fails most signally—The boat finished—Curious conversation with the cat, and other matters.

FOR many days after this Jack applied himself with unremitting assiduity to the construction of our boat, which at length began to look somewhat like one. But those only who have had the thing to do can entertain a right idea of the difficulty involved in such an undertaking, with no other implements than an axe, a bit of hoop iron, a sail-needle, and a broken penknife. But Jack did it. He was of that disposition which *will* not be conquered. When he believed himself to be acting rightly, he overcame all obstacles. I have seen Jack, when doubtful whether what he was about to do were right or wrong, as timid and vacillating as a little girl ; and I honour him for it !

As this boat was a curiosity in its way, a few words here relative to the manner of its construction may not be amiss.

I have already mentioned the chestnut tree with its wonderful buttresses or planks. This tree, then, furnished us with the chief part of our material. First of all, Jack sought out a limb of a tree of such form and size as, while it should form the keel, a bend at either end should form the stem and stern posts.

Such a piece, however, was not easy to obtain; but at last he procured it, by rooting up a small tree which had a branch growing at the proper angle about ten feet up its stem, with two strong roots growing in such a form as enabled him to make a flat-sterned boat. This placed, he procured three branching roots of suitable size, which he fitted to the keel at equal distances, thus forming three strong ribs. Now the squaring and shaping of these, and the cutting of the grooves in the keel, was an easy enough matter, as it was all work for the axe, in the use of which Jack was become wonderfully expert; but it was quite a different affair when he came to nailing the ribs to the keel, for we had no instrument capable of boring a large hole, and no nails to fasten them with. We were, indeed, much perplexed here; but Jack at length devised an instrument that served very well. He took the remainder of our hoop iron and beat it into the form of a pipe or cylinder, about as thick as a man's finger. This he did by means of our axe and the old rusty axe we had found at the house of the poor man at the other side of the island. This, when made red hot, bored slowly through the timbers; and, the better to retain the heat, Jack shut up one end of it and filled it with sand. True, the work was very slowly done; but it mattered not, we had little else to do. Two holes were bored in each timber, about an inch and a half apart, and also down into the keel, but not quite through. In these were placed stout pegs made of a tree called iron-wood; and, when they were hammered well home, the timbers were as firmly fixed as if they had been nailed with iron. The gunwales, which were very stout, were fixed in a similar manner. But, besides the wooden nails, they were firmly lashed to the stem and stern posts and ribs by means of a species of cordage which we had contrived to make out of the fibrous husk of the cocoa nut. This husk was very tough, and when a number of the threads were joined together they formed excellent cordage. At first we tied the different lengths together ; but this was such a clumsy and awkward complication of knots, that we contrived, by careful interlacing of the ends together before twisting, to make good cordage of any size or length we chose. Of course it cost us much time and infinite labour, but Jack kept up our spirits when we grew weary, and so all that we required was at last constructed.

Planks were now cut off the chestnut trees of about an inch thick. These were dressed with the axe— but clumsily, for an axe is ill adapted for such work. Five of these planks on each side were sufficient ; and we formed the boat in a very rounded, barrel-like shape, in order to have as little twisting of the planks as possible, for although we could easily bend them, we could not easily twist them. Having no nails to rivet the planks with, we threw aside the ordinary fashion of boat-building, and adopted one of our own. The planks were therefore placed on each other's edges, and sewed together with the tough cordage already mentioned. They were also thus sewed to the stem, the stern, and the keel.

Each stitch or tie was six inches apart, and was formed thus :—Three holes were bored in the upper plank and three in the lower—the holes being above each other, that is, in a vertical line. Through these holes the cord was passed, and, when tied, formed a powerful stitch of three ply. Besides this, we placed between the edges of the planks layers of cocoa-nut fibre, which, as it swelled when wetted, would, we hoped, make our little vessel water-tight. But in order further to secure this end, we collected a large quantity of pitch from the bread-fruit tree, with which, when boiled in our old iron pot, we paid the whole of the inside of the boat, and, while it was yet hot, placed large pieces of cocoa-nut cloth on it, and then gave it another coat above that. Thus the interior was covered with a tough, water-tight material ; while the exterior, being uncovered, and so exposed to the swelling action of the water, was, we hoped, likely to keep the boat quite dry. I may add that our hopes were not disappointed.

While Jack was thus engaged, Peterkin and I sometimes assisted him ; but as our assistance was not much required, we more frequently went a-hunting on the extensive mud-flats at the entrance of the long valley which lay nearest to our bower. Here we found large flocks of ducks of various kinds, some of them bearing so much resemblance to the wild ducks of our own country that I think they must have been the same. On these occasions we took the bow and the sling, with both of which we were often successful, though I must confess that I was the least so. Our suppers were thus pleasantly varied, and sometimes we had such a profusion spread out before us that we frequently knew not with which of the dainties to begin.

I must also add that the poor old cat which we had brought home had always a liberal share of our good things, and so well was it looked after, especially by Peterkin, that it recovered much of its former strength, and seemed to improve in sight as well as in hearing.

The large flat stone, or rock of coral, which stood just in front of the entrance to our bower, was our table. On this rock we had spread out the few articles we possessed the day we were shipwrecked ; and on the same rock, during many a day afterwards, we spread out the bountiful supply with which we had been blessed on our Coral Island. Sometimes we sat down at this table to a feast consisting of hot rolls —as Peterkin called the newly-baked bread-fruit— a roast pig, roast duck, boiled and roasted yams, cocoa nuts, taro, and sweet potatoes ; which we followed up with a dessert of plums, apples, and plantains—the last being a large-sized and delightful fruit, which grew on a large shrub or tree not more than twelve feet high, with light-green leaves of enormous length and breadth. These luxurious feasts were usually washed down with cocoa-nut lemonade.

Occasionally Peterkin tried to devise some new dish—"a conglomerate," as he used to say; but these generally turned out such atrocious compounds that he was ultimately induced to give up his attempts in extreme disgust—not forgetting, however, to point out to Jack that his failure was a direct contradiction to the proverb which he, Jack, was constantly thrusting down his throat—namely, that "where there's a will there's a way." For he had a great will to become a cook, but could by no means find a way to accomplish that end.

One day, while Peterkin and I were seated beside our table on which dinner was spread, Jack came up from the beach, and, flinging down his axe, exclaimed,—

"There, lads, the boat's finished at last! so we've nothing to do now but shape two pair of oars, and then we may put to sea as soon as we like."

This piece of news threw us into a state of great joy; for although we were aware that the boat had been gradually getting near its completion, it had taken so long that we did not expect it to be quite ready for at least two or three weeks. But Jack had wrought hard and said nothing, in order to surprise us.

"My dear fellow," cried Peterkin, "you're a perfect trump. But why did you not tell us it was so nearly ready? Won't we have a jolly sail to-morrow, eh?"

"Don't talk so much, Peterkin," said Jack; "and, pray, hand me a bit of that pig."

"Certainly, my dear," cried Peterkin, seizing the axe. "What part will you have? a leg, or a wing, or a piece of the breast—which?"

"A hind leg, if you please," answered Jack; "and, pray, be so good as to include the tail."

"With all my heart," said Peterkin, exchanging the

axe for his hoop-iron knife, with which he cut off the desired portion. " I'm only too glad, my dear boy, to see that your appetite is so wholesale, and there's no chance whatever of its dwindling down into re-tail again, at least in so far as this pig is concerned.— Ralph, lad, why don't you laugh, eh ? " he added, turning suddenly to me with a severe look of inquiry.

" Laugh ! " said I ; " what at, Peterkin ? Why should I laugh ? "

Both Jack and Peterkin answered this inquiry by themselves laughing so immoderately that I was induced to believe I had missed noticing some good joke, so I begged that it might be explained to me ; but as this only produced repeated roars of laughter, I smiled, and helped myself to another slice of plantain.

" Well, but," continued Peterkin, " I was talking of a sail to-morrow. Can't we have one, Jack ? "

" No," replied Jack, " we can't have a sail ; but I hope we shall have a row, as I intend to work hard at the oars this afternoon, and, if we can't get them finished by sunset, we'll light our candle-nuts, and turn them out of hands before we turn into bed."

" Very good," said Peterkin, tossing a lump of pork to the cat, who received it with a mew of satisfaction. " I'll help you, if I can."

" Afterwards," continued Jack, " we will make a sail out of the cocoa-nut cloth, and rig up a mast, and then we shall be able to sail to some of the other islands, and visit our old friends the penguins."

The prospect of being so soon in a position to extend our observations to the other islands and enjoy a sail over the beautiful sea afforded us much delight, and after dinner we set about making the oars in good earnest. Jack went into the woods and blocked them roughly out with the axe, and I smoothed them down with the knife, while Peterkin remained in the bower spinning, or rather twisting, some strong thick cordage with which to fasten them to the boat.

We worked hard and rapidly, so that when the sun went down Jack and I returned to the bower with four stout oars, which required little to be done to them save a slight degree of polishing with the knife. As we drew near we were suddenly arrested by the sound of a voice. We were not a little surprised at this—indeed I may almost say alarmed—for, although Peterkin was undoubtedly fond of talking, we had never up to this time found him talking to himself. We listened intently, and still heard the sound of a voice, as if in conversation. Jack motioned me to be silent, and advancing to the bower on tiptoe, we peeped in.

The sight that met our gaze was certainly not a little amusing. On the top of a log which we sometimes used as a table sat the black cat, with a very demure expression on its countenance, and in front of it, sitting on the ground with his legs extended on either side of the log, was Peterkin. At the moment we saw him he was gazing intently into the cat's face, with his nose about four inches from it, his hands being thrust into his breeches pockets.

" Cat," said Peterkin, turning his head a little on one side, " I love you ! "

There was a pause, as if Peterkin awaited a reply to this affectionate declaration. But the cat said nothing.

" Do you hear me ? " cried Peterkin sharply. " I love you—I do. Don't you love me ? "

To this touching appeal the cat said " Mew " faintly.

" Ah ! that's right. You're a jolly old rascal. Why did you not speak at once, eh ? " and Peterkin put forward his mouth and kissed the cat on the nose !

" Yes," continued Peterkin, after a pause, " I love you. D'you think I'd say so if I didn't, you black villain ? I love you because I've got to take care of you, and to look after you, and to think about you, and to see that you don't die—"

" Mew, me-a-w ! " said the cat.

" Very good," continued Peterkin ; " quite true, I have no doubt ; but you've no right to interrupt me, sir. Hold your tongue till I have done speaking. Moreover, cat, I love you because you came to me the first time you ever saw me, and didn't seem to be afraid, and appeared to be fond of me, though you didn't know that I wasn't going to kill you. Now that was brave, that was bold, and very jolly,. old boy, and I love you for it—I do ! "

Again there was a pause of a few minutes, during which the cat looked placid, and Peterkin dropped his eyes upon its toes as if in contemplation. Suddenly he looked up.

" Well, cat, what are you thinking about now ? won't speak, eh ? Now tell me, don't you think it's a monstrous shame that these two scoundrels, Jack and Ralph, should keep us waiting for our supper so long ? "

Here the cat arose, put up its back and stretched itself, yawned slightly, and licked the point of Peterkin's nose !

" Just so, old boy ; you're a clever fellow. I really do believe the brute understands me ! " said Peterkin, while a broad grin overspread his face as he drew back and surveyed the cat.

At this point Jack burst into a loud fit of laughter. The cat uttered an angry fuff and fled, while Peterkin sprang up and exclaimed,—

" Bad luck to you, Jack ! you've nearly made the heart jump out of my body, you have."

" Perhaps I have," replied Jack, laughing, as we entered the bower ; " but as I don't intend to keep you or the cat any longer from your supper, I hope that you'll both forgive me."

Peterkin endeavoured to turn this affair off with a laugh, but I observed that he blushed very deeply at the time we discovered ourselves, and he did not seem to relish any allusion to the subject afterwards ; so we refrained from remarking on it ever after, though it tickled us not a little at the time.

After supper we retired to rest, and to dream of wonderful adventures in our little boat and distant voyages upon the sea.

CHAPTER XVI

The boat launched—We visit the coral reef—The great breaker that never goes down—Coral insects—The way in which coral islands are made—The boat's sail—We tax our ingenuity to form fish-hooks—Some of the fish we saw—And a monstrous whale—Wonderful shower of little fish—Waterspouts.

IT was a bright, clear, beautiful morning when we first launched our little boat and rowed out upon the placid waters of the lagoon. Not a breath of wind ruffled the surface of the deep. Not a cloud spotted the deep blue sky. Not a sound that was discordant broke the stillness of the morning, although there were many sounds, sweet, tiny, and melodious, that mingled in the universal harmony of nature. The sun was just rising from the Pacific's ample bosom and tipping the mountain tops with a red glow. The sea was shining like a sheet of glass, yet heaving with the long, deep swell that, all the world around, indicates the life of ocean ; and the bright seaweeds and the brilliant corals shone in the depths of that pellucid water, as we rowed over it, like rare and precious gems. Oh, it was a sight fitted to stir the soul of man to its profoundest depths, and, if he owned a heart at all, to lift that heart in adoration and gratitude to the great Creator of this magnificent and glorious universe !

At first, in the strength of our delight, we rowed hither and thither without aim or object. But after the effervescence of our spirits was abated, we began to look about us and to consider what we should do.

" I vote that we row to the reef," cried Peterkin.

" And I vote that we visit the islands within the lagoon," said I.

" And I vote we do both," cried Jack ; " so pull away, boys."

As I have already said, we had made four oars, but our boat was so small that only two were necessary. The extra pair were reserved in case any accident should happen to the others. It was therefore only needful that two of us should row, while the third steered, by means of an oar, and relieved the rowers occasionally.

First we landed on one of the small islands and ran all over it, but saw nothing worthy of particular notice. Then we landed on a larger island, on which were growing a few cocoa-nut trees. Not having eaten anything that morning, we gathered a few of the nuts and breakfasted. After this we pulled straight out to sea, and landed on the coral reef.

This was indeed a novel and interesting sight to us. We had now been so long on shore that we had almost forgotten the appearance of breakers, for there were none within the lagoon ; but now, as we stood beside the foam-crested billow of the open sea, all the enthusiasm of the sailor was awakened in our breasts, and as we gazed on the widespread ruin of that single magnificent breaker that burst in thunder at our feet, we forgot the Coral Island behind us ; we forgot our bower and the calm repose of the scented woods ; we forgot all that had passed during the last few months, and remembered nothing but the storms, the calms, the fresh breezes, and the surging billows of the open sea.

This huge, ceaseless breaker, to which I have so often alluded, was a much larger and more sublime object than we had at all imagined it to be. It rose many yards above the level of the sea, and could be seen approaching at some distance from the reef. Slowly and majestically it came on, acquiring greater volume and velocity as it advanced, until it assumed the form of a clear watery arch, which sparkled in the bright sun. On it came with resistless and solemn majesty, the upper edge lipped gently over, and it fell with a roar that seemed as though the heart of Ocean were broken in the crash of tumultuous water, while the foam-clad coral reef appeared to tremble beneath the mighty shock !

We gazed long and wonderingly at this great sight, and it was with difficulty we could tear ourselves away from it. As I have once before mentioned, this wave broke in many places over the reef and scattered some of its spray into the lagoon, but in most places the reef was sufficiently broad and elevated to receive and check its entire force. In many places the coral rocks were covered with vegetation—the beginning, as it appeared to us, of future islands. Thus, on this reef, we came to perceive how most of the small islands of those seas are formed. On one part we saw the spray of the breaker washing over the rocks, and millions of little, active, busy creatures continuing the work of building up this living rampart. At another place, which was just a little too high for the waves to wash over it, the coral insects were all dead ; for we found that they never did their work above water. They had faithfully completed the mighty work which their Creator had given them to do, and they were now all dead. Again, in other spots the ceaseless lashing of the sea had broken the dead coral in pieces, and cast it up in the form of sand. Here sea-birds had alighted, little pieces of seaweed and stray bits of wood had been washed up, seeds of plants had been carried by the wind, and a few lovely blades of bright green had already sprung up, which, when they died, would increase the size and fertility of these emeralds of Ocean. At other places these islets had grown apace, and were shaded by one or two cocoa-nut trees, which grew literally in the sand, and were constantly washed by the ocean spray ; yet, as I have before remarked, their fruit was most refreshing and sweet to our taste.

Again at this time Jack and I pondered the formation of the large coral islands. We could now understand how the low ones were formed ; but the larger islands cost us much consideration, yet we could arrive at no certain conclusion on the subject.

Having satisfied our curiosity and enjoyed ourselves during the whole day, in our little boat, we returned, somewhat wearied, and withal rather hungry, to our bower.

"Now," said Jack, "as our boat answers so well, we will get a mast and sail made immediately."

"So we will," cried Peterkin, as we all assisted to drag the boat above high-water mark ; "we'll light our candle and set about it this very night. Hurrah, my boys, pull away ! "

As we dragged our boat, we observed that she grated heavily on her keel ; and as the sands were in this place mingled with broken coral rocks, we saw portions of the wood being scraped off.

"Hallo ! " cried Jack, on seeing this ; "that won't do. Our keel will be worn off in no time at this rate."

"So it will," said I, pondering deeply as to how this might be prevented. But I am not of a mechanical turn naturally, so I could conceive no remedy save that of putting a plate of iron on the keel ; but as we had no iron, I knew not what was to be done. "It seems to me, Jack," I added, "that it is impossible to prevent the keel being worn off thus."

"Impossible ! " cried Peterkin. "My dear Ralph, you are mistaken ; there is nothing so easy."

"How ? " I inquired, in some surprise.

"Why, by not using the boat at all ! " replied Peterkin.

"Hold your impudent tongue, Peterkin," said Jack, as he shouldered the oars ; "come along with me, and I'll give you work to do. In the first place, you will go and collect cocoa-nut fibre, and set to work to make sewing twine with it—"

" Please, captain," interrupted Peterkin, " I've got lots of it made already—more than enough, as a little friend of mine used to be in the habit of saying every day after dinner."

" Very well," continued Jack ; " then you'll help Ralph to collect cocoa-nut cloth, and cut it into shape, after which we'll make a sail of it. I'll see to getting the mast and the gearing ; so let's to work."

And to work we went right busily, so that in three days from that time we had set up a mast and sail, with the necessary rigging, in our little boat. The sail was not, indeed, very handsome to look at, as it was formed of a number of oblong patches of cloth ; but we had sewed it well by means of our sail-needle, so that it was strong, which was the chief point. Jack had also overcome the difficulty about the keel, by pinning to it a *false* keel. This was a piece of tough wood, of the same length and width as the real keel, and about five inches deep. He made it of this depth because the boat would be thereby rendered not only much more safe, but more able to beat against the wind ; which, in a sea where the trade-winds blow so long and so steadily in one direction, was a matter of great importance. This piece of wood was pegged very firmly to the keel ; and we now launched our boat with the satisfaction of knowing that when the false keel should be scraped off we could easily put on another ; whereas, should the real keel have been scraped away, we could not have renewed it without taking our boat to pieces, which Peterkin said made his "marrow quake to think upon."

The mast and sail answered excellently, and we now sailed about in the lagoon with great delight, and examined with much interest the appearance of our island from a distance. Also, we gazed into the depths of the water, and watched for hours the gambols of the curious and bright-coloured fish among the corals and seaweed. Peterkin also made a fishing-line, and Jack constructed a number of hooks, some of which were very good, others remarkably bad. Some of these hooks were made of iron-wood, which did pretty well, the wood being extremely hard, and Jack made them very thick and large. Fish there are not particular. Some of the crooked bones in fish-heads also answered for this purpose pretty well. But that which formed our best and most serviceable hook was the brass finger-ring belonging to Jack. It gave him not a little trouble to manufacture it. First he cut it with the axe, then twisted it into the form of a hook. The barb took him several hours to cut. He did it by means of constant sawing with the broken penknife. As for the point, an hour's rubbing on a piece of sandstone made an excellent one.

It would be a matter of much time and labour to describe the appearance of the multitudes of fish that were day after day drawn into our boat by means of the brass hook. Peterkin always caught

them—for we observed that he derived much pleasure from fishing—while Jack and I found ample
amusement in looking on, also in gazing down at
the coral groves, and in baiting the hook. Among
the fish that we saw, but did not catch, were porpoises and swordfish, whales and sharks. The porpoises came frequently into our lagoon in shoals,
and amused us not a little by their bold leaps into
the air and their playful gambols in the sea. The
swordfish were wonderful creatures ; some of them
apparently ten feet in length, with an ivory spear
six or eight feet long projecting from their noses.
We often saw them darting after other fish, and no
doubt they sometimes killed them with their ivory
swords. Jack remembered having heard once of a
swordfish attacking a ship—which seemed strange
indeed ; but as they are often in the habit of attacking whales, perhaps it mistook the ship for one.
This swordfish ran against the vessel with such force
that it drove its sword quite through the thick
planks, and when the ship arrived in harbour, long
afterwards, the sword was found still sticking in it !

Sharks did not often appear, but we took care
never again to bathe in deep water without leaving
one of our number in the boat, to give us warning
if he should see a shark approaching. As for the
whales, they never came into our lagoon, but we
frequently saw them spouting in the deep water
beyond the reef. I shall never forget my surprise
the first day I saw one of these huge monsters close
to me. We had been rambling about on the reef

during the morning, and were about to re-embark in our little boat, to return home, when a loud blowing sound caused us to wheel rapidly round. We were just in time to see a shower of spray falling, and the flukes or tail of some monstrous fish disappear in the sea a few hundred yards off. We waited some time to see if he would rise again. As we stood, the sea seemed to open up at our very feet ; an immense spout of water was sent with a snort high into the air, and the huge blunt head of a sperm whale rose before us. It was so large that it could easily have taken our little boat, along with ourselves, into its mouth ! It plunged slowly back into the sea, like a large ship foundering, and struck the water with its tail so forcibly as to cause a sound like a cannon shot.

We also saw a great number of flying-fish, although we caught none ; and we noticed that they never flew out of the water except when followed by their bitter foe the dolphin, from whom they thus endeavoured to escape. But of all the fish that we saw, none surprised us so much as those that we used to find in shallow pools after a shower of rain ; and this not on account of their appearance, for they were ordinary-looking and very small, but on account of their having descended in a shower of rain ! We could account for them in no other way, because the pools in which we found these fish were quite dry before the shower, and at some distance above high-water mark. Jack, however, suggested a cause which seemed to me very probable. We used often to see waterspouts in the sea. A waterspout is a whirling body of water, which rises from the sea like a sharp-pointed pillar. After rising a good way, it is met by a long tongue, which comes down from the clouds; and when the two have joined, they appear something like an hour-glass. The waterspout is then carried by the wind, sometimes gently, sometimes with violence, over the sea, sometimes up into the clouds, and then, bursting asunder, it descends in a deluge. This often happens over the land as well as over the sea; and it sometimes does much damage, but frequently it passes gently away. Now, Jack thought that the little fish might perhaps have been carried up in a waterspout, and so sent down again in a shower of rain. But we could not be certain as to this point, yet we thought it likely.

During these delightful fishing and boating excursions we caught a good many eels, which we found to be very good to eat. We also found turtles among the coral rocks, and made excellent soup in our iron kettle. Moreover, we discovered many shrimps and prawns, so that we had no lack of variety in our food; and, indeed, we never passed a week without making some new and interesting discovery of some sort or other, either on the land or in the sea.

CHAPTER XVII

A monster wave and its consequences—The boat lost and found—
Peterkin's terrible accident—Supplies of food for a voyage in
the boat—We visit Penguin Island, and are amazed beyond
measure—Account of the penguins.

ONE day, not long after our little boat was finished,
we were sitting on the rocks at Spouting Cliff, and
talking of an excursion which we intended to make
to Penguin Island the next day.

" You see," said Peterkin, " it might be all very
well for a stupid fellow like me to remain here and
leave the penguins alone, but it would be quite
inconsistent with your characters as philosophers to
remain any longer in ignorance of the habits and
customs of these birds ; so the sooner we go the
better."

" Very true," said I ; " there is nothing I desire
so much as to have a closer inspection of them."

" And I think," said Jack, " that you had better
remain at home, Peterkin, to take care of the cat ;
for I'm sure the hogs will be at it in your absence, out
of revenge for your killing their great-grandmother
so recklessly."

" Stay at home ! " cried Peterkin. " My dear
fellow, you would certainly lose your way, or get
upset, if I were not there to take care of you."

"Ah, true," said Jack gravely; "that did not occur to me; no doubt you must go. Our boat does require a good deal of ballast; and all that you say, Peterkin, carries so much weight with it, that we won't need stones if you go."

Now, while my companions were talking, a notable event occurred, which, as it is not generally known, I shall be particular in recording here.

While we were talking, as I have said, we noticed a dark line, like a low cloud or fog-bank, on the seaward horizon. The day was a fine one, though cloudy, and a gentle breeze was blowing, but the sea was not rougher or the breaker on the reef higher than usual. At first we thought that this looked like a thundercloud, and as we had had a good deal of broken weather of late, accompanied by occasional peals of thunder, we supposed that a storm must be approaching. Gradually, however, this line seemed to draw nearer without spreading up over the sky, as would certainly have been the case if it had been a storm-cloud. Still nearer it came, and soon we saw that it was moving swiftly towards the island; but there was no sound till it reached the islands out at sea. As it passed these islands, we observed, with no little anxiety, that a cloud of white foam encircled them, and burst in spray into the air: it was accompanied by a loud roar. This led us to conjecture that the approaching object was an enormous wave of the sea; but we had no idea how large it was till it came near to ourselves. When it approached the outer reef, however, we were awestruck with its unusual magnitude; and we sprang to our feet, and clambered hastily up to the highest point of the precipice, under an indefinable feeling of fear.

I have said before that the reef opposite Spouting Cliff was very near to the shore, while just in front of the bower it was at a considerable distance out to sea. Owing to this formation, the wave reached the reef at the latter point before it struck at the foot of Spouting Cliff. The instant it touched the reef we became aware, for the first time, of its awful magnitude. It burst completely over the reef at all points, with a roar that seemed louder to me than thunder; and this roar continued for some seconds, while the wave rolled gradually along towards the cliff on which we stood. As its crest reared before us, we felt that we were in great danger, and turned to flee; but we were too late. With a crash that seemed to shake the solid rock the gigantic billow fell, and instantly the spouting-holes sent up a gush of waterspouts with such force that they shrieked on issuing from their narrow vents. It seemed to us as if the earth had been blown up with water. We were stunned and confused by the shock, and so drenched and blinded with spray that we knew not for a few moments whither to flee for shelter. At length we all three gained an eminence beyond the reach of the water; but what a scene of devastation met our gaze as we looked along the shore! This enormous wave not only burst over the reef, but continued its way across the lagoon, and fell on the sandy beach of the island with such force that it passed completely over it and dashed into the woods, levelling the smaller trees and bushes in its headlong course.

On seeing this, Jack said he feared our bower must have been swept away, and that the boat, which was on the beach, must have been utterly destroyed. Our hearts sank within us as we thought of this, and we hastened round through the woods towards our home. On reaching it we found, to our great relief of mind, that the force of the wave had been expended just before reaching the bower ; but the entrance to it was almost blocked up by the torn-up bushes and tangled heaps of seaweed. Having satisfied ourselves as to the bower, we hurried to the spot where the boat had been left ; but no boat was there. The spot on which it had stood was vacant, and no sign of it could we see on looking around us.

" It may have been washed up into the woods," said Jack, hurrying up the beach as he spoke. Still no boat was to be seen, and we were about to give ourselves over to despair, when Peterkin called to Jack and said,—

" Jack, my friend, you were once so exceedingly sagacious and wise as to make me acquainted with the fact that cocoa nuts grow upon trees ; will you now be so good as to inform me what sort of fruit that is growing on the top of yonder bush ? for I confess to being ignorant, or at least doubtful, on the point."

We looked towards the bush indicated, and there,

to our surprise, beheld our little boat snugly nestled among the leaves. We were very much overjoyed at this, for we would have suffered any loss rather than the loss of our boat. We found that the wave had actually borne the boat on its crest from the beach into the woods, and there launched it into the heart of this bush ; which was extremely fortunate, for had it been tossed against a rock or a tree, it would have been dashed to pieces, whereas it had not received the smallest injury. It was no easy matter, however, to get it out of the bush and down to the sea again. This cost us two days of hard labour to accomplish.

We had also much ado to clear away the rubbish from before the bower, and spent nearly a week in constant labour ere we got the neighbourhood to look as clean and orderly as before ; for the uprooted bushes and seaweed that lay on the beach formed a more dreadfully confused-looking mass than one who had not seen the place after the inundation could conceive.

Before leaving the subject I may mention, for the sake of those who interest themselves in the curious natural phenomena of our world, that this gigantic wave occurs regularly on some of the islands of the Pacific once and sometimes twice in the year. I heard this stated by the missionaries during my career in those seas. They could not tell me whether it visited all of the islands, but I was certainly assured that it occurred periodically in some of them.

After we had got our home put to rights and

cleared of the *débris* of the inundation, we again
turned our thoughts to paying the penguins a visit.
The boat was therefore overhauled and a few repairs
done. Then we prepared a supply of provisions,
for we intended to be absent at least a night or two,
perhaps longer. This took us some time to do,
for while Jack was busy with the boat, Peterkin
was sent into the woods to spear a hog or two, and
had to search long, sometimes, ere he found them.
Peterkin was usually sent on this errand when we
wanted a pork chop (which was not seldom), because
he was so active and could run so wonderfully fast
that he found no difficulty in overtaking the hogs ;
but being dreadfully reckless, he almost invariably
tumbled over stumps and stones in the course of
his wild chase, and seldom returned home without
having knocked the skin off his shins. Once, indeed,
a more serious accident happened to him. He had
been out all morning alone, and did not return at
the usual time to dinner. We wondered at this,
for Peterkin was always very punctual at the dinner-
hour. As supper-time drew near we began to be
anxious about him, and at length sallied forth to
search the woods. For a long time we sought in
vain, but a little before dark we came upon the
tracks of the hogs, which we followed up until we
came to the brow of a rather steep bank or precipice.
Looking over this we beheld Peterkin lying in a state
of insensibility at the foot, with his cheek resting
on the snout of a little pig, which was pinned to the
earth by the spear. We were dreadfully alarmed,

but hastened to bathe his forehead with water, and had soon the satisfaction of seeing him revive. After we had carried him home he related to us how the thing had happened.

"You must know," said he, "I walked about all the forenoon, till I was as tired as an old donkey, without seeing a single grunter, not so much as a track of one ; but as I was determined not to return empty-handed, I resolved to go without my dinner, and—"

"What ! " exclaimed Jack, " did you *really* resolve to do that ? "

"Now, Jack, hold your tongue," returned Peterkin. " I say that I resolved to forego my dinner and to push to the head of the small valley, where I felt pretty sure of discovering the hogs. I soon found that I was on the right scent, for I had scarcely walked half a mile in the direction of the small plum tree we found there the other day, when a squeak fell on my ear. ' Ho, ho,' said I, ' there you go, my boys ; ' and I hurried up the glen. I soon started them, and singling out a fat pig, ran tilt at him. In a few seconds I was up with him, and stuck my spear right through his dumpy body. Just as I did so, I saw that we were on the edge of a precipice, whether high or low I knew not ; but I had been running at such a pace that I could not stop, so the pig and I gave a howl in concert, and went plunging over together. I remembered nothing more after that, till I came to my senses and found you bathing my temples, and Ralph wringing his hands over me."

But although Peterkin was often unfortunate in the way of getting tumbles, he was successful on the present occasion in hunting, and returned before evening with three very nice little hogs. I also was successful in my visit to the mud-flats, where I killed several ducks. So that, when we launched and loaded our boat at sunrise the following morning, we found our store of provisions to be more than sufficient. Part had been cooked the night before, and on taking note of the different items, we found the account to stand thus :—

    10 Bread-fruits (two baked, eight unbaked).
    20 Yams (six roasted, the rest raw).
     6 Taro roots.
    50 Fine large plums.
     6 Cocoa nuts, ripe.
     6 Ditto green (for drinking).
     4 Large ducks and two small ones, raw.
     3 Cold roast pigs, with stuffing.

I may here remark that the stuffing had been devised by Peterkin specially for the occasion. He kept the manner of its compounding a profound secret, so I cannot tell what it was ; but I can say, with much confidence, that we found it to be atrociously bad, and, after the first tasting, scraped it carefully out and threw it overboard. We calculated that this supply would last us for several days ; but we afterwards found that it was much more than we required, especially in regard to the cocoa nuts, of which we found large supplies wherever we went. However, as Peterkin remarked, it was

better to have too much than too little, as we knew
not to what straits we might be put during our voyage.

It was a very calm, sunny morning when we
launched forth and rowed over the lagoon towards
the outlet in the reef, and passed between the two
green islets that guarded the entrance. We experienced some difficulty and no little danger in
passing the surf of the breaker, and shipped a good
deal of water in the attempt ; but, once past the
billow, we found ourselves floating placidly on the
long, oily swell that rose and fell slowly as it rolled
over the wide ocean.

Penguin Island lay on the other side of our own
island, at about a mile beyond the outer reef, and we
calculated that it must be at least twenty miles
distant by the way we should have to go. We
might, indeed, have shortened the way by coasting
round our island inside of the lagoon, and going out
at the passage in the reef nearly opposite to Penguin
Island ; but we preferred to go by the open sea—
first, because it was more adventurous, and secondly,
because we should have the pleasure of again feeling
the motion of the deep, which we all loved very
much, not being liable to sea-sickness.

" I wish we had a breeze," said Jack.

" So do I," cried Peterkin, resting on his oar
and wiping his heated brow ; " pulling is hard work.
Oh dear, if we could only catch a hundred or two of
these gulls, tie them to the boat with long strings
and make them fly as we want them, how capital
it would be ! "

" Or bore a hole through a shark's tail, and reeve a rope through it, eh ? " remarked Jack. " But, I say, it seems that my wish is going to be granted, for here comes a breeze. Ship your oar, Peterkin. Up with the mast, Ralph ; I'll see to the sail. Mind your helm , look out for squalls ! "

This last speech was caused by the sudden appearance of a dark-blue line on the horizon, which, in an incredibly short space of time, swept down on us, lashing up the sea in white foam as it went. We presented the stern of the boat to its first violence, and, in a few seconds, it moderated into a steady breeze, to which we spread our sail and flew merrily over the waves. Although the breeze died away soon afterwards, it had been so stiff while it lasted that we were carried over the greater part of our way before it fell calm again ; so that, when the flapping of the sail against the mast told us that it was time to resume the oars, we were not much more than a mile from Penguin Island.

" There go the soldiers ! " cried Peterkin, as we came in sight of it ; " how spruce their white trousers look this morning ! I wonder if they will receive us kindly. D'you think they are hospitable, Jack ? "

" Don't talk, Peterkin, but pull away, and you shall see shortly."

As we drew near to the island we were much amused by the manœuvres and appearance of these strange birds. They seemed to be of different species: for some had crests on their heads, while others had none ; and while some were about the size of a goose, others appeared nearly as large as a swan. We also saw a huge albatross soaring above the heads of the penguins. It was followed and sur-rounded by numerous flocks of sea-gulls. Having approached to within a few yards of the island, which was a low rock, with no other vegetation on it than a few bushes, we lay on our oars and gazed at the birds with surprise and pleasure, they returning our gaze with interest. We now saw that their soldier-like appearance was owing to the stiff, erect manner in which they sat on their short legs— " bolt-upright," as Peterkin expressed it. They had black heads, long sharp beaks, white breasts, and bluish backs. Their wings were so short that they looked more like the fins of a fish, and, indeed, we soon saw that they used them for the purpose of swimming under water. There were no quills on these wings, but a sort of scaly feathers ; which also thickly covered their bodies. Their legs were short, and placed so far back that the birds, while on land, were obliged to stand quite upright in order to keep their balance ; but in the water they floated like other water-fowl. At first we were so stunned with the clamour which they and other sea-birds kept up around us, that we knew not which way to look—for they covered the rocks in thousands ; but as we continued to gaze, we observed several quadrupeds (as we thought) walking in the midst of the penguins.

" Pull in a bit," cried Peterkin, " and let's see what these are. They must be fond of noisy com-pany, to consort with such creatures."

To our surprise we found that these were no other than penguins which had gone down on all fours, and were crawling among the bushes on their feet and wings, just like quadrupeds. Suddenly one big old bird, that had been sitting on a point very near to us, gazing in mute astonishment, became alarmed, and scuttling down the rocks, plumped or fell, rather than ran, into the sea. It dived in a moment, and, a few seconds afterwards, came out of the water far ahead, with such a spring, and such a dive back into the sea again, that we could scarcely believe it was not a fish that had leaped in sport.

" That beats everything," said Peterkin, rubbing his nose, and screwing up his face with an expression of exasperated amazement. " I've heard of a thing being neither fish, flesh, nor fowl, but I never did expect to live to see a brute that was all three together—at once—in one ! But look there ! " he continued, pointing with a look of resignation to the shore—" look there ! there's no end to it. What *has* that brute got under its tail ? "

We turned to look in the direction pointed out, and there saw a penguin walking slowly and very sedately along the shore with an egg under its tail. There were several others, we observed, burdened in the same way ; and we found afterwards that these were a species of penguins that always carried their eggs so. Indeed, they had a most convenient cavity for the purpose, just between the tail and the legs. We were very much impressed with the regularity and order of this colony. The island seemed to be apportioned out into squares, of which each penguin possessed one, and sat in stiff solemnity in the middle of it, or took a slow march up and down the spaces between. Some were hatching their eggs, but others were feeding their young ones in a manner that caused us to laugh not a little. The mother stood on a mound or raised rock, while the young one stood patiently below her on the ground. Suddenly the mother raised her head and uttered a series of the most discordant cackling sounds.

" She's going to choke," cried Peterkin.

But this was not the case, although, I confess, she looked like it. In a few seconds she put down her head, and opened her mouth, into which the young one thrust its beak and seemed to suck something from her throat. Then the cackling was renewed, the sucking continued, and so the operation of feeding was carried on till the young one was satisfied ; but what she fed her little one with we could not tell.

" Now, just look yonder ! " said Peterkin, in an excited tone ; " if that isn't the most abominable piece of maternal deception I ever saw ! That rascally old lady penguin has just pitched her young one into the sea, and there's another about to follow her example."

This indeed seemed to be the case, for on the top of a steep rock close to the edge of the sea we observed an old penguin endeavouring to entice her young one into the water ; but the young one seemed very unwilling to go, and, notwithstanding the enticements of its mother, moved very slowly towards her. At last she went gently behind the young bird and pushed it a little towards the water, but with great tenderness, as much as to say, ' Don't be afraid, darling ; I won't hurt you, my pet ! ' But no sooner did she get it to the edge of the rock, where it stood looking pensively down at the sea, than she gave it a sudden and violent push, sending it headlong down the slope into the water, where its mother left it to scramble ashore as it best could. We observed many of them employed in doing this, and we came to the conclusion that this is the way in which old penguins teach their children to swim.

Scarcely had we finished making our remarks on this, when we were startled by about a dozen of the old birds hopping in the most clumsy and ludicrous manner towards the sea. The beach here was a sloping rock, and when they came to it some of them succeeded in hopping down in safety, but others lost their balance, and rolled and scrambled down the slope in the most helpless manner. The instant they reached the water, however, they seemed to be in their proper element. They dived and bounded out of it and into it again with the utmost agility ; and so, diving and bounding and sputtering—for they could not fly—they went rapidly out to sea.

On seeing this, Peterkin turned with a grave face to us and said, " It's my opinion that these birds are all stark, staring mad, and that this is an enchanted island. I therefore propose that we should either put about ship and fly in terror from the spot, or land valorously on the island, and sell our lives as dearly as we can."

" I vote for landing ; so pull in, lads," said Jack, giving a stroke with his oar that made the boat spin. In a few seconds we ran the boat into a little creek, where we made her fast to a projecting piece of coral, and running up the beach, entered the ranks of the penguins armed with our cudgels and our spear. We were greatly surprised to find that, instead of attacking us or showing signs of fear at our approach, these curious birds did not move from their places until we laid hands on them, and merely turned their eyes on us in solemn, stupid wonder as we passed. There was one old penguin, however, that began to walk slowly towards the sea, and Peterkin took it into his head that he would try to interrupt its progress, so he ran between it and the sea and brandished his cudgel in its face. But this proved to be a resolute old bird. It would not retreat ; nay, more, it would not cease to advance, but battled with Peterkin bravely, and drove him before it until it reached the sea. Had Peterkin used his club he could easily have felled it, no doubt ; but as he had no wish to do so cruel an act merely out of sport, he let the bird escape.

We spent fully three hours on this island in watching the habits of these curious birds, and when we finally left them, we all three concluded, after much consultation, that they were the most wonderful creatures we had ever seen ; and further, we thought it probable that they were the most wonderful creatures in the world !

CHAPTER XVIII

An awful storm and its consequences—Narrow escape—A rock proves a sure foundation—A fearful night and a bright morning—Deliverance from danger.

It was evening before we left the island of the penguins. As we had made up our minds to encamp for the night on a small island, whereon grew a few cocoa-nut trees, which was about two miles off, we lay to our oars with some energy. But a danger was in store for us which we had not anticipated. The wind, which had carried us so quickly to Penguin Island, freshened as evening drew on to a stiff breeze, and before we had made half the distance to the small island, it became a regular gale. Although it was not so directly against us as to prevent our rowing in the course we wished to go, yet it checked us very much ; and although the force of the sea was somewhat broken by the island, the waves soon began to rise, and to roll their broken crests against our small craft, so that she began to take in water, and we had much ado to keep ourselves afloat. At last the wind and sea together became so violent that we found it impossible to make the island ; so Jack suddenly put the head of the boat round and ordered

Peterkin and me to hoist a corner of the sail, intending to run back to Penguin Island.

" We shall at least have the shelter of the bushes," he said, as the boat flew before the wind, " and the penguins will keep us company."

As Jack spoke, the wind suddenly shifted, and blew so much against us that we were forced to hoist more of the sail in order to beat up for the island, being by this change thrown much to leeward of it. What made matters worse was, that the gale came in squalls, so that we were more than once nearly upset.

" Stand by, both of you," cried Jack, in a quick, earnest tone ; " be ready to douse the sail. I very much fear we won't make the island after all."

Peterkin and I were so much in the habit of trusting everything to Jack, that we had fallen into the way of not considering things, especially such things as were under Jack's care. We had, therefore, never doubted for a moment that all was going well, so that it was with no little anxiety that we heard him make the above remark. However, we had no time for question or surmise, for at the moment he spoke a heavy squall was bearing down upon us, and as we were then flying with our lee gunwale dipping occasionally under the waves, it was evident that we should have to lower our sail altogether. In a few seconds the squall struck the boat, but Peterkin and I had the sail down in a moment, so that it did not upset us ; but when it was past we were more than half full of water. This I soon bailed out, while

Peterkin again hoisted a corner of the sail; but the evil which Jack had feared came upon us. We found it quite impossible to make Penguin Island. The gale carried us quickly past it towards the open sea, and the terrible truth flashed upon us that we should be swept out and left to perish miserably in a small boat in the midst of the wide ocean.

This idea was forced very strongly upon us because we saw nothing in the direction whither the wind was blowing us save the raging billows of the sea; and, indeed, we trembled as we gazed around us, for we were now beyond the shelter of the islands, and it seemed as though any of the huge billows, which curled over in masses of foam, might swallow us up in a moment. The water, also, began to wash in over our sides, and I had to keep constantly bailing, for Jack could not quit the helm nor Peterkin the sail for an instant without endangering our lives. In the midst of this distress Jack uttered an exclamation of hope, and pointed towards a low island or rock which lay directly ahead. It had been hitherto unobserved, owing to the dark clouds that obscured the sky and the blinding spray that seemed to fill the whole atmosphere.

As we neared this rock we observed that it was quite destitute of trees and verdure, and so low that the sea broke completely over it. In fact, it was nothing more than the summit of one of the coral formations, which rose only a few feet above the level of the water, and was, in stormy weather, all but invisible. Over this island the waves were breaking in the utmost fury, and our hearts sank within us as we saw that there was not a spot where we could thrust our little boat without its being dashed to pieces.

"Show a little bit more sail," cried Jack, as we swept past the weather side of the rock with fearful speed.

"Ay, ay," answered Peterkin, hoisting about a foot more of our sail.

Little though the addition was, it caused the boat to lie over and creak so loudly, as we cleft the foaming waves, that I expected to be upset every instant; and I blamed Jack in my heart for his rashness. But I did him injustice, for although during two seconds the water rushed inboard in a torrent, he succeeded in steering us sharply round to the leeward side of the rock, where the water was comparatively calm and the force of the breeze broken.

"Out your oars now, lads! that's well done. Give way!" We obeyed instantly. The oars splashed into the waves together. One good hearty pull, and we were floating in a comparatively calm creek, that was so narrow as to be barely able to admit our boat. Here we were in perfect safety, and as we leaped on shore and fastened our cable to the rocks, I thanked God in my heart for our deliverance from so great danger. But although I have said we were now in safety, I suspect that few of my readers would have envied our position. It is true we had no lack of food, but we were drenched to the skin; the sea was foaming round us and the

spray flying over our heads, so that we were completely enveloped, as it were, in water ; the spot on
which we had landed was not more than twelve yards
in diameter, and from this spot we could not move
without the risk of being swept away by the storm.
At the upper end of the creek was a small hollow or
cave in the rock, which sheltered us from the fury
of the winds and waves ; and as the rock extended in
a sort of ledge over our heads, it prevented the spray
from falling upon us.

"Why," said Peterkin, beginning to feel cheery
again, " it seems to me that we have got into a
mermaid's cave, for there is nothing but water all
round us ; and as for earth or sky, they are things of
the past."

Peterkin's idea was not inappropriate, for what
with the sea roaring in white foam up to our very
feet, and the spray flying in white sheets continually
over our heads, and the water dripping heavily from
the ledge above like a curtain in front of our cave,
it did seem to us very much more like being below
than above water.

" Now, boys," cried Jack, " bestir yourselves, and
let's make ourselves comfortable. Toss out our
provisions, Peterkin ; and here, Ralph, lend a hand
to haul up the boat. Look sharp."

" Ay, ay, captain," we cried, as we hastened to
obey, much cheered by the hearty manner of our
comrade.

Fortunately the cave, although not very deep, was
quite dry, so that we succeeded in making ourselves

much more comfortable than could have been expected. We landed our provisions, wrung the water
out of our garments, spread our sail below us for a
carpet, and after having eaten a hearty meal, began
to feel quite cheerful. But as night drew on our
spirits sank again, for with the daylight all evidence
of our security vanished away. We could no longer
see the firm rock on which we lay, while we were
stunned with the violence of the tempest that raged
around us. The night grew pitchy dark as it
advanced, so that we could not see our hands when
we held them up before our eyes, and were obliged
to feel each other occasionally to make sure that we
were safe, for the storm at last became so terrible
that it was difficult to make our voices audible. A
slight variation of the wind, as we supposed, caused
a few drops of spray ever and anon to blow into our
faces ; and the eddy of the sea, in its mad boiling,
washed up into our little creek until it reached our
feet and threatened to tear away our boat. In
order to prevent this latter calamity, we hauled the
boat further up and held the cable in our hands.
Occasional flashes of lightning shone with a ghastly
glare through the watery curtains around us, and
lent additional horror to the scene. Yet we longed
for those dismal flashes, for they were less appalling
than the thick blackness that succeeded them.
Crashing peals of thunder seemed to tear the skies
in twain, and fell upon our ears through the wild
yelling of the hurricane as if it had been but a gentle
summer breeze ; while the billows burst upon the

weather side of the island until we fancied that
the solid rock was giving way, and in our agony we
clung to the bare ground, expecting every moment
to be whirled away and whelmed in the black howling sea. Oh, it was a night of terrible anxiety! and
no-one can conceive the feelings of intense gratitude and relief with which we at last saw the dawn
of day break through the vapoury mists around us.

For three days and three nights we remained on
this rock, while the storm continued to rage with un-
abated fury. On the morning of the fourth day it
suddenly ceased, and the wind fell altogether; but
the waves still ran so high that we did not dare to
put off in our boat. During the greater part of this
period we scarcely slept above a few minutes at a
time, but on the third night we slept soundly, and
awoke early on the fourth morning to find the sea
very much down, and the sun shining brightly again
in the clear blue sky.

It was with light hearts that we launched forth
once more in our little boat and steered away for
our island home, which, we were overjoyed to find,
was quite visible on the horizon, for we had feared
that we had been blown out of sight of it altogether.
As it was a dead calm, we had to row during the
greater part of the day; but towards the afternoon
a fair breeze sprang up, which enabled us to hoist our
sail. We soon passed Penguin Island and the other
island which we had failed to reach on the day the
storm commenced; but as we had still enough of
provisions, and were anxious to get home, we did

not land, to the great disappointment of Peterkin, who seemed to entertain quite an affection for the penguins.

Although the breeze was pretty fresh for several hours, we did not reach the outer reef of our island till nightfall, and before we had sailed more than a hundred yards into the lagoon, the wind died away altogether, so that we had to take to our oars again. It was late, and the moon and stars were shining brightly, when we arrived opposite the bower and leaped upon the strand. So glad were we to be safe back again on our beloved island, that we scarcely took time to drag the boat a short way up the beach, and then ran up to see that all was right at the bower. I must confess, however, that my joy was mingled with a vague sort of fear lest our home had been visited and destroyed during our absence; but on reaching it we found everything just as it had been left, and the poor black cat curled up, sound asleep, on the coral table in front of our humble dwelling.

CHAPTER XIX

Shoemaking—The even tenor of our way suddenly interrupted—
An unexpected visit and an appalling battle—We all become
warriors, and Jack proves himself to be a hero.

FOR many months after this we continued to live on
our island in uninterrupted harmony and happiness.
Sometimes we went out a-fishing in the lagoon, and
sometimes went a-hunting in the woods, or ascended
to the mountain-top, by way of variety, although
Peterkin always asserted that we went for the purpose
of hailing any ship that might chance to heave in
sight. But I am certain that none of us wished to
be delivered from our captivity, for we were extremely
happy, and Peterkin used to say that as we were
very young we should not feel the loss of a year or
two. Peterkin, as I have said before, was thirteen
years of age, Jack eighteen, and I fifteen. But Jack
was very tall, strong, and manly for his age, and
might easily have been mistaken for twenty.

The climate was so beautiful that it seemed to be
a perpetual summer, and as many of the fruit-trees
continued to bear fruit and blossom all the year round,
we never wanted for a plentiful supply of food.
The hogs, too, seemed rather to increase than di-
minish, although Peterkin was very frequent in his

attacks on them with his spear. If at any time we failed in finding a drove, we had only to pay a visit to the plum-tree before mentioned, where we always found a large family of them asleep under its branches.

We employed ourselves very busily during this time in making various garments of cocoa-nut cloth, as those with which we had landed were beginning to be very ragged. Peterkin also succeeded in making excellent shoes out of the skin of the old hog, in the following manner :—He first cut a piece of the hide, of an oblong form, a few inches longer than his foot. This he soaked in water, and while it was wet he sewed up one end of it, so as to form a rough imitation of that part of the heel of a shoe where the seam is. This done, he bored a row of holes all round the edge of the piece of skin, through which a tough line was passed. Into the sewed-up part of this shoe he thrust his heel ; then drawing the string tight, the edges rose up and overlapped his foot all round. It is true there were a great many ill-looking puckers in these shoes, but we found them very serviceable notwithstanding, and Jack came at last to prefer them to his long boots. We also made various other useful articles, which added to our comfort, and once or twice spoke of building us a house ; but we had so great an affection for the bower, and withal found it so serviceable, that we determined not to leave it, nor to attempt the building of a house, which in such a climate might turn out to be rather disagreeable than useful.

We often examined the pistol that we had found

in the house on the other side of the island, and Peterkin wished much that we had powder and shot, as it would render pig-killing much easier ; but after all, we had become so expert in the use of our sling and bow and spear, that we were independent of more deadly weapons.

Diving in the Water Garden also continued to afford us as much pleasure as ever ; and Peterkin began to be a little more expert in the water from constant practice. As for Jack and me, we began to feel as if water were our native element, and revelled in it with so much confidence and comfort that Peterkin said he feared we would turn into fish some day, and swim off and leave him ; adding that he had been for a long time observing that Jack was becoming more and more like a shark every day. Whereupon Jack remarked that if he, Peterkin, were changed into a fish, he would certainly turn into nothing better or bigger than a shrimp. Poor Peterkin did not envy us our delightful excursions under water, except, indeed, when Jack would dive down to the bottom of the Water Garden, sit down on a rock and look up and make faces at him. Peter-kin did feel envious then, and often said he would give anything to be able to do that. I was much amused when Peterkin said this ; for if he could only have seen his own face when he happened to take a short dive, he would have seen that Jack's was far surpassed by it : the great difference being, however, that Jack made faces on purpose—Peterkin couldn't help it !

Now, while we were engaged with these occupations

and amusements, an event occurred one day which was as unexpected as it was exceedingly alarming and very horrible.

Jack and I were sitting, as we were often wont to do, on the rocks at Spouting Cliff, and Peterkin was wringing the water from his garments, having recently fallen by accident into the sea—a thing he was constantly doing—when our attention was suddenly arrested by two objects which appeared on the horizon.

" What are yon, think you ? " I said, addressing Jack.

" I can't imagine," answered he. " I've noticed them for some time, and fancied they were black sea-gulls, but the more I look at them the more I feel convinced they are much larger than gulls."

" They seem to be coming towards us," said I.

" Hallo ! what's wrong ? " inquired Peterkin, coming up.

" Look there," said Jack.

" Whales ! " cried Peterkin, shading his eyes with his hand. " No—eh—*can* they be boats, Jack ? "

Our hearts beat with excitement at the very thought of seeing human faces again.

" I think you are about right, Peterkin. But they seem to me to move strangely for boats," said Jack, in a low tone, as if he were talking to himself.

I noticed that a shade of anxiety crossed Jack's countenance as he gazed long and intently at the two objects, which were now nearing us fast. At last he sprang to his feet. " They are canoes, Ralph !

whether war-canoes or not I cannot tell ; but this I know, that all the natives of the South Sea Islands are fierce cannibals, and they have little respect for strangers. We must hide if they land here, which I earnestly hope they will not do."

I was greatly alarmed at Jack's speech, but I confess I thought less of what he said than of the earnest, anxious manner in which he said it, and it was with very uncomfortable feelings that Peterkin and I followed him quickly into the woods.

" How unfortunate," said I, as we gained the shelter of the bushes, " that we have forgotten our arms ! "

" It matters not," said Jack ; " here are clubs enough and to spare." As he spoke, he laid his hand on a bundle of stout poles of various sizes, which Peterkin's ever-busy hands had formed during our frequent visits to the cliff, for no other purpose, apparently, than that of having something to do.

We each selected a stout club according to our several tastes, and lay down behind a rock, whence we could see the canoes approach, without ourselves being seen. At first we made an occasional remark on their appearance, but after they entered the lagoon and drew near the beach, we ceased to speak, and gazed with intense interest at the scene before us.

We now observed that the foremost canoe was being chased by the other, and that it contained a few women and children, as well as men—perhaps forty souls altogether ; while the canoe which pursued it contained only men. They seemed to be about

the same in number, but were better armed, and had
the appearance of being a war-party. Both crews
were paddling with all their might, and it seemed as
if the pursuers were exerting themselves to overtake the fugitives ere they could land. In this,
however, they failed. The foremost canoe made
for the beach close beneath the rocks behind which
we were concealed. Their short paddles flashed
like meteors in the water, and sent up a constant
shower of spray. The foam curled from the prow,
and the eyes of the rowers glistened in their black
faces as they strained every muscle of their naked
bodies ; nor did they relax their efforts till the canoe
struck the beach with a violent shock ; then with a
shout of defiance the whole party sprang, as if by
magic, from the canoe to the shore. Three women,
two of whom carried infants in their arms, rushed
into the woods ; and the men crowded to the water's
edge, with stones in their hands, spears levelled,
and clubs brandished, to resist the landing of their
enemies.

The distance between the two canoes had been
about half a mile, and, at the great speed they were
going, this was soon passed. As the pursuers neared
the shore, no sign of fear or hesitation was noticeable.
On they came like a wild charger—received but
recked not of a shower of stones. The canoe struck,
and with a yell that seemed to issue from the throats
of incarnate fiends, they leaped into the water, and
drove their enemies up the beach.

The battle that immediately ensued was frightful

to behold. Most of the men wielded clubs of enormous size and curious shapes, with which they dashed out each other's brains. As they were almost entirely naked, and had to bound, stoop, leap, and run in their terrible hand-to-hand encounters, they looked more like demons than human beings. I felt my heart grow sick at the sight of this bloody battle, and would fain have turned away, but a species of fascination seemed to hold me down and glue my eyes upon the combatants. I observed that the attacking party was led by a most extraordinary being, who, from his size and peculiarity, I concluded was a chief. His hair was frizzed out to an enormous extent, so that it resembled a large turban. It was of a light-yellow hue, which surprised me much, for the man's body was as black as coal, and I felt convinced that the hair must have been dyed. He was tattooed from head to foot ; and his face, besides being tattooed, was besmeared with red paint, and streaked with white. Altogether, with his yellow turban-like hair, his Herculean black frame, his glittering eyes and white teeth, he seemed the most terrible monster I ever beheld. He was very active in the fight, and had already killed four men.

Suddenly the yellow-haired chief was attacked by a man quite as strong and large as himself. He flourished a heavy club something like an eagle's beak at the point. For a second or two these giants eyed each other warily, moving round and round, as if to catch each other at a disadvantage ; but seeing that nothing was to be gained by this caution, and that the loss of time might effectually turn the tide of battle either way, they apparently made up their minds to attack at the same instant, for with a wild shout and simultaneous spring, they swung their heavy clubs, which met with a loud report. Suddenly the yellow-haired savage tripped, his enemy sprang forward, the ponderous club was swung, but it did not descend, for at that moment the savage was felled to the ground by a stone from the hand of one who had witnessed his chief's danger. This was the turning-point in the battle. The savages who landed first turned and fled towards the bush, on seeing the fall of their chief. But not one escaped. They were all overtaken and felled to the earth. I saw, however, that they were not all killed. Indeed, their enemies, now that they were conquered, seemed anxious to take them alive ; and they succeeded in securing fifteen, whom they bound hand and foot with cords, and carrying them up into the woods, laid them down among the bushes. Here they left them, for what purpose I knew not, and returned to the scene of the late battle, where the remnant of the party were bathing their wounds.

Out of the forty blacks that composed the attacking party, only twenty-eight remained alive, two of whom were sent into the bush to hunt for the women and children. Of the other party, as I have said, only fifteen survived, and these were lying bound and helpless on the grass.

Jack and Peterkin and I now looked at each other, and whispered our fears that the savages might clamber up the rocks to search for fresh water, and so discover our place of concealment ; but we were so much interested in watching their movements that we agreed to remain where we were,—and, indeed, we could not easily have risen without exposing ourselves to detection. One of the savages now went up to the wood, and soon returned with a bundle of firewood, and we were not a little surprised to see him set fire to it by the very same means used by Jack the time we made our first fire—namely, with the bow and drill. When the fire was kindled, two of the party went again to the woods, and returned with one of the bound men. A dreadful feeling of horror crept over my heart as the thought flashed upon me that they were going to burn their enemies. As they bore him to the fire my feelings almost overpowered me. I gasped for breath, and seizing my club, endeavoured to spring to my feet ; but Jack's powerful arm pinned me to the earth. Next moment one of the savages raised his club, and fractured the wretched creature's skull. He must have died instantly ; and strange though it may seem, I confess to a feeling of relief when the deed was done, because I now knew that the poor savage could not be burned alive. Scarcely had his limbs ceased to quiver when the monsters cut slices of flesh from his body, and, after roasting them slightly over the fire, devoured them.

Suddenly there arose a cry from the woods, and in a few seconds the two savages hastened towards the fire, dragging the three women and their two infants

along with them. One of those women was much
younger than her companions, and we were struck
with the modesty of her demeanour and the gentle
expression of her face, which, although she had the
flattish nose and thick lips of the others, was of a
light-brown colour, and we conjectured that she must
be of a different race. She and her companions wore
short petticoats, and a kind of tippet on their
shoulders. Their hair was jet black, but instead of
being long, was short and curly—though not woolly
—somewhat like the hair of a young boy. While
we gazed with interest and some anxiety at those
poor creatures, the big chief advanced to one of the
elder females and laid his hand upon the child. But
the mother shrank from him, and clasping the little
one to her bosom, uttered a wail of fear. With a
savage laugh, the chief tore the child from her arms
and tossed it into the sea. A low groan burst from
Jack's lips as he witnessed this atrocious act and
heard the mother's shriek, as she fell insensible on
the sand. The rippling waves rolled the child on the
beach, as if they refused to be a party in such a
foul murder, and we could observe that the little one
still lived.

The young girl was now brought forward, and the
chief addressed her ; but although we heard his
voice and even the words distinctly, of course we
could not understand what he said. The girl made
no answer to his fierce questions, and we saw by the
way in which he pointed to the fire that he threatened
her life.

" Peterkin," said Jack, in a hoarse whisper, " have you got your knife ? "

" Yes," replied Peterkin, whose face was pale as death.

" That will do. Listen to me, and do my bidding quick.—Here is the small knife, Ralph.—Fly both of you through the bush, cut the cords that bind the prisoners, and set them free. There ! quick, ere it be too late." Jack sprang up and seized a heavy but short bludgeon, while his strong frame trembled with emotion, and large drops rolled down his forehead.

At this moment the man who had butchered the savage a few minutes before advanced towards the girl with his heavy club. Jack uttered a yell that rang like a death-shriek among the rocks. With one bound he leaped over a precipice full fifteen feet high, and before the savages had recovered from their surprise, was in the midst of them ; while Peterkin and I dashed through the bushes towards the prisoners. With one blow of his staff Jack felled the man with the club ; then turning round with a look of fury, he rushed upon the big chief with the yellow hair. Had the blow which Jack aimed at his head taken effect, the huge savage would have needed no second stroke ; but he was agile as a cat, and avoided it by springing to one side, while, at the same time, he swung his ponderous club at the head of his foe. It was now Jack's turn to leap aside, and well was it for him that the first outburst of his blind fury was over, else he had become an easy prey

to his gigantic antagonist ; but Jack was cool now.
He darted his blows rapidly and well, and the superiority of his light weapon was strikingly proved in
this combat ; for while he could easily evade the
blows of the chief's heavy club, the chief could not
so easily evade those of his light one. Nevertheless,
so quick was he, and so frightfully did he fling about
the mighty weapon, that although Jack struck him
almost every blow, the strokes had to be delivered
so quickly that they wanted force to be very effec-
tual.

It was lucky for Jack that the other savages
considered the success of their chief in this encounter
to be so certain that they refrained from interfering.
Had they doubted it, they would have probably ended
the matter at once by felling him. But they con-
tented themselves with awaiting the issue.

The force which the chief expended in wielding
his club now began to be apparent. His movements
became slower, his breath hissed through his clinched
teeth, and the surprised savages drew nearer in order
to render assistance. Jack observed this movement.
He felt that his fate was sealed, and resolved to cast
his life upon the next blow. The chief's club was
again about to descend on his head. He might have
evaded it easily, but instead of doing so, he suddenly
shortened his grasp of his own club, rushed in under
the blow, struck his adversary right between the eyes
with all his force, and fell to the earth, crushed
beneath the senseless body of the chief. A dozen
clubs flew high in air, ready to descend on the head

of Jack ; but they hesitated a moment, for the massive body of the chief completely covered him. That moment saved his life. Ere the savages could tear the chief's body away, seven of their number fell prostrate beneath the clubs of the prisoners whom Peterkin and I had set free, and two others fell under our own hand. We could never have accomplished this had not our enemies been so engrossed with the fight between Jack and their chief that they had failed to observe us until we were upon them. They still outnumbered our party by three ; but we were flushed with victory, while they were taken by surprise and dispirited by the fall of their chief. Moreover, they were awestruck by the sweeping fury of Jack, who seemed to have lost his senses altogether, and had no sooner shaken himself free of the chief's body than he rushed into the midst of them, and in three blows equalized our numbers. Peterkin and I flew to the rescue, the savages followed us, and in less than ten minutes the whole of our opponents were knocked down or made prisoners, bound hand and foot, and extended side by side upon the seashore.

CHAPTER XX

AFTER the battle was over, the savages crowded round us, and gazed at us in surprise, while they continued to pour upon us a flood of questions, which, being wholly unintelligible, of course we could not answer. However, by way of putting an end to it, Jack took the chief (who had recovered from the effects of his wound) by the hand and shook it warmly. No sooner did the blacks see that this was meant to express good-will than they shook hands with us all round. After this ceremony was gone through. Jack went up to the girl, who had never once moved from the rock where she had been left, but had continued an eager spectator of all that had passed. He made signs to her to follow him, and then, taking the chief by the hand, was about to conduct him to the bower, when his eye fell on the poor infant which had been thrown into the sea and was still lying on the shore. Dropping the chief's hand he hastened towards it, and to his great joy found it to be still alive. We also found that the mother was beginning to recover slowly.

" Here, get out o' the way," said Jack, pushing us

aside, as we stooped over the poor woman and endeavoured to restore her; "I'll soon bring her
round." So saying, he placed the infant on her
bosom and laid its warm cheek on hers. The effect
was wonderful. The woman opened her eyes, felt
the child, looked at it, and with a cry of joy clasped
it in her arms, at the same time endeavouring to
rise, for the purpose, apparently, of rushing into the
woods.

"There, that's all right," said Jack, once more
taking the chief by the hand.—"Now, Ralph and
Peterkin, make the women and these fellows follow
me to the bower. We'll entertain them as hospitably
as we can."

In a few minutes the savages were all seated on the
ground in front of the bower making a hearty meal
off a cold roast pig, several ducks, and a variety of
cold fish, together with an unlimited supply of cocoa
nuts, bread-fruits, yams, taro, and plums; with all
of which they seemed to be quite familiar and perfectly satisfied.

Meanwhile, we three, being thoroughly knocked up
with our day's work, took a good draught of cocoa-
nut lemonade, and throwing ourselves on our beds
fell fast asleep. The savages, it seems, followed our
example, and in half an hour the whole camp was
buried in repose.

How long we slept I cannot tell, but this I know,
that when we lay down the sun was setting, and
when we awoke it was high in the heavens. I
awoke Jack, who started up in surprise, being unable

at first to comprehend our situation. " Now then,"
said he, springing up, " let's see after breakfast.
—Hallo, Peterkin, lazy fellow ! how long do you
mean to lie there ? "

Peterkin yawned heavily. " Well," said he,
opening his eyes and looking up after some trouble,
" if it isn't to-morrow morning, and me thinking
it was to-day all this time !—Hallo, Venus ! where
did you come from ? You seem tolerably at home,
anyhow. Bah ! might as well speak to the cat as
to you—better, in fact, for it understands me, and
you don't."

This remark was called forth by the sight of one of
the elderly females, who had seated herself on the
rock in front of the bower, and, having placed her
child at her feet, was busily engaged in devouring
the remains of a roast pig.

By this time the natives outside were all astir,
and breakfast in an advanced state of preparation.
During the course of it we made sundry attempts to
converse with the natives by signs, but without
effect. At last we hit upon a plan of discovering
their names. Jack pointed to his breast and said
" Jack " very distinctly ; then he pointed to Peterkin
and to me, repeating our names at the same time.
Then he pointed to himself again, and said " Jack,"
and laying his finger on the breast of the chief, looked
inquiringly into his face. The chief instantly understood him, and said " Tararo " twice distinctly.
Jack repeated it after him, and the chief, nodding
his head approvingly, said " Chuck." On hearing

which Peterkin exploded with laughter; but Jack turned, and with a frown rebuked him, saying, "I must look even more indignantly at you than I feel, Peterkin, you rascal, for these fellows don't like to be laughed at." Then turning towards the youngest of the women, who was seated at the door of the bower, he pointed to her; whereupon the chief said, "Avatea," and pointing towards the sun, raised his finger slowly towards the zenith, where it remained steadily for a minute or two.

"What can that mean, I wonder?" said Jack, looking puzzled.

"Perhaps," said Peterkin, "the chief means she is an angel come down to stay here for a while. If so, she's an uncommonly black one!"

We did not feel quite satisfied with this explanation, so Jack went up to her and said, "Avatea." The woman smiled sadly, and nodded her head, at the same time pointing to her breast and then to the sun, in the same manner as the chief had done. We were much puzzled to know what this could signify, but as there was no way of solving our difficulty, we were obliged to rest content.

Jack now made signs to the natives to follow him, and taking up his axe, he led them to the place where the battle had been fought. Here we found the prisoners, who had passed the night on the beach, having been totally forgotten by us, as our minds had been full of our guests, and were ultimately overcome by sleep. They did not seem the worse for their exposure, however, as we judged by the

hearty appetite with which they devoured the breakfast that was soon after given to them. Jack then
began to dig a hole in the sand, and after working
a few seconds, he pointed to it and to the dead
bodies that lay exposed on the beach. The natives
immediately perceived what he wanted, and running
for their paddles, dug a hole in the course of half an
hour that was quite large enough to contain all the
bodies of the slain. When it was finished they tossed
their dead enemies into it with so much indifference
that we felt assured they would not have put
themselves to this trouble had we not asked them to
do so. The body of the yellow-haired chief was the
last thrown in. This wretched man would have
recovered from the blow with which Jack felled him,
and indeed he did endeavour to rise during the *mêleé*
that followed his fall ; but one of his enemies, happening to notice the action, dealt him a blow with
his club that killed him on the spot.

While they were about to throw the sand over this
chief, one of the savages stooped over him, and with
a knife, made apparently of stone, cut a large slice
of flesh from his thigh. We knew at once that he
intended to make use of this for food, and could not
repress a cry of horror and disgust.

"Come, come, you blackguard!" cried Jack,
starting up and seizing the man by the arm, "pitch
that into the hole. Do you hear?"

The savage, of course, did not understand the
command, but he perfectly understood the look of
disgust with which Jack regarded the flesh, and his

fierce gaze as he pointed towards the hole. Nevertheless he did not obey. Jack instantly turned to Tararo, and made signs to him to enforce obedience. The chief seemed to understand the appeal, for he stepped forward, raised his club, and was on the point of dashing out the brains of his offending subject, when Jack sprang forward and caught his uplifted arm.

"Stop," he shouted, "you blockhead! I don't want you to kill the man." He then pointed again to the flesh and to the hole. The chief uttered a few words, which had the desired effect; for the man threw the flesh into the hole, which was immediately filled up. This man was of a morose, sulky disposition, and during all the time he remained on the island regarded us, especially Jack, with a scowling visage. His name, we found, was Mahine.

The next three or four days were spent by the savages in mending their canoe, which had been damaged by the violent shock it had sustained on striking the shore. This canoe was a very curious structure. It was about thirty feet long, and had a high towering stern. The timbers, of which it was partly composed, were fastened much in the same way as those of our little boat were put together; but the part that seemed most curious to us was a sort of outrigger, or long plank, which was attached to the body of the canoe by means of two stout cross-beams. These beams kept the plank parallel with the canoe, but not in contact with it,

for it floated in the water with an open space between ;
thus forming a sort of double canoe. This we found
was intended to prevent the upsetting of the canoe,
which was so narrow that it could not have maintained an upright position without the outrigger.
We could not help wondering both at the ingenuity
and the clumsiness of this contrivance.

When the canoe was ready, we assisted the natives
to carry the prisoners into it, and helped them
to load it with provisions and fruit. Peterkin also
went to the plum-tree for the purpose of making
a special onslaught upon the hogs, and killed no less
than six of them. These we baked and presented
to our friends on the day of their departure. On that
day Tararo made a great many energetic signs to us,
which, after much consideration, we came to understand were proposals that we should go away with
him to his island ; but having no desire to do so,
we shook our heads very decidedly. However,
we consoled him by presenting him with our rusty
axe, which we thought we could spare, having the
excellent one which had been so providentially
washed ashore to us the day we were wrecked.
We also gave him a piece of wood with our names
carved on it, and a piece of string to hang it round
his neck as an ornament.

In a few minutes more we were all asembled on
the beach. Being unable to speak to the savages,
we went through the ceremony of shaking hands,
and expected they would depart ; but before doing
so, Tararo went up to Jack and rubbed noses with

him, after which he did the same with Peterkin and me ! Seeing that this was their mode of salutation, we determined to conform to their custom ; so we rubbed noses heartily with the whole party, women and all ! The only disagreeable part of the process was when we came to rub noses with Mahine, and Peterkin afterwards said that when he saw his wolfish eyes glaring so close to his face, he felt much more inclined to *bang* than to *rub* his nose. Avatea was the last to take leave of us, and we experienced a feeling of real sorrow when she approached to bid us farewell. Besides her modest air and gentle manners, she was the only one of the party who exhibited the smallest sign of regret at parting from us. Going up to Jack, she put out her flat little nose to be rubbed, and thereafter paid the same compliment to Peterkin and me.

An hour later the canoe was out of sight, and we, with an indefinable feeling of sadness creeping round our hearts, were seated in silence beneath the shadow of our bower, meditating on the wonderful events of the last few days.

CHAPTER XXI

Sagacious and moral remarks in regard to life—A sail!—An
  unexpected salute—The end of the black cat—A terrible dive
  —An incautious proceeding and a frightful catastrophe.

LIFE is a strange compound. Peterkin used to say
of it that it beat a druggist's shop all to sticks;
for whereas the first is a compound of good and
bad, the other is a horrible compound of all that is
utterly detestable. And indeed the more I consider
it, the more I am struck with the strange mixture
of good and evil that exists not only in the material
earth but in our own natures. In our own Coral
Island we had experienced every variety of good
that a bountiful Creator could heap on us. Yet on
the night of the storm we had seen how almost, in
our case—and altogether, no doubt, in the case of
others less fortunate—all this good might be swept
away for ever. We had seen the rich fruit-trees
waving in the soft air, the tender herbs shooting
upwards under the benign influence of the bright sun;
and the next day we had seen these good and beautiful
trees and plants uprooted by the hurricane, crushed
and hurled to the ground in destructive devastation.
We had lived for many months in a clime for the
most part so beautiful that we had often wondered

whether Adam and Eve had found Eden more sweet; and we had seen the quiet solitudes of our paradise suddenly broken in upon by ferocious savages, and the white sands stained with blood and strewed with lifeless forms; yet among these cannibals we had seen many symptoms of a kindly nature. I pondered these things much, and while I considered them there recurred to my memory those words which I had read in my Bible—the works of God are wonderful, and His ways past finding out.

After these poor savages had left us, we used to hold long and frequent conversations about them, and I noticed that Peterkin's manner was now much altered. He did not, indeed, jest less heartily than before, but he did so less frequently, and often there was a tone of deep seriousness in his manner, if not in his words, which made him seem to Jack and me as if he had grown two years older within a few days. But indeed I was not surprised at this, when I reflected on the awful realities which we had witnessed so lately. We could by no means shake off a tendency to gloom for several weeks afterwards; but as time wore away our usual good spirits returned somewhat, and we began to think of the visit of the savages with feelings akin to those with which we recall a terrible dream.

One day we were all enjoying ourselves in the Water Garden, preparatory to going on a fishing excursion; for Peterkin had kept us in such constant supply of hogs that we had become quite tired of pork, and desired a change. Peterkin was sunning himself on the ledge of rock, while we were creeping among the rocks below. Happening to look up, I observed Peterkin cutting the most extraordinary capers and making violent gesticulations for us to come up ; so I gave Jack a push and rose immediately.

" A sail ! a sail !—Ralph, look.—Jack, away on the horizon there, just over the entrance to the lagoon ! " cried Peterkin, as we scrambled up the rocks.

" So it is, and a schooner too ! " said Jack, as he proceeded hastily to dress.

Our hearts were thrown into a terrible flutter by this discovery, for we had no doubt that, should it touch at our island, the captain would be happy to give us a passage to some of the civilized islands, where we could find a ship sailing for England or some other part of Europe. Home, with all its associations, rushed in upon my heart like a flood, and much though I loved the Coral Island and the bower which had now been our home so long, I felt that I could have quitted all at that moment without a sigh. With joyful anticipations we hastened to the highest point of rock near our dwelling, and awaited the arrival of the vessel ; for we now perceived that she was making straight for the island, under a steady breeze.

In less than an hour she was close to the reef, where she rounded to, and backed her topsails in order to survey the coast. Seeing this, and fearing that they might not perceive us, we all three waved pieces of cocoa-nut cloth in the air, and soon had the satisfaction of seeing them beginning to lower a boat and bustle about the decks as if they meant to land. Suddenly a flag was run up to the peak, a little cloud of white smoke rose from the schooner's side, and before we could guess their intentions a cannon-shot came crashing through the bushes, carried away several cocoa-nut trees in its passage, and burst in atoms against the cliff a few yards below the spot on which we stood.

With feelings of terror we now observed that the flag at the schooner's peak was black, with a death's-head and cross-bones upon it. As we gazed at each other in blank amazement, the word " pirate " escaped our lips simultaneously.

" What is to be done ? " cried Peterkin, as we observed a boat shoot from the vessel's side and make for the entrance of the reef. " If they take us off the island, it will either be to throw us overboard for sport, or to make pirates of us."

I did not reply, but looked at Jack, as being our only source in this emergency. He stood with folded arms, and his eyes fixed with a grave, anxious expression on the ground. " There is but one hope," said he, turning with a sad expression of countenance to Peterkin ; " perhaps, after all, we may not have to resort to it. If these villains are anxious to take us, they will soon overrun the whole island. But come, follow me."

Stopping abruptly in his speech, Jack bounded into the woods, and led us by a circuitous route to Spouting Cliff. Here he halted, and advancing cautiously to the rocks, glanced over their edge. We were soon by his side, and saw the boat, which was crowded with armed men, just touching the shore. In an instant the crew landed, formed line, and rushed up to our bower.

In a few seconds we saw them hurrying back to the boat, one of them swinging the poor cat round his head by the tail. On reaching the water's edge, he tossed it far into the sea, and joined his companions, who appeared to be holding a hasty council.

" You see what we may expect," said Jack bitterly. " The man who will wantonly kill a poor brute for sport will think little of murdering a fellow-creature. Now, boys, we have but one chance left—the Diamond Cave."

" The Diamond Cave ! " cried Peterkin ; " then my chance is a poor one, for I could not dive into it if all the pirates on the Pacific were at my heels."

" Nay, but," said I, " we will take you down, Peterkin, if you will only trust us."

As I spoke, we observed the pirates scatter over the beach, and radiate, as if from a centre, towards the woods and along shore.

" Now, Peterkin," said Jack, in a solemn tone, " you must make up your mind to do it, or we must make up our minds to die in your company."

" O Jack, my dear friend," cried Peterkin, turning pale, " leave me ; I don't believe they'll think it worth while to kill me. Go, you and Ralph, and dive into the cave."

" That will not I," answered Jack quietly, while

he picked up a stout cudgel from the ground.—" So now, Ralph, we must prepare to meet these fellows. Their motto is, ' No quarter.' If we can manage to floor those coming in this direction, we may escape into the woods for a while."

" There are five of them," said I ; " we have no chance."

" Come, then," cried Peterkin, starting up, and grasping Jack convulsively by the arm, " let us dive ; I will go."

Those who are not naturally expert in the water know well the feelings of horror that overwhelm them, when in it, at the bare idea of being held down even for a few seconds—that spasmodic, involuntary recoil from compulsory immersion which has no connection whatever with cowardice ; and they will understand the amount of resolution that it required in Peterkin to allow himself to be dragged down to a depth of ten feet, and then, through a narrow tunnel, into an almost pitch-dark cavern. But there was no alternative. The pirates had already caught sight of us, and were now within a short distance of the rocks.

Jack and I seized Peterkin by the arms.

" Now, keep quite still, no struggling," said Jack, " or we are lost."

Peterkin made no reply, but the stern gravity of his marble features, and the tension of his muscles, satisfied us that he had fully made up his mind to go through with it. Just as the pirates gained the foot of the rocks, which hid us for a moment from their view, we bent over the sea, and plunged down together head foremost. Peterkin behaved like a hero. He floated passively between us like a log of wood, and we passed the tunnel and rose into the cave in a shorter space of time than I had ever done it before.

Peterkin drew a long, deep breath on reaching the surface, and in a few seconds we were all standing on the ledge of rock in safety. Jack now searched for the tinder and torch which always lay in the cave. He soon found them, and lighting the torch, revealed to Peterkin's wondering gaze the marvels of the place. But we were too wet to waste much time in looking about us. Our first care was to take off our clothes and wring them as dry as we could. This done, we proceeded to examine into the state of our larder, for, as Jack truly remarked, there was no knowing how long the pirates might remain on the island.

"Perhaps," said Peterkin, "they may take it into their heads to stop here altogether, and so we shall be buried alive in this place."

"Don't you think, Peterkin, that it's the nearest thing to being drowned alive that you ever felt?" said Jack, with a smile. "But I've no fear of that. These villains never stay long on shore. The sea is their home, so you may depend upon it that they won't stay more than a day or two at the furthest."

We now began to make arrangements for spending the night in the cavern. At various periods Jack and I had conveyed cocoa nuts and other fruits, besides rolls of cocoa-nut cloth, to this submarine cave, partly for amusement, and partly from a feeling that we might possibly be driven one day to take shelter here from the savages. Little did we imagine that the first savages who would drive us into it would be white savages, perhaps our own countrymen. We found the cocoa nuts in good condition, and the cooked yams, but the bread-fruits were spoiled. We also found the cloth where we had left it, and on opening it out there proved to be sufficient to make a bed; which was important, as the rock was damp. Having collected it all together, we spread out our bed, placed our torch in the midst of us, and ate our supper. It was indeed a strange chamber to feast in; and we could not help remarking on the cold, ghastly appearance of the walls, and the black water at our side, with the thick darkness beyond, and the sullen sound of the drops that fell at long intervals from the roof of the cavern into the still water, and the strong contrast between all this and our bed and supper, which, with our faces, were lit up with the deep red flame of the torch.

We sat long over our meal, talking together in subdued voices, for we did not like the dismal echoes that rang through the vault above when we happened to raise them. At last the faint light that came through the opening died away, warning us that it was night, and time for rest. We therefore put out our torch and lay down to sleep.

On awaking, it was some time ere we could collect our faculties so as to remember where we were, and we were in much uncertainty as to whether it was early or late. We saw by the faint light that it was day, but could not guess at the hour ; so Jack proposed that he should dive out and reconnoitre.

" No, Jack," said I ; " do you rest here. You've had enough to do during the last few days. Rest yourself now, and take care of Peterkin, while I go out to see what the pirates are about. I'll be very careful not to expose myself, and I'll bring you word again in a short time."

" Very well, Ralph," answered Jack : " please yourself, but don't be long ; and if you'll take my advice you'll go in your clothes, for I would like to have some fresh cocoa nuts, and climbing trees without clothes is uncomfortable, to say the least of it."

" The pirates will be sure to keep a sharp lookout," said Peterkin, " so, pray, be careful."

" No fear," said I ; " good-bye."

" Good-bye," answered my comrades.

And while the words were yet sounding in my ears, I plunged into the water, and in a few seconds found myself in the open air. On rising, I was careful to come up gently and to breathe softly, while I kept close in beside the rocks ; but as I observed no-one near me, I crept slowly out, and ascended the cliff a step at a time, till I obtained a full view of the shore. No pirates were to be seen—even their boat was gone ; but as it was possible they might have hidden themselves, I did not venture too boldly forward. Then it occurred to me to look out to sea, when, to my surprise, I saw the pirate schooner sailing away almost hull down on the horizon! On seeing this I uttered a shout of joy. Then my first impulse was to dive back to tell my companions the good news; but I checked myself, and ran to the top of the cliff, in order to make sure that the vessel I saw was indeed the pirate schooner. I looked long and anxiously at her, and giving vent to a deep sigh of relief, said aloud, " Yes, there she goes; the villains have been balked of their prey this time at least."

" Not so sure of that ! " said a deep voice at my side, while at the same moment a heavy hand grasped my shoulder, and held it as if in a vice.

CHAPTER XXII

I fall into the hands of pirates—How they treated me, and what
   I said to them—The result of the whole ending in a melancholy
   separation and in a most unexpected gift.

MY heart seemed to leap into my throat at the
words ; and turning round, I beheld a man of
immense stature and fierce aspect regarding me
with a smile of contempt. He was a white man—
that is to say, he was a man of European blood,
though his face, from long exposure to the weather,
was deeply bronzed. His dress was that of a common
seaman, except that he had on a Greek skull-cap,
and wore a broad shawl of the richest silk round his
waist. In this shawl were placed two pairs of pistols
and a heavy cutlass. He wore a beard and moustache, which, like the locks on his head, were short,
curly, and sprinkled with gray hairs.

" So, youngster," he said, with a sardonic smile,
while I felt his grasp tighten on my shoulder, " the
villains have been balked of their prey, have they ?
We shall see, we shall see. Now, you whelp, look
yonder." As he spoke, the pirate uttered a shrill
whistle. In a second or two it was answered, and
the pirate boat rowed round the point at the Water
Garden, and came rapidly towards us. " Now,

go, make a fire on that point ; and hark'ee, youngster, if you try to run away, I'll send a quick and
sure messenger after you," and he pointed significantly at his pistols.

I obeyed in silence, and as I happened to have
the burning-glass in my pocket, a fire was speedily
kindled, and a thick smoke ascended into the air.
It had scarcely appeared for two minutes when the
boom of a gun rolled over the sea, and looking up,
I saw that the schooner was making for the island
again.   It now flashed across me that this was a
ruse on the part of the pirates, and that they had
sent their vessel away, knowing that it would lead us
to suppose that they had left altogether. But there
was no use of regret now.   I was completely in their
power, so I stood helplessly beside the pirate, watching the crew of the boat as they landed on the beach.
For an instant I contemplated rushing over the cliff
into the sea, but this I saw I could not now accomplish, as some of the men were already between me
and the water.

There was a good deal of jesting at the success of
their scheme, as the crew ascended the rocks and
addressed the man who had captured me by the
title of captain.   They were a ferocious set of men,
with shaggy beards and scowling brows.   All of them
were armed with cutlasses and pistols, and their
costumes were, with trifling variations, similar to
that of the captain.   As I looked from one to the
other, and observed the low, scowling brows, that
never unbent, even when the men laughed, and the

mean, rascally expression that sat on each face, I felt that my life hung by a hair.

" But where are the other cubs ? " cried one of the men, with an oath that made me shudder. " I'll swear to it there were three at least, if not more."

" You hear what he says, whelp : where are the other dogs ? " said the captain.

" If you mean my companions," said I, in a low voice, " I won't tell you."

A loud laugh burst from the crew at this answer.

The pirate captain looked at me in surprise. Then drawing a pistol from his belt, he cocked it and said, " Now, youngster, listen to me. I've no time to waste here. If you don't tell me all you know, I'll blow your brains out ! Where are your comrades ? "

For an instant I hesitated, not knowing what to do in this extremity. Suddenly a thought occurred to me.

" Villain," said I, shaking my clinched fist in his face, " to blow my brains out would make short work of me, and be soon over ; death by drowning is as sure, and the agony prolonged ; yet, I tell you to your face, if you were to toss me over yonder cliff into the sea, I would not tell you where my companions are, and I dare you to try me ! "

The pirate captain grew white with rage as I spoke. " Say you so ? " cried he, uttering a fierce oath.—" Here, lads, take him by the legs and heave him in—quick ! "

The men, who were utterly silenced with surprise

at my audacity, advanced and seized me, and as they carried me towards the cliff, I congratulated myself not a little on the success of my scheme, for I knew that once in the water I should be safe, and could rejoin Jack and Peterkin in the cave. But my hopes were suddenly blasted by the captain crying out, "Hold on, lads, hold on! We'll give him a taste of the thumbscrews before throwing him to the sharks. Away with him into the boat. Look alive! the breeze is freshening."

The men instantly raised me shoulder high, and hurrying down the rocks, tossed me into the bottom of the boat, where I lay for some time stunned with the violence of my fall.

On recovering sufficiently to raise myself on my elbow, I perceived that we were already outside the coral reef, and close alongside the schooner, which was of small size and clipper built. I had only time to observe this much, when I received a severe kick on the side from one of the men, who ordered me, in a rough voice, to jump aboard. Rising hastily, I clambered up the side. In a few minutes the boat was hoisted on deck, the vessel's head put close to the wind, and the Coral Island dropped slowly astern as we beat up against a head sea.

Immediately after coming aboard, the crew were too busily engaged in working the ship and getting in the boat to attend to me ; so I remained leaning against the bulwarks close to the gangway, watching their operations. I was surprised to find that there were no guns or carronades of any kind in the vessel,

which had more of the appearance of a fast-sailing
trader than a pirate. But I was struck with the
neatness of everything. The brass work of the binnacle and about the tiller, as well as the copper
belaying-pins, were as brightly polished as if they had
just come from the foundry. The decks were pure
white, and smooth. The masts were clean-scraped
and varnished, except at the cross-trees and truck,
which were painted black. The standing and running
rigging was in the most perfect order, and the sails
white as snow. In short, everything, from the single
narrow red stripe on her low black hull to the trucks
on her tapering masts, evinced an amount of care
and strict discipline that would have done credit to
a ship of the Royal Navy. There was nothing lumbering or unseemly about the vessel, excepting,
perhaps, a boat, which lay on the deck with its
keel up between the fore and main masts. It seemed
disproportionately large for the schooner ; but when
I saw that the crew amounted to between thirty and
forty men, I concluded that this boat was held in
reserve in case of any accident compelling the crew
to desert the vessel.

As I have before said, the costumes of the men were
similar to that of the captain. But in head-gear
they differed not only from him but from each other,
some wearing the ordinary straw hat of the merchant
service, while others wore cloth caps and red worsted
nightcaps. I observed that all their arms were sent
below ; the captain only retaining his cutlass and a
single pistol in the folds of his shawl. Although the

captain was the tallest and most powerful man in the ship, he did not strikingly excel many of his men in this respect, and the only difference that an ordinary observer would have noticed was a certain degree of open candour, straightforward daring, in the bold, ferocious expression of his face, which rendered him less repulsive than his low-browed associates, but did not by any means induce the belief that he was a hero. This look was, however, the indication of that spirit which gave him the pre-eminence among the crew of desperadoes who called him captain. He was a lion-like villain ; totally devoid of personal fear, and utterly reckless of consequences, and therefore a terror to his men, who individually hated him, but unitedly felt it to be to their advantage to have him at their head.

But my thoughts soon reverted to the dear companions whom I had left on shore, and as I turned towards the Coral Island, which was now far away to leeward, I sighed deeply, and the tears rolled slowly down my cheeks as I thought that I might never see them more.

" So you're blubbering, are you, you obstinate whelp ? " said the deep voice of the captain, as he came up and gave me a box on the ear that nearly felled me to the deck. " I don't allow any such weakness aboard o' this ship. So clap a stopper on your eyes, or I'll give you something to cry for."

I flushed with indignation at this rough and cruel treatment, but felt that giving way to anger would only make matters worse, so I made no reply, but took out my handkerchief and dried my eyes.

" I thought you were made of better stuff," continued the captain angrily. " I'd rather have a mad bull-dog aboard than a water-eyed puppy. But I'll cure you, lad, or introduce you to the sharks before long. Now go below, and stay there till I call you."

As I walked forward to obey, my eye fell on a small keg standing by the side of the mainmast, on which the word *gunpowder* was written in pencil. It immediately flashed across me that, as we were beating up against the wind, anything floating in the sea would be driven on the reef encircling the Coral Island. I also recollected—for thought is more rapid than the lightning—that my old companions had a pistol. Without a moment's hesitation, therefore, I lifted the keg from the deck and tossed it into the sea ! An exclamation of surprise burst from the captain and some of the men who witnessed this act of mine.

Striding up to me, and uttering fearful imprecations, the captain raised his hand to strike me, while he shouted, " Boy ! whelp ! what mean you by that ? "

" If you lower your hand," said I, in a loud voice, while I felt the blood rush to my temples, " I'll tell you. Until you do so I'm dumb."

The captain stepped back and regarded me with a look of amazement.

" Now," continued I, " I threw that keg into the sea because the wind and waves will carry it to my

friends on the Coral Island, who happen to have a
pistol but no powder. I hope that it will reach them
soon ; and my only regret is that the keg was not a
bigger one. Moreover, pirate, you said just now
that you thought I was made of better stuff. I
don't know what stuff I am made of—I never thought
much about that subject—but I'm quite certain of
this, that I am made of such stuff as the like of you
shall never tame, though you should do your worst."

To my surprise, the captain, instead of flying into
a rage, smiled, and thrusting his hand into the
voluminous shawl that encircled his waist, turned
on his heel and walked aft, while I went below.

Here, instead of being rudely handled, as I had
expected, the men received me with a shout of
laughter, and one of them, patting me on the back,
said, " Well done, lad ! you're a brick, and I have
no doubt will turn out a rare cove. Bloody Bill
there was just such a fellow as you are, and he's
now the biggest cutthroat of us all."

" Take a can of beer, lad," cried another, " and
wet your whistle after that speech o' your'n to the
captain. If any one o' us had made it, youngster,
he would have had no whistle to wet by this time."

" Stop your clapper, Jack," vociferated a third.
" Give the boy a junk o' meat. Don't you see he's
a'most goin' to kick the bucket ? "

" And no wonder," said the first speaker, with an
oath, " after the tumble you gave him into the boat. I
guess it would have broke *your* neck if you had got it."

I did indeed feel somewhat faint, which was

owing, doubtless, to the combined effects of ill-usage
and hunger ; for it will be recollected that I had
dived out of the cave that morning before breakfast,
and it was now near midday. I therefore gladly
accepted a plate of boiled pork and a yam, which
were handed to me by one of the men from the locker
on which some of the crew were seated eating their
dinner. But I must add that the zest with which
I ate my meal was much abated in consequence of
the frightful oaths and the terrible language that
flowed from the lips of these godless men, even in the
midst of their hilarity and good-humour. The man
who had been alluded to as Bloody Bill was seated
near me, and I could not help wondering at the
moody silence he maintained among his comrades.
He did indeed reply to their questions in a careless,
off-hand tone, but he never volunteered a remark.
The only difference between him and the others was
his taciturnity and his size, for he was nearly, if
not quite, as large a man as the captain.

During the remainder of the afternoon I was left
to my own reflections, which were anything but
agreeable ; for I could not banish from my mind the
threat about the thumbscrews, of the nature and use
of which I had a vague but terrible conception. I
was still meditating on my unhappy fate, when, just
after nightfall, one of the watch on deck called down
the hatchway,—

    " Hallo, there ! one o' you tumble up and light the
cabin lamp, and send that boy aft to the captain—
sharp ! "

" Now then, do you hear, youngster ? the captain wants you. Look alive," said Bloody Bill, raising his huge frame from the locker on which he had been asleep for the last two hours. He sprang up the ladder, and I instantly followed him, and going aft was shown into the cabin by one of the men, who closed the door after me.

A small silver lamp which hung from a beam threw a dim soft light over the cabin, which was a small apartment, and comfortably but plainly furnished. Seated on a camp-stool at the table, and busily engaged in examining a chart of the Pacific, was the captain, who looked up as I entered, and in a quiet voice bade me be seated, while he threw down his pencil, and rising from the table, stretched himself on a sofa at the upper end of the cabin.

" Boy," said he, looking me full in the face, " what is your name ? "

" Ralph Rover," I replied.

" Where did you come from, and how came you to be on that island ? How many companions had you on it ? Answer me, now, and mind you tell no lies."

" I never tell lies," said I firmly.

The captain received this reply with a cold, sarcastic smile, and bade me answer his questions.

I then told him the history of myself and my companions from the time we sailed till the day of his visit to the island, taking care, however, to make no mention of the Diamond Cave. After I had concluded, he was silent for a few minutes ; then looking up, he said, " Boy, I believe you."

I was surprised at this remark, for I could not imagine why he should not believe me. However, I made no reply.

" And what," continued the captain, " makes you think that this schooner is a pirate ? "

" The black flag," said I, " showed me what you are ; and if any further proof were wanting, I have had it in the brutal treatment I have received at your hands."

The captain frowned as I spoke, but subduing his anger he continued, " Boy, you are too bold. I admit that we treated your roughly, but that was because you made us lose time and gave us a good deal of trouble. As to the black flag, that is merely a joke that my fellows play off upon people sometimes in order to frighten them. It is their humour, and does no harm. I am no pirate, boy, but a lawful trader—a rough one, I grant you, but one can't help that in these seas, where there are so many pirates on the water and such murderous blackguards on the land. I carry on a trade in sandal-wood with the Feejee Islands ; and if you choose, Ralph, to behave yourself and be a good boy, I'll take you along with me and give you a good share of the profits. You see I'm in want of an honest boy like you to look after the cabin and keep the log and superintend the traffic on shore sometimes. What say you, Ralph : would you like to become a sandal-wood trader ? "

I was much surprised by this explanation, and a good deal relieved to find that the vessel, after all,

was not a pirate; but instead of replying I said,
" If it be as you state, then why did you take me
from my island, and why do you not now take me
back ? "

The captain smiled as he replied, " I took you off
in anger, boy, and I'm sorry for it. I would even
now take you back, but we are too far away from it.
See, there it is," he added, laying his finger on the
chart, " and we are now here—fifty miles at least.
It would not be fair to my men to put about now,
for they have all an interest in the trade."

I could make no reply to this; so, after a little
more conversation I agreed to become one of the
crew, at least until we could reach some civilized
island where I might be put ashore. The captain
assented to this proposition, and after thanking
him for the promise, I left the cabin and went on
deck with feelings that ought to have been lighter,
but which were, I could not tell why, marvellously
heavy and uncomfortable still.

CHAPTER XXIII

Bloody Bill—Dark surmises—A strange sail, and a strange crew, and a still stranger cargo—New reasons for favouring missionaries—A murderous massacre, and thoughts thereon.

THREE weeks after the conversation narrated in the last chapter, I was standing on the quarter-deck of the schooner watching the gambols of a shoal of porpoises that swam round us. It was a dead calm—one of those still, hot, sweltering days so common in the Pacific, when nature seems to have gone to sleep, and the only thing in water or in air that proves her still alive is her long, deep breathing in the swell of the mighty sea. No cloud floated in the deep blue above, no ripple broke the reflected blue below. The sun shone fiercely in the sky, and a ball of fire blazed with almost equal power from out the bosom of the water. So intensely still was it, and so perfectly transparent was the surface of the deep, that had it not been for the long swell already alluded to, we might have believed the surrounding universe to be a huge blue liquid ball, and our little ship the one solitary material speck in all creation, floating in the midst of it.

No sound broke on our ears save the soft puff now

and then of a porpoise, the slow creak of the masts as we swayed gently on the swell, the patter of the reef-points, and the occasional flap of the hanging sails. An awning covered the fore and after parts of the schooner, under which the men composing the watch on deck lolled in sleepy indolence, overcome with excessive heat. Bloody Bill, as the men invariably called him, was standing at the tiller ; but his post for the present was a sinecure, and he whiled away the time by alternately gazing in dreamy abstraction at the compass in the binnacle, and by walking to the taffrail in order to spit into the sea. In one of these turns he came near to where I was standing, and leaning over the side, looked long and earnestly down into the blue wave.

This man, although he was always taciturn and often surly, was the only human being on board with whom I had the slightest desire to become better acquainted. The other men, seeing that I did not relish their company, and knowing that I was a *protégé* of the captain, treated me with total indifference. Bloody Bill, it is true, did the same ; but as this was his conduct to every one else, it was not peculiar in reference to me. Once or twice I tried to draw him into conversation, but he always turned away after a few cold monosyllables. As he now leaned over the taffrail close beside me, I said to him,—

" Bill, why is it that you are so gloomy ? Why do you never speak to any one ? "

Bill smiled slightly as he replied, " Why, I s'pose it's because I hain't got nothin' to say ! "

"That's strange," said I, musingly; "you look like a man that could think, and such men can usually speak."

"So they can, youngster," rejoined Bill, somewhat sternly; "and I could speak too if I had a mind to, but what's the use o' speakin' here? The men only open their mouths to curse and swear, an' they seem to find it entertainin'; but I don't, so I hold my tongue."

"Well, Bill, that's true, and I would rather not hear you speak at all than hear you speak like the other men; but *I* don't swear, Bill, so you might talk to me sometimes, I think. Besides, I'm weary of spending day after day in this way, without a single soul to say a pleasant word to. I've been used to friendly conversation, Bill, and I really would take it kind if you would talk with me a little now and then."

Bill looked at me in surprise, and I thought I observed a sad expression pass across his sunburned face.

"An' where have you been used to friendly conversation?" said Bill, looking down again into the sea; "not on that Coral Island, I take it?"

"Yes, indeed," said I energetically. "I have spent many of the happiest months in my life on that Coral Island;" and without waiting to be further questioned, I launched out into a glowing account of the happy life that Jack and Peterkin and I had spent together, and related minutely every circumstance that befell us while on the island.

"Boy, boy," said Bill, in a voice so deep that it startled me, "this is no place for you."

"That's true," said I. "I am of little use on board, and I don't like my comrades; but I can't help it, and at any rate I hope to be free again soon."

"Free?" said Bill, looking at me in surprise.

"Yes, free," returned I: "the captain said he would put me ashore after this trip was over."

"*This trip!* Hark'ee, boy," said Bill, lowering his voice, "what said the captain to you the day you came aboard?"

"He said that he was a trader in sandal-wood, and no pirate, and told me that if I would join him for this trip he would give me a good share of the profits or put me on shore in some civilized island if I chose."

Bill's brows lowered savagely as he muttered, "Ay, he said truth when he told you he was a sandal-wood trader, but he lied when—"

"Sail ho!" shouted the lookout at the masthead.

"Where away?" cried Bill, springing to the tiller; while the men, startled by the sudden cry, jumped up and gazed round the horizon.

"On the starboard quarter, hull down, sir," answered the lookout.

At this moment the captain came on deck, and mounting into the rigging, surveyed the sail through the glass. Then sweeping his eye round the horizon, he gazed steadily at a particular point.

"Take in topsails," shouted the captain, swinging himself down on the deck by the main-back stay.

"Take in topsails," roared the first mate.

" Ay, ay, sir-r-r," answered the men, as they sprang into the rigging and went aloft like cats.

Instantly all was bustle on board the hitherto quiet schooner. The topsails were taken in and stowed, the men stood by the sheets and halyards, and the captain gazed anxiously at the breeze, which was now rushing towards us like a sheet of dark blue. In a few seconds it struck us. The schooner trembled as if in surprise at the sudden onset, while she fell away, then bending gracefully to the wind, as though in acknowledgment of her subjection, she cut through the waves with her sharp prow like a dolphin, while Bill directed her course towards the strange sail.

In half an hour we neared her sufficiently to make out that she was a schooner, and from the clumsy appearance of her masts and sails we judged her to be a trader. She evidently did not like our appearance, for the instant the breeze reached her she crowded all sail and showed us her stern. As the breeze had moderated a little, our topsails were again shaken out, and it soon became evident—despite the proverb, " A stern chase is a long one "—that we doubled her speed and would overhaul her speedily. When within a mile we hoisted British colours, but receiving no acknowledgment, the captain ordered a shot to be fired across her bows. In a moment, to my surprise, a large portion of the bottom of the boat amidships was removed, and in the hole thus exposed appeared an immense brass gun. It worked on a swivel, and was elevated by

means of machinery. It was quickly loaded and
fired. The heavy ball struck the water a few yards
ahead of the chase, and ricochetting into the air,
plunged into the sea a mile beyond it.

This produced the desired effect. The strange
vessel backed her topsails and hove to, while we
ranged up and lay to about a hundred yards off.

" Lower the boat," cried the captain.

In a second the boat was lowered and manned by
a part of the crew, who were all armed with cutlasses
and pistols. As the captain passed me to get into it,
he said, " Jump into the stern-sheets, Ralph ; I may
want you." I obeyed, and in ten minutes more we
were standing on the stranger's deck. We were all
much surprised at the sight that met our eyes. Instead
of a crew of such sailors as we were accustomed to
see, there were only fifteen blacks, standing on the
quarter-deck and regarding us with looks of undis-
guised alarm. They were totally unarmed, and most
of them unclothed ; one or two, however, wore
portions of European attire. One had on a pair of
duck trousers which were much too large for him,
and stuck out in a most ungainly manner. Another
wore nothing but the common scanty native garment
round the loins and a black beaver hat. But the
most ludicrous personage of all, and one who seemed
to be chief, was a tall, middle-aged man, of a mild,
simple expression of countenance, who wore a white
cotton shirt, a swallow-tail coat, and a straw hat,
while his black brawny legs were totally uncovered
below the knees.

" Where's the commander of this ship ? " inquired our captain, stepping up to this individual.

" I is capin," he answered, taking off his straw hat and making a low bow.

" You ! " said our captain, in surprise. " Where do you come from, and where are you bound ? What cargo have you aboard ? "

" We is come," answered the man with the swallow-tail, " from Aitutaki ; we was go for Rarotonga. We is native miss'nary ship ; our name is de *Olive Branch ;* an' our cargo is two tons cocoa nuts, seventy pigs, twenty cats, and de Gosp'l."

This announcement was received by the crew of our vessel with a shout of laughter, which, however, was peremptorily checked by the captain, whose expression instantly changed from one of severity to that of frank urbanity as he advanced towards the missionary and shook him warmly by the hand.

" I am very glad to have fallen in with you," said he, " and I wish you much success in your missionary labours. Pray take me to your cabin, as I wish to converse with you privately."

The missionary immediately took him by the hand, and as he led him away I heard him saying, " Me most glad to find you trader ; we t'ought you be pirate. You very like one 'bout the masts."

What conversation the captain had with this man I never heard, but he came on deck again in a quarter of an hour, and shaking hands cordially with the missionary, ordered us into our boat and returned to the schooner, which was immediately put before the wind. In a few minutes the *Olive Branch* was left far behind us.

That afternoon, as I was down below at dinner, I heard the men talking about this curious ship.

" I wonder," said one, " why our captain looked so sweet on yon swallow-tailed supercargo o' pigs and Gospels. If it had been an ordinary trader, now, he would have taken as many o' the pigs as he required and sent the ship with all on board to the bottom."

" Why, Dick, you must be new to these seas if you don't know that," cried another. " The captain cares as much for the gospel as you do (an' that's precious little), but he knows, and everybody knows, that the only place among the southern islands where a ship can put in and get what she wants in comfort is where the gospel has been sent to. There are hundreds o' islands, at this blessed moment, where you might as well jump straight into a shark's maw as land without a band o' thirty comrades armed to the teeth to back you."

" Ay," said a man with a deep scar over his right eye, " Dick's new to the work. But if the captain takes us for a cargo o' sandal-wood to the Feejees, he'll get a taste o' these black gentry in their native condition. For my part, I don't know and I don't care what the gospel does to them, but I know that when any o' the islands chance to get it, trade goes all smooth and easy ; but where they hain't got it, Beelzebub himself could hardly desire better company."

" Well, you ought to be a good judge," cried another, laughing, " for you've never kept any company but the worst all your life ! "

" Ralph Rover ! " shouted a voice down the hatchway, " captain wants you, aft."

Springing up the ladder, I hastened to the cabin, pondering as I went the strange testimony borne by these men to the effect of the gospel on savage natures—testimony which, as it was perfectly disinterested, I had no doubt whatever was strictly true.

On coming again on deck, I found Bloody Bill at the helm, and as we were alone together I tried to draw him into conversation. After repeating to him the conversation in the forecastle about the missionaries, I said,—

" Tell me, Bill, is this schooner really a trader in sandal-wood ? "

" Yes, Ralph, she is ; but she's just as really a pirate. The black flag you saw flying at the peak was no deception."

" Then how can you say she's a trader ? " asked I.

" Why, as to that, she trades when she can't take by force ; but she takes by force when she can, in preference. Ralph," he added, lowering his voice, " if you had seen the bloody deeds that I have witnessed done on these decks, you would not need to ask if we were pirates. But you'll find it out soon enough. As for the missionaries, the captain favours them because they are useful to him. The South Sea islanders are such incarnate fiends that they are the better of being tamed, and the missionaries are the only men who can do it."

Our track after this lay through several clusters of small islets, among which we were becalmed more than once. During this part of our voyage the watch on deck and the lookout at the masthead were more than usually vigilant, as we were not only in danger of being attacked by the natives, who, I learned from the captain's remarks, were a bloody and deceitful tribe at this group, but we were also exposed to much risk from the multitudes of coral reefs that rose up in the channels between the islands, some of them just above the surface, others a few feet below it. Our precautions against the savages I found were indeed necessary.

One day we were becalmed among a group of small islands, most of which appeared to be uninhabited. As we were in want of fresh water, the captain sent the boat ashore to bring off a cask or two. But we were mistaken in thinking there were no natives; for scarcely had we drawn near to the shore when a band of naked blacks rushed out of the bush and assembled on the beach, brandishing their clubs and spears in a threatening manner. Our men were well armed, but refrained from showing any signs of hostility, and rowed nearer in order to converse with the natives; and I now found that more than one of the crew could imperfectly speak dialects of the language peculiar to the South Sea islanders. When within forty yards of the shore we ceased rowing, and the first mate stood up to address the multitude ; but instead of answering us, they replied with a shower of stones, some of which cut the men severely. Instantly our muskets were levelled, and a volley was about to be fired, when the captain hailed us in a loud voice from the schooner, which lay about five or six hundred yards off the shore.

"Don't fire!" he shouted angrily. "Pull off to the point ahead of you."

The men looked surprised at this order, and uttered deep curses as they prepared to obey ; for their wrath was roused, and they burned for revenge. Three or four of them hesitated, and seemed disposed to mutiny.

"Don't distress yourselves, lads," said the mate, while a bitter smile curled his lip. "Obey orders. The captain's not the man to take an insult tamely. If Long Tom does not speak presently, I'll give myself to the sharks."

The men smiled significantly as they pulled from the shore, which was now crowded with a dense mass of savages, amounting probably to five or six hundred. We had not rowed off above a couple of hundred yards when a loud roar thundered over the sea, and the big brass gun sent a withering shower of grape point-blank into the midst of the living mass, through which a wide lane was cut, while a yell, the like of which I could not have imagined, burst from the miserable survivors as they fled to the woods. Amongst the heaps of dead that lay on the sand just where they had fallen, I could distinguish mutilated forms writhing in agony, while ever and anon one and another rose convulsively from out the mass, endeavoured to stagger towards the wood, and ere they had taken a few steps, fell and wallowed on the bloody sand. My blood curdled within me as I witnessed this frightful and wanton slaughter ; but I had little time to think, for the captain's deep voice came again over the water towards us : " Pull ashore, lads, and fill your water-casks." The men obeyed in silence, and it seemed to me as if even their hard hearts were shocked by the ruthless deed. On gaining the mouth of the rivulet at which we intended to take in water, we found it flowing with blood, for the greater part of those who were slain had been standing on the banks of the stream, a short way above its mouth. Many of the wretched creatures had fallen into it, and we found one body, which had been carried down, jammed between two rocks, with the staring eyeballs turned towards us, and his black hair waving in the ripples of the blood-red stream. No-one dared to oppose our landing now, so we carried our casks to a pool above the murdered group, and having filled them, returned on board. Fortunately a breeze sprang up soon afterwards and carried us away from the dreadful spot ; but it could not waft me away from the memory of what I had seen.

" And this," thought I, gazing in horror at the captain, who, with a quiet look of indifference, leaned upon the taffrail smoking a cigar and contemplating the fertile green islets as they passed like a lovely picture before our eyes—" this is the man who favours the missionaries because they are useful to him and can tame the savages better than any one else can do it ! " Then I wondered in my mind whether it were possible for any missionary to tame *him* !

CHAPTER XXIV

Bloody Bill is communicative and sagacious—Unpleasant prospects—Retrospective meditations interrupted by volcanic agency—The pirates negotiate with a Feejee chief—Various etceteras that are calculated to surprise and horrify.

IT was many days after the events just narrated ere I recovered a little of my wonted spirits. I could not shake off the feeling for a long time that I was in a frightful dream, and the sight of our captain filled me with so much horror that I kept out of his way as much as my duties about the cabin would permit. Fortunately he took so little notice of me that he did not observe my changed feelings towards him, otherwise it might have been worse for me.

But I was now resolved that I would run away the very first island we should land at, and commit myself to the hospitality of the natives rather than remain an hour longer than I could help in the pirate schooner. I pondered this subject a good deal, and at last made up my mind to communicate my intention to Bloody Bill; for during several talks I had had with him of late, I felt assured that he too would willingly escape if possible. When I told him of my design he shook his head. " No, no, Ralph," said he, " you must not think of running away here. Among some of the groups of islands you might do so with safety, but if you tried it here you would find that you had jumped out of the fryin'-pan into the fire."

" How so, Bill ? " said I ; " would the natives not receive me ? "

" That they would, lad ; but they would eat you too."

" Eat me ! " said I, in surprise. " I thought the South Sea islanders never ate anybody except their enemies."

" Humph ! " ejaculated Bill. " I s'pose 'twas yer tender-hearted friends in England that put that notion into your head. There's a set o' soft-hearted folk at home that I knows on who don't like to have their feelin's ruffled, and when you tell them anything they don't like—that shocks them, as they call it—no matter how true it be, they stop their ears and cry out, ' Oh, that is *too* horrible ! We can't believe that ! ' An' they say truth. They can't believe it 'cause they won't believe it. Now, I believe there's thousands o' the people in England who are such born drivellin' *won't-believers* that they think the black fellows hereaway at the worst eat an enemy only now an' then, out o' spite ; whereas I know for certain, and many captains of the British and American navies know as well as me, that the Feejee islanders eat not only their enemies but one another ; and they do it not for spite, but for pleasure. It's a *fact* that they prefer human flesh to any other. But they don't like white men's flesh so well as black ; they say it makes them sick."

"Why, Bill," said I, "you told me just now that they would eat *me* if they caught me."

"So I did, and so I think they would. I've only heard some o' them say they don't like white men *so well* as black ; but if they was hungry they wouldn't be particular. Anyhow, I'm sure they would kill you. You see, Ralph, I've been a good while in them parts, and I've visited the different groups of islands oftentimes as a trader. And thorough-goin' blackguards some o' them traders are ; no better than pirates, I can tell you. One captain that I sailed with was not a chip better than the one we're now with. He was trading with a friendly chief one day, aboard his vessel. The chief had swum off to us with the things for trade tied atop of his head, for them chaps are like otters in the water. Well, the chief was hard on the captain, and would not part with some o' his things. When their bargainin' was over they shook hands, and the chief jumped overboard to swim ashore ; but before he got forty yards from the ship the captain seized a musket and shot him dead. He then hove up anchor and put to sea, and as we sailed along shore he dropped six black fellows with his rifle, remarkin' that 'that would spoil the trade for the next comers.' But, as I was sayin', I'm up to the ways o' these fellows. One o' the laws o' the country is, that every shipwrecked person who happens to be cast ashore, be he dead or alive, is doomed to be roasted and eaten. There was a small tradin' schooner wrecked off one of these islands when we were lyin' there in harbour during a storm. The crew was lost, all but three men, who swam ashore. The moment they landed they were seized by the natives and carried up into the woods. We knew pretty well what their fate would be, but we could not help them, for our crew was small, and if we had gone ashore they would likely have killed us all. We never saw the three men again ; but we heard frightful yelling and dancing and merry-making that night ; and one of the natives, who came aboard to trade with us next day, told us that the *long pigs*, as he called the men, had been roasted and eaten, and their bones were to be converted into sail-needles. He also said that white men were bad to eat, and that most o' the people on shore were sick.

I was very much shocked and cast down in my mind at this terrible account of the natives, and asked Bill what he would advise me to do. Looking round the deck to make sure that we were not overheard, he lowered his voice and said, " There are two or three ways that we might escape, Ralph, but none o' them's easy. If the captain would only sail for some o' the islands near Tahiti, we might run away there well enough, because the natives are all Christians ; an' we find that wherever the savages take up with Christianity they always give over their bloody ways, and are safe to be trusted. I never cared for Christianity myself," he continued, in a soliloquizing voice, " and I don't well know what it means ; but a man with half an eye can see what it does for these black critters. However, the captain always keeps a sharp lookout after us when we get to these islands, for he half suspects that one or two o' us are tired of his company. Then we might manage to cut the boat adrift some fine night when it's our watch on deck, and clear off before they discovered that we were gone. But we would run the risk o' bein' caught by the blacks. I wouldn't like to try that plan. But you and I will think over it, Ralph, and see what's to be done. In the meantime it's our watch below, so I'll go and turn in."

Bill then bade me good-night, and went below, while a comrade took his place at the helm; but feeling no desire to enter into conversation with him, I walked aft, and leaning over the stern, looked down into the phosphorescent waves that gurgled around the rudder, and streamed out like a flame of blue light in the vessel's wake. My thoughts were very sad, and I could scarce refrain from tears as I contrasted my present wretched position with the happy, peaceful time I had spent on the Coral Island with my dear companions. As I thought upon Jack and Peterkin anxious forebodings crossed my mind, and I pictured to myself the grief and dismay with which they would search every nook and corner of the island, in a vain attempt to discover my dead body; for I felt assured that if they did not see any sign of the pirate schooner or boat when they came out of the cave to look for me, they would never imagine that I had been carried away. I wondered, too, how Jack would succeed in getting Peterkin out of the cave without my assistance; and I trembled

when I thought that he might lose presence of mind,
and begin to kick when he was in the tunnel ! These
thoughts were suddenly interrupted and put to
flight by a bright red blaze which lighted up the
horizon to the southward and cast a crimson glow
far over the sea. This appearance was accompanied
by a low growling sound, as of distant thunder, and at
the same time the sky above us became black, while
a hot, stifling wind blew around us in fitful gusts.

The crew assembled hastily on deck, and most
of them were under the belief that a frightful hurricane was pending ; but the captain coming on deck,
soon explained the phenomena.

" It's only a volcano," said he. " I knew there
was one hereabouts, but thought it was extinct.—
Up there and furl top-gallant-sails ; we'll likely
have a breeze, and it's well to be ready."

As he spoke a shower began to fall, which we
quickly observed was not rain but fine ashes. As
we were many miles distant from the volcano, these
must have been carried to us from it by the wind.
As the captain had predicted, a stiff breeze soon
afterwards sprang up, under the influence of which
we speedily left the volcano far behind us ; but
during the greater part of the night we could see its
lurid glare and hear its distant thunder. The shower
did not cease to fall for several hours, and we must
have sailed under it for nearly forty miles, perhaps
further. When we emerged from the cloud, our decks
and every part of the rigging were completely covered
with a thick coat of ashes. I was much interested

in this, and recollected that Jack had often spoken
of many of the islands of the Pacific as being vol-
canoes, either active or extinct, and had said that the
whole region was more or less volcanic, and that
some scientific men were of opinion that the islands
of the Pacific were nothing more or less than the
mountain-tops of a huge continent which had sunk
under the influence of volcanic agency.

Three days after passing the volcano, we found
ourselves a few miles to windward of an island of
considerable size and luxuriant aspect. It consisted
of two mountains, which seemed to be nearly four
thousand feet high. They were separated from
each other by a broad valley, whose thick-growing
trees ascended a considerable distance up the moun-
tain-sides ; and rich level plains, or meadow-land,
spread round the base of the mountains, except at
the point immediately opposite the large valley,
where a river seemed to carry the trees, as it were,
along with it down to the white sandy shore. The
mountain-tops, unlike those of our Coral Island,
were sharp, needle-shaped, and bare, while their
sides were more rugged and grand in outline than
anything I had yet seen in those seas. Bloody Bill
was beside me when the island first hove in sight.

" Ha ! " he exclaimed, " I know that island well.
They call it Emo."

" Have you been there before, then ? " I inquired.

" Ay, that I have, often, and so has this schooner.
'Tis a famous island for sandal-wood. We have
taken many cargoes off it already, and have paid for

them too ; for the savages are so numerous that we dared not try to take it by force. But our captain has tried to cheat them so often that they're beginnin' not to like us overmuch now. Besides, the men behaved ill the last time we were here, and I wonder the captain is not afraid to venture. But he's afraid o' nothing earthly, I believe."

We soon ran inside the barrier coral reef, and let go our anchor in six fathoms water, just opposite the mouth of a small creek, whose shores were densely covered with mangroves and tall umbrageous trees. The principal village of the natives lay about half a mile from this point. Ordering the boat out, the captain jumped into it, and ordered me to follow him. The men, fifteen in number, were well armed ; and the mate was directed to have Long Tom ready for emergencies.

" Give way, lads," cried the captain.

The oars fell into the water at the word, the boat shot from the schooner's side, and in a few minutes reached the shore. Here, contrary to our expectation, we were met with the utmost cordiality by Romata, the principal chief of the island, who conducted us to his house and gave us mats to sit upon. I observed in passing that the natives, of whom there were two or three thousand, were totally unarmed.

After a short preliminary palaver, a feast of baked pigs and various roots was spread before us ; of which we partook sparingly, and then proceeded to business. The captain stated his object in visiting the island, regretted that there had been a slight misunderstanding during the last visit, and hoped that no ill-will was borne by either party, and that a satisfactory trade would be accomplished.

Romata answered that he had forgotten there had been any differences between them, protested that he was delighted to see his friends again, and assured them they should have every assistance in cutting and embarking the wood. The terms were afterwards agreed on, and we rose to depart. All this conversation was afterwards explained to me by Bill, who understood the language pretty well.

Romata accompanied us on board, and explained that a great chief from another island was then on a visit to him, and that he was to be ceremoniously entertained on the following day. After begging to be allowed to introduce him to us, and receiving permission, he sent his canoe ashore to bring him off. At the same time he gave orders to bring on board his two favourites, a cock and a paroquet. While the canoe was gone on this errand, I had time to regard the savage chief attentively. He was a man of immense size, with massive but beautifully moulded limbs and figure, only parts of which, the broad chest and muscular arms, were uncovered ; for although the lower orders generally wore no other clothing than a strip of cloth called *maro* round their loins, the chief, on particular occasions, wrapped his person in voluminous folds of a species of native cloth made from the bark of the Chinese paper-mulberry. Romata wore a magnificent black beard and moustache, and his hair was frizzed out to such an extent

that it resembled a large turban, in which was stuck
a long wooden pin! I afterwards found that this
pin served for scratching the head, for which purpose
the fingers were too short without disarranging the
hair. But Romata put himself to much greater in-
convenience on account of his hair, for we found that
he slept with his head resting on a wooden pillow,
in which was cut a hollow for the neck, so that the
hair of the sleeper might not be disarranged.

In ten minutes the canoe returned, bringing the
other chief, who certainly presented a most extraordinary appearance, having painted one half of
his face red and the other half yellow, besides
ornamenting it with various designs in black!
Otherwise he was much the same in appearance as
Romata, though not so powerfully built. As this
chief had never seen a ship before, except, perchance,
some of the petty traders that at long intervals
visit these remote islands, he was much taken up
with the neatness and beauty of all the fittings of
the schooner. He was particularly struck with a
musket which was shown to him, and asked where
the white men got hatchets hard enough to cut the
tree of which the barrel was made! While he was
thus engaged, his brother chief stood aloof, talking
with the captain, and fondling a superb cock and a
little blue-headed paroquet, the favourites of which
I have before spoken. I observed that all the other
natives walked in a crouching posture while in the
presence of Romata. Before our guests left us, the
captain ordered the brass gun to be uncovered and

fired for their gratification ; and I have every reason
to believe he did so for the purpose of showing our
superior power, in case the natives should harbour
any evil designs against us. Romata had never seen
this gun before, as it had not been uncovered on
previous visits, and the astonishment with which
he viewed it was very amusing. Being desirous of
knowing its power, he begged that the captain would
fire it. So a shot was put into it. The chiefs were
then directed to look at a rock about two miles out
at sea, and the gun was fired. In a second the top
of the rock was seen to burst asunder, and to fall in
fragments into the sea.

Romata was so delighted with the success of this
shot, that he pointed to a man who was walking on
the shore, and begged the captain to fire at him,
evidently supposing that his permission was quite
sufficient to justify the captain in such an act. He
was therefore surprised, and not a little annoyed,
when the captain refused to fire at the native, and
ordered the gun to be housed.

Of all the things, however, that afforded matter
of amusement to these savages, that which pleased
Romata's visitor most was the ship's pump. He
never tired of examining it and pumping up the
water. Indeed, so much was he taken up with this
pump, that he could not be prevailed on to return
on shore, but sent a canoe to fetch his favourite stool,
on which he seated himself, and spent the remainder of
the day in pumping the bilge-water out of the ship !

Next day the crew went ashore to cut sandal-wood

while the captain, with one or two men, remained
on board, in order to be ready, if need be, with the
brass gun, which was unhoused and conspicuously
elevated, with its capacious muzzle directed point-
blank at the chief's house. The men were fully
armed as usual ; and the captain ordered me to
go with them, to assist in the work. I was much
pleased with this order, for it freed me from the
captain's company, which I could not now endure,
and it gave me an opportunity of seeing the natives.

As we wound along in single file through the rich
fragrant groves of banana, cocoa-nut, bread-fruit,
and other trees, I observed that there were many of
the plum and banian trees, with which I had become
familiar on the Coral Island. I noticed also large
quantities of taro-roots, yams, and sweet potatoes
growing in enclosures. On turning into an open
glade of the woods, we came abruptly upon a cluster
of native houses. They were built chiefly of bamboos,
and were thatched with the large thick leaves of the
pandanus ; but many of them had little more than a
sloping roof and three sides with an open front, being
the most simple shelter from the weather that could
well be imagined. Within these and around them
were groups of natives—men, women, and children—
who all stood up to gaze at us as we marched along,
followed by the party of men whom the chief had
sent to escort us. About half a mile inland we arrived
at the spot where the sandal-wood grew, and while
the men set to work I clambered up an adjoining
hill to observe the country.

About midday the chief arrived with several followers, one of whom carried a baked pig on a wooden platter, with yams and potatoes on several plantain leaves, which he presented to the men, who sat down under the shade of a tree to dine. The chief sat down to dine also ; but to my surprise, instead of feeding himself, one of his wives performed that office for him ! I was seated beside Bill, and asked him the reason of this.

" It is beneath his dignity, I believe, to feed himself," answered Bill ; " but I daresay he's not particular, except on great occasions. They've a strange custom among them, Ralph, which is called *tabu*, and they carry it to great lengths. If a man chooses a particular tree for his god, the fruit o' that tree is tabued to him ; and if he eats it, he is sure to be killed by his people, and eaten, of course, for killing means eating hereaway. Then, you see that great mop o' hair on the chief's head ? Well, he has a lot o' barbers to keep it in order ; and it's a law that whoever touches the head of a living chief or the body of a dead one, his hands are tabued ; so in that way the barbers' hands are always tabued, and they daren't use them for their lives, but have to be fed like big babies, as they are, sure enough ! "

" That's odd, Bill. But look here," said I, pointing to a man whose skin was of a much lighter colour than the generality of the natives. " I've seen a few of these light-skinned fellows among the Feejeeans. They seem to me to be of quite a different race."

" So they are," answered Bill. " These fellows

come from the Tongan Islands, which lie a long way
to the eastward. They come here to build their big
war-canoes ; and as these take two and sometimes
four years to build, there's always some o' the brown-
skins among the black sarpents o' these islands."

"By the way, Bill," said I, "your mentioning
serpents reminds me that I have not seen a reptile
of any kind since I came to this part of the
world."

"No more there are any," said Bill ; "if ye except
the niggers themselves, there's none on the islands
but a lizard or two and some sich harmless things.
But I never seed any myself. If there's none on
the land, however, there's more than enough in the
water, and that minds me of a wonderful brute they
have here. But come, I'll show it to you." So
saying, Bill arose, and leaving the men still busy
with the baked pig, led me into the forest. After
proceeding a short distance we came upon a small
pond of stagnant water. A native lad had followed us,
to whom we called, and beckoned him to come to us.
On Bill saying a few words to him, which I did not
understand, the boy advanced to the edge of the
pond, and gave a low, peculiar whistle. Immediately the water became agitated, and an enormous
eel thrust its head above the surface and allowed the
youth to touch it. It was about twelve feet long,
and as thick round the body as a man's thigh.

"There !" said Bill, his lip curling with contempt; "what do you think of that for a god,
Ralph ? This is one o' their gods, and it has been

fed with dozens o' livin' babies already. How many more it'll get afore it dies is hard to say."

"Babies!" said I, with an incredulous look.

"Ay, babies," returned Bill. "Your soft-hearted folk at home would say, ' Oh, horrible! impossible!' to that, and then go away as comfortable and unconcerned as if their sayin' ' Horrible! impossible!' had made it a lie. But I tell you, Ralph, it's a *fact*. I've seed it with my own eyes the last time I was here, an' mayhap if you stop awhile at this accursed place, and keep a sharp lookout, you'll see it too. They don't feed it regularly with livin' babies, but they give it one now and then as a treat. Bah, you brute!" cried Bill in disgust, giving the reptile a kick on the snout with his heavy boot that sent it sweltering back in agony into its loathsome pool. I thought it lucky for Bill, indeed for all of us, that the native youth's back happened to be turned at the time; for I am certain that if the poor savages had come to know that we had so rudely handled their god, we should have had to fight our way back to the ship. As we retraced our steps I questioned my companion further on this subject.

"How comes it, Bill, that the mothers allow such a dreadful thing to be done?"

"Allow it? the mothers *do* it! It seems to me that there's nothing too fiendish or diabolical for these people to do. Why, in some of the islands they have an institution called the *Areoi*, and the persons connected with that body are ready for any wickedness that mortal man can devise. In fact they stick at nothing ; and one o' their customs is to murder their infants the moment they are born. The mothers agree to it, and the fathers do it. And the mildest ways they have of murdering them is by sticking them through the body with sharp splinters of bamboo, strangling them with their thumbs, or burying them alive and stamping them to death while under the sod."

I felt sick at heart while my companion recited these horrors.

" But it's a curious fact," he continued, after a pause, during which we walked in silence towards the spot where we had left our comrades—" it's a curious fact, that wherever the missionaries get a footin' all these things come to an end at once, an' the savages take to doin' each other good and singin' psalms, just like Methodists."

" God bless the missionaries ! " said I, while a feeling of enthusiasm filled my heart, so that I could speak with difficulty. " God bless and prosper the missionaries till they get a footing in every island of the sea ! "

" I would say Amen to that prayer, Ralph, if I could," said Bill, in a deep, sad voice ; " but it would be a mere mockery for a man to ask a blessing for others who dare not ask one for himself. But, Ralph," he continued, " I've not told you half o' the abominations I have seen durin' my life in these seas. If we pull long together, lad, I'll tell you more ; and if times have not changed very much since I was here last, it's like that you'll have a chance o' seeing a little for yourself before long."

CHAPTER XXV

The sandal-wood party—Native children's games somewhat
   surprising—Desperate amusements suddenly and fatally
   brought to a close—An old friend recognized—News—
   Romata's mad conduct.

NEXT day the wood-cutting party went ashore again,
and I accompanied them as before. During the
dinner-hour I wandered into the woods alone, being
disinclined for food that day. I had not rambled
far when I found myself unexpectedly on the seashore, having crossed a narrow neck of land which
separated the native village from a large bay.
Here I found a party of the islanders busy with one
of their war-canoes, which was almost ready for
launching. I stood for a long time, watching this
party with great interest, and observed that they
fastened the timbers and planks to each other very
much in the same way in which I had seen Jack
fasten those of our little boat. But what surprised
me most was its immense length, which I measured
very carefully, and found to be a hundred feet long ;
and it was so capacious that it could have held
three hundred men. It had the unwieldy outrigger
and enormously high stern-posts which I had remarked on the canoe that came to us while I was on

the Coral Island. Observing some boys playing at
games a short way along the beach, I resolved to
go and watch them ; but as I turned from the natives
who were engaged so busily and cheerfully at their
work, I little thought of the terrible event that hung
on the completion of that war-canoe.

Advancing towards the children, who were so
numerous that I began to think this must be the
general playground of the village, I sat down on a
grassy bank under the shade of a plantain tree to
watch them. And a happier or more noisy crew
I have never seen. There were at least two hundred of them, both boys and girls, all of whom were
clad in no other garments than their own glossy
little black skins, except the maro, or strip of cloth
round the loins of the boys, and a very short petti-
coat or kilt on the girls. They did not all play at
the same game, but amused themselves in different
groups.

One band was busily engaged in a game exactly
similar to our blind man's buff. Another set were
walking on stilts, which raised the children three
feet from the ground. They were very expert at
this amusement, and seldom tumbled. In another
place I observed a group of girls standing together,
and apparently enjoying themselves very much ;. so
I went up to see what they were doing, and found
that they were opening their eyelids with their fingers
till their eyes appeared of an enormous size, and then
thrusting pieces of straw between the upper and
lower lids, across the eyeball, to keep them in that

position! This seemed to me, I must confess, a very foolish as well as dangerous amusement. Nevertheless the children seemed to be greatly delighted with the hideous faces they made. I pondered this subject a good deal, and thought that if little children knew how silly they seem to grown-up people when they make faces, they would not be so fond of doing it. In another place were a number of boys engaged in flying kites, and I could not help wondering that some of the games of those little savages should be so like to our own, although they had never seen us at play. But the kites were different from ours in many respects, being of every variety of shape. They were made of very thin cloth, and the boys raised them to a wonderful height in the air by means of twine made from the cocoa-nut husk. Other games there were, some of which showed the natural depravity of the hearts of these poor savages, and made me wish fervently that missionaries might be sent out to them. But the amusement which the greatest number of the children of both sexes seemed to take chief delight in was swimming and diving in the sea, and the expertness which they exhibited was truly amazing. They seemed to have two principal games in the water, one of which was to dive off a sort of stage which had been erected near a deep part of the sea, and chase each other in the water. Some of them went down to an extraordinary depth; others skimmed along the surface, or rolled over and over like porpoises, or diving under each other, came up

unexpectedly and pulled each other down by a leg
or an arm. They never seemed to tire of this sport,
and from the great heat of the water in the South
Seas, they could remain in it nearly all day without
feeling chilled. Many of these children were almost
infants, scarce able to walk ; yet they staggered
down the beach, flung their round, fat little black
bodies fearlessly into deep water and struck out to
sea with as much confidence as ducklings.

The other game to which I have referred was
swimming in the surf. But as this is an amusement
in which all engage, from children of ten to gray-
headed men of sixty, and as I had an opportunity
of witnessing it in perfection the day following, I
shall describe it more minutely.

I suppose it was in honour of their guest that this
grand swimming-match was got up, for Romata came
and told the captain that they were going to engage
in it, and begged him to " come and see."

" What sort of amusement is this surf-swimming ? " I inquired of Bill, as we walked together to
a part of the shore on which several thousands of
the natives were assembled.

" It's a very favourite lark with these 'xtr'or'nary
critters," replied Bill, giving a turn to the quid of
tobacco that invariably bulged out of his left cheek.
" Ye see, Ralph, them fellows take to the water as
soon a'most as they can walk, an' long before they
can do that anything respectably, so that they are
as much at home in the sea as on the land. Well,
ye see, I 'spose they found swimmin' for miles out to

sea, and divin' fathoms deep, wasn't exciting enough, so they invented this game o' swimmin' on the surf. Each man and boy, as you see, has got a short board or plank, with which he swims out for a mile or more to sea, and then, gettin' on the top o' yon thunderin' breaker, they come to shore on the top of it, yellin' and screechin' like fiends. It's a marvel to me that they're not dashed to shivers on the coral reef, for sure an' sartin am I that if any o' us tried it, we wouldn't be worth the fluke of a broken anchor after the wave fell. But there they go ! "

As he spoke, several hundreds of the natives, amongst whom we were now standing, uttered a loud yell, rushed down the beach, plunged into the surf, and were carried off by the seething foam of the retreating wave.

At the point where we stood, the encircling coral reef joined the shore, so that the magnificent breakers, which a recent stiff breeze had rendered larger than usual, fell in thunder at the feet of the multitudes who lined the beach. For some time the swimmers continued to strike out to sea, breasting over the swell like hundreds of black seals. Then they all turned, and watching an approaching billow, mounted its white crest, and each laying his breast on the short flat board, came rolling towards the shore, careering on the summit of the mighty wave, while they and the onlookers shouted and yelled with excitement. Just as the monster wave curled in solemn majesty to fling its bulky length upon the beach, most of the swimmers slid back into the trough behind ; others, slipping off their boards, seized them in their hands, and plunging through the watery waste, swam out to repeat the amusement ; but a few, who seemed to me the most reckless, continued their career until they were launched upon the beach, and enveloped in the churning foam and spray. One of these last came in on the crest of the wave most manfully, and landed with a violent bound almost on the spot where Bill and I stood. I saw by his peculiar head-dress that he was the chief whom the tribe entertained as their guest. The sea-water had removed nearly all the paint with which his face had been covered, and as he rose panting to his feet, I recognized, to my surprise, the features of Tararo, my old friend of the Coral Island !

Tararo at the same moment recognized me, and advancing quickly, took me round the neck and rubbed noses ; which had the effect of transferring a good deal of the moist paint from his nose to mine. Then, recollecting that this was not the white man's mode of salutation, he grasped me by the hand and shook it violently.

" Hallo, Ralph ! " cried Bill, in surprise, " that chap seems to have taken a sudden fancy to you, or he must be an old acquaintance."

" Right, Bill," I replied : " he is indeed an old acquaintance ; " and I explained in a few words that he was the chief whose party Jack and Peterkin and I had helped to save.

Tararo having thrown away his surf-board,

entered into an animated conversation with Bill, pointing frequently during the course of it to me ; whereby I concluded he must be telling him about the memorable battle and the part we had taken in it. When he paused, I begged of Bill to ask him about the woman Avatea, for I had some hope that she might have come with Tararo on this visit. "And ask him," said I, "who she is, for I am persuaded she is of a different race from the Fee-jeeans." On the mention of her name the chief frowned darkly, and seemed to speak with much anger.

"You're right, Ralph," said Bill, when the chief had ceased to talk : "she's not a Feejee girl, but a Samoan. How she ever came to this place the chief does not very clearly explain, but he says she was taken in war, and that he got her three years ago, an' kept her as his daughter ever since. Lucky for her, poor girl, else she'd have been roasted and eaten like the rest."

"But why does Tararo frown and look so angry ? " said I.

"Because the girl's somewhat obstinate, like most o' the sex, an' won't marry the man he wants her to. It seems that a chief of some other island came on a visit to Tararo and took a fancy to her, but she wouldn't have him on no account, bein' already in love, and engaged to a young chief whom Tararo hates, and she kicked up a desperate shindy ; so, as he was going on a war-expedition in his canoe, he left her to think about it, sayin' he'd be back in

six months or so, when he hoped she wouldn't be
so obstropolous. This happened just a week ago;
an' Tararo says that if she's not ready to go, when
the chief returns, as his bride, she'll be sent to him
as a *long pig.*"

" As a long pig ! " I exclaimed, in surprise ; " why,
what does he mean by that ? "

" He means somethin' very unpleasant," answered Bill, with a frown. " You see these blackguards eat men an' women just as readily as they
eat pigs ; and as baked pigs and baked men are
very like each other in appearance, they call men
long pigs. If Avatea goes to this fellow as a long
pig, it's all up with her, poor thing."

" Is she on the island now ? " I asked eagerly.

" No ; she's at Tararo's island."

" And where does it lie ? "

" About fifty or sixty miles to the south'ard o'
this," returned Bill ; " but I—"

At this moment we were startled by the cry of
" Mao ! mao !—a shark ! a shark ! " which was
immediately followed by a shriek that rang clear
and fearfully loud above the tumult of cries that
arose from the savages in the water and on the land.
We turned hastily towards the direction whence the
cry came, and had just time to observe the glaring
eyeballs of one of the swimmers as he tossed his
arms in the air. Next instant he was pulled under
the waves. A canoe was instantly launched, and the
hand of the drowning man was caught, but only half
of his body was dragged from the maw of the monster,

which followed the canoe until the water became so shallow that it could scarcely swim. The crest of the next billow was tinged with red as it rolled towards the shore.

In most countries of the world this would have made a deep impression on the spectators, but the only effect it had upon these islanders was to make them hurry with all speed out of the sea, lest a similar fate should befall some of the others ; but so utterly reckless were they of human life, that it did not for a moment suspend the progress of their amusements. It is true the surf-swimming ended for that time somewhat abruptly, but they immediately proceeded with other games. Bill told me that sharks do not often attack the surf-swimmers, being frightened away by the immense numbers of men and boys in the water, and by the shouting and splashing that they make. " But," said he, " such a thing as you have seen just now don't frighten them much. They'll be at it again to-morrow or next day, just as if there wasn't a single shark between Feejee and Nova Zembla."

After this the natives had a series of wrestling and boxing matches ; and being men of immense size and muscle, they did a good deal of injury to each other, especially in boxing, in which not only the lower orders but several of the chiefs and priests engaged. Each bout was very quickly terminated, for they did not pretend to a scientific knowledge of the art, and wasted no time in sparring, but hit straight out at each other's heads, and their blows were delivered with great force. Frequently one of the combatants was knocked down with a single blow; and one gigantic fellow hit his adversary so severely that he drove the skin entirely off his forehead. This feat was hailed with immense applause by the spectators.

During these exhibitions, which were very painful to me, though I confess I could not refrain from beholding them, I was struck with the beauty of many of the figures and designs that were tattooed on the persons of the chiefs and principal men. One figure, that seemed to me very elegant, was that of a palm tree tattooed on the back of a man's leg, the roots rising, as it were, from under his heel, the stem ascending the tendon of the ankle, and the graceful head branching out upon the calf. I afterwards learned that this process of tattooing is very painful, and takes long to do, commencing at the age of ten, and being continued at intervals up to the age of thirty. It is done by means of an instrument made of bone, with a number of sharp teeth with which the skin is punctured. Into these punctures a preparation made from the kernel of the candle-nut, mixed with cocoa-nut oil, is rubbed, and the mark thus made is indelible. The operation is performed by a class of men whose profession it is, and they tattoo as much at a time as the person on whom they are operating can bear: which is not much, the pain and inflammation caused by tattooing being very great, sometimes causing death. Some of the chiefs were tattooed with an ornamental stripe down

the legs, which gave them the appearance of being
clad in tights; others had marks round the ankles
and insteps which looked like tight-fitting and elegant
boots. Their faces were also tattooed, and their
breasts were very profusely marked with every
imaginable species of device—muskets, dogs, birds,
pigs, clubs, and canoes, intermingled with lozenges,
squares, circles, and other arbitrary figures.

The women were not tattooed so much as the
men, having only a few marks on their feet and arms.
But I must say, however objectionable this strange
practice may be, it nevertheless had this good effect,
that it took away very much from their appearance
of nakedness.

Next day, while we were returning from the
woods to our schooner, we observed Romata rushing
about in the neighbourhood of his house, apparently
mad with passion.

" Ah ! " said Bill to me, " there he's at his old tricks
again. That's his way when he gets drink. The
natives make a sort of drink o' their own, and it
makes him bad enough; but when he gets brandy
he's like a wild tiger. The captain, I suppose, has
given him a bottle, as usual, to keep him in good-
humour. After drinkin' he usually goes to sleep,
and the people know it well, and keep out of his
way, for fear they should waken him. Even the
babies are taken out of ear-shot; for when he's
waked up he rushes out just as you see him now,
and spears or clubs the first person he meets."

It seemed at the present time, however, that no

deadly weapon had been in his way, for the infuriated chief was raging about without one. Suddenly he caught sight of an unfortunate man who was trying to conceal himself behind a tree. Rushing towards him, Romata struck him a terrible blow on the head, which knocked out the poor man's eye and also dislocated the chief's finger. The wretched creature offered no resistance ; he did not even attempt to parry the blow. Indeed, from what Bill said, I found that he might consider himself lucky in having escaped with his life, which would certainly have been forfeited had the chief been possessed of a club at the time.

"Have these wretched creatures no law among themselves," said I, "which can restrain such wickedness ? "

"None," replied Bill. "The chief's word is law. He might kill and eat a dozen of his own subjects any day for nothing more than his own pleasure, and nobody would take the least notice of it."

This ferocious deed took place within sight of our party as we wended our way to the beach, but I could not observe any other expression on the faces of the men than that of total indifference or contempt. It seemed to me a very awful thing that it should be possible for men to come to such hardness of heart and callousness to the sight of bloodshed and violence ; but, indeed, I began to find that such constant exposure to scenes of blood was having a slight effect upon myself, and I shuddered when I came to think that I too was becoming callous.

I thought upon this subject much that night while I walked up and down the deck during my hours of watch, and I came to the conclusion that if I, who hated, abhorred, and detested such bloody deeds as I had witnessed within the last few weeks, could so soon come to be less sensitive about them, how little wonder that these poor ignorant savages, who were born and bred in familiarity therewith, should think nothing of them at all, and should hold human life in so very slight esteem.

CHAPTER XXVI

Mischief brewing—My blood is made to run cold—Evil consultations and wicked resolves—Bloody Bill attempts to do good, and fails—The attack—Wholesale murder—The flight—The escape.

NEXT morning I awoke with a feverish brow and a feeling of deep depression at my heart, and the more I thought on my unhappy fate, the more wretched and miserable did I feel.

I was surrounded on all sides by human beings of the most dreadful character, to whom the shedding of blood was mere pastime. On shore were the natives, whose practices were so horrible that I could not think of them without shuddering. On board were none but pirates of the blackest dye, who, although not cannibals, were foul murderers, and more blameworthy even than the savages, inasmuch as they knew better. Even Bill, with whom I had, under the strange circumstances of my lot, formed a kind of intimacy, was so fierce in his nature as to have acquired the title of "Bloody" from his vile companions. I felt very much cast down the more I considered the subject and the impossibility of delivery, as it seemed to me, at least for a long time to come. At last, in my feeling of utter helplessness, I prayed fervently to the Almighty that He would deliver me out of my miserable condition ; and when I had done so I felt some degree of comfort.

When the captain came on deck, before the hour at which the men usually started for the woods, I begged of him to permit me to remain aboard that day, as I did not feel well ; but he looked at me angrily, and ordered me, in a surly tone, to get ready to go on shore as usual. The fact was that the captain had been out of humour for some time past. Romata and he had had some differences, and high words had passed between them, during which the chief had threatened to send a fleet of his war-canoes, with a thousand men, to break up and burn the schooner ; whereupon the captain smiled sarcastically, and going up to the chief, gazed sternly in his face, while he said, " I have only to raise my little finger just now, and my big gun will blow your whole village to atoms in five minutes ! " Although the chief was a bold man, he quailed before the pirate's glance and threat, and made no reply ; but a bad feeling had been raised, and old sores had been opened.

I had, therefore, to go with the woodcutters that day. Before starting, however, the captain called me into the cabin, and said,—

" Here, Ralph ; I've got a mission for you, lad. That blackguard Romata is in the dumps, and nothing will mollify him but a gift ; so do you go up to his house and give him these whale's teeth, with my compliments. Take with you one of the men who can speak the language."

I looked at the gift in some surprise, for it consisted of six white whale's teeth, and two of the same dyed bright red, which seemed to me very paltry things. However, I did not dare to hesitate, or to ask any questions; so gathering them up, I left the cabin, and was soon on my way to the chief's house, accompanied by Bill. On expressing my surprise at the gift, he said,—

" They're paltry enough to you or me, Ralph, but they're considered of great value by them chaps. They're a sort o' cash among them. The red ones are the most prized, one of them bein' equal to twenty o' the white ones. I suppose the only reason for their bein' valuable is that there ain't many of them, and they're hard to be got."

On arriving at the house we found Romata sitting on a mat, in the midst of a number of large bales of native cloth and other articles, which had been brought to him as presents from time to time by inferior chiefs. He received us rather haughtily, but on Bill explaining the nature of our errand he became very condescending, and his eyes glistened with satisfaction when he received the whale's teeth, although he laid them aside with an assumption of kingly indifference.

" Go," said he, with a wave of the hand—" go tell your captain that he may cut wood to-day, but not to-morrow. He must come ashore; I want to have a palaver with him."

As we left the house to return to the woods, Bill shook his head.

" There's mischief brewin' in that black rascal's head. I know him of old. But what comes here ? "

As he spoke, we heard the sound of laughter and shouting in the wood, and presently there issued from it a band of savages, in the midst of whom were a number of men bearing burdens on their shoulders. At first I thought that these burdens were poles with something rolled round them, the end of each pole resting on a man's shoulder ; but on a nearer approach I saw that they were human beings, tied hand and foot, and so lashed to the poles that they could not move. I counted twenty of them as they passed.

" More murder ! " said Bill, in a voice that sounded between a hoarse laugh and a groan.

" Surely they are not going to murder them ? " said I, looking anxiously into Bill's face.

" I don't know, Ralph," replied Bill, " what they're goin' to do with them ; but I fear they mean no good when they tie fellows up in that way."

As we continued our way towards the wood-cutters, I observed that Bill looked anxiously over his shoulder in the direction where the procession had disappeared. At last he stopped, and turning abruptly on his heel, said,—

" I tell ye what it is, Ralph : I must be at the bottom o' that affair. Let us follow these black scoundrels and see what they're goin' to do."

I must say I had no wish to pry further into their

bloody practices ; but Bill seemed bent on it, so I turned and went. We passed rapidly through the bush, being guided in the right direction by the shouts of the savages. Suddenly there was a dead silence, which continued for some time, while Bill and I involuntarily quickened our pace until we were running at the top of our speed across the narrow neck of land previously mentioned. As we reached the verge of the wood, we discovered the savages surrounding the large war-canoe, which they were apparently on the point of launching. Suddenly the multitude put their united strength to the canoe ; but scarcely had the huge machine began to move, when a yell, the most appalling that ever fell upon my ear, rose high above the shouting of the savages. It had not died away when another and another smote upon my throbbing ear ; and then I saw that these inhuman monsters were actually launching their canoe over the living bodies of their victims. But there was no pity in the breasts of these men. Forward they went in ruthless indifference, shouting as they went, while high among their voices rang the dying shrieks of those wretched creatures, as, one after another, the ponderous canoe passed over them, burst the eyeballs from their sockets, and sent the life-blood gushing from their mouths. O reader, this is no fiction. I would not, for the sake of thrilling you with horror, invent so terrible a scene. It was witnessed. It is true—true as that accursed sin which has rendered the human heart capable of such diabolical enormities !

When it was over I turned round and fell upon the grass with a deep groan ; but Bill seized me by the arm, and lifting me up as if I had been a child, cried,—

" Come along, lad ; let's away ! "—and so, staggering and stumbling over the tangled underwood, we fled from the fatal spot.

During the remainder of that day I felt as it I were in a horrible dream. I scarce knew what was said to me, and was more than once blamed by the men for idling my time. At last the hour to return aboard came. We marched down to the beach, and I felt relief for the first time when my feet rested on the schooner's deck.

In the course of the evening I overheard part of a conversation between the captain and the first mate, which startled me not a little. They were down in the cabin, and conversed in an undertone ; but the skylight being off, I overheard every word that was said.

" I don't half like it," said the mate. " It seems to me that we'll only have hard fightin' and no pay."

" No pay ! " repeated the captain, in a voice of suppressed anger. " Do you call a good cargo all for nothing no pay ? "

" Very true," returned the mate ; " but we've got the cargo aboard. Why not cut your cable and take French leave o' them ? What's the use o' tryin' to lick the blackguards when it'll do us no manner o' good ? "

"Mate," said the captain in a low voice, "you talk like a fresh-water sailor. I can only attribute this shyness to some strange delusion ; for surely " (his voice assumed a slightly sneering tone as he said this), " surely I am not to suppose that *you* have become soft-hearted ! Besides, you are wrong in regard to the cargo being aboard ; there's a good quarter of it lying in the woods, and that blackguard chief knows it and won't let me take it off. He defied us to do our worst yesterday."

"Defied us ! did he ? " cried the mate, with a bitter laugh. "Poor, contemptible thing ! "

"And yet he seems not so contemptible but that you are afraid to attack him."

"Who said I was afraid ? " growled the mate sulkily. "I'm as ready as any man in the ship. But, captain, what is it that you intend to do ? "

"I intend to muffle the sweeps and row the schooner up to the head of the creek there, from which point we can command the pile of sandal-wood with our gun. Then I shall land with all the men except two, who shall take care of the schooner and be ready with the boat to take us off. We can creep through the woods to the head of the village, where these cannibals are always dancing round their suppers of human flesh, and if the carbines of the men are loaded with a heavy charge of buckshot, we can drop forty or fifty at the first volley. After that the thing will be easy enough. The savages will take to the mountains in a body, and we shall take what we require, up anchor, and away."

To this plan the mate at length agreed. As he left the cabin I heard the captain say,—

" Give the men an extra glass of grog, and don't forget the buckshot."

The reader may conceive the horror with which I heard this murderous conversation. I immediately repeated it to Bill, who seemed much perplexed about it. At length he said,—

" I'll tell you what I'll do, Ralph. I'll swim ashore after dark and fix a musket to a tree not far from the place where we'll have to land, and I'll tie a long string to the trigger, so that when our fellows cross it they'll let it off, and so alarm the village in time to prevent an attack, but not in time to prevent us gettin' back to the boat. So, Master Captain," added Bill, with a smile that for the first time seemed to me to be mingled with good-natured cheerfulness, " you'll be balked at least for once in your life by Bloody Bill."

After it grew dark, Bill put this resolve in practice. He slipped over the side with a musket in his left hand, while with his right he swam ashore and entered the woods. He soon returned, having accomplished his purpose, and got on board without being seen, I being the only one on deck.

When the hour of midnight approached, the men were mustered on deck, the cable was cut and the muffled sweeps got out. These sweeps were immensely large oars, each requiring a couple of men to work it. In a few minutes we entered the mouth of the creek, which was indeed the mouth of a small

river, and took about half an hour to ascend it,
although the spot where we intended to land was
not more than six hundred yards from the mouth,
because there was a slight current against us, and
the mangroves which narrowed the creek impeded
the rowers in some places. Having reached the
spot, which was so darkened by overhanging trees
that we could see with difficulty, a small kedge
anchor attached to a thin line was let softly down
over the stern.

" Now, lads," whispered the captain, as he walked
along the line of men, who were all armed to the
teeth, " don't be in a hurry, aim low, and don't
waste your first shots."

He then pointed to the boat, into which the men
crowded in silence. There was no room to row ; but
oars were not needed, as a slight push against the side
of the schooner sent the boat gliding to the shore.

" There's no need of leaving two in the boat,"
whispered the mate, as the men stepped out ; " we
shall want all our hands. Let Ralph stay."

The captain assented, and ordered me to stand in
readiness with the boat-hook, to shove ashore at a
moment's notice if they should return, or to shove
off if any of the savages should happen to approach.
He then threw his carbine into the hollow of his
arm, and glided through the bushes, followed by his
men. With a throbbing heart I awaited the result
of our plan. I knew the exact locality where the
musket was placed, for Bill had described it to me,
and I kept my straining eyes fixed upon the spot.

But no sound came, and I began to fear that either
they had gone in another direction or that Bill
had not fixed the string properly. Suddenly I heard
a faint click, and observed one or two bright sparks
among the bushes. My heart immediately sank
within me, for I knew at once that the trigger had
indeed been pulled, but that the priming had not
caught. The plan, therefore, had utterly failed. A
feeling of dread now began to creep over me as I
stood in the boat, in that dark, silent spot, awaiting
the issue of this murderous expedition. I shuddered
as I glanced at the water that glided past like a dark
reptile. I looked back at the schooner, but her hull
was just barely visible, while her tapering masts
were lost among the trees which overshadowed her.
Her lower sails were set, but so thick was the gloom
that they were quite invisible.

Suddenly I heard a shot. In a moment a thousand voices raised a yell in the village ; again the cry
rose on the night air, and was followed by broken
shouts as of scattered parties of men bounding
into the woods. Then I heard another shout loud
and close at hand. It was the voice of the captain
cursing the man who had fired the premature shot.
Then came the order, " Forward ! " followed by a
wild hurrah of our men as they charged the savages.
Shots now rang in quick succession, and at last a
loud volley startled the echoes of the woods. It
was followed by a multitude of wild shrieks, which
were immediately drowned in another hurrah from
the men ; the distance of the sound proving that

they were driving their enemies before them towards the sea.

While I was listening intently to these sounds, which were now mingled in confusion, I was startled by the rustling of the leaves not far from me. At first I thought it was a party of savages who had observed the schooner, but I was speedily undeceived by observing a body of natives—apparently several hundreds, as far as I could guess in the uncertain light—bounding through the woods towards the scene of battle. I saw at once that this was a party who had outflanked our men, and would speedily attack them in the rear. And so it turned out; for in a short time the shouts increased tenfold, and among them I thought I heard a death-cry uttered by voices familiar to my ear.

At length the tumult of battle ceased, and from the cries of exultation that now arose from the savages, I felt assured that our men had been conquered. I was immediately thrown into dreadful consternation. What was I now to do? To be taken by the savages was too horrible to be thought of; to flee to the mountains was hopeless, as I should soon be discovered; and to take the schooner out of the creek without assistance was impossible. I resolved, however, to make the attempt, as being my only hope, and was on the point of pushing off, when my hand was stayed, and my blood chilled by an appalling shriek, in which I recognized the voice of one of the crew. It was succeeded by a shout from the savages. Then came another and another shriek of agony, making my ears to tingle, as I felt convinced they were murdering the pirate crew in cold blood. With a bursting heart and my brain whirling as if on fire, I seized the boat-hook to push from shore, when a man sprang from the bushes.

"Stop! Ralph, stop!—there now, push off," he cried, and bounded into the boat so violently as nearly to upset her. It was Bill's voice! In another moment we were on board—the boat made fast, the line of the anchor cut, and the sweeps run out. At the first stroke of Bill's giant arm the schooner was nearly pulled ashore, for in his haste he forgot that I could scarcely move the unwieldy oar. Springing to the stern, he lashed the rudder in such a position that, while it aided me, it acted against him, and so rendered the force of our strokes nearly equal. The schooner now began to glide quickly down the creek; but before we reached its mouth, a yell from a thousand voices on the bank told that we were discovered. Instantly a number of the savages plunged into the water and swam toward us; but we were making so much way that they could not overtake us. One, however, an immensely powerful man, succeeded in laying hold of the cut rope that hung from the stern, and clambered quickly upon deck. Bill caught sight of him the instant his head appeared above the taffrail. But he did not cease to row, and did not appear even to notice the savage until he was within a yard of him; then dropping the sweep, he struck him a blow on the forehead with his clinched fist that felled him to the deck. Lifting him up he hurled him overboard and resumed the oar. But now a greater danger awaited us, for the savages had outrun us on the bank, and were about to plunge into the water ahead of the schooner. If they succeeded in doing so our fate was sealed. For one moment Bill stood irresolute. Then drawing a pistol from his belt, he sprang to the brass gun, held the pan of his pistol over the touch-hole and fired. The shot was succeeded by the hiss of the cannon's priming; then the blaze and the crashing thunder of the monstrous gun burst upon the savages with such deafening roar that it seemed as if their very mountains had been rent asunder.

This was enough. The moment of surprise and hesitation caused by the unwonted sound gave us time to pass the point; a gentle breeze, which the dense foliage had hitherto prevented us from feeling, bulged out our sails; the schooner bent before it, and the shouts of the disappointed savages grew fainter and fainter in the distance as we were slowly wafted out to sea.

CHAPTER XXVII

Reflections—The wounded man—The squall—True consolation—
Death.

THERE is a power of endurance in human beings, both in their bodies and in their minds, which, I have often thought, seems to be wonderfully adapted and exactly proportioned to the circumstances in which individuals may happen to be placed—a power which, in most cases, is sufficient to carry a man through and over every obstacle that may happen to be thrown in his path through life, no matter how high or how steep the mountain may be, but which often forsakes him the moment the summit is gained, the point of difficulty passed, and leaves him prostrated, with energies gone, nerves unstrung, and a feeling of incapacity pervading the entire frame that renders the most trifling effort almost impossible.

During the greater part of that day I had been subjected to severe mental and much physical excitement, which had almost crushed me down by the time I was relieved from duty in the course of the evening. But when the expedition whose failure has just been narrated was planned, my anxieties and energies had been so powerfully aroused that I went through the protracted scenes of that terrible night without a feeling of the slightest fatigue. My mind and body were alike active and full of energy. No sooner was the last thrilling fear of danger past, however, than my faculties were utterly relaxed ; and when I felt the cool breezes of the Pacific playing around my fevered brow, and heard the free waves rippling at the schooner's prow, as we left the hated island behind us, my senses forsook me, and I fell in a swoon upon the deck.

From this state I was quickly aroused by Bill, who shook me by the arm, saying,—

" Hallo, Ralph boy ! rouse up, lad ; we're safe now. Poor thing ! I believe he's fainted." And raising me in his arms he laid me on the folds of the gaff-topsail, which lay upon the deck near the tiller. " Here, take a drop o' this ; it'll do you good, my boy," he added, in a voice of tenderness which I had never heard him use before, while he held a brandy-flask to my lips.

I raised my eyes gratefully as I swallowed a mouthful ; next moment my head sank heavily upon my arm, and I fell fast asleep. I slept long, for when I awoke the sun was a good way above the horizon. I did not move on first opening my eyes, as I felt a delightful sensation of rest pervading me, and my eyes were riveted on and charmed with the gorgeous splendour of the mighty ocean, that burst upon my sight. It was a dead calm ; the sea seemed a sheet of undulating crystal, tipped and streaked

with the saffron hues of sunrise, which had not
yet merged into the glowing heat of noon ; and there
was a deep calm in the blue dome above that was
not broken even by the usual flutter of the sea-fowl.
How long I would have lain in contemplation of
this peaceful scene I know not, but my mind was
recalled suddenly and painfully to the past and the
present by the sight of Bill, who was seated on the
deck at my feet, with his head reclining, as if in sleep,
on his right arm, which rested on the tiller. As he
seemed to rest peacefully, I did not mean to disturb
him, but the slight noise I made in raising myself
on my elbow caused him to start and look round.

"Well, Ralph, awake at last, my boy ; you have
slept long and soundly," he said, turning towards me.

On beholding his countenance I sprang up in
anxiety. He was deadly pale, and his hair, which
hung in dishevelled locks over his face, was clotted
with blood. Blood also stained his hollow cheeks
and covered the front of his shirt, which, with the
greater part of his dress, was torn and soiled with
mud.

"O Bill!" said I, with deep anxiety, "what is
the matter with you? You are ill. You must
have been wounded."

"Even so, lad," said Bill, in a deep, soft voice,
while he extended his huge frame on the couch from
which I had just risen. "I've got an ugly wound,
I fear ; and I've been waiting for you to waken, to
ask you to get me a drop o' brandy and a mouthful
o' bread from the cabin lockers. You seemed to

sleep so sweetly, Ralph, that I didn't like to disturb you. But I don't feel up to much just now."

I did not wait till he had done talking, but ran below immediately, and returned in a few seconds with a bottle of brandy and some broken biscuit. He seemed much refreshed after eating a few morsels and drinking a long draught of water mingled with a little of the spirits. Immediately afterwards he fell asleep, and I watched him anxiously until he awoke, being desirous of knowing the nature and extent of his wound.

"Ha!" he exclaimed, on awaking suddenly after a slumber of an hour, "I'm the better of that nap, Ralph; I feel twice the man I was:" and he attempted to rise, but sank back again immediately with a deep groan.

"Nay, Bill, you must not move, but lie still while I look at your wound. I'll make a comfortable bed for you here on deck, and get you some breakfast. After that you shall tell me how you got it. Cheer up, Bill," I added, seeing that he turned his head away; "you'll be all right in a little, and I'll be a capital nurse to you though I'm no doctor."

I then left him, and lighted a fire in the caboose. While it was kindling, I went to the steward's pantry and procured the materials for a good breakfast, with which, in little more than half an hour, I returned to my companion. He seemed much better, and smiled kindly on me as I set before him a cup of coffee and a tray with several eggs and some bread on it.

" Now then, Bill," said I cheerfully, sitting down beside him on the deck, " let's fall to. I'm very hungry myself, I can tell you ; but—I forgot—your wound," I added, rising ; " let me look at it."

I found that the wound was caused by a pistol-shot in the chest. It did not bleed much, and as it was on the right side, I was in hopes that it might not be very serious. But Bill shook his head. " However," said he, " sit down, Ralph, and I'll tell you all about it."

" You see, after we left the boat an' began to push through the bushes, we went straight for the line of my musket, as I had expected ; but by some unlucky chance it didn't explode, for I saw the line torn away by the men's legs, and heard the click o' the lock ; so I fancy the priming had got damp and didn't catch. I was in a great quandary now what to do, for I couldn't concoct in my mind, in the hurry, any good reason for firin' off my piece. But they say necessity's the mother of invention ; so just as I was givin' it up and clinchin' my teeth to bide the worst o't and take what should come, a sudden thought came into my head. I stepped out before the rest, seemin' to be awful anxious to be at the savages, tripped my foot on a fallen tree, plunged head foremost into a bush, an', ov coorse, my carbine exploded ! Then came such a screechin' from the camp as I never heard in all my life. I rose at once, and was rushing on with the rest, when the captain called a halt.

" ' You did that a-purpose, you villain ! ' he said,

with a tremendous oath, and drawin' a pistol from his belt, let fly right into my breast. I fell at once, and remembered no more till I was startled and brought round by the most awful yell I ever heard in my life—except, maybe, the shrieks o' them poor critters that were crushed to death under yon big canoe. Jumpin' up, I looked round, and through the trees saw a fire gleamin' not far off, the light of which showed me the captain and men tied hand and foot, each to a post, and the savages dancin' round them like demons. I had scarce looked for a second when I saw one o' them go up to the captain flourishing a knife, and before I could wink he plunged it into his breast, while another yell, like the one that roused me, rang upon my ear. I didn't wait for more, but bounding up, went crashing through the bushes into the woods. The black fellows caught sight of me, however, but not in time to prevent me jumpin' into the boat, as you know."

Bill seemed to be much exhausted after this recital, and shuddered frequently during the narrative ; so I refrained from continuing the subject at that time, and endeavoured to draw his mind to other things.

" But now, Bill," said I, " it behoves us to think about the future, and what course of action we shall pursue. Here we are, on the wide Pacific, in a well-appointed schooner, which is our own—at least no-one has a better claim to it than we have—and the world lies before us. Moreover, here comes a breeze, so we must wake up our minds which way to steer."

"Ralph, boy," said my companion, "it matters not to me which way we go. I fear that my time is short now. Go where you will; I'm content."

"Well then, Bill, I think we had better steer to the Coral Island, and see what has become of my dear old comrades, Jack and Peterkin. I believe the island has no name, but the captain once pointed it out to me on the chart, and I marked it afterwards; so, as we know pretty well our position just now, I think I can steer to it. Then, as to working the vessel, it is true I cannot hoist the sails single-handed, but luckily we have enough of sail set already; and if it should come on to blow a squall, I could at least drop the peaks of the main and fore sails, and clew them up partially without help, and throw her head close into the wind, so as to keep her all shaking till the violence of the squall is past. And if we have continued light breezes, I'll rig up a complication of blocks and fix them to the top-sail halyards, so that I shall be able to hoist the sails without help. 'Tis true I'll require half a day to hoist them, but we don't need to mind that. Then I'll make a sort of erection on deck to screen you from the sun, Bill; and if you can only manage to sit beside the tiller and steer for two hours every day, so as to let me get a nap, I'll engage to let you off duty all the rest of the twenty-four hours. And if you don't feel able for steering, I'll lash the helm and heave to, while I get you your breakfasts and dinners; and so we'll manage famously, and soon reach the Coral Island."

Bill smiled faintly as I ran on in this strain.

" And what will you do," said he, " if it comes on to blow a storm ? "

This question silenced me, while I considered what I should do in such a case. At length I laid my hand on his arm, and said, " Bill, when a man has done all that he *can* do, he ought to leave the rest to God."

" O Ralph," said my companion, in a faint voice, looking anxiously into my face, " I wish that I had the feelin's about God that you seem to have, at this hour. I'm dyin', Ralph ; yet I, who have braved death a hundred times, am afraid to die. I'm afraid to enter the next world. Something within tells me there will be a reckoning when I go there. But it's all over with me, Ralph. I feel that there's no chance o' my bein' saved."

" Don't say that, Bill," said I, in deep compassion; " don't say that. I'm quite sure there's hope even for you, but I can't remember the words of the Bible that make me think so. Is there not a Bible on board, Bill ? "

" No ; the last that was in the ship belonged to a poor boy that was taken aboard against his will. He died, poor lad—I think through ill-treatment and fear. After he was gone the captain found his Bible and flung it overboard."

I now reflected, with great sadness and self-re-proach, on the way in which I had neglected my

Bible ; and it flashed across me that I was actually in the sight of God a greater sinner than this blood-stained pirate ; for, thought I, he tells me that he never read the Bible, and was never brought up to care for it ; whereas I was carefully taught to read it by my own mother, and had read it daily as long as I possessed one, yet to so little purpose that I could not now call to mind a single text that would meet this poor man's case, and afford him the consolation he so much required. I was much distressed, and taxed my memory for a long time. At last a text did flash into my mind, and I wondered much that I had not thought of it before.

" Bill," said I, in a low voice, " ' Believe on the Lord Jesus Christ, and thou shalt be saved.' "

" Ay, Ralph, I've heard the missionaries say that before now, but what good can it do me ? It's not for me that ; it's not for the likes o' me."

I knew not now what to say, for although I felt sure that that word was for him as well as for me, I could not remember any other word whereby I could prove it.

After a short pause, Bill raised his eyes to mine and said, " Ralph, I've led a terrible life. I've been a sailor since I was a boy, and I've gone from bad to worse ever since I left my father's roof. I've been a pirate three years now. It is true I did not choose the trade, but I was inveigled aboard this schooner and kept here by force till I became reckless and at last joined them. Since that time my hand has been steeped in human blood again and again.

Your young heart would grow cold if I— But why should I go on? 'Tis of no use, Ralph; my doom is fixed."

"Bill," said I, "'Though your sins be red like crimson, they shall be white as snow.' 'Only believe.'"

"Only believe!" cried Bill, starting up on his elbow. "I've heard men talk o' believing as if it was easy. Ha! 'tis easy enough for a man to point to a rope and say, 'I believe that would bear my weight;' but 'tis another thing for a man to catch hold o' that rope and swing himself by it over the edge of a precipice!"

The energy with which he said this, and the action with which it was accompanied, were too much for Bill. He sank back with a deep groan. As if the very elements sympathized with this man's sufferings, a low moan came sweeping over the sea.

"Hist, Ralph!" said Bill, opening his eyes; "there's a squall coming, lad. Look alive, boy! Clew up the foresail. Drop the main-sail peak. Them squalls come quick sometimes."

I had already started to my feet, and saw that a heavy squall was indeed bearing down on us. It had hitherto escaped my notice, owing to my being so much engrossed by our conversation. I instantly did as Bill desired, for the schooner was lying motionless on the glassy sea. I observed with some satisfaction that the squall was bearing down on the larboard bow, so that it would strike the vessel in the position in which she would be best able to stand the shock. Having done my best to shorten sail, I returned aft, and took my stand at the helm.

" Now, boy," said Bill, in a faint voice, " keep her close to the wind."

A few seconds afterwards he said, " Ralph, let me hear those two texts again."

I repeated them.

" Are ye sure, lad, ye saw them in the Bible ? "

" Quite sure," I replied.

Almost before the words had left my lips the wind burst upon us, and the spray dashed over our decks. For a time the schooner stood it bravely, and sprang forward against the rising sea like a war-horse. Meanwhile, clouds darkened the sky and the sea began to rise in huge billows. There was still too much sail on the schooner, and as the gale increased, I feared that the masts would be torn out of her or carried away, while the wind whistled and shrieked through the strained rigging. Suddenly the wind shifted a point, a heavy sea struck us on the bow, and the schooner was almost laid on her beam-ends, so that I could scarcely keep my legs. At the same moment Bill lost his hold of the belaying-pin which had served to steady him, and he slid with stunning violence against the skylight. As he lay on the deck close beside me, I could see that the shock had rendered him insensible ; but I did not dare to quit the tiller for an instant, as it required all my faculties, bodily and mental, to manage the schooner. For an hour the blast drove us along, while, owing to the sharpness of the vessel's bow and the press of canvas, she dashed through the waves instead of breasting over them, thereby drenching the decks with water fore and aft. At the end of that time the squall passed away, and left us rocking on the bosom of the agitated sea.

My first care, the instant I could quit the helm, was to raise Bill from the deck and place him on the couch. I then ran below for the brandy-bottle, and rubbed his face and hands with it, and endeavoured to pour a little down his throat. But my efforts, although I continued them long and assiduously, were of no avail ; as I let go the hand which I had been chafing, it fell heavily on the deck. I laid my hand over his heart, and sat for some time quite motionless ; but there was no flutter there—the pirate was dead !

CHAPTER XXVIII

IT was with feelings of awe, not unmingled with
fear, that I now seated myself on the cabin skylight
and gazed upon the rigid features of my late comrade, while my mind wandered over his past history
and contemplated with anxiety my present position.
Alone, in the midst of the wide Pacific, having a most
imperfect knowledge of navigation, and in a schooner
requiring at least eight men as her proper crew!
But I will not tax the reader's patience with a minute
detail of my feelings and doings during the first
few days that followed the death of my companion.
I will merely mention that I tied a cannon-ball to
his feet, and with feelings of the deepest sorrow
consigned him to the deep.

For fully a week after that a steady breeze blew
from the east, and as my course lay west and by
north, I made rapid progress towards my destina-
tion. I could not take an observation, which I
very much regretted, as the captain's quadrant was
in the cabin; but from the day of setting sail from
the island of the savages I had kept a dead reckoning,

and as I knew pretty well now how much leeway the schooner made, I hoped to hit the Coral Island without much difficulty. In this I was the more confident that I knew its position on the chart (which I understood was a very good one), and so had its correct bearings by compass.

As the weather seemed now quite settled and fine, and as I had got into the trade-winds, I set about preparations for hoisting the top-sails. This was a most arduous task, and my first attempts were complete failures, owing, in a great degree, to my reprehensible ignorance of mechanical forces. The first error I made was in applying my apparatus of blocks and pulleys to a rope which was too weak, so that the very first heave I made broke it in two, and sent me staggering against the after-hatch, over which I tripped, and striking against the main-boom, tumbled down the companion-ladder into the cabin. I was much bruised and somewhat stunned by this untoward accident. However, I considered it fortunate that I was not killed. In my next attempt I made sure of not coming by a similar accident, so I unreeved the tackling and fitted up larger blocks and ropes. But although the principle on which I acted was quite correct, the machinery was now so massive and heavy that the mere friction and stiffness of the thick cordage prevented me from moving it at all. Afterwards, however, I came to proportion things more correctly ; but I could not avoid reflecting at the time how much better it would have been had I learned all this from observation and study, instead

of waiting till I was forced to acquire it through the
painful and tedious lessons of experience.

After the tackling was prepared and in good
working order, it took me the greater part of a day
to hoist the main-top sail. As I could not steer and
work at this at the same time, I lashed the helm
in such a position that, with a little watching now
and then, it kept the schooner in her proper course.
By this means I was enabled also to go about the
deck and down below for things that I wanted, as
occasion required ; also to cook and eat my victuals.
But I did not dare to trust to this plan during the
three hours of rest that I allowed myself at night, as
the wind might have shifted, in which case I should
have been blown far out of my course ere I awoke.
I was, therefore, in the habit of *heaving to* during
those three hours—that is, fixing the rudder and the
sails in such a position as that by acting against
each other they would keep the ship stationary.
After my night's rest, therefore, I had only to make
allowance for the leeway she had made, and so
resume my course.

Of course, I was to some extent anxious lest another squall should come, but I made the best provision I could in the circumstances, and concluded
that by letting go the weather-braces of the top-sails
and the top-sail halyards at the same time, I should
thereby render these sails almost powerless. Besides
this, I proposed to myself to keep a sharp look-out
on the barometer in the cabin, and if I observed
at any time a sudden fall in it, I resolved that I

would instantly set about my multiform appliances
for reducing sail, so as to avoid being taken at unawares. Thus I sailed prosperously for two weeks,
with a fair wind, so that I calculated I must be
drawing near to the Coral Island ; at the thought of
which my heart bounded with joyful expectation.

The only book I found on board, after a careful
search, was a volume of Captain Cook's voyages.
This, I suppose, the pirate captain had brought with
him in order to guide him, and to furnish him with
information regarding the islands of these seas. I
found this a most delightful book indeed, and I not
only obtained much interesting knowledge about
the sea in which I was sailing, but I had many of
my own opinions, derived from experience, corroborated, and not a few of them corrected. Besides
the reading of this charming book, and the daily
routine of occupations, nothing of particular note
happened to me during this voyage, except once,
when on rising one night, after my three hours' nap,
while it was yet dark, I was amazed and a little
alarmed to find myself floating in what appeared to
be a sea of blue fire ! I had often noticed the beautiful appearance of phosphorescent light, but this far
exceeded anything of the sort I had ever seen. The
whole sea appeared somewhat like milk, and was
remarkably luminous.

I rose in haste, and letting down a bucket into the
sea, brought some of the water on board and took
it down to the cabin to examine it ; but no sooner
did I approach the light than the strange appearance

disappeared, and when I removed the cabin lamp the luminous light appeared again. I was much puzzled with this, and took up a little of the water in the hollow of my hand and then let it run off, when I found that the luminous substance was left behind on my palm. I ran with it to the lamp, but when I got there it was gone. I found, however, that when I went into the dark my hand shone again; so I took the large glass of the ship's telescope and examined my hand minutely, when I found that there were on it one or two small patches of a clear, transparent substance like jelly, which were so thin as to be almost invisible to the naked eye. Thus I came to know that the beautiful phosphoric light, which I had so often admired before, was caused by animals, for I had no doubt that these were of the same kind as the Medusæ or jelly-fish which are seen in all parts of the world.

On the evening of my fourteenth day I was awakened out of a nap into which I had fallen by a loud cry, and starting up I gazed around me. I was surprised and delighted to see a large albatross soaring majestically over the ship. I immediately took it into my head that this was the albatross I had seen at Penguin Island. I had, of course, no good reason for supposing this, but the idea occurred to me, I know not why, and I cherished it, and regarded the bird with as much affection as if he had been an old friend. He kept me company all that day, and left me as night fell.

Next morning, as I stood motionless and with

heavy eyes at the helm—for I had not slept well—
I began to weary anxiously for daylight, and peered
towards the horizon, where I thought I observed
something like a black cloud against the dark sky.
Being always on the alert for squalls, I ran to the
bow. There could be no doubt it was a squall, and
as I listened I thought I heard the murmur of the
coming gale. Instantly I began to work might and
main at my cumbrous tackle for shortening sail, and
in the course of an hour and a half had the most of
it reduced—the top-sail yards down on the caps, the
top-sails clewed up, the sheets hauled in, the main and
fore peaks lowered, and the flying-jib down. While
thus engaged the dawn advanced, and I cast an occasional furtive glance ahead in the midst of my labour.
But now that things were prepared for the worst, I
ran forward again and looked anxiously over the
bow. I now heard the roar of the waves distinctly.
and as a single ray of the rising sun gleamed over
the ocean, I saw—what! could it be that I was
dreaming?—that magnificent breaker with its ceaseless roar!—that mountain top!—yes, once more I
beheld the Coral Island!

CHAPTER XXIX

I ALMOST fell upon the deck with the tumult of mingled emotions that filled my heart as I gazed ardently towards my beautiful island. It was still many miles away, but sufficiently near to enable me to trace distinctly the well-remembered outlines of the two mountains. My first impulse was to utter an exclamation of gratitude for being carried to my former happy home in safety ; my second, to jump up, clap my hands, shout, and run up and down the deck, with no other object in view than that of giving vent to my excited feelings. Then I went below for the telescope, and spent nearly ten minutes of the utmost impatience in vainly trying to get a focus, and in rubbing the skin nearly off my eyes, before I discovered that having taken off the large glass to examine the phosphoric water with I had omitted to put it on again.

After that I looked up impatiently at the sails, which I now regretted having lowered so hastily, and for a moment thought of hoisting the main-top sail again ; but recollecting that it would take me full half a day to accomplish, and that, at the present rate of sailing, two hours would bring me to the island, I immediately dismissed the idea.

The remainder of the time I spent in making feverish preparations for arriving and seeing my dear comrades. I remembered that they were not in the habit of rising before six, and as it was now only three, I hoped to arrive before they were awake. Moreover, I set about making ready to let go the anchor, resolving in my own mind that, as I knew the depth of water in the passage of the reef and within the lagoon, I would run the schooner in and bring up opposite the bower. Fortunately the anchor was hanging at the cat-head, otherwise I should never have been able to use it. Now I had only to cut the tackling, and it would drop of its own weight. After searching among the flags, I found the terrible black one, which I ran up to the peak. While I was doing this a thought struck me. I went to the powder-magazine, brought up a blank cartridge and loaded the big brass gun, which, it will be remembered, was unhoused when we set sail; and as I had no means of housing it, there it had stood, bristling alike at fair weather and foul all the voyage. I took care to grease its mouth well, and before leaving the fore part of the ship, thrust the poker into the fire.

All was now ready. A steady five-knot breeze was blowing, so that I was now not more than quarter of a mile from the reef. I was soon at the entrance, and as the schooner glided quickly through, I glanced affectionately at the huge breaker, as if it had been the same one I had seen there when I bade adieu, as I feared for ever, to the island. On coming opposite the Water Garden, I put the helm hard down. The schooner came round with a rapid, graceful bend, and lost way just opposite the bower. Running forward, I let go the anchor, caught up the red-hot poker, applied it to the brass gun, and saluted the mountains with a *bang* such as had only once before broke their slumbering echoes !

Effective although it was, however, it was scarcely equal to the bang with which, instantly after, Peterkin bounded from the bower, in scanty costume, his eyeballs starting from his head with surprise and terror. One gaze he gave, one yell, and then fled into the bushes like a wild cat. The next moment Jack went through exactly the same performance, the only difference being that his movements were less like those of Jack-in-the-box, though not less vigorous and rapid than those of Peterkin.

" Hallo ! " I shouted, almost mad with joy, " what ho ! Peterkin ! Jack ! hallo ! it's *me* ! "

My shout was just in time to arrest them. They halted and turned round, and the instant I repeated the cry I saw that they recognized my voice, by both of them running at full speed towards the beach. I could no longer contain myself. Throwing off my jacket, I jumped overboard at the same moment that Jack bounded into the sea. In another moment we met in deep water, clasped each other round the neck, and sank, as a matter of course, to the bottom ! We were well-nigh choked, and instantly struggled to the surface, where Peterkin was sputtering about like a wounded duck, laughing and crying by turns, and choking himself with salt water !

It would be impossible to convey to my reader, by description, an adequate conception of the scene that followed my landing on the beach, as we stood embracing each other indiscriminately in our dripping garments, and giving utterance to incoherent rhapsodies, mingled with wild shouts. It can be more easily imagined than described, so I will draw a curtain over this part of my history, and carry the reader forward over an interval of three days.

During the greater part of that period Peterkin did nothing but roast pigs, taro, and bread-fruit, and ply me with plantains, plums, potatoes, and cocoa nuts, while I related to him and Jack the terrible and wonderful adventures I had gone through since we last met. After I had finished the account, they made me go all over it again ; and when I had concluded the second recital, I had to go over it again, while they commented upon it piecemeal. They were much affected by what I told them of the probable fate of Avatea, and Peterkin could by no means brook the idea of the poor girl being converted into a *long pig* ! As for Jack, he clinched his teeth, and shook his fist towards the sea, saying at the same time that he was sorry he had not broken Tararo's head, and he only hoped that one day he should be able to plant his knuckles on the bridge of that chief's nose ! After they had " pumped me dry," as Peterkin said, I begged to be informed of what had happened to them during my long absence, and particularly as to how they got out of the Diamond Cave.

"Well, you must know," began Jack, "after you had dived out of the cave, on the day you were taken away from us, we waited very patiently for half an hour, not expecting you to return before the end of that time. Then we began to upbraid you for staying so long, when you knew we would be anxious; but when an hour passed, we became alarmed, and I resolved at all hazards to dive out, and see what had become of you, although I felt for poor Peterkin, because, as he truly said, ' If you never come back I'm shut up here for life.' However, I promised not to run any risk, and he let me go; which, to say truth, I thought very courageous of him!"

"I should just think it was," interrupted Peterkin, looking at Jack over the edge of a monstrous potato which he happened to be devouring at the time.

"Well," continued Jack, "you may guess my consternation when you did not answer to my halloo. At first I imagined that the pirates must have killed you, and left you in the bush or thrown you into the sea; then it occurred to me that this would have served no end of theirs, so I came to the conclusion that they must have carried you away with them. As this thought struck me, I observed the pirate schooner standing away to the nor'ard, almost hull down on the horizon, and I sat down on the rocks to watch her as she slowly sank from my sight. And I tell you, Ralph, my boy, that I shed more tears that time at losing you than I have done, I verily believe, all my life before—"

"Pardon me, Jack, for interrupting," said Peterkin; "surely you must be mistaken in that: you've often told me that when you were a baby you used to howl and roar from morning to—"

"Hold your tongue, Peterkin," cried Jack. "Well, after the schooner had disappeared, I dived back into the cave, much to Peterkin's relief, and told him what I had seen. We sat down and had a long talk over this matter, and then we agreed to make a regular, systematic search through the woods, so as to make sure at least that you had not been killed. But now we thought of the difficulty of getting out of the cave without your help. Peterkin became dreadfully nervous when he thought of this; and I must confess that I felt some alarm, for, of course, I could not hope alone to take him out so quickly as we two together had brought him in; and he himself vowed that, if we had been a moment longer with him that time, he would have had to take a breath of salt water. However, there was no help for it, and I endeavoured to calm his fears as well as I could: 'for,' said I, 'you can't live here, Peterkin'; to which he replied, 'Of course not, Jack; I can only die here, and as that's not at all desirable, you had better propose something.' So I suggested that he should take a good long breath, and trust himself to me.

"'Might we not make a large bag of cocoa-nut cloth, into which I could shove my head, and tie it tight round my neck?' he asked, with a haggard smile. 'It might let me get one breath under water!'

"'No use,' said I; 'it would fill in a moment and suffocate you. I see nothing for it, Peterkin, if you really can't keep your breath so long, but to let me knock you down, and carry you out while in a state of insensibility.'

"But Peterkin didn't relish this idea. He seemed to fear that I would not be able to measure the exact force of the blow, and might, on the one hand, hit him so softly as to render a second or third blow necessary, which would be very uncomfortable; or, on the other hand, give him such a smash as would entirely spoil his figurehead, or mayhap knock the life out of him altogether! At last I got him persuaded to try to hold his breath, and commit himself to me; so he agreed, and down we went. But I had not got him half-way through when he began to struggle and kick like a wild bull, burst from my grasp, and hit against the roof of the tunnel. I was therefore obliged to force him violently back into the cave again, where he rose panting to the surface. In short, he had lost his presence of mind, and—"

"Nothing of the sort!" cried Peterkin indignantly; "I had only lost my wind; and if I had not had presence of mind enough to kick as I did, I should have bu'st in your arms!"

"Well, well, so be it," resumed Jack, with a smile; "but the upshot of it was that we had to hold another consultation on the point, and I really believe that had it not been for a happy thought of mine we should have been consulting there yet."

"I wish we had!" again interrupted Peterkin, with a sigh.—"I'm sure, Ralph, if I had thought that you were coming back again, I would willingly have awaited your return for months, rather than have endured the mental agony which I went through. But proceed."

"The thought was this," continued Jack—"that I should tie Peterkin's hands and feet with cords, and then lash him firmly to a stout pole about five feet long, in order to render him quite powerless, and keep him straight and stiff. You should have seen his face of horror, Ralph, when I suggested this; but he came to see that it was his only chance, and told me to set about it as fast as I could—'for,' said he, "this is no jokin', Jack, I can tell you, and the sooner it's done the better.' I soon procured the cordage and a suitable pole, with which I returned to the cave, and lashed him as stiff and straight as an Egyptian mummy; and, to say truth, he was no bad representation of what an English mummy would be, if there were such things, for he was as white as a dead man.

"'Now,' said Peterkin, in a tremulous voice 'swim with me as near to the edge of the hole as you can before you dive, then let me take a long breath, and as I shan't be able to speak after I've taken it, you'll watch my face, and the moment you see me wink—dive! And oh,' he added earnestly, 'pray don't be long!'

"I promised to pay the strictest attention to his wishes, and swam with him to the outlet of the cave. Here I paused. 'Now then,' said I, 'pull away at the wind, lad.'

"Peterkin drew in a breath so long that I could not help thinking of the frog in the fable, that wanted to swell itself as big as the ox. Then I looked into his face earnestly. Slap went the lid of his right eye; down went my head, and up went my heels. We shot through the passage like an arrow, and rose to the surface of the open sea before you could count twenty.

" Peterkin had taken in such an awful load of wind that, on reaching the free air, he let it out with a yell loud enough to have been heard a mile off; and then the change in his feelings was so sudden and great, that he did not wait till we landed, but began, tied up as he was, to shout and sing for joy as I supported him with my left arm to the shore. However, in the middle of a laugh that a hyena might have envied, I let him accidentally slip, which extinguished him in a moment.

" After this happy deliverance, we immediately began our search for your dead body, Ralph; and you have no idea how low our hearts sank as we set off, day after day, to examine the valleys and mountain sides with the utmost care. In about three weeks we completed the survey of the whole island, and had at least the satisfaction of knowing that you had not been killed. But it occurred to us that you might have been thrown into the sea, so we examined the sands and the lagoon carefully, and afterwards went all round the outer reef. One day, while we were upon the reef, Peterkin espied a small dark object lying among the rocks, which seemed to be quite different from the surrounding stones. We hastened towards the spot, and found it to be a small keg. On knocking out the head we discovered that it was gunpowder."

"It was I who sent you that, Jack," said I, with a smile.

"Fork out!" cried Peterkin energetically, starting to his feet and extending his open hand to Jack. "Down with the money, sir, else I'll have you shut up for life in a debtor's prison the moment we return to England!"

"I'll give you an I O U in the meantime," returned Jack, laughing, "so sit down and be quiet.—The fact is, Ralph, when we discovered this keg of powder, Peterkin immediately took me a bet of a thousand pounds that you had something to do with it, and I took him a bet of ten thousand that you had not."

"Peterkin was right, then," said I, explaining how the thing had occurred.

"Well, we found it very useful," continued Jack, "although some of it had got a little damp; and we furbished up the old pistol, with which Peterkin is a crack shot now. But to continue :—We did not find any other vestige of you on the reef, and finally gave up all hope of ever seeing you again. After this the island became a dreary place to us, and we began to long for a ship to heave in sight and take us off. But now that you're back again, my dear fellow, it looks as bright and cheerful as it used to do, and I love it as much as ever.

"And now," continued Jack, "I have a great desire to visit some of the other islands of the South Seas. Here we have a first-rate schooner at our disposal, so I don't see what should hinder us."

"Just the very thing I was going to propose," cried Peterkin. "I vote for starting at once."

"Well, then," said Jack, "it seems to me that we could not do better than shape our course for the island on which Avatea lives, and endeavour to persuade Tararo to let her marry the black fellow to whom she is engaged, instead of making a long pig of her. If he has a spark of gratitude in him he'll do it. Besides, having become champions for this girl once before, it behoves us, as true knights, not to rest until we set her free; at least, all the heroes in all the story-books I have ever read would count it foul disgrace to leave such a work unfinished."

"I'm sure I don't know or care what your knights in story-books would do," said Peterkin; "but I'm certain that it would be capital fun, so I'm your man whenever you want me."

This plan of Jack's was quite in accordance with his romantic, impulsive nature; and having made up his mind to save this black girl, he could not rest until the thing was commenced.

"But there may be great danger in this attempt," he said, at the end of a long consultation on the subject. "Will you, lads, go with me in spite of this?"

"Go with you?" we repeated in the same breath.

"Can you doubt it?" said I.

"For a moment," added Peterkin.

I need scarcely say that having made up our minds to go on this enterprise, we lost no time in making preparations to quit the island; and as the schooner was well laden with stores of every kind

for a long cruise, we had little to do except to
add to our abundant supply a quantity of cocoa
nuts, bread-fruit, taro, yams, plums, and potatoes,
chiefly with the view of carrying the fragrance of
our dear island along with us as long as we could.

When all was ready we paid a farewell visit to the
different familiar spots where most of our time had
been spent. We ascended the mountain top, and
gazed for the last time at the rich green foliage in the
valleys, the white sandy beach, the placid lagoon, and
the barrier coral reef with its crested breakers. Then
we descended to Spouting Cliff, and looked down at
the pale-green monster which we had made such
fruitless efforts to spear in days gone by. From
this we hurried to the Water Garden, and took a last
dive into its clear waters, and a last gambol amongst
its coral groves. I hurried out before my companions, and dressed in haste, in order to have a long
examination of my tank, which Peterkin, in the
fullness of his heart, had tended with the utmost
care, as being a vivid remembrancer of me rather
than out of love for natural history. It was in
superb condition—the water as clear and pellucid
as crystal ; the red and green seaweed of the most
brilliant hues ; the red, purple, yellow, green, and
striped anemones fully expanded, and stretching out
their arms as if to welcome and embrace their former
master ; the starfish, zoophytes, sea-pens, and other
innumerable marine insects looking fresh and beautiful ; and the crabs, as Peterkin said, looking as wide-
awake, impertinent, rampant, and pugnacious as ever.

It was, indeed, so lovely and so interesting that I would scarcely allow myself to be torn away from it.

Last of all, we returned to the bower and collected the few articles we possessed—such as the axe, the pencil-case, the broken telescope, the penknife, the hook made from the brass ring, and the sail-needle, with which we had landed on the island ; also the long boots and the pistol, besides several curious articles of costume which we had manufactured from time to time.

These we conveyed on board in our little boat, after having carved our names on a chip of iron-wood, thus :—

> JACK MARTIN,
> RALPH ROVER,
> PETERKIN GAY,

which we fixed up inside of the bower. The boat was then hoisted on board and the anchor weighed ; which latter operation cost us great labour and much time, as the anchor was so heavy that we could not move it without the aid of my complex machinery of blocks and pulleys. A steady breeze was blowing off shore when we set sail, at a little before sunset. It swept us quickly past the reef and out to sea. The shore grew rapidly more indistinct as the shades of evening fell, while our clipper bark bounded lightly over the waves. Slowly the mountain top sank on the horizon, until it became a mere speck. In another moment the sun and the Coral Island sank together into the broad bosom of the Pacific.

CHAPTER XXX

The voyage—The island, and a consultation in which danger is
scouted as a thing unworthy of consideration—Rats and
cats—The native teacher—Awful revelations—Wonderful
effects of Christianity.

OUR voyage during the next two weeks was most
interesting and prosperous. The breeze continued
generally fair, and at all times enabled us to lie out
course ; for being, as I have said before, clipper-
built, the pirate schooner could lie very close to the
wind and make little leeway. We had no difficulty
now in managing our sails, for Jack was heavy and
powerful, while Peterkin was active as a kitten.
Still, however, we were a very insufficient crew for
such a vessel, and if any one had proposed to us to
make such a voyage in it before we had been forced
to go through so many hardships from necessity,
we would have turned away with pity from the
individual making such proposal as from a madman.
I pondered this a good deal, and at last concluded
that men do not know how much they are capable
of doing till they try, and that we should never give
way to despair in any undertaking, however difficult
it may seem—always supposing, however, that our

cause is a good one, and that we can ask the divine blessing on it.

Although, therefore, we could now manage our sails easily, we nevertheless found that my pulleys were of much service to us in some things ; though Jack did laugh heartily at the uncouth arrangement of ropes and blocks, which had, to a sailor's eye, a very lumbering and clumsy appearance. But I will not drag my reader through the details of this voyage. Suffice it to say that, after an agreeable sail of about three weeks, we arrived off the island of Mango, which I recognized at once from the description that the pirate Bill had given me of it during one of our conversations.

As soon as we came within sight of it we hove the ship to and held a council of war.

" Now, boys," said Jack, as we seated ourselves beside him on the cabin skylight, " before we go further in this business, we must go over the pros and cons of it ; for although you have so generously consented to stick by me through thick and thin, it would be unfair did I not see that you thoroughly understand the danger of what we are about to attempt."

" Oh, bother the danger ! " cried Peterkin. " I wonder to hear *you*, Jack, talk of danger. When a fellow begins to talk about it, he'll soon come to magnify it to such a degree that he'll not be fit to face it when it comes, no more than a suckin' baby."

" Nay, Peterkin," replied Jack gravely, " I won't

be jested out of it. I grant you that when we've once resolved to act, and have made up our minds what to do, we should think no more of danger. But before we have so resolved it behoves us to look at it straight in the face, and examine into it, and walk round it; for if we flinch at a distant view, we're sure to run away when the danger is near.— Now, I understand from you, Ralph, that the island is inhabited by thoroughgoing, out-and-out cannibals, whose principal law is, ' Might is right, and the weakest goes to the wall ' ? "

" Yes," said I; " so Bill gave me to understand. He told me, however, that at the southern side of it the missionaries had obtained a footing amongst an insignificant tribe. A native teacher had been sent there by the Wesleyans, who had succeeded in persuading the chief at that part to embrace Christianity. But instead of that being of any advantage to our enterprise, it seems the very reverse; for the chief, Tararo, is a determined heathen, and persecutes the Christians—who are far too weak in numbers to offer any resistance—and looks with dislike upon all white men, whom he regards as propagators of the new faith."

" 'Tis a pity," said Jack, " that the Christian tribe is so small, for we shall scarcely be safe under their protection, I fear. If Tararo takes it into his head to wish for our vessel, or to kill ourselves, he could take us from them by force. You say that the native missionary talks English ? "

" So I believe."

" Then, what I propose is this," said Jack. " We
will run round to the south side of the island, and cast
anchor off the Christian village. We are too far
away just now to have been descried by any of the
savages, so we shall get there unobserved, and have
time to arrange our plans before the heathen tribes
know of our presence. But in doing this we run the
risk of being captured by the ill-disposed tribes, and
being very ill-used, if not—a—"

" Roasted alive and eaten," cried Peterkin.
" Come, out with it, Jack. According to your own
showing, it's well to look the danger straight in the
face ! "

" Well, that *is* the worst of it, certainly. Are you
prepared, then, to take your chance of that ? "

" I've been prepared and had my mind made up
long ago," cried Peterkin, swaggering about the
deck with his hands thrust into his breeches pockets.
" The fact is, Jack, I don't believe that Tararo will
be so ungrateful as to eat us, and I'm quite sure that
he'll be too happy to grant us whatever we ask ; so
the sooner we go in and win the better."

Peterkin was wrong, however, in his estimate of
savage gratitude, as the sequel will show.

The schooner was now put before the wind, and
after making a long run to the southward, we put
about and beat up for the south side of Mango, where
we arrived before sunset, and hove to off the coral
reef. Here we awaited the arrival of a canoe, which
immediately put off on our rounding to. When it
arrived, a mild-looking native, of apparently forty

years of age, came on board, and taking off his straw hat, made us a low bow. He was clad in a respectable suit of European clothes ; and the first words he uttered, as he stepped up to Jack and shook hands with him, were,—

" Good day, gentlemen. We are happy to see you at Mango ; you are heartily welcome."

After returning his salutation, Jack exclaimed, " You must be the native missionary teacher of whom I have heard ; are you not ? "

" I am. I have the joy to be a servant of the Lord Jesus at this station."

" You're the very man I want to see then," replied Jack ; " that's lucky. Come down to the cabin, friend, and have a glass of wine. I wish particularly to speak with you. My men there " (pointing to Peterkin and me) " will look after your people."

" Thank you," said the teacher, as he followed Jack to the cabin ; " I do not drink wine or any strong drink."

" Oh ! then there's lots of water, and you can have biscuit."

" Now, 'pon my word, that's cool ! " said Peterkin : " his *men*, forsooth ! Well, since we are to be men, we may as well come it as strong over these black chaps as we can.—Hallo, there ! " he cried to the half-dozen of natives who stood upon the deck, gazing in wonder at all they saw, " here's for you," and he handed them a tray of broken biscuits and a can of water. Then thrusting his hands into his pockets, he walked up and down the deck with an enormous swagger, whistling vociferously.

In about half an hour Jack and the teacher came on deck, and the latter, bidding us a cheerful good-evening, entered his canoe and paddled to the shore. When he was gone, Peterkin stepped up to Jack, and touching his cap, said,—

" Well, captain, have you any communications to make to your *men* ? "

" Yes," cried Jack : " ready about, mind the helm and clew up your tongue, while I con the schooner through the passage in the reef. The teacher, who seems a first-rate fellow, says it's quite deep, and good anchorage within the lagoon close to the shore."

While the vessel was slowly advancing to her anchorage, under a light breeze, Jack explained to us that Avatea was still on the island, living amongst the heathens ; that she had expressed a strong desire to join the Christians, but Tararo would not let her, and kept her constantly in close confinement.

" Moreover," continued Jack, " I find that she belongs to one of the Samoan Islands, where Christianity had been introduced long before her capture by the heathens of a neighbouring island ; and the very day after she was taken, she was to have joined the church which had been planted there by that excellent body the London Missionary Society. The teacher tells me, too, that the poor girl has fallen in love with a Christian chief, who lives on an island some fifty miles or so to the south of this one, and that she is meditating a desperate attempt at escape.

So, you see, we have come in the nick of time.—I
fancy that this chief is the fellow whom you heard
of, Ralph, at the island of Emo.—Besides all this,
the heathen savages are at war among themselves,
and there's to be a battle fought the day after to-
morrow, in which the principal leader is Tararo ;
so that we'll not be able to commence our negotia-
tions with the rascally chief till the day after.''

The village off which we anchored was beautifully
situated at the head of a small bay, from the margin
of which trees of every description peculiar to the
tropics rose in the richest luxuriance to the summit
of a hilly ridge, which was the line of demarcation
between the possessions of the Christians and those
of the neighbouring heathen chief.

The site of the settlement was an extensive plot
of flat land, stretching in a gentle slope from the sea
to the mountain. The cottages stood several hundred yards from the beach, and were protected from
the glare of the sea by the rich foliage of rows of
large Barringtonia and other trees which girt the
shore. The village was about a mile in length, and
perfectly straight, with a wide road down the middle,
on either side of which were rows of the tufted-
topped tree, whose delicate and beautiful blossoms,
hanging beneath their plume-crested tops, added
richness to the scene. The cottages of the natives
were built beneath these trees, and were kept in the
most excellent order, each having a little garden in
front, tastefully laid out and planted, while the
walks were covered with black and white pebbles.

Every house had doors and Venetian windows, painted partly with lamp black made from the candle-nut, and partly with red ochre, which contrasted powerfully with the dazzling coral lime that covered the walls. On a prominent position stood a handsome church, which was quite a curiosity in its way. It was a hundred feet long by fifty broad, and was seated throughout to accommodate upwards of two thousand persons. It had six large folding-doors, and twelve windows with Venetian blinds; and although a large and substantial edifice, it had been built, we were told by the teacher, in the space of two months! There was not a single iron nail in the fabric, and the natives had constructed it chiefly with their stone and bone axes and other tools, having only one or two axes or tools of European manufacture. Everything around this beautiful spot wore an aspect of peace and plenty; and as we dropped our anchor within a stone's-cast of the substantial coral wharf, I could not avoid contrasting it with the wretched village of Emo, where I had witnessed so many frightful scenes. When the teacher afterwards told me that the people of this tribe had become converts only a year previous to our arrival, and that they had been living before that in the practice of the most bloody system of idolatry, I could not refrain from exclaiming, " What a convincing proof that Christianity is of God ! "

On landing from our little boat, we were received with a warm welcome by the teacher and his wife ; the latter being also a native, clothed in a simple

European gown and a straw bonnet. The shore was lined with hundreds of natives, whose persons were all more or less clothed with native cloth. Some of the men had on a kind of poncho formed of this cloth, their legs being uncovered; others wore clumsily-fashioned trousers, and no upper garment except hats made of straw and cloth. Many of the dresses, both of women and men, were grotesque enough, being very bad imitations of the European garb; but all wore a dress of some sort or other. They seemed very glad to see us, and crowded round us as the teacher led the way to his dwelling, where we were entertained, in the most sumptuous manner, on baked pig and all the varieties of fruits and vegetables ·that the island produced. We were much annoyed, however, by the rats: they seemed to run about the house like domestic animals. As we sat at table, one of them peeped up at us over the edge of the cloth, close to Peterkin's elbow, who floored it with a blow on the snout from his knife, exclaiming as he did so,—

"I say, Mister Teacher, why don't you set traps for these brutes? Surely you are not fond of them!"

"No," replied the teacher, with a smile—"we would be glad to get rid of them if we could; but if we were to trap all the rats on the island, it would occupy our whole time."

"Are they, then, so numerous?" inquired Jack.

"They swarm everywhere. The poor heathens on the north side eat them, and think them very sweet. So did my people formerly; but they do not eat so many now, because the missionary who was last here expressed disgust at it. The poor people asked if it was wrong to eat rats; and he told them that it was certainly not wrong, but that the people of England would be much disgusted were they asked to eat rats."

We had not been an hour in the house of this kind-hearted man when we were convinced of the truth of his statement as to their numbers; for the rats ran about the floors in dozens, and during our meal two men were stationed at the table to keep them off!

"What a pity you have no cats!" said Peterkin, as he aimed a blow at another reckless intruder, and missed it.

"We would indeed be glad to have a few," rejoined the teacher, "but they are difficult to be got. The hogs, we find, are very good rat-killers, but they do not seem to be able to keep the numbers down. I have heard that they are better than cats."

As the teacher said this, his good-natured black face was wrinkled with a smile of merriment. Observing that I had noticed it, he said,—

"I smiled just now when I remembered the fate of the first cat that was taken to Rarotonga. This is one of the stations of the London Missionary Society. It, like our own, is infested with rats, and a cat was brought at last to the island. It was a large black one. On being turned loose, instead of being content to stay among men, the cat took to the mountains, and lived in a wild state, sometimes paying visits during the night to the houses of the natives ; some of whom, living at a distance from the settlement, had not heard of the cat's arrival, and were dreadfully frightened in consequence, calling it a ' monster of the deep,' and flying in terror away from it. One night the cat—feeling a desire for company, I suppose—took its way to the house of a chief who had recently been converted to Christianity, and had begun to learn to read and pray. The chief's wife, who was sitting awake at his side while he slept, beheld with horror two fires glistening in the doorway, and heard with surprise a mysterious voice. Almost petrified with fear, she awoke her husband, and began to upbraid him for forsaking his old religion and burning his god, who, she declared, was now come to be avenged of them. ' Get up and pray ! get up and pray ! ' she cried. The chief arose, and on opening his eyes beheld the same glaring lights and heard the same ominous sound. Impelled by the extreme urgency of the case, he commenced, with all possible vehemence, to vociferate the alphabet, as a prayer to God to deliver them from the vengeance of Satan ! On hearing this, the cat, as much alarmed as themselves, fled precipitately away, leaving the chief and his wife congratulating themselves on the efficacy of their prayer.''

We were much diverted with this anecdote, which the teacher related in English so good that we certainly could not have supposed him a native but for the colour of his face and the foreign accent in his tone. Next day we walked out with this interesting

man, and were much entertained and instructed by
his conversation, as we rambled through the cool
shady groves of bananas, citrons, limes, and other
trees, or sauntered among the cottages of the natives,
and watched them while they laboured diligently
in the taro beds or manufactured the tapa or native
cloth. To some of these Jack put questions through
the medium of the missionary ; and the replies were
such as to surprise us at the extent of their knowledge.
Indeed, Peterkin very truly remarked that "they
seemed to know a considerable deal more than Jack
himself ! "

Among other pieces of interesting information
that we obtained was the following in regard to
coral formations :—

" The islands of the Pacific," said our friend,
" are of three different kinds or classes. Those of
the first class are volcanic, mountainous, and wild ;
some shooting their jagged peaks into the clouds
at an elevation of ten and fifteen thousand feet.
Those of the second class are of crystallized limestone, and vary in height from one hundred to five
hundred feet. The hills on these are not so wild or
broken as those of the first class, but are richly clothed
with vegetation, and very beautiful. I have no doubt
that the Coral Island on which you were wrecked
was one of this class. They are supposed to have
been upheaved from the bottom of the sea by volcanic agency, but they are not themselves volcanic
in their nature, neither are they of coral formation.
Those of the third class are the low coralline islands,

usually having lagoons of water in their midst ; they are very numerous.

" As to the manner in which coral islands and reefs are formed, there are various opinions on this point. I will give you what seems to me the most probable theory—a theory, I may add, which is held by some of the good and scientific missionaries. It is well known that there is much lime in salt water ; it is also known that coral is composed of lime. It is supposed that the polypes, or coral insects, have the power of attracting this lime to their bodies ; and with this material they build their little cells or habitations. They choose the summit of a volcano, or the top of a submarine mountain, as a foundation on which to build ; for it is found that they never work at any great depth below the surface. On this they work ; the polypes on the mountain top, of course, reach the surface first, then those at the outer edges reach the top sooner than the others between them and the centre, thus forming the coral reef surrounding the lagoon of water and the central island ; after that the insects within the lagoon cease working. When the surface of the water is reached, these myriads of wonderful creatures die. Then birds visit the spot, and seeds are thus conveyed thither, which take root, and spring up, and flourish. Thus are commenced those coralline islets of which you have seen so many in these seas. The reefs round the large islands are formed in a similar manner. When we consider," added the missionary, " the smallness of the archi-

tects used by our heavenly Father in order to form
those lovely and innumerable islands, we are filled
with much of that feeling which induced the ancient
king to exclaim, ' How manifold, O Lord, are thy
works ! in wisdom hast thou made them all.' "

We all heartily agreed with the missionary in this
sentiment, and felt not a little gratified to find that
the opinions which Jack and I had been led to form
from personal observation on our Coral Island were
thus to a great extent corroborated.

The missionary also gave us an account of the
manner in which Christianity had been introduced
among them. He said : " When missionaries
were first sent here, three years ago, a small vessel
brought them ; and the chief, who is now dead,
promised to treat well the two native teachers who
were left with their wives on the island. But scarcely
had the boat which landed them returned to the
ship, than the natives began to maltreat their
guests, taking away all they possessed, and offering
them further violence, so that, when the boat was
sent in haste to fetch them away, the clothes of both
men and women were torn nearly off their backs.

" Two years after this the vessel visited them
again, and I, being in her, volunteered to land
alone, without any goods whatever, begging that
my wife might be brought to me the following year
—that is, *this* year ; and, as you see, she is with
me. But the surf was so high that the boat could
not land me ; so with nothing on but my trousers
and shirt, and with a few catechisms and a Bible,

besides some portions of the Scripture translated into the Mango tongue, I sprang into the sea, and swam ashore on the crest of a breaker. I was instantly dragged up the beach by the natives; who, on finding I had nothing worth having upon me, let me alone. I then made signs to my friends in the ship to leave me; which they did. At first the natives listened to me in silence, but laughed at what I said while I preached the gospel of our blessed Saviour Jesus Christ to them. Afterwards they treated me ill sometimes; but I persevered, and continued to dwell among them, and dispute, and exhort them to give up their sinful ways of life, burn their idols, and come to Jesus.

"About a month after I landed, I heard that the chief was dead. He was the father of the present chief, who is now a most consistent member of the church. It is a custom here that when a chief dies his wives are strangled and buried with him. Knowing this, I hastened to his house, to endeavour to prevent such cruelty if possible. When I arrived, I found two of the wives had already been killed, while another was in the act of being strangled. I pleaded hard for her, but it was too late; she was already dead. I then entreated the son to spare the fourth wife; and, after much hesitation, my prayer was granted: but in half an hour afterwards this poor woman repented of being unfaithful, as she termed it, to her husband, and insisted on being strangled; which was accordingly done.

" All this time the chief's son was walking up and down before his father's house with a brow black as thunder. When he entered I went in with him, and found, to my surprise, that his father was *not* dead ! The old man was sitting on a mat in a corner, with an expression of placid resignation on his face.

" ' Why,' said I, ' have you strangled your father's wives before he is dead ? '

" To this the son replied, ' He is dead. That is no longer my father. He is as good as dead now. He is to be *buried alive.*'

" I now remembered having heard that it is a custom among the Feejee islanders, that when the reigning chief grows old or infirm, the heir to the chieftainship has a right to depose his father ; in which case he is considered as dead, and is buried alive. The young chief was now about to follow this custom, and despite my earnest entreaties and pleadings, the old chief was buried that day before my eyes in the same grave with his four strangled wives ! Oh, my heart groaned when I saw this ! and I prayed to God to open the hearts of these poor creatures, as He had already opened mine, and pour into them the light and the love of the gospel of Jesus. My prayer was answered very soon. A week afterwards, the son, who was now chief of the tribe, came to me, bearing his god on his shoulders, and groaning beneath its weight. Flinging it down at my feet, he desired me to burn it !

" You may conceive how overjoyed I was at this.

I sprang up and embraced him, while I shed tears of joy. Then we made a fire, and burned the god to ashes, amid an immense concourse of the people, who seemed terrified at what was being done, and shrank back when we burned the god, expecting some signal vengeance to be taken upon us ; but seeing that nothing happened, they changed their minds, and thought that our God must be the true one after all. From that time the mission prospered steadily ; and now, while there is not a single man in the tribe who has not burned his household gods and become a convert to Christianity, there are not a few, I hope, who are true followers of the Lamb, having been plucked as brands from the burning by Him who can save unto the uttermost. I will not tell you more of our progress at this time ; but you see," he said, waving his hand around him, " the village and the church did not exist a year ago ! "

We were indeed much interested in this account, and I could not help again in my heart praying God to prosper those missionary societies that send such inestimable blessings to these islands of dark and bloody idolatry. The teacher also added that the other tribes were very indignant at this one for having burned its gods, and threatened to destroy it altogether, but they had done nothing yet. " And if they should," said the teacher, " the Lord is on our side ; of whom shall we be afarid ? "

" Have the missionaries many stations in these seas ? " inquired Jack.

" Oh yes. The London Missionary Society have

a great many in the Tahiti group, and other islands in that quarter. Then the Wesleyans have the Feejee Islands all to themselves, and the Americans have many stations in other groups. But still, my friend, there are hundreds of islands here the natives of which have never heard of Jesus, or the good word of God, or the Holy Spirit ; and thousands are living and dying in the practice of those terrible sins and bloody murders of which you have already heard. I trust, my friends," he added, looking earnestly into our faces—" I trust that if you ever return to England, you will tell your Christian friends that the horrors which they hear of in regard to these islands are *literally true*, and that when they have heard the worst, the ' *half has not been told them* ' ; for there are perpetrated here foul deeds of darkness of which man may not speak. You may also tell them," he said, looking around with a smile, while a tear of gratitude trembled in his eye and rolled down his coal-black cheek—" tell them of the blessings that the gospel has wrought *here* ! "

We assured our friend that we would certainly not forget his request. On returning towards the village, about noon, we remarked on the beautiful whiteness of the cottages.

" That is owing to the lime with which they are plastered," said the teacher. " When the natives were converted, as I have described, I set them to work to build cottages for themselves, and also this handsome church which you see. When the framework and other parts of the house were up,

I sent the people to fetch coral from the sea. They brought immense quantities. Then I made them cut wood, and piling the coral above it, set it on fire.

" ' Look ! look ! ' cried the poor people, in amazement ; ' what wonderful people the Christians are ! He is roasting stones. We shall not need taro or bread-fruit any more ; we may eat stones ! '

" But their surprise was still greater when the coral was reduced to a fine soft white powder. They immediately set up a great shout, and mingling the lime with water, rubbed their faces and their bodies all over with it, and ran through the village screaming with delight. They were also much surprised at another thing they saw me do. I wished to make some household furniture, and constructed a turning-lathe to assist me. The first thing that I turned was the leg of a sofa ; which was no sooner finished than the chief seized it with wonder and delight, and ran through the village exhibiting it to the people, who looked upon it with great admiration. The chief then, tying a string to it, hung it round his neck as an ornament ! He afterwards told me that if he had seen it before he became a Christian, he would have made it his god ! ' "

As the teacher concluded this anecdote we reached his door. Saying that he had business to attend to, he left us to amuse ourselves as we best could.

" Now, lads," said Jack, turning abruptly towards us, and buttoning up his jacket as he spoke, " I'm off to see the battle. I've no particular fondness for seein' bloodshed, but I must find out the nature o' these fellows and see their customs with my own eyes, so that I may be able to speak of it again, if need be, authoritatively. It's only six miles off, and we don't run much more risk than that of getting a rap with a stray stone or an overshot arrow. Will you go ? "

" To be sure we will," said Peterkin.

" If they chance to see us we'll cut and run for it," added Jack.

" Dear me ! " cried Peterkin—" *you* run ! I thought you would scorn to run from any one."

" So I would, if it were my duty to fight," returned Jack coolly ; " but as I don't want to fight, and don't intend to fight, if they offer to attack us I'll run away like the veriest coward that ever went by the name of Peterkin. So come along."

CHAPTER XXXI

A strange and bloody battle—The lion bearded in his den—
Frightful scenes of cruelty, and fears for the future.

WE had ascertained from the teacher the direction
to the spot on which the battle was to be fought,
and after a walk of two hours reached it. The
summit of a bare hill was the place chosen; for,
unlike most of the other islanders, who are addicted
to bush-fighting, those of Mango are in the habit
of meeting on open ground. We arrived before the
two parties had commenced the deadly struggle,
and creeping as close up as we dared among the
rocks, we lay and watched them.

The combatants were drawn up face to face, each
side ranged in rank four deep. Those in the first
row were armed with long spears; the second with
clubs to defend the spearmen; the third row was
composed of young men with slings; and the fourth
consisted of women, who carried baskets of stones
for the slingers, and clubs and spears with which
to supply the warriors. Soon after we arrived
the attack was made with great fury. There was no
science displayed. The two bodies of savages rushed
headlong upon each other, and engaged in a general

mêlée ; and a more dreadful set of men I have never seen. They wore grotesque war-caps made of various substances and decorated with feathers. Their faces and bodies were painted so as to make them look as frightful as possible ; and as they brandished their massive clubs, leaped, shouted, yelled, and dashed each other to the ground, I thought I had never seen men look so like demons before.

We were much surprised at the conduct of the women, who seemed to be perfect furies, and hung about the heels of their husbands in order to defend them. One stout young woman we saw whose husband was hard pressed and about to be overcome : she lifted a large stone, and throwing it at his opponent's head, felled him to the earth. But the battle did not last long. The band most distant from us gave way and were routed, leaving eighteen of their comrades dead upon the field. These the victors brained as they lay ; and putting some of their brains on leaves went off with them, we were afterwards informed, to their temples, to present them to their gods as an earnest of the human victims who were soon to be brought there.

We hastened back to the Christian village with feelings of the deepest sadness at the sanguinary conflict which we had just witnessed.

Next day, after breakfasting with our friend the teacher, we made preparations for carrying out our plan. At first the teacher endeavoured to dissuade us.

" You do not know," said he, turning to Jack, " the danger you run in venturing amongst these ferocious savages. I feel much pity for poor Avatea ; but you are not likely to succeed in saving her, and you may die in the attempt."

" Well," said Jack quietly, " I am not afraid to die in a good cause."

The teacher smiled approvingly at him as he said this, and after a little further conversation agreed to accompany us as interpreter ; saying that, although Tararo was unfriendly to him, he had hitherto treated him with respect.

We now went on board the schooner, having resolved to sail round the island and drop anchor opposite the heathen village. We manned her with natives, and hoped to overawe the savages by displaying our brass gun to advantage. The teacher soon after came on board, and setting our sails we put to sea. In two hours more we made the cliffs reverberate with the crash of the big gun, which we fired by way of salute, while we ran the British ensign up to the peak and cast anchor. The commotion on shore showed us that we had struck terror into the hearts of the natives ; but seeing that we did not offer to molest them, a canoe at length put off and paddled cautiously towards us. The teacher showed himself, and explaining that we were friends and wished to palaver with the chief, desired the native to go and tell him to come on board.

We waited long and with much impatience for an answer. During this time the native teacher conversed with us again, and told us many things concerning the success of the gospel among those islands; and perceiving that we were by no means so much gratified as we ought to have been at the hearing of such good news, he pressed us more closely in regard to our personal interest in religion, and exhorted us to consider that our souls were certainly in as great danger as those of the wretched heathen whom we pitied so much, if we had not already found salvation in Jesus Christ. "Nay, further," he added, "if such be your unhappy case, you are, in the sight of God, much worse than these savages (forgive me, my young friends, for saying so): for they have no knowledge, no light, and do not profess to believe; while you, on the contrary, have been brought up in the light of the blessed gospel, and call yourselves Christians. These poor savages are indeed the enemies of our Lord; but you, if ye be not true believers, are traitors!"

I must confess that my heart condemned me while the teacher spoke in this earnest manner, and I knew not what to reply. Peterkin, too, did not seem to like it, and I thought would willingly have escaped; but Jack seemed deeply impressed, and wore an anxious expression on his naturally grave countenance, while he assented to the teacher's remarks and put to him many earnest questions. Meanwhile the natives who composed our crew, having nothing particular to do, had squatted down on the deck and taken out their little books containing the translated portions of the New Testament, along with hymns and spelling-books, and were now busily engaged, some vociferating the alphabet, others learning prayers off by heart, while a few sang hymns—all of them being utterly unmindful of our presence. The teacher soon joined them, and soon afterwards they all engaged in a prayer which was afterwards translated to us, and proved to be a petition for the success of our undertaking and for the conversion of the heathen.

While we were thus engaged a canoe put off from shore and several savages leaped on deck, one of whom advanced to the teacher and informed him that Tararo could not come on board that day, being busy with some religious ceremonies before the gods, which could on no account be postponed. He was also engaged with a friendly chief who was about to take his departure from the island, and therefore begged that the teacher and his friends would land and pay a visit to him. To this the teacher returned answer that we would land immediately.

" Now, lads," said Jack, as we were about to step into our little boat, " I'm not going to take any weapons with me, and I recommend you to take none either. We are altogether in the power of these savages, and the utmost we could do, if they were to attack us, would be to kill a few of them before we were ourselves overpowered. I think that our only chance of success lies in mild measures ; don't you think so ? "

To this I assented gladly, and Peterkin replied by laying down a huge bell-mouthed blunderbuss, and divesting himself of a pair of enormous horse-pistols with which he had purposed to overawe the natives! We then jumped into our boat and rowed ashore.

On reaching the beach we were received by a crowd of naked savages, who shouted a rude welcome, and conducted us to a house or shed where a baked pig and a variety of vegetables were prepared for us. Having partaken of these, the teacher begged to be conducted to the chief; but there seemed some hesitation, and after some consultation among themselves one of the men stood forward and spoke to the teacher.

" What says he ? " inquired Jack when the savage had concluded.

" He says that the chief is just going to the temple of his god, and cannot see us yet ; so we must be patient, my friend."

" Well," cried Jack, rising, " if he won't come to see me, I'll e'en go and see him. Besides, I have a great desire to witness their proceedings at this temple of theirs. Will you go with me, friend ? "

" I cannot," said the teacher, shaking his head ; " I must not go to the heathen temples and witness their inhuman rites, except for the purpose of condemning their wickedness and folly."

" Very good," returned Jack ; " then I'll go alone, for I cannot condemn their doings till I have seen them."

Jack arose, and we, having determined to go also, followed him through the banana groves to a rising ground immediately behind the village, on the top of which stood the Bure, or temple, under the dark shade of a group of iron-wood trees. As we went through the village, I was again led to contrast the rude huts and sheds and their almost naked, savage-looking inhabitants with the natives of the Christian village, who, to use the teacher's scriptural expression, were now " clothed and in their right mind."

As we turned into a broad path leading towards the hill, we were arrested by the shouts of an approaching multitude in the rear. Drawing aside into the bushes, we awaited their coming up, and as they drew near we observed that it was a procession of the natives, many of whom were dancing and gesticulating in the most frantic manner. They had an exceedingly hideous aspect, owing to the black, red, and yellow paints with which their faces and naked bodies were bedaubed. In the midst of these came a band of men carrying three or four planks, on which were seated in rows upwards of a dozen men. I shuddered involuntarily as I recollected the sacrifice of human victims at the island of Emo, and turned with a look of fear to Jack as I said,—

" O Jack ! I have a terrible dread that they are going to commit some of their cruel practices on these wretched men. We had better not go to the temple. We shall only be horrified without being able to do any good, for I fear they are going to kill them."

Jack's face wore an expression of deep compassion as he said in a low voice, " No fear, Ralph ; the sufferings of these poor fellows are over long ago."

I turned with a start as he spoke, and glancing at
the men, who were now quite near to the spot
where we stood, saw that they were all dead. They
were tied firmly with ropes in a sitting posture on
the planks, and seemed, as they bent their sightless
eyeballs and grinning mouths over the dancing crew
below, as if they were laughing in ghastly mockery
at the utter inability of their enemies to hurt them
now. These, we discovered afterwards, were the
men who had been slain in the battle of the previous
day, and were now on their way to be first presented
to the gods and then eaten. Behind these came two
men leading between them a third, whose hands
were pinioned behind his back. He walked with a
firm step, and wore a look of utter indifference on
his face as they led him along ; so that we concluded
he must be a criminal who was about to receive some
slight punishment for his faults. The rear of the
procession was brought up by a shouting crowd of
women and children, with whom we mingled and
followed to the temple.

Here we arrived in a few minutes. The temple
was a tall circular building, open at one side. Around
it were strewn heaps of human bones and skulls.
At a table inside sat the priest, an elderly man with
a long gray beard. He was seated on a stool, and
before him lay several knives, made of wood, bone,
and splinters of bamboo, with which he performed
his office of dissecting dead bodies. Further in lay
a variety of articles that had been dedicated to the
god, and among them were many spears and clubs.

I observed among the latter some with human teeth sticking in them, where the victims had been clubbed in their mouths.

Before this temple the bodies, which were painted with vermillion and soot, were arranged in a sitting posture ; and a man, called a " dan-vosa " (orator), advanced, and laying his hands on their heads, began to chide them, apparently, in a low, bantering tone. What he said we knew not, but as he went on he waxed warm, and at last shouted to them at the top of his lungs, and finally finished by kicking the bodies over and running away, amid the shouts and laughter of the people, who now rushed forward. Seizing the bodies by a leg or an arm, or by the hair of the head, they dragged them over stumps and stones and through sloughs, until they were exhausted. The bodies were then brought back to the temple and dissected by the priest, after which they were taken out to be baked.

Close to the temple a large fire was kindled, in which stones were heated red hot. When ready these were spread out on the ground, and a thick coating of leaves strewn over them to slack the heat. On this " lovo," or oven, the bodies were then placed, covered over, and left to bake.

The crowd now ran with terrible yells towards a neighbouring hill or mound, on which we observed the framework of a house lying ready to be erected. Sick with horror, yet fascinated by curiosity, we staggered after them mechanically, scarce knowing where we were going or what we did, and feeling a sort of impression that all we saw was a dreadful dream.

Arrived at the place, we saw the multitude crowding round a certain spot. We pressed forward, and obtained a sight of what they were doing. A large wooden beam or post lay on the ground, beside the other parts of the framework of the house, and close to the end of it was a hole about seven feet deep and upwards of two feet wide. While we looked, the man whom we had before observed with his hands pinioned was carried into the circle. His hands were now free, but his legs were tightly strapped together. The post of the house was then placed in the hole, and the man put in beside it. His head was a good way below the surface of the hole, and his arms were clasped round the post. Earth was now thrown in until all was covered over and stamped down ; and this, we were afterwards told, was a *ceremony* usually performed at the dedication of a new temple or the erection of a chief's house !

"Come, come," cried Jack, on beholding this horrible tragedy ; "we have seen enough, enough— far more than enough ! Let us go."

Jack's face looked ghastly pale and haggard as we hurried back to rejoin the teacher, and I have no doubt that he felt terrible anxiety when he considered the number and ferocity of the savages, and the weakness of the few arms which were ready indeed to essay, but impotent to effect, Avatea's deliverance from these ruthless men.

CHAPTER XXXII

WHEN we returned to the shore and related to our friend what had passed, he was greatly distressed, and groaned in spirit ; but we had not sat long in conversation when we were interrupted by the arrival of Tararo on the beach, accompanied by a number of followers bearing baskets of vegetables and fruits on their heads.

We advanced to meet him, and he expressed, through our interpreter, much pleasure in seeing us.

" And what is it that my friends wish to say to me ? " he inquired.

The teacher explained that we came to beg that Avatea might be spared.

" Tell him," said Jack, " that I consider that I have a right to ask this of him, having not only saved the girl's life, but the lives of his own people also ; and say that I wish her to be allowed to follow her own wishes, and join the Christians."

While this was being translated, the chief's brow lowered, and we could see plainly that our request met with no favourable reception. He replied with considerable energy, and at some length.

" What says he ? " inquired Jack.

" I regret to say that he will not listen to the proposal. He says he has pledged his word to his friend that the girl shall be sent to him, and a deputy is even now on this island awaiting the fulfilment of the pledge."

Jack bit his lip in suppressed anger. " Tell Tararo," he exclaimed, with flashing eye, " that if he does not grant my demand it will be worse for him. Say I have a big gun on board my schooner that will blow his village into the sea, if he does not give up the girl."

" Nay, my friend," said the teacher gently, " I will not tell him that ; we must ' overcome evil with good.' "

" What does my friend say ? " inquired the chief, who seemed nettled by Jack's looks of defiance.

" He is displeased," replied the teacher.

Tararo turned away with a smile of contempt, and walked towards the men who carried the baskets of vegetables, and who had now emptied the whole on the beach in an enormous pile.

" What are they doing there ? " I inquired.

" I think that they are laying out a gift which they intend to present to some one," said the teacher.

At this moment a couple of men appeared leading a young girl between them, and going towards the heap of fruits and vegetables, placed her on the top of it. We started with surprise and fear, for in the young female before us we recognized the Samoan girl Avatea.

We stood rooted to the earth with surprise and thick-coming fears.

" O my dear young friend," whispered the teacher, in a voice of deep emotion, while he seized Jack by the arm, " she is to be made a sacrifice even now ! "

" Is she ? " cried Jack, with a vehement shout, spurning the teacher aside, and dashing over two natives who stood in his way, while he rushed towards the heap, sprang up its side, and seized Avatea by the arm. In another moment he dragged her down, placed her back to a large tree, and wrenching a war-club from the hand of a native who seemed powerless and petrified with surprise, whirled it above his head, and yelled, rather than shouted, while his face blazed with fury, " Come on, the whole nation of you, an ye like it, and do your worst ! "

It seemed as though the challenge had been literally accepted ; for every savage on the ground ran precipitately at Jack with club and spear, and doubtless would speedily have poured out his brave blood on the sod, had not the teacher rushed in between them, and raising his voice to its utmost, cried,—

" Stay your hands, warriors ! It is not your part to judge in this matter. It is for Tararo, the chief, to say whether or not the young man shall live or die."

The natives were arrested, and I know not whether it was the gratifying acknowledgment of his superiority thus made by the teacher, or some lingering feeling of gratitude for Jack's former aid in time of need, that influenced Tararo, but he stepped forward, and waving his hand, said to his people, " Desist. The young man's life is mine." Then turning to Jack, he said, " You have forfeited your liberty and life to me. Submit yourself, for we are more numerous than the sand upon the shore. You are but one ; why should you die ? "

" Villain ! " exclaimed Jack passionately, " I may die, but assuredly I shall not perish alone. I will not submit until you promise that this girl shall not be injured."

" You are very bold," replied the chief haughtily, " but very foolish. Yet I will say that Avatea shall not be sent away, at least for three days."

" You had better accept these terms," whispered the teacher entreatingly. " If you persist in this mad defiance, you will be slain, and Avatea will be lost. Three days are worth having."

Jack hesitated a moment, then lowered his club, and throwing it moodily to the ground, crossed his arms on his breast and hung down his head in silence.

Tararo seemed pleased by his submission, and told the teacher to say that he did not forget his former services, and therefore would leave him free as to his person, but that the schooner would be detained till he had further considered the matter.

While the teacher translated this, he approached as near to where Avatea was standing as possible, without creating suspicion, and whispered to her a few words in the native language. Avatea, who during the whole of the foregoing scene had stood leaning against the tree perfectly passive, and seemingly quite uninterested in all that was going on, replied by a single rapid glance of her dark eye, which was instantly cast down again on the ground at her feet.

Tararo now advanced, and taking the girl by the hand, led her unresistingly away; while Jack, Peterkin, and I returned with the teacher on board the schooner.

On reaching the deck, we went down to the cabin, where Jack threw himself, in a state of great dejection, on a couch; but the teacher seated himself by his side, and laying his hand upon his shoulder, said,—

"Do not give way to anger, my young friend. God has given us three days, and we must use the means that are in our power to free this poor girl from slavery. We must not sit in idle disappointment, we must act—"

"Act!" cried Jack, raising himself and tossing back his hair wildly; "it is mockery to talk of acting when one is bound hand and foot. How can I act? I cannot fight a whole nation of savages single-handed. Yes," he said, with a bitter smile, "I *can* fight them, but I cannot conquer them or save Avatea."

"Patience, my friend; your spirit is not a good one just now. You cannot expect that blessing which alone can insure success unless you are more submissive. I will tell you my plans if you will listen."

" Listen ! " cried Jack eagerly ; " of course I will, my good fellow ; I did not know you had any plans. Out with them. I only hope you will show me how I can get the girl on board of this schooner, and I'd up anchor and away in no time. But proceed with your plans."

The teacher smiled sadly. " Ah, my friend, if one fathom of your anchor chain were to rattle as you drew it in, a thousand warriors would be standing on your deck ! No, no, that could not be done. Even now your ship would be taken from you were it not that Tararo has some feeling of gratitude toward you. But I know Tararo well. He is a man of falsehood, as all the unconverted savages are. The chief to whom he has promised this girl is very powerful, and Tararo *must* fulfil his promise. He has told you that he would do nothing to the girl for three days ; but that is because the party who are to take her away will not be ready to start for three days. Still, as he might have made you a prisoner during those three days, I say that God has given them to us."

" Well, but what do you propose to do ? " said Jack impatiently.

" My plan involves much danger, but I see no other, and I think you have courage to brave it. It is this. There is an island about fifty miles to the south of this, the natives of which are Christians, and have been so for two years or more, and the principal chief is Avatea's lover. Once there, Avatea would be safe. Now, I suggest that you should abandon your schooner. Do you think that you can make so great a sacrifice ? "

" Friend," replied Jack, " when I make up my mind to go through with a thing of importance, I can make any sacrifice."

The teacher smiled. " Well, then, the savages could not conceive it possible that for the sake of a girl you would voluntarily lose your fine vessel ; therefore as long as she lies here they think they have you all safe ; so I suggest that we get a quantity of stores conveyed to a sequestered part of the shore, provide a small canoe, put Avatea on board, and you three would paddle to the Christian island."

" Bravo ! " cried Peterkin, springing up and seizing the teacher's hand. " Missionary, you're a regular brick. I didn't think you had so much in you."

" As for me," continued the teacher, " I will remain on board till they discover that you are gone. Then they will ask me where you are gone to, and I will refuse to tell."

" And what'll be the result of that ? " inquired Jack.

" I know not. Perhaps they will kill me ; but," he added, looking at Jack with a peculiar smile, " I, too, am not afraid to die in a good cause ! "

" But how are we to get hold of Avatea ? " inquired Jack.

" I have arranged with her to meet us at a particular spot, to which I will guide you to-night. We shall then arrange about it. She will easily manage to elude her keepers, who are not very strict in watching her, thinking it impossible that she could escape from the island. Indeed, I am sure that such an idea will never enter their heads. But, as I have said, you run great danger. Fifty miles in a small canoe, on the open sea, is a great voyage to make. You may miss the island, too, in which case there is no other in that direction for a hundred miles or more; and if you lose your way and fall among other heathens, you know the law of Feejee— a castaway who gains the shore is doomed to die, You must count the cost, my young friend."

"I have counted it," replied Jack. "If Avatea consents to run the risk, most certainly I will; and so will my comrades also. Besides," added Jack, looking seriously into the teacher's face, "your Bible—*our* Bible—tells of ONE who delivers those who call on Him in the time of trouble; who holds the winds in His fists, and the waters in the hollow of His hand."

We now set about active preparations for the intended voyage; collected together such things as we should require, and laid out on the deck provisions sufficient to maintain us for several weeks, purposing to load the canoe with as much as she could hold consistently with speed and safety. These we covered with a tarpaulin, intending to convey them to the canoe only a few hours before starting. When night spread her sable curtain over the scene, we prepared to land; but first kneeling along with the natives and the teacher, the latter implored a blessing on our enterprise. Then we rowed quietly to the shore and followed our sable guide, who led us by a long detour, in order to avoid the village, to the place of rendezvous. We had not stood more than five minutes under the gloomy shade of the thick foliage when a dark figure glided noiselessly up to us.

" Ah! here you are," said Jack, as Avatea approached—" Now, then, tell her what we've come about, and don't waste time."

" I understan' leetl English," said Avatea, in a low voice.

" Why, where did you pick up English ? " exclaimed Jack, amazed ; " you were dumb as a stone when I saw you last."

" She has learned all she knows of it from me," said the teacher, " since she came to the island."

We now gave Avatea a full explanation of our plans, entering into all the details, and concealing none of the danger, so that she might be fully aware of the risk she ran. As we had anticipated, she was too glad of the opportunity thus afforded her to escape from her persecutors to think of the danger or risk.

" Then you're willing to go with us, are you ? " said Jack.

" Yis, I willing to go."

" And you're not afraid to trust yourself out on the deep sea so far ? "

" No, I not 'fraid to go. Safe with Christian."

After some further consultation the teacher sug-

gested that it was time to return; so we bade
Avatea good-night, and having appointed to meet
at the cliff where the canoe lay on the following night,
just after dark, we hastened away—we to row on
board the schooner with muffled oars, Avatea to glide
back to her prison-hut among the Mango savages.

CHAPTER XXXIII

The flight—The pursuit—Despair and its results—The lion
bearded in his den again—Awful danger threatened and
wonderfully averted—A terrific storm.

As the time for our meditated flight drew near, we
became naturally very fearful lest our purpose should
be discovered, and we spent the whole of the following day in a state of nervous anxiety. We resolved
to go ashore and ramble about the village, as if to
observe the habits and dwellings of the people, as we
thought that an air of affected indifference to the
events of the previous day would be more likely
than any other course of conduct to avert suspicion
as to our intentions. While we were thus occupied,
the teacher remained on board with the Christian
natives, whose powerful voices reached us ever and
anon as they engaged in singing hymns or in prayer.

At last the long and tedious day came to a close,
the sun sank into the sea, and the short-lived twilight
of those regions, to which I have already referred,
ended abruptly in a dark night. Hastily throwing
a few blankets into our little boat, we stepped into
it, and whispering farewell to the natives in the
schooner, rowed gently over the lagoon, taking care
to keep as near to the beach as possible. We rowed
in the utmost silence and with muffled oars, so that
had any one observed us at the distance of a few

yards, he might have almost taken us for a phantom-
boat or a shadow on the dark water. Not a breath
of air was stirring; but fortunately the gentle
ripple of the sea upon the shore, mingled with the
soft roar of the breaker on the distant reef, effectually
drowned the slight plash that we unavoidably made
in the water by the dipping of our oars.

Quarter of an hour sufficed to bring us to the
overhanging cliff under whose black shadow our little
canoe lay, with her bow in the water ready to be
launched, and most of her cargo already stowed
away. As the keel of our little boat grated on the
sand, a hand was laid upon the bow, and a dim form
was seen.

" Ha ! " said Peterkin in a whisper, as he stepped
upon the beach, " is that you, Avatea ? "

" Yis, it am me," was the reply.

" All right ! Now, then, gently. Help me to
shove off the canoe," whispered Jack to the teacher ;
" and, Peterkin, do you shove these blankets
aboard—we may want them before long. Avatea,
step into the middle ;—that's right."

" Is all ready ? " whispered the teacher.

" Not quite," replied Peterkin.—" Here, Ralph,
lay hold o' this pair of oars, and stow them away if
you can. I don't like paddles. After we're safe
away I'll try to rig up rollicks for them."

" Now, then, in with you and shove off."

One more earnest squeeze of the kind teacher's
hand, and with his whispered blessing yet sounding
in our ears, we shot like an arrow from the shore,

sped over the still waters of the lagoon, and paddled as swiftly as strong arms and willing hearts could urge us over the long swell of the open sea.

All that night and the whole of the following day we plied our paddles in almost total silence and without halt, save twice to recruit our failing energies with a mouthful of food and a draught of water. Jack had taken the bearing of the island just after starting, and laying a small pocket-compass before him, kept the head of the canoe due south, for our chance of hitting the island depended very much on the faithfulness of our steersman in keeping our tiny bark exactly and constantly on its proper course. Peterkin and I paddled in the bow, and Avatea worked untiringly in the middle.

As the sun's lower limb dipped on the gilded edge of the sea Jack ceased working, threw down his paddle, and called a halt.

" There ! " he cried, heaving a deep, long-drawn sigh, " we've put a considerable breadth of water between us and these black rascals, so now we'll have a hearty supper and a sound sleep."

" Hear, hear ! " cried Peterkin. " Nobly spoken, Jack.—Hand me a drop water, Ralph.—Why, girl, what's wrong with you ? you look just like a black owl blinking in the sunshine."

Avatea smiled. " I sleepy," she said ; and as if to prove the truth of this, she laid her head on the edge of the canoe and fell fast asleep.

" That's uncommon sharp practice," said Peterkin, with a broad grin. " Don't you think we should awake her to make her eat something first ? or perhaps," he added, with a grave, meditative look,— " perhaps we might put some food in her mouth, which is so elegantly open at the present moment, and see if she'd swallow it while asleep. If so, Ralph, you might come round to the front here and feed her quietly, while Jack and I are tucking into the victuals. It would be a monstrous economy of time."

I could not help smiling at Peterkin's idea, which indeed, when I pondered it, seemed remarkably good in theory ; nevertheless I declined to put it in practice, being fearful of the result should the victual chance to go down the wrong throat. But on suggesting this to Peterkin, he exclaimed,—

" Down the wrong throat, man ! why, a fellow with half an eye might see that if it went down Avatea's throat it could not go down the wrong throat !—unless, indeed, you have all of a sudden become inordinately selfish, and think that all the throats in the world are wrong ones except your own. However, don't talk so much, and hand me the pork before Jack finishes it. I feel myself entitled to at least one minute morsel."

" Peterkin, you're a villain—a paltry little villain," said Jack quietly, as he tossed the hind legs (including the tail) of a cold roast pig to his comrade ; " and I must again express my regret that unavoidable circumstances have thrust your society upon me, and that necessity has compelled me to cultivate your acquaintance. Were it not that you are incapable of walking upon the water, I would order you, sir, out of the canoe."

"There! you've wakened Avatea with your long tongue," retorted Peterkin, with a frown, as the girl gave vent to a deep sigh. "No," he continued, "it was only a snore. Perchance she dreameth of her black Apollo.—I say, Ralph, do leave just one little slice of that yam. Between you and Jack I run a chance of being put on short allowance, if not— yei—a—a—ow!"

Peterkin's concluding remark was a yawn of so great energy that Jack recommended him to postpone the conclusion of his meal till next morning—a piece of advice which he followed so quickly that I was forcibly reminded of his remark, a few minutes before, in regard to the sharp practice of Avatea.

My readers will have observed, probably, by this time that I am much given to meditation; they will not, therefore, be surprised to learn that I fell into a deep reverie on the subject of sleep, which was continued without intermission into the night, and prolonged without interruption into the following morning. But I cannot feel assured that I actually slept during that time, although I am tolerably certain that I was not awake.

Thus we lay like a shadow on the still bosom of the ocean, while the night closed in, and all around was calm, dark, and silent.

A thrilling cry of alarm from Peterkin startled us in the morning, just as the gray dawn began to glimmer in the east.

" What's wrong ? " cried Jack, starting up.

Peterkin replied by pointing with a look of anxious dread towards the horizon ; and a glance sufficed to show us that one of the largest sized war-canoes was approaching us !

With a groan of mingled despair and anger Jack seized his paddle, glanced at the compass, and in a suppressed voice commanded us to " give way." But we did not require to be urged. Already our four paddles were glancing in the water, and the canoe bounded over the glassy sea like a dolphin, while a shout from our pursuers told that they had observed our motions.

" I see something like land ahead," said Jack, in a hopeful tone. " It seems impossible that we could have made the island yet ; still, if it is so, we may reach it before these fellows can catch us, for our canoe is light and our muscles are fresh."

No-one replied ; for, to say truth, we felt that in a long chase we had no chance whatever with a canoe which held nearly a hundred warriors. Nevertheless, we resolved to do our utmost to escape, and paddled with a degree of vigour that kept us well in advance of our pursuers. The war-canoe was so far behind us that it seemed but a little speck on the sea, and the shouts, to which the crew occasionally gave vent, came faintly towards us on the morning breeze. We therefore hoped that we should be able to keep in advance for an hour or two, when we might perhaps reach the land ahead. But this hope was suddenly crushed by the supposed land not long after rising up into the sky, thus proving itself to be a fog-bank !

A bitter feeling of disappointment filled each heart, and was expressed on each countenance, as we beheld this termination to our hopes. But we had little time to think of regret. Our danger was too great and imminent to permit of a moment's relaxation from our exertions. No hope now animated our bosoms ; but a feeling of despair, strange to say, lent us power to work, and nerved our arms with such energy that it was several hours ere the savages overtook us. When we saw that there was indeed no chance of escape, and that paddling any longer would only serve to exhaust our strength, without doing any good, we turned the side of our canoe towards the approaching enemy, and laid down our paddles.

Silently, and with a look of bitter determination on his face, Jack lifted one of the light boat-oars that we had brought with us, and resting it on his shoulder, stood up in an attitude of bold defiance. Peterkin took the other oar and also stood up, but there was no anger visible on his countenance. When not sparkling with fun, it usually wore a mild, sad expression, which was deepened on the present occasion, as he glanced at Avatea, who sat with her face resting in her hands upon her knees. Without knowing very well what I intended to do, I also arose and grasped my paddle with both hands.

On came the large canoe like a war-horse of the deep, with the foam curling from its sharp bow, and the spear-heads of the savages glancing in the beams of the rising sun. Perfect silence was maintained on both sides. and we could hear the hissing water, and see the frowning eyes of the warriors, as they came rushing on. When about twenty yards distant, five or six of the savages in the bow rose, and, laying aside their paddles, took up their spears. Jack and Peterkin raised their oars, while, with a feeling of madness whirling in my brain, I grasped my paddle and prepared for the onset. But before any of us could strike a blow, the sharp prow of the war-canoe struck us like a thunderbolt on the side, and hurled us into the sea!

What occurred after this I cannot tell, for I was nearly drowned; but when I recovered from the state of insensibility into which I had been thrown, I found myself stretched on my back, bound hand and foot between Jack and Peterkin, in the bottom of the large canoe.

In this condition we lay the whole day, during which time the savages only rested one hour. When night came, they rested again for another hour, and appeared to sleep just as they sat. But we were neither unbound nor allowed to speak to each other during the voyage, nor was a morsel of food or a draught of water given to us. For food, however, we cared little, but we would have given much for a drop of water to cool our parched lips; and we would have been glad, too, had they loosened the cords that bound us, for they were tightly fastened, and occasioned us much pain. The air, also, was

unusually hot, so much so that I felt convinced that
a storm was brewing. This also added to our sufferings. However, these were at length relieved by our
arrival at the island from which we had fled.

While we were being led ashore, we caught a
glimpse of Avatea, who was seated in the hinder part
of the canoe. She was not fettered in any way.
Our captors now drove us before them towards the
hut of Tararo, at which we speedily arrived, and
found the chief seated with an expression on his face
that boded us no good. Our friend the teacher
stood beside him, with a look of anxiety on his mild
features.

" How comes it," said Tararo, turning to the teacher,
" that these youths have abused our hospitality ? "

" Tell him," replied Jack, " that we have not
abused his hospitality, for his hospitality has not
been extended to us. I came to the island to deliver
Avatea, and my only regret is that I have failed to
do so. If I get another chance, I will try to save
her yet."

The teacher shook his head. " Nay, my young
friend, I had better not tell him that ; it will only
incense him."

" I care not," replied Jack. " If you don't tell
him that, you'll tell him nothing, for I won't say
anything softer."

On hearing Jack's speech, Tararo frowned and his
eye flashed with anger.

" Go," he said, " presumptuous boy. My debt to
you is cancelled. You and your companions shall die."

As he spoke he rose and signed to several of his attendants, who seized Jack and Peterkin and me violently by the collars, and dragging us from the hut of the chief, led us through the wood to the outskirts of the village. Here they thrust us into a species of natural cave in a cliff, and having barricaded the entrance, left us in total darkness.

After feeling about for some time—for our legs were unshackled, although our wrists were still bound with thongs—we found a low ledge of rock running along one side of the cavern. On this we seated ourselves, and for a long time maintained unbroken silence.

At last I could restrain my feelings no longer. "Alas! dear Jack and Peterkin," said I, " what is to become of us ? I fear that we are doomed to die."

" I know not," replied Jack, in a tremulous voice, " I know not. Ralph, I regret deeply the hastiness of my violent temper, which, I must confess, has been the chief cause of our being brought to this sad condition. Perhaps the teacher may do something for us. But I have little hope."

"Ah no ! " said Peterkin, with a heavy sigh ; " I am sure he can't help us. Tararo doesn't care more for him than for one of his dogs."

"Truly," said I, "there seems no chance of deliverance, unless the Almighty puts forth His arm to save us. Yet I must say that I have great hope, my comrades ; for we have come to this dark place by no fault of ours—unless it be a fault to try to succour a woman in distress."

I was interrupted in my remarks by a noise at the entrance to the cavern, which was caused by the removal of the barricade. Immediately after, three men entered, and taking us by the collars of our coats, led us away through the forest. As we advanced, we heard much shouting and beating of native drums in the village, and at first we thought that our guards were conducting us to the hut of Tararo again. But in this we were mistaken. The beating of drums gradually increased, and soon after we observed a procession of the natives coming towards us. At the head of this procession we were placed, and then we all advanced together towards the temple where human victims were wont to be sacrificed !

A thrill of horror ran through my heart as I recalled to mind the awful scenes that I had before witnessed at that dreadful spot. But deliverance came suddenly from a quarter whence we little expected it. During the whole of that day there had been an unusual degree of heat in the atmosphere, and the sky assumed that lurid aspect which portends a thunderstorm. Just as we were approaching the horrid temple, a growl of thunder burst overhead, and heavy drops of rain began to fall.

Those who have not witnessed gales and storms in tropical regions can form but a faint conception of the fearful hurricane that burst upon the island of Mango at this time. Before we reached the temple, the storm burst upon us with a deafening roar, and the natives, who knew too well the devastation that was to follow, fled right and left through the woods in order to save their property, leaving us alone in the midst of the howling storm. The trees around us bent before the blast like willows, and we were about to flee in order to seek shelter, when the teacher ran toward us with a knife in his hand.

" Thank the Lord," he said, cutting our bonds, " I am in time ! Now, seek the shelter of the nearest rock."

This we did without a moment's hesitation, for the whistling wind burst, ever and anon, like thunder-claps among the trees, and tearing them from their roots, hurled them with violence to the ground. Rain cut across the land in sheets, and lightning played liked forked serpents in the air, while high above the roar of the hissing tempest the thunder crashed and burst and rolled in awful majesty.

In the village the scene was absolutely appalling. Roofs were blown completely off the houses in many cases ; and in others the houses themselves were levelled with the ground. In the midst of this the natives were darting to and fro, in some instances saving their goods, but in many others seeking to save themselves from the storm of destruction that whirled around them. But terrific although the tempest was on land, it was still more tremendous on the mighty ocean. Billows sprang, as it were, from the great deep, and while their crests were absolutely scattered into white mist, they fell upon the beach with a crash that seemed to shake the solid land. But they did not end there. Each suc-

cessive wave swept higher and higher on the beach,
until the ocean lashed its angry waters among the
trees and bushes, and at length, in a sheet of white
curdled foam, swept into the village and upset and
carried off, or dashed into wreck, whole rows of the
native dwellings ! It was a sublime, an awful scene,
calculated, in some degree at least, to impress the
mind of beholders with the might and the majesty
of God.

We found shelter in a cave that night and all the
next day, during which time the storm raged in fury ;
but on the night following it abated somewhat, and
in the morning we went to the village to seek for
food, being so famished with hunger that we lost all
feeling of danger and all wish to escape in our desire
to satisfy the cravings of nature. But no sooner had
we obtained food than we began to wish that we had
rather endeavoured to make our escape into the
mountains. This we attempted to do soon afterwards ; but the natives were now able to look after
us, and on our showing a disposition to avoid observation and make towards the mountains, we were
seized by three warriors, who once more bound our
wrists and thrust us into our former prison.

It is true Jack made a vigorous resistance, and
knocked down the first savage who seized him with a
well-directed blow of his fist, but he was speedily
overpowered by others. Thus we were again prisoners, with the prospect of torture and a violent
death before us.

CHAPTER XXXIV

Imprisonment—Sinking hopes—Unexpected freedom to more than one, and in more senses than one.

For a long, long month we remained in our dark and dreary prison, during which dismal time we did not see the face of a human being, except that of the silent savage who brought us our daily food.

There have been one or two seasons in my life during which I have felt as if the darkness of sorrow and desolation that crushed my inmost heart could never pass away until death should make me cease to feel. The present was such a season.

During the first part of our confinement we felt a cold chill at our hearts every time we heard a footfall near the cave—dreading lest it should prove to be that of our executioner. But as time dragged heavily on we ceased to feel this alarm, and began to experience such a deep, irrepressible longing for freedom that we chafed and fretted in our confinement like tigers. Then a feeling of despair came over us, and we actually longed for the time when the savages would take us forth to die! But these changes took place very gradually, and were mingled sometimes with brighter thoughts ; for there were times when we sat in that dark cavern on our ledge of rock and conversed almost pleasantly about the past,

until we well-nigh forgot the dreary present. But
we seldom ventured to touch upon the future.

A few decayed leaves and boughs formed our bed,
and a scanty supply of yams and taro, brought to us
once a day, constituted our food.

" Well, Ralph, how have you slept ? " said Jack,
in a listless tone, on rising one morning from his
humble couch. " Were you much disturbed by the
wind last night ? "

" No," said I. " I dreamed of home all night, and
I thought that my mother smiled upon me, and
beckoned me to go to her ; but I could not, for I
was chained."

" And I dreamed, too," said Peterkin ; " but it was
of our happy home on the Coral Island. I thought
we were swimming in the Water Garden ; then the
savages gave a yell, and we were immediately in the
cave at Spouting Cliff, which, somehow or other,
changed into this gloomy cavern ; and I awoke to
find it true."

Peterkin's tone was so much altered by the
depressing influence of his long imprisonment, that,
had I not known it was he who spoke, I should
scarcely have recognized it, so sad was it, and so
unlike to the merry, cheerful voice we had been
accustomed to hear. I pondered this much, and
thought of the terrible decline of happiness that
may come on human beings in so short a time ; how
bright the sunshine in the sky at one time, and in a
short space how dark the overshadowing cloud ! I
had no doubt that the Bible would have given me

much light and comfort on this subject, if I had possessed one, and I once more had occasion to regret deeply having neglected to store my memory with its consoling truths.

While I meditated thus, Peterkin again broke the silence of the cave, by saying, in a melancholy tone, " Oh, I wonder if we shall ever see our dear island more ! "

His voice trembled, and covering his face with both hands, he bent down his head and wept. It was an unusual sight for me to see our once joyous companion in tears, and I felt a burning desire to comfort him ; but, alas ! what could I say ? I could hold out no hope ; and although I essayed twice to speak, the words refused to pass my lips. While I hesitated, Jack sat down beside him and whispered a few words in his ear ; while Peterkin threw himself on his friend's breast, and rested his head on his shoulder.

Thus we sat for some time in deep silence. Soon after, we heard footsteps at the entrance of the cave, and immediately our jailer entered. We were so much accustomed to his regular visits, however, that we paid little attention to him, expecting that he would set down our meagre fare as usual and depart. But to our surprise, instead of doing so, he advanced towards us with a knife in his hand, and going up to Jack, he cut the thongs that bound his wrists ; then he did the same to Peterkin and me ! For fully five minutes we stood in speechless amazement, with our freed hands hanging idly by our

sides. The first thought that rushed into my mind
was, that the time had come to put us to death;
and although, as I have said before, we actually
wished for death in the strength of our despair, now
that we thought it drew really near I felt all the
natural love of life revive in my heart, mingled with
a chill of horror at the suddenness of our call.

But I was mistaken. After cutting our bonds,
the savage pointed to the cave's mouth, and we
marched, almost mechanically, into the open air.
Here, to our surprise, we found the teacher standing under a tree, with his hands clasped before him,
and the tears trickling down his dark cheeks. On
seeing Jack, who came out first, he sprang towards
him, and clasping him in his arms, exclaimed,—

"O my dear young friend, through the great
goodness of God you are free!"

"Free!" cried Jack.

"Ay, free," repeated the teacher, shaking us
warmly by the hands again and again—"free to go
and come as you will. The Lord has unloosed the
bands of the captive and set the prisoners free.
A missionary has been sent to us, and Tararo has
embraced the Christian religion! The people are
even now burning their gods of wood. Come, my
dear friends, and see the glorious sight."

We could scarcely credit our senses. So long
had we been accustomed in our cavern to dream of
deliverance, that we imagined for a moment this
must surely be nothing more than another vivid
dream. Our eyes and minds were dazzled, too, by

the brilliant sunshine, which almost blinded us after
our long confinement to the gloom of our prison, so
that we felt giddy with the variety of conflicting
emotions that filled our throbbing bosoms ; but as
we followed the footsteps of our sable friend, and
beheld the bright foliage of the trees, and heard the
cries of the paroquets, and smelt the rich perfume
of the flowering shrubs, the truth, that we were really
delivered from prison and from death, rushed with
overwhelming power into our souls, and with one
accord, while tears sprang to our eyes, we uttered a
loud long cheer of joy.

It was replied to by a shout from a number of the
natives who chanced to be near. Running towards
us, they shook us by the hand with every demon-
stration of kindly feeling. They then fell behind,
and forming a sort of procession, conducted us to the
dwelling of Tararo.

The scene that met our eyes here was one that I
shall never forget. On a rude bench in front of his
house sat the chief. A native stood on his left hand,
who from his dress seemed to be a teacher. On his
right stood an English gentleman, who I at once
and rightly concluded was a missionary. He was
tall, thin, and apparently past forty, with a bald
forehead and thin gray hair. The expression of his
countenance was the most winning I ever saw,
and his clear gray eye beamed with a look that was
frank, fearless, loving, and truthful. In front of the
chief was an open space, in the centre of which lay
a pile of wooden idols, ready to be set on fire ; and

around these were assembled thousands of natives, who had come to join in or to witness the unusual sight. A bright smile overspread the missionary's face as he advanced quickly to meet us, and he shook us warmly by the hands.

" I am overjoyed to meet you, my dear young friends," he said. " My friend and *your* friend, the teacher, has told me your history ; and I thank our Father in heaven with all my heart, that He has guided me to this island, and made me the instrument of saving you."

We thanked the missionary most heartily, and asked him in some surprise how he had succeeded in turning the heart of Tararo in our favour.

" I will tell you that at a more convenient time," he answered ; " meanwhile we must not forget the respect due to the chief. He waits to receive you."

In the conversation that immediately followed between us and Tararo, the latter said that the light of the gospel of Jesus Christ had been sent to the island, and that to it we were indebted for our freedom. Moreover, he told us that we were at liberty to depart in our schooner whenever we pleased, and that we should be supplied with as much provision as we required. He concluded by shaking hands with us warmly, and performing the ceremony of rubbing noses.

This was indeed good news to us, and we could hardly find words to express our gratitude to the chief and to the missionary.

" And what of Avatea ? " inquired Jack.

The missionary replied by pointing to a group of natives, in the midst of whom the girl stood. Beside her was a tall, strapping fellow, whose noble mien and air of superiority bespoke him a chief of no ordinary kind.

" That youth is her lover. He came this very morning in his war-canoe to treat with Tararo for Avatea. He is to be married in a few days, and afterwards returns to his island home with his bride ! "

" That's capital," said Jack, as he stepped up to the savage and gave him a hearty shake of the hand. " I wish you joy, my lad ; and you too, Avatea."

As Jack spoke, Avatea's lover took him by the hand, and led him to the spot where Tararo and the missionary stood, surrounded by most of the chief men of the tribe. The girl herself followed, and stood on his left hand while her lover stood on his right, and, commanding silence, made the following speech, which was translated by the missionary :—

" Young friend, you have seen few years, but your head is old. Your heart also is large and very brave. I and Avatea are your debtors, and we wish, in the midst of this assembly, to acknowledge our debt, and to say that it is one which we can never repay. You have risked your life for one who was known to you only for a few days. But she was a woman in distress, and that was enough to secure to her the aid of a Christian man. We, who live in these islands of the sea, know that the true Christians always act thus. Their religion is one of love and kindness. We thank God that so many Christians have been sent here ; we hope many more will come. Remember that I and Avatea will think of you and pray for you and your brave comrades when you are far away."

To this kind speech Jack returned a short, sailor-like reply, in which he insisted that he had only done for Avatea what he would have done for any woman under the sun. But Jack's forte did not lie in speech-making, so he terminated rather abruptly by seizing the chief's hand and shaking it violently, after which he made a hasty retreat.

" Now, then, Ralph and Peterkin," said Jack, as we mingled with the crowd, " it seems to me that the object we came here for having been satisfactorily accomplished, we have nothing more to do but get ready for sea as fast as we can, and hurrah for dear old England ! "

" That's my idea precisely," said Peterkin, endeavouring to wink ; but he had wept so much of late, poor fellow, that he found it difficult. " However, I'm not going away till I see these fellows burn their gods."

Peterkin had his wish, for in a few minutes afterwards fire was put to the pile, the roaring flames ascended, and amid the acclamations of the assembled thousands the false gods of Mango were reduced to ashes !

CHAPTER XXXV

Conclusion.

To part is the lot of all mankind. The world is a scene of constant leave-taking, and the hands that grasp in cordial greeting to-day are doomed ere long to unite for the last time, when the quivering lips pronounce the word—" Farewell." It is a sad thought, but should we on that account exclude it from our minds? May not a lesson worth learning be gathered in the contemplation of it? May it not, perchance, teach us to devote our thoughts more frequently and attentively to that land where we meet but part no more?

How many do we part from in this world with a light good-bye whom we never see again! Often do I think, in my meditations on this subject, that if we realized more fully the shortness of the fleeting intercourse that we have in this world with many of our fellow-men, we would try more earnestly to do them good, to give them a friendly smile, as it were, in passing (for the longest intercourse on earth is little more than a passing word and glance), and show that we have sympathy with them in the

short, quick struggle of life, by our kindly words
and looks and actions.

The time soon drew near when we were to quit
the islands of the South Seas ; and strange though it
may appear, we felt deep regret at parting with the
natives of the island of Mango : for after they embraced the Christian faith, they sought, by showing
us the utmost kindness, to compensate for the harsh
treatment we had experienced at their hands ; and
we felt a growing affection for the native teachers
and the missionary, and especially for Avatea and
her husband.

Before leaving we had many long and interesting
conversations with the missionary, in one of which
he told us that he had been making for the island of
Rarotonga, when his native-built sloop was blown
out of its course, during a violent gale, and driven
to this island. At first the natives refused to listen
to what he had to say ; but after a week's residence
among them, Tararo came to him and said that he
wished to become a Christian, and would burn his
idols. He proved himself to be sincere, for, as we
have seen, he persuaded all his people to do likewise.
I use the word " persuaded " advisedly ; for, like all
the other Feejee chiefs, Tararo was a despot, and
might have commanded obedience to his wishes ;
but he entered so readily into the spirit of the new
faith, that he perceived at once the impropriety of
using constraint in the propagation of it. He set
the example, therefore ; and that example was
followed by almost every man of the tribe.

During the short time that we remained at the island, repairing our vessel and getting her ready for sea, the natives had commenced building a large and commodious church, under the superintendence of the missionary, and several rows of new cottages were marked out ; so that the place bid fair to become, in a few months, as prosperous and beautiful as the Christian village at the other end of the island.

After Avatea was married, she and her husband were sent away loaded with presents, chiefly of an edible nature. One of the native teachers went with them, for the purpose of visiting still more distant islands of the sea, and spreading, if possible, the light of the glorious gospel there.

As the missionary intended to remain for several weeks longer, in order to encourage and confirm his new converts, Jack and Peterkin and I held a consultation in the cabin of our schooner—which we found just as we had left her, for everything that had been taken out of her was restored. We now resolved to delay our departure no longer. The desire to see our beloved native land was strong upon us, and we could not wait.

Three natives volunteered to go with us to Tahiti, where we thought it likely that we should be able to procure a crew of sailors sufficient to man our vessel ; so we accepted their offer gladly.

It was a bright clear morning when we hoisted the snow-white sails of the pirate schooner and left the shores of Mango. The missionary and thousands of the natives came down to bid us God-speed, and to see us sail away. As the vessel bent before a light fair wind, we glided quickly over the lagoon under a cloud of canvas.

Just as we passed through the channel in the reef the natives gave us a loud cheer ; and as the missionary waved his hat, while he stood on a coral rock with his gray hairs floating in the wind, we heard the single word " Farewell " borne faintly over the sea.

That night, as we sat on the taffrail gazing out upon the wide sea and up into the starry firmament, a thrill of joy, strangely mixed with sadness, passed through our hearts ; for we were at length " homeward bound," and were gradually leaving far behind us the beautiful, bright green coral islands of the Pacific Ocean.